HELL OF THE LIVING DEAD

A NOVEL BY
BRAD CARTER

Inspired by
the Original Story & Screenplay by
CLAUDIO FRAGASSO and ROSSELLA DRUDI
that became BRUNO MATTEI's
HELL OF THE LIVING DEAD

Encyclopocalypse Publications
www.encyclopocalypse.com

Remembering Virus: Hell of the Living Dead
Rossella Drudi

Publisher's Note: Before beginning to write the novelization of Virus *in April of 2023, Brad Carter corresponded with Rossella Drudi, the writer of the original film treatment. Brad wanted to get a better sense of the themes she wanted to explore when she wrote the story, as well as some of the concrete details about elements that never made it into the final film. Below are excerpts from that correspondence, minimally edited for clarity and better translation. There may be potential spoilers for the film as well as this book.*

The original idea for *Virus* was written in 1979. It was, more or less, as follows:

> For years the most powerful, industrialized and richest governments and states on earth have been trying to solve the problem of hunger in the third world without success, despite great expenditure of resources and humanitarian aid. America, Russia, and Europe unite for the first time and finance a multinational venture, HOPE, with the support and blessing of the UN.
>
> Chemical laboratories are opened for the manufacture of a pill that feeds and nourishes men to satiety. Scientific research

is very expensive, but once the right chemical formula is found, the production of the pills will be almost free. This is why the best scientists are selected to start the research. However, the pills are to be tested on natives.

Unfortunately, these pills do not take away hunger and do not nourish the human body. The real secret purpose of the project is that of genetic mutation. This mutation transforms African people into cannibals, inducing them to devour each other and thus to self-extinguish. In practical terms, the HOPE Project's aims are to carry out the mass extermination of the peoples of the third world, starting with the Africa.

At the beginning of the process, there is mass sterilization without the knowledge of the peoples subject to experimentation. During the second phase, there is genetic mutation of the test subjects into mindless cannibals. Scientists have also developed a second pill that acts as an antidote, in case it is administered by mistake to the white man.

The phases of production and experimentation on the first human guinea pigs are more atrocious and horrendous than the nine circles of Dante's hell. Everything proceeds in absolute secrecy, and when it appears the latest formula finally is the right one, something goes wrong.

A fly contaminates the two different toxic gases which, due to a trivial accident, mix together. This causes gases to escape from the laboratory, affecting the scientists and researchers of the HOPE complex in New Guinea. The substances, mixing with each other, have created a new and different chemical compound, which transforms everyone, regardless of ethnicity, into cannibals. The gases form a toxic cloud which, once raised into the sky, begins to spread. Genetic mutations immediately occur in anyone who comes into contact with the passage of the cloud or breathes its vapors.

Entire populations are transformed into cannibals and

devour each other. A corps of soldiers is sent to New Guinea in an effort to rescue the scientists and fix the problem before it spreads. They know that there is an antidote, and they must find him before it's too late. But they don't have the scientific skills to act and they aren't informed about the top secret purpose of the experiments.

Two French journalists also rushed to the scene to document the incident and spread the truth about what was falsely announced as a nuclear disaster. There's a courageous young female journalist and a young male photographer for a well-known French newspaper. The journalist gets lost, after having been through an ordeal, with a tribe of indigenous people of New Guinea, who recognize her as their savior and goddess.

The photographer teams up with the military, but he's killed before discovering the truth. The military freaks out when they realize they've been sent on a suicide mission. They behave like crazed lunatics, devoid of any sort of inhibition, as if they were facing hallucinogenic trip, which leads them to their death.

Only a few human beings are saved. These few survivors of the contamination, who manage to get a lift from Charon, the ferryman of pure souls, those devoid of greed and sin. Charon awaits them aboard a boat. And after verifying their innocence, he gives them the antidote. Then he takes them on a voyage across the large lake of a volcanic cave, until they arrive in the underworld, where toxic clouds do not enter.

Rain spells the end of everything, because it contaminates the earth as well as the air. In the finale, we see the clouds enveloping the world. Major cities in Europe, America, and Russia are affected by toxic rain. All the peoples of the world are about to turn into cannibals to devour each other.

Poverty will no longer exist. Hunger will no longer exist. But the human race will no longer exist either, and the earth, now purified, will breathe again, regenerating itself.

This original treatment was the starting point for what eventually became *Virus*. The characters were recast to be adapted to newly rewritten scenes, based on the very small budget that was available. It was a great frustration to give up so many scenes from the original script, which in post-production, were replaced by archival images that had nothing to do with what had been previously written. Even the actors were disappointed. Each of them had loved their characters and the original story. Each of the characters had a more extensive and defined role with their respective psychologies and personalities. So, we worked a lot with Franco Garofalo and his character (Zantoro), trying to give him as much depth and madness as possible. And you know the most ironically absurd thing for us? The Spanish producer told us that this film was the biggest success of her career. It cost ten cents and made millions in worldwide sales and theatrical box office receipts.

For the new novelization, I am pleased to see the full breadth of the story restored. For example, the novel shows the first phase of the HOPE Project, specifically the experimentation on human guinea pigs kept hidden in the basement of the laboratory. I wanted it to describe the monstrous genetic mutations these people undergo before reaching cannibalism, including the practice of mass sterilization. I'm particularly eager to see the return of Charon. His philosophy of purity and atonement played a big role in the original story. The same is true of the survivors taking refuge in an underground city which was dug deep into the earth by many different generations.

The sense of social denunciation that was present in the original story appears very little in the film. The story should be a metaphor about the greed of the most industrialized peoples, who are, in a sense, the real cannibals. They are the ones who starve third world countries, robbing them of all their resources and preventing them from developing to become independent. So-called civilized nations lack a sense of inclusion and sharing, especially in the growth of a country for the good of all. These issues are as relevant today as they were when the original story was written.

Rossella Drudi, 2023

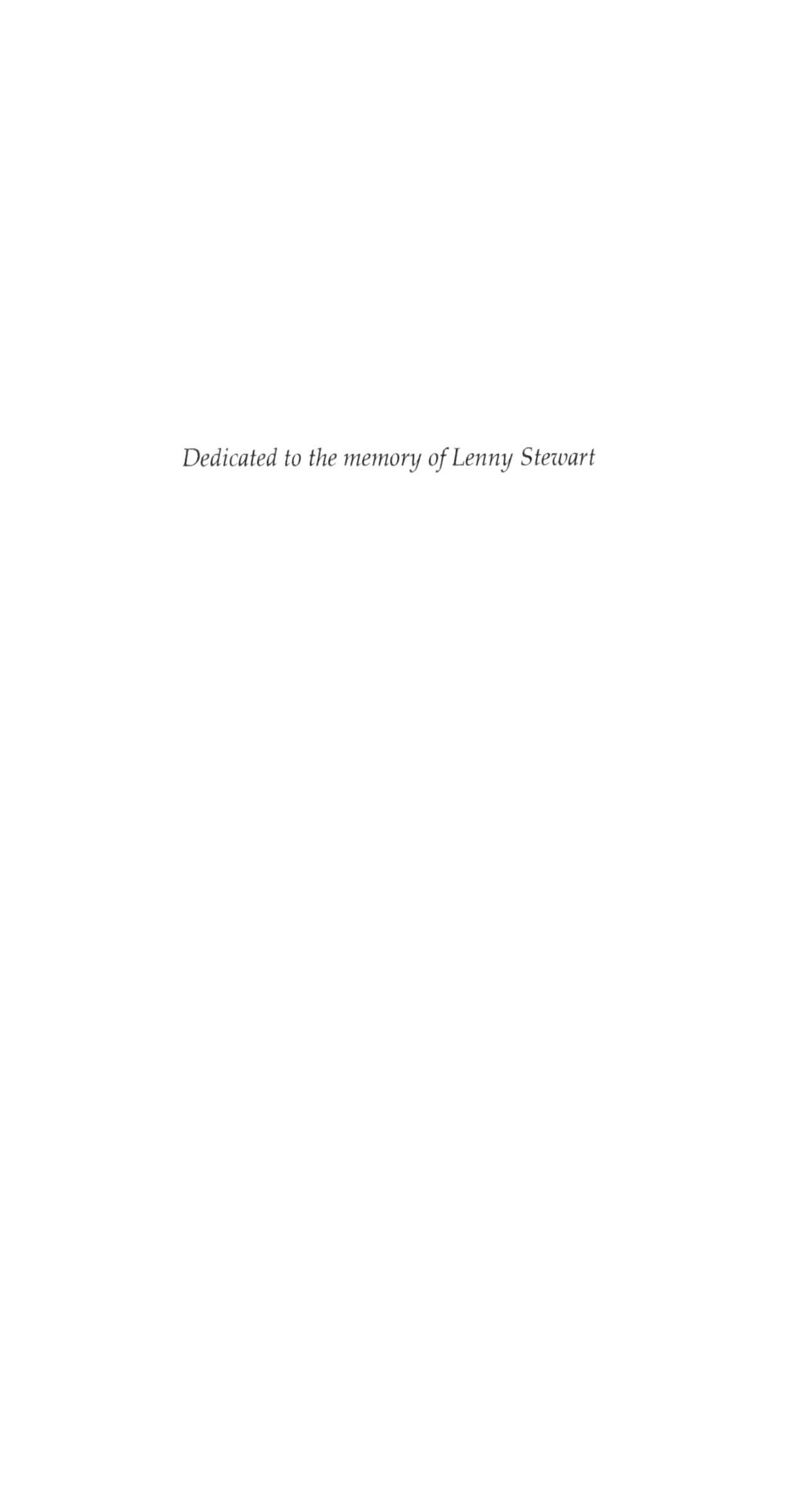

Dedicated to the memory of Lenny Stewart

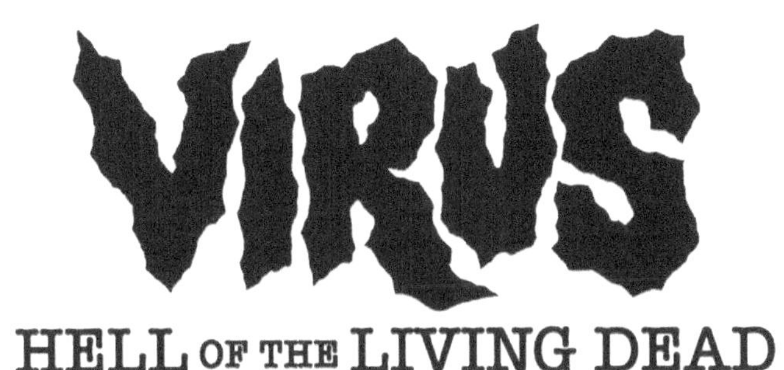

VIRUS
HELL OF THE LIVING DEAD

Turning and turning in the widening gyre
The falcon cannot hear the falconer;
Things fall apart; the centre cannot hold;
Mere anarchy is loosed upon the world,
The blood-dimmed tide is loosed, and everywhere
The ceremony of innocence is drowned;
The best lack all conviction, while the worst
Are full of passionate intensity.

Surely some revelation is at hand;
Surely the Second Coming is at hand.
The Second Coming! Hardly are those words out
When a vast image out of Spiritus Mundi
Troubles my sight: somewhere in sands of the desert
A shape with lion body and the head of a man,
A gaze blank and pitiless as the sun,
Is moving its slow thighs, while all about it
Reel shadows of the indignant desert birds.
The darkness drops again; but now I know
That twenty centuries of stony sleep
Were vexed to nightmare by a rocking cradle,
And what rough beast, its hour come round at last,
Slouches towards Bethlehem to be born?

—William Butler Yeats, "The Second Coming"

And Darkness and Decay and the Red Death held illimitable
dominion over all.

—Edgar Allan Poe, "The Masque of the Red Death"

Prologue

In the darkest, coldest chamber of the nameless city, a being so ancient that its lifespan could only be regarded as eternal awakened. For centuries, it had slumbered dreamlessly, adrift in the starless ether of its inner universe. But now, at long last, the time for slumber had ended. The stars and planets had once again come into alignment, and the time for upheaval and judgment was at hand. The barrier between worlds was growing thin, and soon the gateway would open.

The being's names over millennia had been many, but it preferred the name the Greeks had given it: Charon. There was, after all, a river separating the underground city from the cave that served as an entrance to the world above. But the nameless city itself was older than the Greeks. Older even than the Sumerians, who had worshipped the being as the goddess Tiamat. The grand archways and towering spires that made up the cathedrals of the city had been carved into stone by a vanished race, whose giant bones had been repurposed as building materials for the smaller, though no less architecturally intricate structures that stretched from just beyond the banks of the river to deepest recesses of the chasm below the cradle of civilization.

Charon rose from its resting place, shook the dust from its robes, and began its slow march through the city. From the cold, grey interior of the Chamber of Sleep, past the oldest cathedral, with its garlands of luminescent lichen, through the labyrinthine streets lined by the bone houses of the residential quarter. Charon walked on, its ancient sinews creaking as waking life flowed back into its corporeal form. It breathed the cool air of the empty city and enjoyed the echo of each footfall upon the moist stone.

At last, it settled on the banks of the river, content to watch the burbling water pass while it awaited the arrival of the first humans whose souls were pure enough to enter. In the shallows at the edge of the river, something shiny caught Charon's eye. It stooped to pluck it from the sandy riverbed. The object was a gold coin, its markings worn smooth by centuries of flowing water. Charon wondered which civilization had minted the coin. A smile played across Charon's skeletal features as it remembered a human tradition. It drew back its hand and tossed the coin into the water, silently wishing that the empty city would soon teem with life.

Part One

Things Fall Apart…

"We do what we're told and cash the paycheck."

—Dr. Jeffrey A. Proust

1

The dog was already dead when Dr. Morton Fairbanks' battered Jeep rolled over it. At least he wouldn't have that on his conscience.

The carcass was laid out in the middle of the road, and it exploded in a spray of rancid innards and noxious gases. Fairbanks gagged as the smell hit him. The Jeep was standard military issue, which meant there were no creature comforts like AC or even doors. His eyes were only half on the road as he yawned away the last vestiges of sleep.

It wasn't surprising that he didn't see the dog until it was too late. Hell, it could have been an elephant and he might not have noticed it. Muscle memory got him through the drive from the barracks to the lab these days. After a couple years in country, muscle memory accounted for just about everything outside the lab.

There was a loud pop as the front passenger side tire blew and the Jeep jerked to the right. Fairbanks grabbed at the wheel with both hands and stomped on the brakes. He killed the ignition, unbuckled his seatbelt, and clambered out onto hard packed dirt to check the carnage. Not only was the tire completely blown out, it was splattered with roadkill gore.

"Double whammy," he sighed.

Dawn had just begun to color the bottom edge of the horizon, but it was already hot as hell. The air was thick with humidity, without the faintest hint of a breeze. What a day to come back from a week of vacation.

Vacation? He nearly laughed at the thought. He'd just spent seven days ping-ponging between his quarters and the cafeteria. When he wasn't sleeping or eating, he'd whiled away the hours watching mindless TV shows and masturbating while reading cheap paperback romance novels, an innocuous vice that nevertheless filled him with shame. By the end of the week, he thought he was rested and ready to return to work. But now that he was here, standing in the middle of the road in the stifling African heat, he felt just as tired as he had a week ago.

Fairbanks abandoned the Jeep—keys still in it—and started walking. One of the guards coming off night shift could retrieve the vehicle. It wasn't like the damn thing was blocking traffic or in danger of being stolen. Besides, he could do with a little exercise. The last couple years had taken their toll on his health. During his last company-mandated checkup, Dr. Bouchard had read him the riot act about high blood pressure, obesity, bad cholesterol, and imminent diabetes.

"Too much junk food from the cafeteria, Morton. Try having a salad for dinner instead of an entire pizza," Bouchard had said.

Fairbanks had just mumbled the usual bullshit about how he'd make some changes, knowing full well he intended to do no such thing. The food that Marsh Industries imported was one of the few pleasures available to the employees in Daroka. The irony wasn't lost on Fairbanks. A few miles away, people were literally starving, but he was in danger of eating himself to death.

"Another day in paradise," he muttered, scrubbing beads of sweat from his forehead with the back of his hand.

He fixed his eyes on the Marsh Industries complex and put one foot in front of the other.

See, Bouchard? I'm getting the recommended number of steps!

By the time he made it to the guard station in the lobby of the main building, his shirt was wet under his arms and across his back. The guard on duty—a kid so young his cheeks were still aflame with acne—went through the motions of checking Fairbanks' ID badge.

"Good morning, sir." The kid's voice cracked on the last syllable.

"If you say so." Fairbanks shivered as the building's air condition system turned his sweat-stained shirt to a clammy film on the small of his back. Good thing he kept a set of scrubs in the lab for such emergencies. "I had a flat on the road from the barracks. The keys are still in it."

"Yes, sir. We'll get that taken care of," the guard said.

Fairbanks stepped past the guard desk and walked into the even cooler hallway. Daroka may have been a third world jungle hellhole, but you'd never know it by taking a tour of the lab facility. The first floor looked like it could belong to any number of high-end pharmaceutical research centers. The floor was faux marble, and it caused footfalls to echo softly in the high-ceilinged lobby. Tasteful, nondescript potted plants were set in every corner. The walls were decorated with bland landscape paintings in varnished wood frames. A short hallway in the rear of the lobby contained a pair of low-backed chairs done in imitation black leather. The chairs, in which Fairbanks had never seen anyone actually sit, faced a pair of elevators.

The elevator on the right accessed the upper levels of the building. These three floors contained the pure research science labs. That was where the teams of biochemical engineers toiled away during the regular nine-to-five shift.

The elevator on the left went to the basement level. It was a round-the-clock operation that only employees with the highest security clearance could access. This elevator required a thumbprint and voice ID check before the doors even opened.

Fairbanks pressed his right thumb to the scanner and cleared his throat. "Morton Fairbanks. Access code alpha zero-nine-five-one-five."

The door slid back and Fairbanks stepped inside. There was no control panel in the elevator. It only traveled between the first floor and the basement. Fairbanks' stomach lurched as the elevator began its descent. He'd put away his usual pair of sausage biscuits and hash browns for breakfast, and the walk from the Jeep to the lab complex had churned them to acidic froth in his gut. The three cups of coffee he'd used to wash the food down didn't help matters.

The elevator lurched to a halt, and the doors opened. Fairbanks stepped into the brightly lit lab. The soles of his shoes squeaked on the polished tile floor. No carpet down here. Many of the rooms on this level were sterile facilities, and carpet wasn't conducive to such an environment. That was also why all food and beverages were restricted to the basement's single staff lounge. Not that anyone had any trouble following that rule. Even Fairbanks, whose body demanded feedings at regular intervals, couldn't eat down here. Like the rest of the staff, he made the trip to the canteen on the second floor at meal or snack times.

There were only a baker's dozen people with unfettered access to the room beyond the door. Eleven of them, including Morton Fairbanks, were multi-disciplined scientists who'd spent years working in R&D for government contractors. The twelfth person was Waylon Marsh, the President and CEO of Marsh Industries. The thirteenth was Dr. Gustav Vogel, the scientist whose research formed the basis of the entire project.

Though he'd spent two years—twenty-six months, if you

wanted precision—in Daroka, Fairbanks still got a faint tickle of butterflies in his stomach when he entered this room. Waylon Marsh had dubbed the place, for some unfathomable reason, "Antares Module." The people who actually worked in the basement had another, more appropriate name for it: The Freak Show.

Anyone confused about why the unofficial name was the more appropriate one wouldn't remain so for longer than the time it took to glance around at the Plexiglass-fronted cells lining the walls. The inhabitants of these cells were still recognizable as human in the same way that severely mutilated corpses in the extreme stages of decay still resemble human anatomy. The difference was that the things in the cells—Fairbanks steadfastly refused to think of them as people—were still alive. They still shambled aimlessly around their cells, bumping into the walls and one another like delirious drunks. They clawed at the bulletproof glass separating them from the researchers. And worst of all, they still screamed. Fairbanks, like all his colleagues, thanked the nameless architect or engineer who'd had the foresight to make the cells soundproof.

There was a large semicircular desk in the center of the room. Its surface was crammed full of computers and medical monitoring equipment. Currently, two of the desk's six chairs were occupied. Francine Whittaker—her brick red hair wound into a severe bun atop her head—was busily pecking away at a computer keyboard. Jeff Proust sat with his back to her, flipping through a stack of papers. He was a gangly scarecrow of a man. Fairbanks' method for dealing with the isolation and endless grind of life in Daroka was stuffing his face, while Proust's release valve was endless hours on the treadmill in the staff gym. It took all types to make the world go round, even in this godforsaken place.

Fairbanks stepped behind the desk and took a seat. The chair squeaked beneath his weight.

"Welcome back, Morty," Proust said. "How was the week off? Get into any trouble?"

Fairbanks shrugged. He left it at that. His colleagues knew what passed for vacation in Daroka. No one was allowed off company property without an armed guard detail.

"In case you're wondering," Whittaker said without looking away from her computer, "there has been zero improvement."

"That's not exactly true," Proust countered, rattling a sheet of paper for emphasis. "Wagner and Yokono administered cognitive tests during the overnight, and these numbers show significant slowing in the rates of deterioration. They gave them the usual metabolic panel while they were at it, and guess what, those rates have also slowed."

Well, that's just fucking great, Fairbanks thought. *Instead of dissolving into stinking puddles of goo one week after exposure, the test subjects are just decaying on their feet. Break out the champagne, fellas!*

Whittaker shook her head. "Statistical anomalies. Standard deviation. Take your pick. But don't expect me to start turning cartwheels. At this rate, we'll be stuck in this shithole until judgment day."

Fairbanks tuned them out. The word around the water cooler was that Whittaker and Proust had begun—in clear violation of company policy—a sexual relationship. Fairbanks didn't care much for office gossip, but he could certainly see how that particular rumor started. It didn't make a bit of difference to him if Whittaker and Proust spent all their free time in bed together. Fairbanks' interest in that sort of thing had withered almost entirely away. It had been months since he'd put in a request with the R&R desk to have a native girl brought to his quarters. These days, he was more interested in a bowl of ice cream before bed than having some glassy-eyed pre-teen girl spread her legs for him.

"What do you think, Morty?" Proust asked. "We seeing progress here or not?"

Fairbanks shrugged again. He'd long ago given up asking Proust not to use that nickname. "Hard to say. A single cognitive test and a metabolic is hardly conclusive."

Whittaker swiveled around in her chair and poked Proust in the ribs with her elbow. "See? I told you not to get excited."

"Woman, you haven't seen me get excited," Proust said.

"Oh yeah? Is that a fact?"

Fairbanks cleared his throat. "I'm less concerned with the quantitative stuff. How is the behavioral side of things looking?"

"Well," Whittaker said, swiveling around to face him. "You see that big one in Cell F? He bit Wagner."

"What?" Fairbanks turned his gaze to Cell F.

"He's been a bad boy." Proust laughed. "That's why he's in isolation."

Like all the human test subjects in Antares Module, the occupant of that cell had been drawn from the native population. Technically, Daroka was in the midst of a civil war. General George Mbowi and his troops had executed the President and a good portion of the country's parliament, then assumed control of the government. What the United Nations had chosen to refer to as civil war was actually much closer to a violent purge of Daroka's political dissidents. In simple terms, anyone who made George Mbowi's shitlist was put under arrest and never heard from again. One could reasonably assume that the detainees were executed and tossed into a mass grave in the jungle. That assumption would be wrong, however. The detainees were drugged into unconsciousness and delivered to the gates of the Marsh Industries compound.

The current resident of Cell F might have been a former member of the Daroka parliament or one of the protesters from the riots in the capital city. Maybe he was just someone who looked at one of Mbowi's soldiers wrong. Whatever he'd been in his past life, the man in Cell F—Subject 1349, according to the paperwork in Fairbanks' hand—was now a scientific experiment gone awry, as well as a victim of the Marsh Industries barter system. As Fairbanks understood it, the current rate of exchange was a two AK-47 rifles for each test subject or one shoulder-mounted rocket launcher for a dozen.

"Yeah," Proust continued, "it went down before shift change on Friday. Wagner was in there administering tests, and all the sudden, 1349 decided to have a nibble. Francine and I ran in there to get the subject into restraints, and he had a nip at her too."

Whittaker lifted her left hand, which was partially wrapped in a gauze bandage. "Barely broke the skin, but yeah, he got me. Not like Wagner, though. 1349 took a good chunk out of his right forearm. He had to get stitched up."

"That level of aggression is unprecedented," Fairbanks said. "What strain were you testing on 1349?"

"Just the latest SD-9 to come down from the second floor," Proust answered. "Only this time, we combined it with the prion booster. That was a suggestion that came straight from Vogel himself."

Fairbanks got up from his chair and crossed the room. He needed to get a closer look. The path to Cell F took him past the first five cells. The test subject in these cells were housed four to each unit. Some of them stood, swaying on their feet as they drooled and moaned. Others lay on the concrete floor, their eyes glassy and unblinking as they stared into the fluorescent lights overhead. There were both male and female subjects, and once they'd made it through the initial round of injections, they were housed in coed quarters. Even if the test subjects showed any inclination toward sexual activity, the act was quite impossible. One of the many side effects of the serum was near instant withering of the sexual organs.

After two years, Fairbanks had yet to reach the level of desensitization that his colleagues displayed. He still recoiled when examining the test subjects. There were side effects other than desiccated penises and shrunken vaginas, and they were possibly even more repulsive. The subjects in Cell A were in the advanced stages of serum exposure, and they displayed the worst of the side effects. Fairbanks forced himself to pause in front of the cell. Desensitized or not, he felt a need—a compulsion, really—to examine his work.

There were three male subjects and a lone female. All four were stumbling into one another as they shuffled aimlessly in the tight space. Their mouths hung open, letting their blistered, oozing tongues hang freely. Their heads were mostly bald, their hair having fallen out in clumps during the initial stages of exposure. Their scalps were red raw, crusted with dried blood and pus. The skin on their limbs and torsos was crisscrossed with suppurating wounds bordered by ragged scraps of dried skin. Another few days, and the skin would begin to slough away entirely, exposing the withered musculature beneath. Then, at last, the abdominal cavity would burst, spilling the internal organs onto the floor in a fetid, gooey heap. Fairbanks had seen it before. He'd seen it many times during his time in Daroka.

The residents of Cell B weren't much better off, although they appeared to still have some motor control. One of the male subjects paused in front of the glass partition between him and Fairbanks. The subject stared straight ahead as he scratched slowly, methodically at the shriveled limp penis between his thighs. With a grunt, the subject ripped the organ away from his body and smeared the bloody scraps across the glass.

"Jesus Christ," Fairbanks whispered, stepping away from the cell. He called over his shoulder, "How are this one's vitals?"

"Yeah, about that," Proust said. "That particular one

seems okay, but 1349 has some issues. The old boy must have squashed his chip out of place when he was wrestling with Wagner. His monitor is showing a total flat line, body temp nearing ambient, and next to no metabolic function."

Fairbanks shook his head. The chip Proust was referencing was implanted in the chest cavity of each subject via a quick laparoscopic insertion. There was no way a bit of wrestling could knock it loose. It was grafted into the tissue itself.

"Have you tried a repair?" Fairbanks asked.

This time, it was Whittaker who answered. "You feel like fighting that guy? Because we tried sedating him. Hit him with a heavy cocktail, diazepam and thorazine, but it didn't do a damn thing. We even had some animal tranqs sent down from the third floor and gave those a whirl. No dice."

"That's…" Fairbanks paused, searching for the right word. "That's alarming."

He quickened his pace a bit, still forcing himself to peer into each cell, but no longer pausing for a close examination. Finally, he made it to Cell F, where Subject 1349 was isolated. The male subject displayed most of same defects as his fellow residents of Antares Module: the oozing sores, the unblinking eyes, the shriveled genitalia. But the slack-jawed, seemingly disoriented state wasn't as pronounced. When 1349 turned his eyes at Fairbanks' approach, he actually *saw* the doctor. Fairbanks was sure of it. Perhaps there was no real sense of personal recognition, but the subject was certainly aware of a human presence.

Subject 1349 lunged for the glass, his jaws opening and snapping shut like those of an attack dog. And just like a mad dog, flecks of foam flew from his lips as his head whipped back and forth. The heavy canvas material of the collar restraint bit into the subject's neck, drawing blood that ran in thick rivulets down his bare chest. His hands reached out, clawing at the glass.

"Good Lord, what have we done?" Fairbanks muttered.

"Looks like you got him all fired up, Morty!" Proust jeered. "Maybe he wants to come out and play."

Fairbanks tore himself away from the gruesome spectacle and stalked back to the desk.

"That's neither funny nor appropriate, Proust. Don't forget who outranks whom down here." He poked the younger doctor in the chest with his finger, daring him to protest. Then, he rounded on Whittaker. "And you, why the hell are you not in quarantine? Did exposure protocol go out the window while I was on vacation? This won't do, I tell you. Not at all."

"Hey, just back off," Whittaker said, whipping her glasses off her face and tossing them onto the cluttered desk. "I did a full 48 in quarantine and checked out fine."

"Protocol states that you should still be under observation," Fairbanks countered.

"You mean that's what protocol used to state," Proust said, smiling. "While you were locked away in your room, stuffing donuts into your mouth, a new set of rules came down. And when I say 'came down,' I mean they came straight from the top. Waylon Marsh himself wants all hands on deck around the clock in light of recent developments. Herr Vogel wants us using the prion-boosted serum exclusively."

"Recent developments?" Fairbanks raised his eyebrows. "Meaning what?"

Proust pointed to Cell F. "Meaning that nasty bugger in isolation. Marsh wants to replicate that as quickly as possible. Hence, the switch to the prion-boost."

"Replicate it?" Fairbanks shook his head in confusion. "Why the hell would he want that?"

Proust shrugged. "Hey, you know the score at this laugh factory. We do what we're told and cash the paycheck. Anything else is above our pay-grade."

2

On the southern side of the Marsh Industries compound, in the nondescript dormitory that the employees called "the barracks," Brett Wagner popped his daily antibiotic dose into his mouth and washed it down with a mouthful of tepid coffee. The pills the pharmacy had given him were goddamn horse pills that threatened to choke him every time he took one. The meds might have been fighting off a possible infection, but they also gave him a world-class case of the drizzly shits and made him sweat, even in the dim, air conditioned interior of his room. And, of course, they did fuck-all for the burning itch on his wounded arm.

He flopped back down on his bed and tried to focus on the screen of his television. It was just some taped rerun of an inane British sitcom, but Wagner was willing to try anything to distract him from the itch. The urge to tear back the swaddling of bandages and scratch at his stitched-up wound was overwhelming. He'd given in to that urge twice already, and both times, he'd landed himself back in the infirmary. The last time, Dr. Stilwell had threatened to put Wagner's forearm in a cast if he couldn't leave it alone.

"It's either a cast or I put your right hand in a mitten," Dr.

Stilwell had said. "But you can't keep scratching at that wound. There's no sign of infection yet, but there will be if you don't leave it alone."

"Damn thing itches like there are fire ants under my skin," Wagner had complained.

"I'm sure it does. That's the same thing I heard from Dr. Tasker and those two assistants who got nibbled by their lab rats. And I'll tell you the same thing I told them: I can give you antibiotics to keep you from getting sick and Benadryl to help with the itching. You're just going to have to endure a little discomfort."

Wagner had mumbled something like a promise not to scratch his wound and held out his left arm so it could be bandaged again.

Now, sitting on his bed, he was teetering on the edge of breaking that promise. He felt the invisible fire ants on his forearm, crawling over his skin. Yet, every time he complained, the doctors in the infirmary just assured him there was no sign of infection and that a minor itch was an expected part of the healing process.

"Minor itch?" Wagner laughed. "Minor itch, my ass."

He scooped up the remote control and fired it at the TV screen, putting a merciful end to the snooty British accents and canned laughter. He stood up from his bed and paced the room, eager to get out of here and…well, he didn't quite know what he was eager to do. There wasn't much in the way of distraction out here in the sticks. And he was beginning to think that the fat paycheck wasn't worth the boredom. Sure, each monthly deposit was close to what he'd made in an entire year of teaching at Covington College, but what good was all that money when you were stuck in the armpit of the world on an open-ended contract?

Wagner stepped into his shoes and shuffled out of his room. He walked down the hallway, muttering half-hearted greetings to the colleagues he passed on his way out of the building.

"Hey, Brett, how they hanging?" a cheerful researcher named Quinley asked as Wagner passed her in the first floor lobby.

Wagner grunted.

Unable to take the hint, Quinley fell into step beside him. "You going into work early?"

"Yeah." Wagner quickened his pace as he crossed the open space between him and the front door.

The lobby looked like the waiting room of an upscale dentist office. There were couches and chairs set along the wall, potted plants in the corners, and a large central desk, where the building's concierge sat, ready to help with any problems or requests the residents might have. Like all the accommodations in the barracks, the furnishings were top-shelf. The non-essential staff—the concierge, the cooking and cleaning crews, the personal assistants—were obsequious and eager to please. Marsh Industries spared no expense when it came to the creature comforts of its scientists and researchers. But just like the paycheck, all the fancy furniture and good food amounted to very little after a long stretch in Daroka. Outside the gates of the compound, a bloody civil war was raging. Inside the gates, boredom reigned supreme. Wagner had begun to doubt whether one was preferable to the other.

"Arm still giving you trouble?" Quinley asked as they passed the concierge desk.

The concierge on duty cleared his throat politely and asked if they needed to check a vehicle out of the motor pool.

"Don't know about her plans..." Wagner pointed to Quinley. "But I'm walking."

"Yeah, think I'll walk too," Quinley said. "It's a nice evening."

"Great," Wagner said.

If the antibiotics boiling away in the pit of his stomach

weren't enough to nauseate him, the thought of a fifteen minute walk with one of his colleagues did the trick. After two full years living in these people, Wagner sometimes thought he could happily murder the lot of them. They were, after all, scumbags, one and all. He knew this because he himself was a scumbag. He'd been dismissed from Covington after the number of rape rumors became too much for the administration to ignore. Wagner knew that fat fuck Fairbanks had gotten up to similar hanky-panky at Stanford, only there were rumors that the fat boy preferred them young. Proust and Whittaker had been hit with so many malpractice suits that no hospital would dare employ them. And Quinley? Rumor had it that, once upon a time, she'd killed a string of husbands by poisoning their morning coffee. That was the way Marsh Industries had staffed the research center. They'd collected a group of brilliant but morally bankrupt minds and promised them a big payday in exchange for extended service on a project that might end up giving the scientists of the Third Reich a run for the money. And once their term of service was complete and they'd signed a stack of nondisclosure forms, they would have a blank slate. It had seemed like a no-lose situation when Wagner had signed on.

It was a wonder no one had burned the whole thing to the ground, Wagner often thought. Then again, if Marsh Industries had spared no expense with the living quarters, they'd done even more with the security measures. Word around the campfire was that at least one in five of the scientific staff was actually an undercover security operative.

The automatic front doors of the barracks slid open, and Wagner stepped out into the humid, mosquito-choked air.

"Wow, would you look at that sunset!" Quinley said, trotting a few steps to come alongside him. "You sure don't get them like that back in Omaha."

Wagner slapped away a cloud of insects.

"So, you never told me how that arm was doing." Quinley pointed to the thick bandage. "Almost looks like you got a cast on that thing."

That did it. Wagner had gotten more than his fill of the murderous pixie's sing-song voice. In his past life, he might have found her attractive; although she would never be mistaken for a porn star, she was cute in a girl next door way. But now, her upturned nose with the faint spray of freckles, her little heart-shaped mouth, her perky ass, and even her red-painted fingernails filled him with something close to revulsion.

He glanced to the side, giving her a head-to-toe appraisal, and came to a decision.

"Hey," he said, forcing his mouth to smile. "You feel like taking the long way around?"

"You mean the jungle road?"

Wagner nodded. "That sunset might look pretty through the canopy."

"Wow, I've never been on the jungle road before."

"Up to you." Wagner shrugged. "I'm going that way and thought some company might be nice."

"Okay," Quinley said. "Let's go!"

Although there was only one official road from the barracks to the research center, there was another way to get from Point A to Point B. The official road was a two-lane dirt track cut through the patch of jungle that separated the barracks from the research center. The other road, the so-called jungle road, wasn't really a road at all. It was a path that had been cut through the dense vegetation, possibly by the natives who were displaced when the compound was built. Wagner had often wondered why Marsh Industries hadn't just cleared all the land when they built the compound. He'd heard at least a dozen theories—most of them related to keeping the place relatively hidden from aircraft—but he figured it probably just came down to money.

Expense had to be spared somewhere, or perhaps it was just a matter of trying to get the compound up and running as quickly as possible. Whatever the reason, there was a patch of jungle just inside the perimeter wall, and through this patch of jungle, there was a circuitous trail that led from the barracks to the research center. And it was onto that trail that Wagner led Quinley.

Although she expressed appreciation for the beauty of their natural surroundings, she certainly didn't look around in awed silence. If anything, her inane chatter only ramped up in volume and pace as they went. Wagner had to force himself to wait until they'd put a respectable distance between themselves and the barracks before he pounced.

"You know, Quinley," he said, edging close to her as they walked beneath the thick canopy of trees. "I wonder if you'd mind answering a question."

"It's Roseanne," she said, "and if you want to know if I killed a bunch of rich husbands, the answer is no. I only killed one, and Leroy was far from rich. He was a deadbeat drunk. But I killed him, all right. And the way he used to slap me around, I probably would have gotten away with a slap on the wrist, only Leroy's cousin was a county judge. Thank God for Marsh Industries, though. After this project wraps up, I'll be able to buy and sell Leroy's cousin."

"I guess that's…"

"What? Disappointing?" she laughed. "Well, I'm sorry I'm not a bad girl."

"Still…" Wagner grabbed her arm, spinning her around to face him. "I think I'm going to do this anyway."

She pulled her arm out of his grasp. "Hey, look, I'm not that kind of girl."

Wagner drew back his fist and brought it around in what the rednecks back in Covington had called "a real haymaker." It connected with Quinley's—*it's Roseanne*—face with a soft smack. Wagner had never punched someone in the face before, and the sound was nothing like it was in the movies. It was anticlimactic in a way. Nevertheless, the blow did what it was intended to do. It landed with enough force to spin Quinley around on her heels and nearly knock her off balance. Wagner wrapped his arms around her waist and dragged her off the trail and into the jungle vegetation. Creeping vines and thorny weeds caught at his feet and ankles. Quinley recovered and began to squirm and thrash in Wagner's arms. But neither the plants nor her violent movements were enough to deter his assault.

He pressed forward, leaving the trail far behind, until he found a small clearing and threw Quinley to the ground. She screamed, and he gave her a kick to the ribs.

"Not that it matters," he said, looming over her. "There's no one out here. We're still a couple hours away from shift change. But I'd rather not hear all that racket."

She pushed herself up on her elbows and screamed again anyway. Wagner sighed and kicked again. This time, his aim was off. He'd meant to give her another shot to the ribs, to knock the wind out of her. But his foot went high, and the toe of his mud-streaked sneaker broke her cute freckly nose flat against her face and smashed both her lips in the bargain. She fell back hard, her head slamming onto the ground. It didn't knock her unconscious—Wagner could hear her soft moaning —but it sure as hell took the fight out of her. That much was evident when he knelt beside her and removed her pants and underwear. Her eyes didn't even open when he tore off her shirt and bra.

"Well, Quinley…excuse me, *Roseanne,* you may not have murdered a bunch of rich husbands, but I most certainly did have my way with a bunch of coeds." He forced her legs apart and moved between them. "Some of them just needed a little gentle persuasion, others required some force. But in the end, I got my way."

He unbuttoned his pants and eased them down to his

knees. To his utter dismay, his cock still hung limply. He grunted as he took it in his hand and gave it a few gentle tugs. Not only did the act fail to produce any change, it also failed to give him the slightest sensation. It was like the doctor had injected lidocaine into his dick. He stroked furiously, but to no avail. Something squirmed in his belly. He felt like he was going to—

He fell forward, vomiting a steady stream as he landed on Quinley. His stomach continued to heave and contract. Hot bile filled his mouth and nose. He rolled onto his side and spewed until he was sure that his guts would come up. Finally, the convulsions in his belly stopped. And then gradually, the nausea abated. He stood up, rocking unsteadily on his feet.

"What the fuck?" he wheezed, looking down at himself.

His shirt was soaked in stinking, blood-streaked vomit. He peeled it off and flung it into the trees. His pants had made it through the ordeal mostly unscathed, and he tugged them up, trying not to look too closely at the strange grey color that his limp cock had taken on. Finally, he looked down at Quinley. Her eyes were open now, staring accusatorily at Wagner, but she lay there unmoving.

This time, when Wagner's belly contracted and growled, it wasn't from nausea. This time, it was hunger. No, that wasn't right. The sensation that had taken hold of Wagner's guts— his whole body, actually—was something so far beyond hunger that it defied description.

He dropped to his knees again. His hands moved as if of their own volition, rubbing and scratching at Quinley's vomit-spattered body.

"No," she moaned, feebly squirming beneath him.

Wagner dropped down to his belly, his face pressed close to one of Quinley's breasts. The twin sensations of hunger and disgust fought a pitched battle in the depths of Wagner's stomach. He opened his mouth and gagged, knowing that he had to obey the hunger, but fighting against it with his last reserves of strength. In the end, the hunger won out.

Wagner buried his face in the soft flesh of Quinley's breast and bit down. She screamed and writhed beneath him as he pulled back, straining to bring his teeth together around the mouthful of flesh. Something like an orgasm rocked him back as he tore that first chunk of flesh free and chomped it down. His throat bulged as he swallowed. He took a deep breath and went back for more. That same nearly sexual bliss washed over him as he bit into her shoulder. His dick still hung useless and limp in his pants, but he no longer cared.

Eventually, Quinley stopped screaming. By that time, her body had been savaged, covered in bites from neck to ankles, and Wagner lay beside her, his distended belly straining at the button of his pants. And then, as the jungle grew dark around them, Quinley began to moan. Wagner smiled as he felt the scrape of her teeth against his arm.

3

Fairbanks checked his watch. Then he checked the clock on the wall.

"Wagner is a full hour late," he announced.

Proust looked up from his work station. "Yeah, and I'm telling you right now, I don't care if Waylon Marsh himself said he wants this phase of the project going twenty-four hours until completion, I'm not working overtime. Francine and I got a date in the barracks' rec room. They're showing *Pretty Woman* on the big screen. After that, maybe a midnight stroll down the jungle road with our flashlights and a bottle of wine."

Fairbanks rolled his eyes.

The lady in question was all the way across the lab, prepping the residents of Cell Z for their dose of the prion-boosted serum. Their orders were to begin immediate injection of all the basement test subjects—108 individuals, all in various stages of development. The order was so sudden—and reckless, even—that Fairbanks had felt it necessary to get Pete Sorenson, the Marsh Industries corporate liaison in Daroka on the phone.

"Look, Dr. Fairbanks," Sorenson had said in his clipped,

semi-European accent, "you may not be one of our ex-military men, but surely you understand the chain of command. This directive came from the Board of Directors, which meant it came from Waylon Marsh himself. Not that it matters, but the order has the express approval of Dr. Vogel. So, with all due respect to your expertise, inject the serum."

While Fairbanks had been troubled by the order, he knew he had little choice but to follow it. And Whittaker, who'd been acting jittery all morning, had been eager to get started, volunteering to start the injections while Proust and Fairbanks monitored the subjects' vitals, which were broadcasted from their implant chip to one of the desk computers.

"Do you ever wonder, Proust," Fairbanks began as he tried to focus on the computer in front of him, "what the purpose of this project really is? We've speculated, of course, but have you ever really asked yourself why our base of operations is here in Daroka?"

Proust sniffed. "I don't really give a fuck what Waylon Marsh's endgame is. All I know is that once this tour of duty is up, I get to go home with seven figures in my bank account and a clear record with the American Medical Association. If a few primitives happen to die along the way, it's all for the greater good, right?"

Fairbanks sighed. When he'd started his work at Antares Module, he'd had a similar attitude, but lately, he'd begun to wonder about the long term repercussions of their work. *For the Greater Good!* was the Marsh Industries motto, and it had, for Fairbanks, taken on an increasingly sinister edge.

"Just look at her working," Proust said, nodding in Whittaker's direction. "I know she's a little flat up top, but I've always been more of an ass man myself. And just get a look at that caboose."

"Primitives, indeed."

"Fuck you, Fairbanks. You can take your holier-than-thou

bullshit and stick it where the sun don't shine. Or are you the only scientist in this joint without a skeleton in the closet? Tell me, Morty, what did Marsh dig up on you? Were you fucking undergrads? Or maybe it was little boys, huh?"

Fairbanks stood up. "I'm not going to dignify that with a response."

"Is that so?" Proust snickered. "Well, where are you going?"

"To help your lady fair, the one with the magnificent caboose, get on with the injections. I don't see a point in drawing this out any longer than necessary."

4

Bill Parker emptied the big red barrel marked "Warning: Biohazardous Waste" into a regular black plastic garbage bag. He wrinkled his nose at the sight of the contents. It was the usual slop: a bunch of used-up hypodermics, discarded latex gloves, cracked and leaking glass vials, and a whole pile of dead rats.

Rats.

Bill was just a janitor with the overnight cleaning crew, but that didn't mean he was too stupid to have a sense of irony. And tonight, as he pushed his supply cart, through the hallways of the third floor, going from lab to lab, emptying trashcans and collecting abandoned coffee cups, his sense of irony was red hot. It was all down to the rats. In this place, the rat test subjects got the third floor, with its scenic views and cushy staff lounges. The human test subjects, however, were confined to the basement, where there were no windows, and what passed for a staff lounge was a cramped room with flickering fluorescent lighting, a mini-fridge, and a basic coffee maker. Not that the test subjects gave a shit about staff lounges or views. They were—rats and humans alike—

confined to cages, spending what remained of their lives on death row.

Still, it was sort of funny when you thought about it.

There was, however, nothing funny about the restrooms on the third floor. For a bunch of college-educated research scientists, the people working up here were fucking slobs. Especially the women. Bill had cleaned truck stop bathrooms that couldn't hold a candle to what the stuck up bitches on the—

He paused with his cart halfway through the doorway to the women's restroom. Something was rustling around in the black trash bag hanging from the back of the cart. He stood there for a moment, sure that his imagination was playing tricks on him, then pushed the cart into the restroom. But then it happened again, a faint rustling, scratching sound. This time, there was no doubt about it. The bag even moved.

"Fucking eggheads left a live one in the trash can," he muttered, shaking his head.

He opened the bag and peered inside. On one hand, he could just ignore it and go on with his duties. All the trash was bound for the incinerator anyway. But what if the critter chewed his way out of the bag and got loose? He'd end up chasing the goddamn thing all over the place. Besides, wasn't it enough that the eggheads had injected the rat with all their potions and elixirs then tossed it into the garbage? Did the little bastard really need to burn to death on top of that? Sure, it was just a rat, but there was something about the whole deal that rubbed Bill the wrong way. It didn't seem right.

He sighed. "Goddamn it."

He snapped on a pair of yellow rubber gloves—the ones he used when he had to scrub an especially nasty toilet—and plunged his arm into the trash bag. It didn't take long to find the noisemaker—the rat practically jumped into his hand.

"Sorry about this, partner," Bill said, grasping the squirming rodent's midsection with one hand and preparing to twist its neck with the other. "But it's better than getting barbecued alive, I reckon."

But the rat had other ideas rattling around in its pea-sized brain. It was almost like it knew what was coming, and it thrashed against Bill's grip with a vigor that belied its small size.

"Jesus Christ!" Bill yelped as the rat squirmed out of his hand and fell to the floor.

The rat spun around in a few frantic circles before settling back on its haunches to regard Bill with its beady, rheum-crusted eyes. Bill crouched cautiously, then made a wild grab for the rat, which scuttled backwards, just out of reach. The janitor screamed in frustration and lunged forward, like he was going for an open-field tackle. His pants snagged the side of his supply cart, and the whole thing came crashing down. Bottles of liquid cleaner, boxes of rubber gloves, scrub brushes, and cleaning rags scattered over the tile floor. Worst of all, the trash bag ruptured upon impact, spilling its biohazardous contents. A dozen or more dead rats rolled out, joined their living brother.

Bill growled in frustration. He cursed himself for being merciful, wishing that he'd just let the fucking rat go on digging through its dead brothers and sisters on its way to the incinerator. Now he had a real mess on his hands.

He pushed himself to a seated position, never taking his eyes off the escaped rat.

"Come here, you little fucker," Bill whispered, preparing himself for another grab.

The rat obliged, although not in the way Bill hoped. It ran right at him, scrambling over his boot, and disappeared up into his pant leg. Bill's panicked yelps gave way to cries of shock and pain as the rat sank its teeth into his calf muscle. He shrieked like a terrified child as the rat climbed higher, nipping at his thigh. He pounded against the lump in his trousers as it edged its way higher. Now, the rat wasn't just nibbling; it was chomping. Bill watched in horror and disgust as a dark stain spread over his pants. He wasn't sure it if was just blood or if he'd also pissed himself, but the thought was blasted from his brain when the rat began to move even higher, nosing its way into Bill's underwear.

Through the blinding agony, Bill noticed that the other rats—the ones who'd only moments ago been lying there stone cold dead—were stirring to life. One darted up his arm and sank its teeth into his shoulder. Another climbed his lap and worked its way into his shirt. Bill clawed at his pants with one hand and his shirt with another, jabbering in abject terror as he felt a rat climb up his back and into his hair.

By now, he was bleeding from what seemed like a thousand wounds. His vision was going fuzzy around the edges. He could feel consciousness fading, pulling him closer and closer to the end of his waking nightmare.

5

Mirai Yokono had learned from the barracks' concierge that Wagner had gone for an evening stroll down the jungle road with Roseanne Quinley.

"Everyone thinks they're slick, but I can see where you're going on this monitor." The concierge had tapped the computer screen for emphasis. "Technically, I'm supposed to report anyone who goes off the official road, but I usually just turn a blind eye. I mean, I'm stuck out here just like the rest of you. I know how it is. And nothing's ever gone wrong until now. I really hope you find them, because if they go missing, it's my ass too."

Yokono had tried to summon genuine anger, but the truth was that he himself had been known to take a stroll through the jungle with Bas Lundgren, the big Swedish lunk who worked as a security guard at the research center. It was rumored that there was a little hideaway cabin somewhere out there in the jungle—the fabled "love shack"—but Mirai and Bas had never found it. They'd traded blowjobs right out in the open, climaxing to a soundtrack of shrieking birds and croaking frogs. But that had been just fine with Mirai. It was more exciting that way.

"It's okay," Mirai had told the concierge. "I'm sure they just lost track of time. Maybe they even found the love shack and decided to sleep it off. But if I'm not back here in an hour, you better call it in."

The concierge had looked crestfallen. "Sure hope you find him."

"Don't worry," Mirai had said.

Now, as he traipsed through the dark jungle with only a flashlight to guide him, Mirai had started to think that the time to worry had arrived. He'd made it nearly to the end of the road before doubling back and going off the road and into the jungle. If he was going to find Wagner and Quinley, he wasn't going to do it by sticking to the path. He knew it was a bad idea, but he felt that he owed Wagner this much at least. Though he could be an asshole, Wagner had always protected Mirai from the bullying Proust and the slave-driving Fairbanks.

"Hey, Wagner!" he called. "Time to zip it up and get to work, man! We're already late, and unless you want Fairbanks crawling up our asses, we need to get to the lab!"

No response.

Mirai cursed. He checked his compass and continued his trek through the jungle. His plan—if it could really even be called that—was to go as far as the perimeter wall and then zig-zag back to the barracks. If he kept calling out, maybe Wagner might answer. He didn't have much hope. Despite the oppressive heat, his stomach was cold with dread.

Something was wrong out here. Mirai's instinct told him to beat a hasty retreat, to abandon his search and get back to the barracks as quickly as possible. But he fought down the urge. Damn it, he was a scientist. He shouldn't be scared by a nighttime stroll through the little patch of jungle on the southwest corner of the compound.

Still, there was something that wasn't quite right.

He paused, certain that the rustling sound he heard was

footsteps and not the scurrying of some small animal. He turned slowly, bringing the beam of his flashlight to chest level, and found himself face to face with Wagner and Quinley.

"Damn it, guys," he said, "you really had me worried. Do you have any idea what time…?"

He trailed off as he noticed that something was horribly wrong with his colleagues. And because he was such a diligent worker and had a talent for multitasking, Mirai Yokono was able to do two things at once: curse himself for not obeying the urge to run for the safety of the barracks, and scream in abject fear and agony as Wagner and Quinley pulled him to the ground and began biting him.

6

"Well, that's fucking great," Proust said, slamming the desk phone back onto its cradle. He shoved back from the desk and slung his feet on top of it, scattering a stack of papers. "That was the security desk. The whole building's on lockdown. Something about a disturbance up on the third floor and another one at the barracks. It looks like we're stuck down here for a while."

Fairbanks had a bad feeling, like an itch in his brain. It was as if his subconscious was trying to warn him of impending danger, but his senses couldn't register any immediate threat. Something was wrong—very wrong—but he couldn't define it.

He looked across the room at Whittaker, who had worked her way back from Cell Z to Cell R. So far, she'd administered the serum to over thirty of the test subjects. Some of them were already experiencing side effects. Vomiting, diarrhea, grand mal seizures. None of that was unusual. What was highly unusual, however, was the information on the computer screen in front of Fairbanks. He stared at the screen for a moment, trying to make sense of what he was seeing. He refreshed the program. He logged off and restarted the machine. He ran a diagnostic program; all of the things the heavy-sighing, condescending IT specialists recommended when things got glitchy. But none of the troubleshooting changed the information Fairbanks had in front of him.

"Whittaker," he called across the room. "Stop the injections."

"Why?" Proust objected before Whittaker got a chance. "We're getting close to halfway done."

Fairbanks swiveled the monitor around so Proust could see it. "Have a look at this and tell me if you're seeing something different than I am. Because what I see is subjects flat-lining left and right. Only thing is, they're still on their feet. If it were one or two, maybe it could be a chip malfunction, or something blocking the RFID. But I see a dozen or more showing flat-line and rapidly declining body temp."

"What the fuck?" Proust pulled his feet off the desk and scooted closer to the screen.

"How long do you think before they start displaying the same aggression as 1349?" Fairbanks asked.

"It took 1349 nearly 24 hours to show any change in behavior."

"And how long before you noticed 1349 was showing complete flat-line?"

Proust shrugged. "Maybe a few hours. We thought it was a malfunction, so we put in a call to surgical, but we didn't make a big thing of it. Why?"

"This is just a hypothesis, but..." Fairbanks swallowed, his mouth suddenly dry. The reason for his growing dread was beginning to take definite form. "It seems to me that the new serum—maybe it's the prion booster, I don't know—but maybe it's speeding up. The protein inhibitors, perhaps. Or the replicators. Perhaps it's a mutation we didn't see coming. I don't know."

Proust's eyes widened as realization dawned. "But that would mean…"

Fairbanks watched the younger doctor for a moment as he processed the information and ran various scenarios in his head. He knew Proust was coming to the same conclusions. The outlook was grim.

"Jesus Christ, Morty, what the hell have we been doing down here? They told us this was passive population control as a means for ending world hunger, that it was a way to boost immune systems to the point that vaccines were obsolete, that it was…"

Fairbanks nodded. The second part of the statement—the bit about world hunger—was the publicly stated reason for Marsh Industries' presence in Africa. The first part—the portion about passive population control—was kept under the lock and key of non-disclosure agreements and blackmail. It had an unpleasant ring to it, after all. It carried unpleasant connotations of Nazis and eugenics. The sort of thing that made shareholders run away in panic, especially given the fact that Waylon Marsh's fortune was largely derived from his father's diamond operations in war torn regions of the continent. Environmental groups and human rights organizations alike had Marsh Industries in their crosshairs and would pounce on the first bit of concrete evidence that linked the company to something that so clearly violated international law.

"I guess it makes sense," Proust said. "Remember that scandal when Marsh's father said something about the only problem with Africa was all the damn Africans? It took his son years to crawl out of his father's shadow, but perhaps the apple doesn't fall so far from the tree."

Fairbanks leaned to the side to get a better view of Whittaker. She'd quit administering injections, but she was still standing in front of Cell R, leaning against the wheeled supply cart full of needles and vials.

"I suggest you forget about Leonidas Marsh for the moment and go check on your girlfriend." Fairbanks nodded in Whittaker's direction.

"Probably just tired. We're going into our third hour of overtime." He stood up. "Maybe we should just hit the pause button until this lockdown is over. See if we can't get some answers from the third floor before we continue."

"Yes, that sounds prudent."

But Fairbanks was starting to get the idea that it was too late to hit the pause button. Marsh Industries had crossed some line and there was no going back.

No, he corrected himself. *It wasn't Marsh Industries that crossed a line. Sure, they gave the marching order, but it was we, the morally compromised boots on the ground, who sighted the Rubicon and gleefully marched across. And all for what? A paycheck? A second chance at life with a clean slate?*

Proust had returned to the desk, leading Whittaker by the arm. Several strands of red hair had come loose from the bun atop her head and hung loosely about her face. She'd removed her glasses and tucked them into the breast pocket of her lab coat. Her eyes appeared heavy-lidded and bloodshot, with dark circles underneath. She looked like she hadn't slept in days.

"Sorry, guys," she said, shrugging out of her lab coat as she dropped herself into a chair. "I just got to feeling a little woozy there for a second. Must be something I ate."

Fairbanks glanced at her bandaged forearm. *Or maybe something that tried to eat you.*

"You know what we need?" Proust stood at her side, rubbing his hands together like he was hatching a plan. "Some good, strong coffee. I'm going to the lounge to brew some up."

"Yeah." Whittaker hugged her arms around herself. "Coffee sounds good. All of the sudden, it feels cold down here."

Proust edged his way around Fairbanks and headed for the staff lounge. Fairbanks watched him go then turned his attention back to Whittaker. She was a natural redhead with fair skin, so it was hard to say whether or not she had grown pale, but there was a sheen of sweat on her forehead.

Fairbanks cleared his throat. "Whittaker, I wonder if I might check your vitals. If you don't mind me saying so, you don't look well."

"What are you implying?" She gripped her chair's armrests. "I feel fine."

"Whittaker, you know exactly what I'm implying. Let's be adults here."

"Fuck you, Morty." She emphasized the nickname, surely aware of how much he hated it. Her gaze flicked downward, glancing at her injured arm, then snapped back to stare right into his eyes. "I'm not one of your test subjects."

"*Our* test subjects," he said, careful to keep his voice low and even. "Let's not get too hasty to assign blame. We've all contributed to this project."

"You know what, Morty? Jeff and I have had just about enough…"

She stopped short, gagging as if the words had physically caught in her throat. Then she leaned forward and spewed a steady stream of stringy, stinking vomit onto the floor between them. Instinctively, Fairbanks shoved his chair back, out of the line of fire. He jerked his feet under his chair. Whittaker seemed to run out of steam, breathing heavily as flecks of vomit flew from her lips. She glared at Fairbanks with eyes that were no longer bloodshot and red-rimmed. Now, the whites of her eyes were completely red. Thin lines of blood ran from their corners. She gagged again, and as if getting a second wind, resumed painting the floor with vomit. She twitched and thrashed in her chair, her shoulders jerking up to her ears and then back down with such sudden force that Fairbanks was sure the joints would dislocate.

The commotion brought Proust out of the staff lounge. He stood in the doorway, coffee filter in one hand, can of Maxwell House in the other. His mouth hung open as he stared at the unfolding scene.

Whittaker struggled to her feet, her shoulders still hitching up and down, her mouth still open wide to let loose yet another vile stream. Her feet slid in the puddled vomit and she toppled backwards, her arms flung wide, her hands grasping at the air.

"Don't just stand there, Proust, you goddamn idiot!" Fairbanks shouted. "Help me restrain her!"

Proust shook his head like he was fighting off a trance. He dropped his coffee-brewing supplies and dashed for the desk.

"Help me," Fairbanks said, kneeling beside Whittaker's violently convulsing body. He winced as vomit soaked through the thin fabric of his pants. He wondered if he had any broken skin on his lower legs. Who the hell knew how this thing was spread?

Whittaker heaved one final burst of vomit, then her jaws snapped shut with such sudden force that Fairbanks was sure she broke her teeth.

"She's having a seizure." Proust, jackass that he was, chose to state the obvious. "She's going to swallow her tongue!"

Proust maneuvered himself behind Whittaker. He sat cross-legged and put her head in his lap. Then, with one hand on her forehead and the other on her chin, he began trying to pry her jaws apart.

It seemed to Fairbanks that it happened in slow motion. Proust managed to work Whittaker's mouth open. He glanced away for a moment, maybe to make a comment or suggestion to Fairbanks. But whatever words he had in mind died before they could make it to his throat, replaced by shrieks of pain and disbelief as Whittaker's teeth snapped together, neatly crunching through Proust's index finger. She didn't pause to chew before biting again, this time taking Proust's thumb.

Fairbanks put his hands on the floor and shoved himself away, too horrified by what he'd just witnessed to even notice the hot vomit squelching between his fingers. He grabbed his chair and hauled himself to his feet.

Whittaker reached up and hooked her fingers through Proust's hair. She pulled his face to hers, and in an obscene reenactment of a kiss, bit his lips—first the bottom and then the top—right off his face. Proust, in an act that seemed to Fairbanks to be counter to reflex, opened his mouth to scream. Whittaker pulled him even closer and bit his tongue off. Her throat bulged as she swallowed. It reminded Fairbanks of seeing an anaconda devour a goat.

Proust gurgled as blood pumped from his ravaged mouth. Whittaker rolled off his lap and stood, tottering like a drunk. She stared at Fairbanks, as if noticing him for the first time. A smile spread across her face as stepped closer. Behind her, Proust writhed on the floor, hands pressed to his face. His screams had been reduced to thin, reedy squeaks.

"Whittaker, if you're still in there," Fairbanks stammered, beating a slow retreat. "Please, listen to me. You need to be quarantined."

He almost laughed at the sound of his own voice.

Quarantine? Really? Haven't we gone well past that mark? What was that thought you had earlier, something about gleefully marching across the Rubicon? An awful high moral perch for a man whose last girlfriend was in junior high.

Whittaker made another grab, and this time, Fairbanks recoiled too strongly, and his feet went out from under him. He went down hard, his tailbone cracking against the concrete floor. But the pain spreading across his ass was the least of his concerns. What had seized his attention was the sharp, stabbing sensation in the left side of his chest. He inhaled, struggling to force air into his lungs. Whittaker loomed over him, her red eyes glowing with animal intensity.

"No," he pleaded.

Her face twitched. She squeezed her eyes shut and pressed her hands to her temples like a person suffering a migraine. Then, she moaned. It was the low, guttural sound that Fairbanks had heard a thousand times from their human test subjects. His heart fluttered in his chest. The pain that had set up shop there took on a new jagged, insistent edge.

Whittaker jerked to one side, peering at the control panel on the desk. She stabbed one finger down onto a keyboard. Overhead, warning lights flashed and an alarm blatted. Then, the doors to the holding cells—all 26 of them—slid open.

Fairbanks managed to snag a lungful of air. It gave him the strength he needed to reach out, grasp the edge of the desk, and pull himself to his feet. He focused on the open doorway to the staff lounge. If he could make it across the room before Whittaker—or any of the liberated subjects—got there first, he might have a chance…

But the pain in his chest, and his difficulty breathing, made it seem as though his goal was a million miles away.

Whittaker dropped to her knees and ripped Proust's shirt open. She tore into the flesh of his abdomen with brutal precision, her fingers plunging into the bloody wound and drawing out a handful of glistening, wet intestines. She brought them to her open mouth and began cramming them inside.

Fairbanks focused on putting one foot in front of another. It was thirty feet to the staff lounge, maybe less…

7

The concierge at the Staff Residential Center (known among the staff as "the barracks") was a bright-eyed kid from Chicago named Matt Harding. He was only half-awake when he pressed the button that unlocked the front door.

It was a cushy gig. He might not have gotten it if his father wasn't on the shareholder's board of directors for Marsh Industries. Not that Matt had even wanted the job. He'd been content to snort cocaine and crash cars on his father's dime. But when Matt washed out of school yet again, Dad decided it was time for the kid to get some life experience, and had shipped him over to Africa (*the fucking dark continent, man!*) for some life experience. The pay wasn't bad and the native chicks were willing to spread their legs for a couple bucks (*use a rubber, dude)*, so it wasn't all bad. But scoring coke meant dealing with General Mbowi's people, and those motherfuckers were extra scary. Like it or not, Matt had cleaned up that particular part of his act. Now, he was just trying to run out the clock on his year in Daroka so he could go back to tossing back shots of Malort at DIY punk shows.

So when he gave the security monitor a half-assed glance and saw three of the residents coming up the walk to the front door, he hit the buzzer and went back to turning the pages of last month's issue of *Young Sluts*. It was hard to find a good time on overnight desk duty, but a dude had to try.

The front doors opened, and in staggered three of the egghead scientists who called this dump home. Matt gave them a quick, out-of-the-corner-of-the-eye assessment. It was all he needed to tell him that this trio of nerds was well past their sell-by date. They didn't pass the literal sniff test.

Probably having some sort of geek orgy out there in the jungle, Matt thought. *Motherfuckers smell like they've been rolling around in roadkill. Goddamn nerds in this joint get up to some weird shit.*

But when they started moaning—all three of them, like they were trying to harmonize—Matt tossed aside his magazine and gave them his full attention. What he saw made his stomach lurch and his asshole clench so tightly he was sure that it would vacuum seal. The nerds looked like they'd walked too close to a chainsaw. They were covered in ragged, bloody wounds. The chick was named Quinley; Matt always made it a point to know the chicks' names. She was completely, butt-ass naked. Normally, this would have excited Matt, but there was nothing normal about this. Not only was Quinley covered in wounds crusted with dirt and dried blood, but one of her tits had been torn off. When Matt looked closely—and he didn't want to, but he couldn't help himself —he saw an off-white scrap of rib cage. The two males didn't look much better. One of them was naked from the waist down, and his dick—once again, Matt couldn't help himself— looked like someone had turned it into a scrap of beef jerky.

Matt stood up, looking around frantically for an escape route as the trio of stinking, moaning freaks converged on the desk.

Of course, by then, it was too late. The Asian guy— Chinese, Japanese...Matt couldn't fucking tell the difference —was the first one over the desk. Matt planted his hands on the doctor's chest and shoved. But it wasn't a fair fight. That Wagner asshole, the one who always had some complaint about the air conditioning or the water pressure in the showers, was behind him. Wagner dragged Matt back down into his chair. The Asian dude—*Was it Dr. Yamaha?*—fell to his knees, then sat down between Matt's thighs. Mouth open wide to reveal a set of straight white chompers as the doctor pushed his face into Matt's crotch.

Oh, shit, not there…

Matt screamed as Wagner descended on him. The habitually complaining scientist grabbed Matt by the ears and leaned in to bite a chunk of cheek. He screamed even louder as Dr. Yamaha or whatever his name was finally tore through the fabric of his pants and bit into the soft parts hidden within.

One thought flashed through Matt's panicked brain as Quinley bit down on his neck: *Thanks a lot, Dad.*

8

One of Waylon Marsh's faithful assistants, a Nordic blonde name Svetlana, took the call on the satellite phone. Their flight was still hours away from Daroka, somewhere over the middle of the Atlantic, but whatever it was, it couldn't wait.

Svetlana's face was impassive as she listened to the news conveyed by the frantic caller somewhere inside the Marsh Industries compound. Waylon Marsh watched her intently, though his hands busied themselves peeling an orange. Bits of peel fell to the floor, piling up between his crocodile-skin boots. White strands of pith dropped to his lap, clinging to the pants of his custom-tailored suit. He dropped his orange on the tray table in front of him and grabbed a fresh can of Ignition Energy Drink. He popped the tab and took a long swallow. He stifled a belch then went back to peeling his orange.

"Well?" he asked as Svetlana ended the call and returned the phone to its charging station.

"It's a Code Bruno situation in Daroka."

Marsh cursed and threw the orange across the aircraft's cabin. It splattered against the door to the cockpit. "Are they fucking sure?"

Svetlana nodded.

"Then what are they calling for?" Marsh asked. "They know the protocol. Nuke the whole fucking joint before this thing spreads. We'll set up shop somewhere else and be up and running by the end of the year."

"They tried, but the remote triggers are unresponsive."

"Then get that goddamn darkie Mbowi to send his fucking troops in there to trigger it manually. God knows we've given them enough guns and ammo to shoot up the entire continent."

Svetlana shook her head. "They've lost contact with Mbowi. Sir, I think we might have a situation on our hands. If the serum was as effective as the last reports indicate, and containment has been breached, the shit could really hit the fan. Our plan hinged on our ability to contain and control the serum once administered."

Marsh leaned forward in his seat, grasping the armrest to keep from giving in to the urge to slap Svetlana. "You think I don't know that? Why do you think we had so much remote-trigger ordinance installed? Why do you think we supplied Mbowi with that goddamn arsenal? There were contingencies and fail-safes. This wasn't supposed to happen."

"We still might be able to get ahead of this, sir."

Marsh sat back, his heartrate dropping back down to normal. Sure, Svetlana had fashion model looks, but the real reason he employed her was her ability to strategize on the fly. She was his secret weapon, and he paid her accordingly.

"Let's hear it then, sweetheart," he said.

"We still have our contract with Pendleton Security. We could send in a small strike team. They can manually hit the self-destruct and also retrieve whatever is salvageable. They're also good enough to take out anything that may have escaped containment while they're at it."

Marsh grabbed another orange from the bag on the seat

next to him. He started peeling as he considered Svetlana's plan. It seemed solid enough.

"All right, blondie," he said. "First things first. Let's create a cover for the situation in Daroka. Blame it on Mbowi's people. Something like environmental sabotage. Whatever details you can cook up. Then contact Pendleton and have them send in a team."

Svetlana rose from her seat, smoothing her skirt. "I'll have the pilot put us down in Rome. Our Vatican contacts can help us coordinate from there."

Marsh waved her off and went back to peeling his orange.

9

The ancient being that called itself Charon stood on the bank of the nameless underground river. Possessed of patience on a near geologic scale, it could have stood there, silent and still, for centuries. But it knew it wouldn't need to wait very long. It didn't need to ascend to the mouth of the cave, crawl through the narrow aperture, and stand under the night sky to know that, at long last, the stars were right and the time of reconciliation was at hand. It could feel the change in the very core of its being. The coming of a new age was at hand, as inexorable as the ocean tide.

Charon reached out over the edge of the water, spreading his skeletal fingers above the dark glassy surface of the river. The rushing current ebbed, slowing until the flow stopped altogether. The river was as still as a frozen lake. Charon moved its fingers, tracing in the air the pattern of arcane symbols. The still water rippled. When it was once again still, the flat black surface was replaced by images from the world above.

Charon's features didn't register emotion, but its posture changed ever so slightly, shoulders rising, its neck craning forward, and back straightening as it looked out over the colorful display.

A pair of armed guards, their uniforms emblazed with the Marsh Industries logo, firing rifles indiscriminately into a crowd of walking cadavers...

A young man writhing in agony on a blood-slicked floor as a trio of hollow-eyed ghouls bit into his flesh...

An older, heavy-set man, sweating and clutching the left side of his chest as he cowers in small room, eyes fixed on the locked door in front of him...

A collection of rats, a herd of wild beasts in miniature, scuttling down a hallway, advancing on a group of panicked, screaming people in white lab coats...

A group of naked ghouls shambling up a stairwell, spilling into the spacious lobby of the Marsh Industries research center...

A trio of native children, dressed in outdated American styles, using bolt cutters to snip through the heavy gauge fence surrounding the Marsh Industries compound...

A fire raging through a laboratory full of broken test tubes, malfunctioning equipment, and ruptured canisters filling the air with noxious gas...

Charon watched.

10

Marsh Industries Stock Remains Strong Despite Continued Unrest In Daroka.

Billionaire venture capitalist and controversial public figure Waylon Marsh declined to comment on the continued unrest in the central African nation of Daroka. At the tenth annual Vision Summit in Bern, Switzerland, Marsh refused to take questions from media outlets. According to a press release, "Marsh Industries has not, does not, and will not take up political causes. We remain committed to the betterment of humankind across all borders, both geopolitical and ideological."

Protestors gathered outside the summit to boycott Marsh Industries' continued presence in Daroka, despite the bloody coup staged by General George Mbowi against the country's democratically elected socialist government. The company's public relations department also declined to comment specifically on Mbowi, but said, via press release, that "Marsh Industries condemns violence in all forms."

Regarding the recent chemical spill at Marsh Industries' Daroka facility, the press release stated that the accident was "minor in scope" and that heightened security measures were part of "a cautious approach to help ensure the safety of all our employees."

--Karen Kitteridge, Associated Press

Posted anonymously to the *Up With People's Revolution* online message board:

So most of you probably won't believe this, but here goes.

I've been in contact with someone who works at the HOPE Project facility in Daroka. That place is locked down pretty tight, and that includes internet communications, but my friend does some white hat hacking, so he knows how to get past their security measures. I haven't heard from him in a while and I'm starting to get worried because his last message was all about how there's some weird shit going on in those labs. Basically the HOPE Project is just a cover for some real evil corporate shit. He said they're doing experiments on humans to develop some sort of bio-weapon or new disease or something. Scary shit.

Part Two

The centre cannot hold…

"Things like this have a way of getting bloody."

—Michael K. London

1

The local police had already set up a perimeter by the time Mike London and his team arrived. A dozen vehicles— including a SWAT van—spread out at regular intervals around the house. A helicopter thundered overhead. London didn't need to look up to confirm that there was a sniper on board, hanging half-in, half-out of the chopper, like he might actually be able to hit something smaller than a truck from that vantage point. Probably the most excitement these cops had seen in years. London figured the SWAT van and chopper had come all the way out here from Toronto. No way a town this small had that kind of firepower. Not that it mattered one bit. The guy the terrorists had snatched was a Marsh Industries employee, and therefore, his security was the sole responsibility of the Pendleton Team.

All things considered, London would have rather been back home in Texas. Something about Canada just didn't agree with him. They had weird rules for football, for one thing. And just try getting a decent plate of barbecue.

"Well, boys, it is a beautiful day for a nice quiet drive in the country, don't you think?" Gil Zantoro asked, turning on his driver's seat perch as he brought the van to a halt a few yards behind the line of local cops.

There was a brief round of dutiful laughter from the rest of the team. As the comedian of the group, Zantoro had his moments, but this wasn't one of them. Everyone was on edge. They'd just finished a job in Washington DC, knocking off a couple goons from a Juarez cartel who were trying to put the screws to one of Marsh Industries' lobbyists. Things had gotten hot and heavy towards the end of the operation, and the team had been promised some downtime. They'd barely had time to pop the tops on their first round of celebratory beers when the call came in: some Earth First wannabes had snatched a senior level executive and taken the poor bastard to their headquarters in a piss-ant town called Vernonville. So, they'd poured the beers down the sink, geared up for a fight, and jumped on a company plane. Now, here they were, less than twenty-four hours after a dustup with a bunch of cartel cutthroats, and ready to go at it with some eco-terror collective that called themselves Earth Force.

"Is it just me, or does Earth Force sound like some comic book shit?" Zantoro continued. "Fucking hippies, man."

London switched off the ignition and pocketed the keys. "Stow it, Zantoro."

"You're the boss."

The team clambered out of the van. They stood behind the vehicle, going through their final gear check while London gave them the lowdown.

"All right, guys, listen up," he said. "We have multiple civilians. Our guy was on his way to some fundraiser in New York when he got snatched. His wife and two children were with him, in addition to a driver and personal assistant. That brings us to a grand total of six hostages, two of whom are about the right age for kindergarten. They were dressed in evening wear when they were taken, so unless the Earth

Force is generous with their wardrobe, the hostages should be easy to spot."

"What's our level of engagement?"

The question came from Buzz Osbourne, one of the team's veteran members. He and Zantoro were the only ones who'd been there as long as London. A big corn-fed Midwesterner with zero sense of humor, he was Zantoro's polar opposite.

"We're here to kick ass and take names, right? We're weapons free as soon as we breach," London said. "The company wants their man and his family back in New York safe and sound. They can clean up any mess we make. Now, that doesn't mean we should aim for a bloodbath. Zantoro, I'm talking to you, okay?"

Zantoro clapped a hand to his chest, clutching invisible pearls. "I'm shocked you would say such a thing. Shocked, I tell you."

"Put a fucking cork in it, man," Osbourne said.

The rest of the team murmured their agreement. There were only four of them, but they'd been cooped up with Zantoro for far too long. In a couple weeks, another team from Pendleton would rotate to active duty, and London's squad would get some downtime. London had decided that Zantoro was past due for his yearly psych eval. And maybe it wouldn't be a bad idea for the guy to drop some piss for the doctor. Although he was nearly certain Zantoro was powdering his nose again, London believed in the principle of a man being innocent until proven guilty. For now, he'd have to settle for keeping a close eye on him.

"Standard procedure this time. These guys aren't much above amateur hour, so nothing fancy." London said. "Zantoro, you're with me through the back door. Vincent and Osbourne will take the front."

Osbourne clapped a hand over Zantoro's mouth. "It is too goddamn early in the day for the butt-fucking joke you were about to make."

"Remember," London said, "nothing fancy. Get in, get our people, get out. Anyone interferes with that plan, put them down hard. Now let's go introduce ourselves."

When it came to local law enforcement, the reactions to the Pendleton Team fell into two categories. The first was indignant pushback. This was the local PD's time to shine, and they didn't want some fancy private security firm with a government contract spoiling it. The second category involved a little confusion, followed by a whole lot of slack jawed amazement. Either way, the result was the same: the locals were welcome to provide any support the team needed, but otherwise, they were obliged to step aside and stay out of the fucking way.

London did his best to size up the Vernonville chief of police as the team made their approach. The guy looked like he'd been a real hardass back in the day, but the advancing years had done the same thing they did to everyone in his line of work. He'd made it this far up the food chain by knowing when to pick his battles. So the old guy—Chief of Police Andy Thompson, as he introduced himself— didn't put up a fight when London showed him a federal writ transferring authority in this terrorist action to the Pendleton Team.

"Fine with me," the chief said, glancing over the paperwork then passing it back to London. "Not sure my boys are up to it, to be honest. You need anything from us? What I mean to say is, there are just four of you. Might be stretched a little thin, don't you think?"

London shook his head. "Trust me, four of us is plenty for this situation. Tell the hotshots in the riot gear to stand down. Last thing my team needs is a bunch of friendly fire. You feel the need to help, you might gather up a supply of body bags. Things like this have a way of getting bloody."

"That a fact?" Chief Thompson chuckled, but there wasn't

a trace of levity in it. "Just who the hell are you guys anyway? Bunch of goddamn cowboys?"

"We're just out here earning a paycheck," London answered.

2

London and Zantoro advanced on the back door at a dead sprint. There was no sense in sneaking around. It was broad daylight, and anyone looking out the window would see them, so why bother? Their boots thudded on the wooden stairs leading to the back porch. London slapped a pre-wired explosive to the door then turned away as the charge blew. It wasn't a big explosion, just enough to blow the lock out of the door. But the Earth Force hadn't done much upkeep on their headquarters, and the door frame was worm-eaten and flimsy. The explosion ripped the entire door from its hinges and sent it crashing onto the porch.

They were inside before the dust had cleared, and just in time to see two Earth Forcers stumbling around the kitchen, struggling to clear the dust from their eyes as they raised their pistols. Zantoro fired first, two quick bursts from his M-4 that caught the two men square in their chests. As they fell, London got his first good look at the opposition. He wasn't impressed. They looked like college kids in their concert t-shirts and ripped and faded jeans.

There was a quick burst of gunfire from the front of the house, followed by a voice shouting, "Clear up front!"

Zantoro laughed. "Sounds like Vincent and Osbourne had themselves a little fun, huh, boss?"

"Yeah," London sighed. "Fun."

He and Zantoro met up with Vincent and Osbourne in the large front room. The two men had dropped no fewer than five bodies with that quick burst of fire. Like the two Zantoro had put down in the kitchen, these Earth Force soldiers looked like they hadn't been much more than kids. But they were kids who'd seen fit to take a family hostage. London didn't know if that made it more or less tragic. Truth be told, it didn't matter. That sort of question was above his pay grade.

"This floor is clear," Vincent reported. "We even checked the bathroom."

Vincent was the youngest member of the team. He'd stepped in for Jim Kunz, who'd put in his retirement papers at the end of the prior year. He had the sort of baby face that got him carded when the team went out for beers.

Osbourne pointed across the room at a narrow staircase. "Guess everyone else is upstairs."

London made his way across the room, stepping around the puddles of blood. He looked up the staircase. It was too narrow for more than one of them to go at a time. There were eight steps, then a small landing. After that, the staircase made a sharp L-shaped turn on its way to the second floor. It was a tactical nightmare. If the Earth Force had anyone with a brain for combat strategy, they'd know all they had to do was post lookouts at the windows and keep a couple guns trained on the top of the staircase.

"What do you think, boss?" Zantoro asked.

London craned his neck, trying to get a better view. It was no good. The staircase was too narrow, and the angle of the turn too sharp for him to see anything.

"Vincent, Osbourne, I want you guys outside," he said. "Fire some shots around the windows. Nothing that will do any damage to anyone inside. I just want whoever is waiting for us upstairs to have to worry about every room up there."

They nodded, spun on their heels, and went out the front door. They didn't sound off or salute. The Pendleton Team didn't bother with that bullshit. It wasn't that kind of job.

3

Micah Zetty, known to his friends as Zed, wasn't built for this shit, and he knew it. But when circumstances were dire, they demanded extreme responses. Lori Lund, the founder of Earth Force, had both preached and practiced that principle. And Zed knew that if it wasn't for her public persona, she'd be here alongside her brothers and sisters on the frontline. Lori Lund was a force to be reckoned with. Zed just hoped what he and his friends did here today would make her proud.

He glanced around the room, taking stock of the situation. What he saw didn't exactly fill him with a sense of pride or purpose. In fact, for the first time since joining Earth Force a few years ago, a faint tickle of doubt had wormed its way into his heart. It was the kids that did it. Robby, one of the most gung-ho members from the latest batch of recruits, had the two kids in the corner of the room, facing the wall. He had his gun trained on them, like they were dangerous prisoners of war rather than a pair of terrified kids. The little girl kept crying out for her mother, who was on the opposite side of the room. Her mother—eyes hidden behind a blindfold, hands cuffed behind her back—was doing her best to reassure her children that everything was going to be okay. But the tone of her voice told a different story than her words. The woman was terrified. And nothing about her quavering voice conveyed the sense that things might turn out okay.

The woman's name was Brianna Styles, wife of Howard Styles, senior VP in charge of worldwide planning for Marsh Industries. Howard had ascended the Marsh Industries ladder to one if its highest rungs by spearheading the HOPE project. Humanitarian Operations for Preserving Earth; that was the meaning behind the acronym. But Zed knew all too well that Marsh Industries had zero interest in humanity or the environment, at least nothing beyond extracting the highest dollar value from both. Lori Lund had told him and the other members of Earth Force's strike team the true mission of the HOPE project. Zed knew that Waylon Marsh's evil empire had to be crushed by any means necessary. The fate of humanity hung in the balance.

But, goddamn it, did that have to include terrorizing children?

The third gunman in the room, a grizzled Earth Force veteran called Squirrel, edged up to the side of the window and peered out.

"Goddamn pigs got us surrounded," he said, looking back at Zed. "This thing is going to get bloody. Sure as hell, it's going to get bloody."

"No." Zed shook his head. "As long as the cops hang back, we wait until the media arrives. Once the reporters get here, we make our case."

Squirrel shook his head, a few strands of his long grey hair falling over his wide forehead. "You got a thing or two to learn."

"I don't doubt that," Zed admitted. "But Lori put me in charge of this thing, and I say we keep cool until the reporters arrive."

Squirrel sneered. He stroked the barrel of his gun like he

was caressing a lover's thigh. He draped the rifle over one arm and edged away from the window, moving closer to the crying children.

The pistol in Zed's hand was a Glock 19. It was reliable and accurate. Well, at least it was when Zed took it to the firing range. Now, out here in the real world, it felt light and inconsequential, especially compared to the pump shotgun Squirrel was toting. Nevertheless, Zed half-raised it in Squirrel's direction.

"Squirrel, I want you to get the fuck away from those kids. This room is secure, and I don't need you in here. Go out there with Laney and watch the stairs."

Squirrel's eyes flicked from Zed's face to the Glock and back again. Then he looked towards the corner of the room, where Robby stood over the Styles children.

"How about sending the kid?" Squirrel suggested.

"I told you to quit calling me that," Robby growled, squaring his shoulders. "And I seem to remember Lori putting Zed in charge of this operation. So maybe you should get your old ass moving?"

Zed nodded. "That's a solid argument, Robby."

"Fucking teacher's pet, I swear," Squirrel muttered, stomping out of the room.

Zed let go of the breath he hadn't realized he was holding. He did his best not to look at the kids, but it was hard not to. At first, when they'd grabbed them off the street and shoved them into the van, the kids had screamed. But ever since they'd made it to the house, all they did was whimper and hiccup. It was like they'd progressed from terror to despair. Each little sob was a knife in Zed's heart.

He looked at Brianna and Howard Styles. Bound and blindfolded, they looked pathetic, not at all like an evil titan of a planet-destroying corporation and his vapid trophy wife. Zed wasn't sure what he felt for them anymore. It certainly wasn't the righteous anger he'd felt when his chapter of Earth

Force had planned the mission. But it wasn't sympathy either.

Fuck me, when did this shit get so complicated? Zed shook his head.

He considered going to the children's side, maybe trying to offer some comfort. But an explosion, followed by a burst of gunfire like the hammer of Thor, blasted all his musings about moral ambiguity right out of his brain.

Things were about to get scary.

4

They hit the landing in quick succession, Zantoro going down on one knee while London stood behind him, back to the wall. There were two hostiles at the top of the stairs: a scrawny, grey haired guy who looked like a lesser member of the Grateful Dead, and a woman with a bodybuilder's physique and a headful of multicolored dreadlocks. Both were armed with shotguns. But they were untrained and slow to take aim.

The gunfire from outside was working as intended, panicking the Earth Forcers. That panic slowed them down even more. Not that London and Zantoro needed much more than a fraction of a second to get the drop on them. London's squad had been through so many firefights over the years that London had lost count. They'd faced down narco-guerillas in South America, ethnic cleansers in former Soviet satellite nations, and African warlords with military grade firepower. A couple of college dropouts in tie-dye t-shirts didn't stand a chance. If London was a man given to introspection, he might have felt a twinge of guilt about the way things unfolded. Not that a little guilt would have changed anything. Gunfire has a way of drowning out everything else, conscience included.

Zantoro's first shot punched a hole through the center of the woman's belly. It was almost like he was using the tie-dye pattern of her shirt as a bullseye. Actually, London wouldn't put that past him. Zantoro's sick sense of humor certainly allowed for such shit. Zantoro was using his nine for close quarters work, same as London. The gun's report wasn't as loud as the blast from the woman's shotgun. She fired a wild shot at the ceiling as she staggered backwards.

London snapped off three quick rounds, hitting the Grateful Dead reject in a tight, center-mass cluster. Textbook shots. Clean and effective, just the way London liked them. The target dropped his weapon, staggering a couple steps back in that *Holy shit, I'm dead* stupor that London had seen hundreds of times. It was one of those universal language things. London took careful aim and squeezed the trigger. The bullet caught the target right between the eyes, sending blood, brains, and skull fragments airborne. It was a quick kill shot. Once again, clean and effective.

Zantoro laughed wildly and fired two quick ones. They were, for lack of a better term, tit shots. London sighed, sighted down the barrel of his pistol, and got off another quick kill shot. The big woman collapsed atop the body of her partner.

"You're a sick fuck, Zantoro," London said, taking the lead as they advanced up the stairs.

5

Zed looked at the gun in his hand. If it felt unsubstantial before, it felt like a toy now. Gunfire was erupting all around the house. Bullets slammed into the house's exterior from what seemed like a hundred different directions. His ears rang. His heart raced as his adrenal glands pumped pure speed into his veins. Then a half-dozen shots thundered in the hallway just outside the room, followed by two heavy thumps like overfilled laundry bags hitting the floor.

Zed swallowed. He knew what those thumps meant. Squirrel and Laney were gone. Bang-bang, just like that. He did a quick run-through of his options. When they practiced worse case scenarios in the weeks leading up to the operation, they'd prepared for the possibility of a last stand situation. It had been the general consensus of all the Earth Forcers that one of the Styles children would make the best and/or easiest human shield. They were lighter and easier to control, and Lori assured them that even the most hardened corporate shock trooper wouldn't dare open fire and risk hitting a child. But now that he was in the shit, Zed knew he couldn't do it. In simulations, they'd used a Cabbage Patch doll, even though they knew the Styles children were much larger, not even toddlers anymore. As Zed looked at the terror-stricken children, huddled together and whimpering, he knew that using them as human shields wasn't an option. Robby kept his gun trained on them, but even he looked full of doubt.

"Robby…" Zed began. "I need you to…"

"You don't got to say it. I'll go deal with those pigs coming up the staircase."

Robby walked out of the room in a series of purposeful strides, his gun held out in front of him. A moment later, Zed heard another quick series of gunshots followed by a muffled thump.

He looked at Brianna Styles, sizing her up. She was slender, just this side of model-thin. Bigger than a Cabbage Patch doll, but she didn't look like she'd put up too much resistance.

"Mrs. Styles," he said, "I hate to have to do this, but just remember, the more you cooperate, the less likely they'll be to shoot."

6

London took point, entering the room two paces ahead of
Zantoro. It was a small room, devoid of furniture, and it only
took a couple seconds for London to assess the situation.
They'd whittled the hostiles down to a single man, and he
was standing with his back against the wall. The Styles
woman was playing the part of human shield. The last Earth
Forcer standing had her in a semi-chokehold. He also had a
Glock nine raised. From the way he held it, London knew the
kid was no marksman. In fact, he probably could have
emptied the magazine and failed to hit London, even at a
range of a few feet. Still, it wasn't the sort of thing London
wanted to wager. Especially not when they were so close to
seeing this operation through.

London holstered his gun. He called over his shoulder for
Zantoro to stay put outside the room.

"Check, boss," Zantoro answered.

"And radio the boys outside. Tell them to chill out with
the distraction fire."

Zantoro passed the order along, and the gunfire ceased.

Then London turned his attention to the situation at hand.

"Look, kid, believe it or not, I'd love it if this day could end without another shot being fired. I'm sure whatever grievance you have with Marsh Industries will get sufficient media coverage if we bring you in alive."

The kid sneered, blowing a lock of Brianna Style's hair out of his face. "Oh yeah? Nearly every mainstream conglomerate on this planet bends over backwards to give Marsh Industries positive coverage. They're Waylon's cheerleading squad. Exactly how much airtime will they give me? Because I don't think it will be much."

London kept his hands visible. They were still at that point where this thing could tip in either direction. "You snatched a top-level executive from Marsh Industries. And you're not some towel-head suicide bomber or some neo-Nazi dickhead. You got that All-American look, even if you need a haircut. Seems to me that the public will be very interested in what you have to say. And you know the media. It's all about ratings, right?"

"I wish that was the case." The kid paused to adjust his grip on Mrs. Styles. "But the truth has been out there for everyone to see. Ever since the shit went down in Daroka, it's been right out there in front of us. But how many mainstream media outlets have even run the story?"

So that's what this is about.

As a rule, London kept his nose out of politics and that sort of thing. If he tuned in to the evening news, it was usually just for sports and weather. Politics and world events were above his pay-grade. His bosses had to deal with that bullshit, not him. Still, it was hard to avoid the lunatic fringe these days. They seized on the most innocuous stories and assigned them places in a vast conspiracy to…, well, London usually lost the thread at that point. He wasn't sure what the current prevailing conspiracy theory was. Seemed like the loons couldn't quite agree on who was to blame for the state of the world. For some, it was central banking, which meant the Jews or possibly the Vatican. For others, it was the pharmaceutical industry, who wished to vaccinate the population with microchips. And for still others, it was the radical feminist agenda, who wanted to feed the world with aborted baby nuggets. Different brands of bullshit, London figured. Now it was time to figure out which brand Earth Force was peddling.

"What is it, kid?" London asked. "You got a problem with Marsh Industries buddying up to, shit, what's that general's name?"

"George Mbowi is the least of our concerns. And he should be the least of anyone's concerns compared to what is happening in Daroka. What do you think that disaster was really about?"

London felt like the slow kid in class who finally knew what the teacher was talking about. "Oh, the chemical spill? The HOPE research center, right?"

The kid nodded. "Pretty ironic, huh? Calling your eugenics program HOPE."

"Eugenics? I thought they were doing something to end world hunger."

"Yeah, that's what you'd like to believe..."

London opened his mouth to respond, but he didn't get a chance. Apparently, Mrs. Styles wasn't patient enough to wait for a peaceful resolution. Abruptly, in one fluid motion, she bent her knees and swung her handcuffed fists into the kid's crotch. Although she was surprisingly flexible, there wasn't too much force behind the blow. But given the target area, there didn't need to be. As the kid bent forward in pain, she stood, catching his chin with the top of her head. Then she dove out of the way, giving London a clear line of fire.

"No!" he shouted at the kid, who was doing his best to raise his gun.

But despite having taken an elbow to the goodies and having his teeth rattled, the kid seemed intent on drawing a bead on London. And that was that. London was all out of options. Before the kid could even take aim, London drew his pistol and fired two quick shots, both of which caught the kid square in the chest. He went down like a sack of wet laundry.

London holstered his weapon and sighed. He told himself that it had been the only way, that he'd been left with no choice. It was his standard post-kill pep talk, as perfunctory as sneaking a fart, and done for similar reasons.

He helped Mrs. Styles to her feet. "Are you okay, ma'am?"

She smiled. "Just glad I paid attention in those Krav Maga classes."

7

Eight hours later, the team was back in DC. Everyone but London had gone in search of a decent strip club for some much needed decompression time. London didn't mind missing the titty bar. At forty years of age, he was ready to admit he just wasn't a strip club guy. But he would have gladly tagged along if it meant skipping the debrief. While it had taken him years to figure out that he wasn't a strip club guy, it had only taken one hour in a meeting room full of stuffed suits for him to figure out he wasn't a debrief guy.

As he entered the lobby, he tried to remember if he'd ever been in this particular building before. Even after he'd checked in at the front desk and traded his sidearm for a visitor's badge, he still wasn't sure. For a guy with supposedly top notch observation skills, this was a bit disappointing. But in his defense, these places all looked like they'd been stamped out by some architectural cookie cutter. Same boring metal-and-smoked glass exterior. Same faux-marble floors. Same potted plants and corporate art décor. Same severe-looking secretaries offering the same shitty coffee. And he had to endure all of it while wearing a suit and tie. Fucking DC was the worst.

London rode an express elevator with a stone-faced security guard who looked like he bench pressed cars in his spare time. They rode in stoic silence, a couple of hard asses forced to waste a perfectly good Saturday night so some government contractors could file the correct paperwork. London hoped the rest of the team was enjoying their overpriced liquor and overpriced women.

The elevator came to a stop on the fourth floor. The doors slid back, and the security guard stepped out. He led London down a hallway, past a series of darkened offices, to a conference room. The guard opened the door for London.

"Come on in, Mr. London." The voice from inside the conference room was booming and confident. London knew without looking exactly the type of man it belonged to: aging, overweight, dressed in an expensive suit, doused in cologne, and rich as Croesus.

The security guard waited until London stepped into the room then made himself scarce.

The man with the booming voice was indeed just as London had predicted, and he raised a hand in greeting as London entered.

"Go ahead and make yourself comfortable, Mr. London. Any empty seat will do."

London looked around the table. Three of the men seated at the large rectangular table were cut from the same cloth as the one with the big voice. The other two were much younger and leaner. They wore civilian clothing, but the haircuts and ramrod-straight posture screamed military. The hard stares these two fixed on London said that they weren't all that jazzed about being thrown into a meeting with a contractor.

Well, fellas, London thought, *that feeling is mutual.*

He chose a seat facing the door. He liked being able to see whatever was coming at him.

"My name is Raymond Hollister," the man with the big

voice said. "I won't be offended if you don't recognize it. Just know that Waylon Marsh certainly knows it, and that I'm here in his stead. The other old farts are Casey Johnson, Merle Ferguson, and Dan White. They're all on the board of directors for Marsh Industries."

Each of the three old men nodded as they were introduced. Hollister didn't introduce the two military men, and London wasn't surprised. When it came to this type of military-corporate entanglement, the boys in uniform preferred to keep their names out of it. That was fine with London. He didn't take it personally, and really, he was going to forget all their names the minute he left the conference room.

"Good evening, gentlemen," London said. "I suppose I'll get right to it and give you the highlights of my team's latest operation."

Hollister raised a hand. "Actually, we know pretty much all we need to on that score. Don't get me wrong, it was nice work. You and your men managed to wrap that thing up in a matter of minutes without one casualty aside from the terrorists. We're here to discuss something entirely different. But before we get into that, do I need to remind you of your commitment to confidentiality regarding all matters related to Marsh Industries?"

London didn't like the implication, but he tried to keep that out of his tone of voice when he answered, "I don't need a reminder. And that goes for the rest of my team as well."

Hollister glanced at the other three old men. Each of them nodded in turn. London took the opportunity to pour himself a glass of water from the pitcher at the center of the table. He was starting to get the idea that he might be here for a while.

"Well, let's get down to it then, shall we, gentlemen?" Hollister cleared his throat. "Mr. London, what do you know about Marsh Industries' operations in Daroka?"

London shrugged. "If you're asking for any insight, you got the wrong guy. I've never worked in intelligence. All I can tell you is that a lot of people think Waylon Marsh set up shop in Daroka to avoid any ethical oversight. The same people would probably admit that cozying up to George Mbowi is more a matter of expediency than any indication of Marsh's politics. Try as they might, they've never been able to pin him down to any political party. And then there are the fringe loonies who will tell you that the HOPE project is just a smokescreen for…well, for all sorts of nefarious conspiracies."

The man to Hollister's right leaned over and whispered something into Hollister's ear. Hollister nodded, then said to London, "And this group you just encountered in Canada, they belonged to this group of, um, fringe loonies. Is that correct?"

"Before we engaged the last hostile, he launched into some sermon about the HOPE project." London drank some of his water. "Typical stuff. The chemical spill was a cover for some big disaster and the government is complicit in keeping it all under wraps. I didn't catch all the details since I was more concerned with the gun that was pointed at me."

Hollister listened to another whisper, this one from the man on his left.

"Without getting into too many technical details," Hollister said, "I can tell you that the HOPE project is indeed part of a humanitarian effort. However, the experimental nature of the project involves certain materials and procedures that necessitated our presence in a place like Daroka, unstable though it may be. You understand. A man like Waylon Marsh prefers to cut through the bureaucratic red tape whenever possible."

"You're talking about skirting oversight committees. FDA, EPA, that sort of thing," London replied. "That's why the chemical spill has been all over the news. Marsh Industries burned some bridges and now there's fallout."

"Certain proprietary chemical agents, as well as equipment, was compromised, possibly by outside agents. We need to ensure that the material remains proprietary. Do you understand?"

London nodded. "You need a team to get in there and retrieve anything that's salvageable and destroy the rest. If I had to guess, I'd say you're afraid that Mbowi might backdoor you and auction that material off to the highest bidder. Or maybe you just want to make sure that your tracks are covered before the UN gets peacekeeping troops on the ground in Daroka. But that's all stuff that's above my pay-grade."

Finally, one of the military men spoke up. "At this point, both Marsh Industries and our covert operatives have lost contact with General Mbowi. It's our belief that he can be considered a hostile rogue element. We believe he has already begun the process of looting what he can from the research facility. More worrying is the fact that we've lost contact with the facility entirely. Our security operatives, the research staff…they've all gone radio silent."

Hollister touched a button on the underside of the table. The lights dimmed, and a projection screen lowered from the ceiling on one end of the room. Hollister touched another button and an image appeared on the screen: a black man with snow white hair who was dressed in camouflage fatigue pants and a black shirt with a priest's Roman collar. The man on the screen was surrounded by a group of ragged children, many of whom were armed with guns that appeared comically large in their hands.

"This man is Father Xavier Arnaud," the military man said. "He's was a thorn in the Darokan government's side before Mbowi, and he was even worse once the General took over. The usual stuff: alleging human rights violations, pushing for democratic elections, begging for further UN intervention. Once Marsh Industries set up shop, he made himself scarce. Disappeared into the jungle is our best guess."

Probably because he's not an idiot, London thought. *He knew how much firepower Mbowi was getting from Waylon Marsh, and he took his child army into the jungle to wait out the storm.*

"Since the disaster at the research center last month, Arnaud has popped his head up," Mr. Military continued. "We can assume that Mbowi's control has, at the very least, weakened. Probably why this Arnaud character is so emboldened."

"And this is the part," London said, "where you tell me that we can also consider this Arnaud an active target. I'm telling you right now that my team won't engage kids. I don't care if they're active hostiles or not. You want that sort of dirty work done, look elsewhere. You want me to put Mbowi down, fine. You want me to clean up your mess at that research center, also fine. But if you want me to kill children, you're barking up the wrong goddamn tree."

"Now, now," Hollister broke in. "There's no need for that. We merely want you to be aware that you may face opposition from this Arnaud. We certainly don't want any children harmed. As far as Arnaud himself goes, we would certainly like to see him detained, but we have another team selected for that work."

"Nevertheless," Mr. Military said, "should you encounter Arnaud, you should consider him an active target. Leaving aside his child army, of course."

"This is the last video that Arnaud made," Hollister said, activating the screen. "We pulled it off the phones from one of the hostiles you engaged in Canada."

London swiveled his chair around to get a better view.

On the screen, Father Xavier Arnaud was walking toward some unclear destination. From the angle of the camera, London assumed one of the children was doing the filming.

When Arnaud spoke, he did so in English, but his accent was French. It reminded London of the voices he'd heard during his time in Haiti.

"The time of the great revelation is at hand, people." Arnaud gestured to the sky, which was full of smoke. The angle of the camera changed to show a large building being consumed by flames. "Here, in this building, the corrupt forces of Satan himself have been developing the seed of our destruction. A pill, they say, to end hunger. But they lie. What these men of science are making is an Unholy Eucharist. And though their palace of iniquity is consumed by flames, the fire of their ambition will not be extinguished. Indeed, they have loosed upon this world a plague. The dead will walk. They will feast-"

The video cut abruptly and the screen went black. Hollister brought the lights back up.

"Certainly has the gift of gab," the old man laughed. "Like the tent preachers my mother listened to so much back when I was a child. Still, Arnaud isn't just some backwoods hellfire-and-brimstone pulpit-pounder. General Mbowi certainly took him as a serious threat, and we do too."

"You think he's responsible for the explosions at the research center," London said.

Hollister didn't choose to answer that one. Instead, he produced a manila envelope from somewhere under the table and passed it over to London.

"This dossier is considered eyes-only," he said. "Shred and burn protocol applies. In there, you'll find everything you and your team need to know to get started."

London dropped the folder back on the table. "The thing is, Mr. Hollister, my team is overdue for some downtime. Mikkelson's team is supposed to rotate back to active duty for actions abroad. I've got at least one team member in serious need of some mental health days."

"We think Gilbert Zantoro is just fine," Hollister said. "He'll at least hold up for one more mission."

London wasn't surprised that Hollister knew the situation with Zantoro. If he truly was one of Waylon Marsh's right hand men, Hollister probably knew a hell of a lot more.

"Still, Mikkelson is up, so contact him." London scooted his chair back from the table. "I'm afraid I'm going to have to insist. My guys are getting close to burn out, and in our line of work, that's a recipe for disaster."

One of the other old men, the one Hollister introduced as Dan White, spoke up. "As chief of operations for Pendleton, *I'm* afraid that *I'm* going to have to insist."

London thought of the lyrics to some old country song he'd heard, something about how you spend your life working for a man you've never seen. He felt like the wind had gone out of his sails.

"Mikkelson's team was activated," Hollister countered. "They were deployed to Daroka last week. We lost contact with them after forty-eight hours. Again, we suspect Mbowi, or possibly Arnaud."

Well, that's just fucking great. London wondered why they hadn't mentioned the team's disappearance earlier. *Probably because they didn't want to mention it at all; you just forced their hand by threatening to walk.*

"You'll fly out in forty-eight hours. Once on the ground in Daroka, you'll proceed to research center," White said, reaching across the table to shove the manila envelope closer to London. "Once you've gathered the material outlined in the dossier, you'll place demolition charges at the indicated points in the building. Then you'll blow it sky high and get the hell out. Should you happen to make contact with Arnaud, consider him a secondary target. Our intelligence indicates he may have a small security force, but it's nothing your team can't handle. It should be quick and easy."

London picked up the folder. "Is that the same line you fed Mikkelson?"

The corners of White's mouth tugged up in a reasonable facsimile of a smile. "You're dismissed, Mr. London. There's an agent in the hallway who will escort you to the weapons department for a briefing on the explosive ordinance you'll be carrying in Daroka."

London knew better than to argue. It would be pointless. His two choices were to take his team to Daroka and do what had to be done, or put in his papers. Since the second option meant crossing the sort of people who ordered assassinations with as much thought as most people ordering breakfast, it was really no option at all.

The same musclebound agent who'd ushered him London the briefing was waiting for him in the hallway.

"If you'll follow me, sir, I'll take you downstairs to the weapons department," he said.

"Yeah, sure thing," London answered, following him to the elevator. "Those guys in there called you an agent. What department are you with?"

"That's classified, sir."

"Of course it is."

Their second elevator ride was just as grim and silent as the first. It took them to a basement level that looked like something out of a James Bond movie. Lab coat clad technicians labored over various clever instruments of death while others sat in front of computers, their fingers chattering over the keyboards.

"Jesus Christ, it's a fucking Saturday night," London said. "Don't you people ever sleep?"

His oversized guide just shrugged and took him into a conference room that was much more utilitarian than the one on the upper floor. This room was all cinderblock walls and stainless steel furniture. The table in the center of the room was considerably smaller, and there was no decanter of water on offer. There was only one man in the room. He looked like an absent minded professor with his lab coat worn over an Oxford shirt and plain tie. His glasses rode low on his nose, and his white hair looked like it hadn't seen the business end of a comb in a while.

"I'll wait outside, sir," the agent said.

"Stay classified, my friend," London told him.

The man at the table waited until the door was closed then stood up and launched into his spiel about the explosives. He didn't bother introducing himself, just got right down to it. That was fine with London. One less name for him to forget.

"These explosives are still classified as experimental, so this will be the first time they've been used outside the usual field tests," the professor said as he placed a metal briefcase on the table. "I must say, it's quite exciting. Not even the United States military has access to these yet. Whoever you work for must be powerful indeed."

"Yeah, they're a bunch of swell guys. Tell me what I'm looking at here."

The professor opened the case. Inside were three black spheres swaddled in layers of protective plastic padding. "We call them Thunderballs."

London tried not to roll his eyes. These weapons R & D guys were so nerdy it was painful.

"The material contained within each should be enough to take care of your target, but your superiors insist that you carry extras," the professor said.

"They have a real hard-on for overkill," London explained.

"The Thunderball is lightweight and its housing is quite secure. They are fireproof as well. Basically, you could drop these off the top of the building into a burning car, and they'd still be safe."

London got the idea he should act impressed. "Wow, that's something."

"The core of the Thunderball is one of the most explosive substances known to man…"

London let his mind wander as the professor launched into a lecture about the chemical makeup of the explosives. All he really needed to know was how to make the goddamn things go bang. But he figured the professor probably didn't get out much, and this was what passed for his social hour. He nodded at appropriate intervals and tried not to make it obvious when he glanced at his watch.

8

Arthur's Tavern was a reliable DC watering hole for a guy who just wanted to forget the bullshit daily grind and get wasted. It was too far away from the capitol to be overrun by political hacks, and it was too much of a dive to attract tourists. Still, though, two of the four TVs above the bar were tuned to twenty-four hour news networks. One of these networks was airing a talking head show where partisan journalists screamed at each other about abortion or gun control or whatever divisive issue could whip the audience into a froth. The other was showing footage of a riot in Portland, Oregon.

London signaled the bartender that he was ready for another Jack and Coke.

"On the house," the bartender said, placing the cocktail on the bar. "Neighborhood like this, sometimes it's good for the clientele to see a cop drinking here."

London didn't bother to correct him. For one thing, he wasn't one to look a gift horse in the mouth, especially when that gift horse was carrying a double shot of Tennessee whiskey. And besides, it wasn't too far off the mark. After three tours in Afghanistan, London had taken his discharge and gone back to Texas. He'd breezed through the police academy and joined the force in his hometown of Black Mound. It hadn't taken him long to figure out that small town police departments were havens for high school bullies who'd advanced in age but not in mentality. And the big city departments? Same bullshit, just better equipped. After a couple years of bouncing around from department to department, he put in for a job with Pendleton and had been cruising along ever since. The work wasn't too much different from what he'd done in Special Ops, but the pay was a hell of a lot better. Another three years, five at the most, and London would be able to retire. And then what? He tried not to think too much about that.

He took a sip of his drink and pointed at the footage of the riot. "You got any idea what the fuck that's about? Some trigger-happy cop shoot an unarmed black kid again? Or was that last week?"

"This time, your brothers in blue are in the clear," the bartender said. "It's Marsh Industries that's got the hippies all stirred up this week. I guess they're pissed off about something the company is doing in some African shithole. Like we ain't got problems enough of our own, so we gotta go looking abroad."

London forced a sympathetic laugh, but he had a bad feeling in his gut. He wondered how long it would be before Arnaud's videos went public. If he had to guess, Marsh Industries had all its cyber security people working overtime to swat the videos down, but as powerful as the company was, it couldn't keep that going for long. They were just buying time until London and his team could cover the company's tracks. After that, the UN could send in a million peacekeepers and it wouldn't matter.

London slugged down his drink in two gulps. The whiskey didn't do much to combat his growing feeling of dread.

9

Waylon Marsh could have contented himself with the videos he'd received from Daroka, but he needed to see the results with his own eyes. So he'd hopped on one of his private jets and headed to Washington DC. After getting off his plane, he'd slid into the backseat of a giant black SUV. To the untrained eye, the vehicle would look like any other high-end luxury gas-guzzler, but someone who'd worked a professional security detail would recognize it as armor-reinforced, with bulletproof glass. An identical SUV took to the road in front of the one in which Marsh rode, and a third followed. The drivers were all combat-trained, as were the other six members of the security detail. They were the best men money could buy. Of that, Marsh was certain. According to *Forbes* magazine, Waylon Marsh was the third richest man on the planet.

He reclined in the backseat of his armored transport, sipping from a can of Ignition Energy Drink. It was vile stuff, little more than caffeinated sugar water with some questionable herbal substances tossed in for good measure, but Marsh consumed six cans per day. He resented the concept of sleep, considering it a waste of time, and did his best to curtail it. Once his life's work was complete—and the success of the HOPE project was bringing that moment closer every day—Marsh would relax for a bit and bask in the glory befitting the king of the world. Until then, sleep was just another thing to be endured in a world full of petty, tedious annoyances.

He chugged the last half of his energy drink, wincing as the carbonation burned on the way down. The belch that followed was forceful enough to make his eyes water. Then he rolled down the window and tossed the empty can out. He rolled the window back up and tapped the back of the driver's seat.

"A little privacy, huh?" he said.

The driver hit a switch, and a privacy screen descended, sealing the backseat off. Marsh dug his tablet out of the designer bag on the vacant seat beside him. He activated the device, keyed in his security code, and opened the files containing the security camera footage from the Daroka research center. He'd watched the footage dozens of times, but it never got boring. He'd even added some soundtrack music to enhance the experience—a little Kid Rock, just to amp up the excitement. Yes, the whole thing was a clusterfuck, and it meant potential disasters on every front: the shareholder front, the PR front, and the developmental front. But that didn't mean it wasn't an absolute rush to behold. And besides, so many of Marsh's career breakthroughs had come as a result of what initially appeared to be disasters.

Disaster is just a pessimist's way of defining opportunity. That was a phrase the ghost writer had conjured up for Marsh's autobiography.

Marsh watched the footage of the initial exposure in the basement lab, when the redhead chick opened up all the holding cells. That shit was sexy as hell. Then the way she fell on that guy and started pulling his guts out? Fucking fantastic.

He scrolled back and watched that portion again, transferring the tablet to his left hand so he could rub his crotch with his right. After an encore viewing of Dr. Whittaker's performance, he changed to the footage from the front desk at the staff dormitory. This was another of his favorite sequences. He liked the way the infected woman looked, her naked body covered with blood and dirt. Sure, there was a bloody hole in her chest where one of her tits had been, but still, it was hot.

Next, he opened a file of footage from the hallways at the research center. The screen was split into four separate views.

The first view showed a stampede of scientists in lab coats. They were running for the exits, looking over their shoulders at a group of infected people who had until recently been their coworkers, perhaps even friends.

The second view was of one of the animal laboratories. Some thoughtful research had injected the rhesus monkeys with the serum, and the little bastards were going absolutely bonkers, slamming their fists and faces against the bars of their cages. One of the monkeys was smashing its head against the bars with such force that its scalp had completely torn away, exposing the slick grey surface of its skull.

The third view showed the cafeteria. There was no action in this portion. It was like a still life painting depicting the quiet aftermath of a day at the slaughterhouse. The floor was littered with blood and body parts and bodies so thoroughly maimed that the serum couldn't reanimate them.

The fourth view had nothing to do with the serum at all. It showed footage from one of the staff lounges. A quartet of men had barricaded the door against the chaos. Rather than quietly waiting for help to arrive, they'd chosen to use the opportunity to take turns raping one of their female colleagues. Marsh had cued the music up just right, so that the beat dropped the exact moment the first man forced the woman's legs apart and climbed on top of her.

It was good shit. The serum was working, although not quite as intended. The reanimation of the dead and the subsequent cannibalism was even quicker and more ferocious than expected by anyone privy to real purpose of the HOPE project. It just seemed to have leapfrogged their fail-safes and containment protocols. But Marsh hadn't increased his father's fortune by failing to adapt. Perhaps this new development was, as the kids liked to say, a feature, not a bug.

The whole point of the HOPE project had always been to put the keys to the kingdom in his hands. Not even the lunatic fringe's craziest conspiracy theorists had guessed at Marsh's true motivations. And that made him even more excited than the footage of the naked woman eating the desk clerk. The only thing that had changed was the strategy for forcing the world to crown him god emperor. Money was never the end goal anyway. Power—pure authoritarian power—had always been Marsh's endgame. The serum had just accelerated the plan.

It didn't matter that *Forbes* put him in third place. Very soon, he'd be the richest man on the planet, and by a substantial margin. His wealth would have nothing to do with the amount of money in his bank account or his stock portfolio. No, in short order, he would see the concept of wealth completely uncoupled from money. Mankind was going to enter a new age, when there would only be one measure of wealth: access to the Daroka serum.

But that was all long-term shit. In the meantime, he had to keep the project under his thumb. And that meant reassuring the frontline pawns guarding the king. It meant keeping the bagmen happy and making sure that he alone controlled the flow of information.

He took another can of Ignition from the cooler on the

floorboard. This one was Red Berry Annihilation flavor, his favorite. The first mouthful was always the best, so he drank until his throat burned. His heart fluttered in his chest. He tapped the screen of his tablet, turning up the music.

"Here we go," he said, drumming his fingers on his thigh.

By the time he'd finished his beverage, the limousine was pulling into a parking garage attached to a nondescript office building. The back door swung open, and Marsh slid out. He found himself flanked by a pair of security guards who were built like brick shithouses, and whose faces were impassive. A third guard, this one slightly less imposing but just as cheerful led the way. The grim-faced trio escorted him a short distance through the garage, their footfalls echoing through the cavernous concrete interior.

Marsh had no idea what the name of the building was. He couldn't have recited the street address with a gun to his head. But that didn't matter. Those were minor details, and he had a payroll full of people to keep up with that petty bullshit. He was a big picture, outside-the-box thinker. That wasn't just his opinion, either. *American Entrepreneur* magazine had run a cover story that had described Marsh in exactly those terms. *Wired* had gushed about his FlexPad computer, calling it the biggest breakthrough since the iPhone. And while the FlexPad had fallen short of that prediction, it had still been good enough to send Marsh Industries stock through the roof. The point was, he couldn't have explained how the FlexPad worked. His engineering degree was largely awarded on the basis of his father's donations to the university. But he was the one who came up with the idea. It was his brainchild, so to speak. And it was just one of many brilliant ideas he had. Because he was a *brilliant* man. Of that, he was certain.

The security detail ushered him into an elevator that whooshed them to the one of the upper levels. From there, it was a short walk down a hallway to a luxuriously appointed room; a pristine, modern space with windows revealing a gorgeous nighttime view of Washington DC. The chairs were smooth black leather, and they were arrayed around a table that appeared to have been carved from one massive hunk of teakwood. A crystal decanter full of amber liquid sat in the center of the table, next to a bucket of hand-chopped ice and a set of square bottomed glasses.

Marsh walked into the room and took a seat. His security detail scanned the room then left, closing the door behind them. Two of the chairs on the other side of the table were occupied by Raymond Hollister and General Wesley Strickler. The man in the chair next to Marsh was named Gustav Vogel. He was a tiny old man, just under five feet tall. The glasses perched on his bulbous nose appeared comically large.

"What's up, doc?" Marsh said, slapping Vogel on the back.

The laughter that Vogel managed wasn't fooling anyone. Marsh knew the doctor hated the joke. That was why he insisted on using it as a standard greeting. If the old kraut fucker didn't like it, he was free to return to the fatherland. Of course, the German authorities wouldn't exactly welcome him with open arms. People in those parts took a dim view of doctors with questionable political sympathies who'd been accused of using human test subjects in medical experiments. Vogel was the detail man behind the HOPE project, but it didn't mean he was irreplaceable.

Marsh turned his attention to the other side of the table. "Hey, Ray. Wes, my man, how they hanging these days?"

The two men weren't quite to Vogel's advanced age, but they were still old enough to be what Marsh considered old farts. And it wasn't just their ages that put them in that category. They were a couple of humorless, boring old fucks. Sadly, they were pretty typical of the men Marsh had to deal with in order to keep the wheels of industry grinding forward. He'd long ago decided that when Atlas finally shrugged, these dudes were all going out to pasture.

"I know you're busy, so I'll cut right to the chase," Strickler said. "My people—and I don't think I need to drop names here—want some assurances that the situation in Daroka is contained."

"Is that all?" Marsh poured himself a couple fingers of whatever top shelf liquor was in the decanter. He scooped ice from the bucket with his bare hands. "Okay, then. Tell them it's contained. Tell them to chill the fuck out. Everything is still going to be fine, and everyone is still going to get filthy rich. Well, even filthier, even richer. Whatever."

Hollister cleared his throat. "General, I think what Mr. Marsh is trying to say here is…"

Marsh cut Hollister off before he could formulate a reply. He slapped the table. "Stay in your fucking lane, Ray. I'm not *trying* to say anything. I'm fucking saying it. Now, you got technical questions about viral half-lives, containment protocols coded into protein cases, or any of that boring bullshit, Herr Vogel can fill you in on the details."

"Look here, Marsh." Strickler jabbed a finger in the air. "I think it's best you don't forget who's backing you on this project. These aren't a bunch of tech millionaires looking to blow some of their dot com money. These aren't trust fund kids with hard-ons for Ayn Rand. They're the type of people who don't like seeing their names attached to anything that even smells like scandal, and they move in spheres of influence that even you can't reach."

"Want to bet on that, Wes? Because I got the President's personal cell number. And all those senators that are yanking your chain? Might want to remind them that I know who their mistresses are. I know where the bodies are buried. And hell, I know where the bodies of some mistresses are buried. Beyond that, I know their donors. One phone call from me, and the gravy train goes off the fucking tracks. Permanently." Marsh paused to drink some liquor. It tasted like piss. All things considered, he preferred vodka and Cherry Coke. "It was their genius idea to keep the UN out of Daroka while Mbowi raped and pillaged his way across the country. Now, instead of misleading a few nosy inspectors, we're dealing with the fallout of that decision."

It was bullshit, of course. Marsh had chosen Daroka *because* of its instability, not in spite of it. And Strickler knew it, too, but he had to pretend like he was somehow above that sort of corruption. It was just the way this particular game was played.

"You still think that the situation at the Daroka facility was due to Mbowi?" Strickler asked.

"Shit, who else?" Marsh took another sip. "Ugh, this tastes like drinking a campfire."

Hollister spread his hands in a pacifying gesture. "Well, I'll trust that our security contractors will take care of Mbowi if he isn't already dead. And I'm confident that the situation at the research center will be taken care of by the end of the week. We'll have boots on the ground in less than forty-eight hours."

"Hear that, Wes? Boots on the ground. Ray here is speaking your language." Marsh slung his arm around the back of Vogel's chair. "And the doc here assures me we can be up and running at our Kyrvyiv facility by next month."

Vogel nodded enthusiastically. "Yes, of course."

Marsh glanced around the table as he added more ice to his glass of liquid campfire. He didn't know if they were reassured or not, and he didn't care. They were lucky he even agreed to the meeting in the first place. The truth was, they were all full of shit. Hollister had no choice but to keep pushing. He'd convinced too many of his criminal Wall Street buddies to bet the farm on Marsh Industries. Same with Strickler. There was a trail of bodies leading from Mbowi back to Strickler and any number of his Pentagon jerkoff buddies. And Vogel? He knew exactly what was going on in Daroka. He was the man who'd designed the serum. But none of them could turn back now. All their chips were in the middle of the table.

The silent looks they exchanged with one another were more enlightening than any bullshit discussion.

"I think," Marsh said, "our time is better spent brainstorming ways to keep a lid on this thing until Daroka is back under our control. I have a few ideas to run past you guys. There's a state representative in Mississippi with ties to the Klan. He's got one of those names, Elmer or Buford, where you just know he's some fat, sweaty, cigar-chomping motherfucker. What if a cop in his district could shoot a black kid?"

"I know some people in the Justice Department that could make that happen," Strickler said. "But maybe think bigger, more national. Midterms are coming up. We got representatives in both Georgia and Colorado that are pretty openly courting the Neo-Nazi vote. I think they could be nudged further in that direction."

"Hear that, doc?" Marsh laughed. "Maybe you could give them some pointers."

"I think we can help with the election stuff," Hollister chimed in. "Throw some dark money at these extremist candidates. Really whip up the national debate about what it means to be an American. On the corporate front, maybe we can use back channels to get some retailers to promote diversity in their fall lineups. That always gets good play in the southern states. High visibility protests over rainbow flag t-shirts in the children's apparel section, that sort of nonsense."

"Now, we're talking," Marsh said. "I'll get our social media department cracking. Standard operating procedure. We'll farm some work out to some of our Russian agencies. It's sort of weird how the more transparently fake the accounts are, the more they get amplified. Maybe some of our tech subsidiaries can massage the algorithm. And don't forget the twenty-four hour news networks. We own two of them. About time that investment paid off. If we can't get a complete blackout on the Daroka story, I want to muddy the waters with so many conflicting versions that nobody on either side of the aisle knows what to believe."

Hollister nodded. "I think we can cook up something in time for the Sunday morning shows. Maybe something about how Mbowi was a pipsqueak compared to the warlord next door. Remind the people about the old 'devil you know' adage. The current guy in Borwannah, Isaiah Duchamps, is a bit of a pussycat, but the average American doesn't know that. Hell, the average American can't find Daroka or Borwannah on a map."

Marsh smiled. Sometimes this shit was too easy. "Okay, boys, let's get to work. There's money to be made."

10

Charon waved its hand over the unnamed river, and the images swirling across the surface of the water continued to flicker and change. They were an unending nightmare thread unspooling from a skein of hatred, despair, and violence. Charon had known for millennia what lay at the end of the long, dark tunnel known as the Age of Mankind.

One after another, the images of a world engulfed in disease and unrest swam across the smooth, dark water...

A government building surrounded by protestors, many of them dressed in clothes that were little more than rags...

Men in military uniforms firing weapons into a crowd of people who had converged on a tanker truck carrying potable water...

A hospital so overrun with patients that orderlies were setting up tents in the parking lot...

A ragged band of pirates on a battered, rusty gunboat preparing to fire weapons at a lavish yacht, its deck swarmed with revelers...

A group of armed men surrounding a makeshift morgue in an African village, their guns trained on stacks of body bags that had begun to twitch and writhe on the dusty ground...

A scuttling parade of red-eyed rats climbing aboard a ship, slipping into the cargo hold while men armed with automatic rifles patrolled the dock...

11

Controversial Activist Denies Terrorist Ties

Lori Lund, president of the environmental activist group Earth Force has denied any connection to the kidnapping of Howard Styles and his family. Styles, the senior VP in charge of worldwide planning for Marsh Industries, was abducted along with his wife and children in an attempted ransom plot last Friday. The kidnappers had ties to Earth Force, but no solid connection between the crime and the activist organization has been proven.

"Although we hold people like Howard Styles responsible for the continued corporate rape and pillage of environmental policies and practices, we condemn terrorist action," Lori Lund said via press release. "While the people involved in the kidnapping of the Styles family were at one time involved with Earth Force, their actions were neither sanctioned nor encouraged by our organization."

--Juko Taobi, International News Wire Service

PARTIAL TRANSCRIPT OF

THE SILENT MAJORITY WITH BIG DAVE AND JOE
SIX PACK
RADIO SHOW:

BIG DAVE: I don't care what that crazy *be-otch* Lori Lund says, her tree-hugging hippies have taken up arms against this country. And I'll tell you one thing, listeners: this is just the beginning. It won't stop, because these people hate success. They hate America, too, because this country celebrates success. That's why a guy like Waylon Marsh gets under their skin so much. He's a proud American who innovates, while they're just a bunch of whiny welfare queen commies who can't decide which bathroom to use. You know what I'm saying? They don't want a free market, but they sure as hell want to be free to go into whatever bathroom they feel like fits their gender that particular day. It's disgusting! I'm disgusted!

JOE SIX PACK: You're absolutely correct about the mindset of these people. They're lazy and entitled, so they hate things like freedom and God and success. Guess what? Waylon Marsh is rich because he works harder than all those hippies combined.

BIG DAVE: And if the current administration won't condemn these libtard losers outright, I say it's time for people to start exercising their Second Amendment rights with these loons.

JOE SIX PACK: I'm telling you, most Americans are fed up. They've had enough with these soy-boys and their blue-haired drag queens.

Brad Carter

BIG DAVE: All right, my producers are telling me it's time to take a break so we can pay some bills. When we come back, we'll have another proud American live in the studio. Our guest today is none other than country music sensation Cody James Harmon, whose latest hit "Small Town Saturday Nights" is triggering snowflakes and heating up the charts. We'll get his take on current events and open up the phone lines for your calls.

Part Three

The blood-dimmed tide is loosed…

"We are in a world of trouble, I'm afraid."

—Lia Rousseau

1

Under normal conditions, Mike London had zero problems with air travel. Even if he was packed into coach with a half-dozen screaming infants, he could still focus on the background drone of engines and zone out. He'd never gotten motion sickness, and he understood he was more likely to die in a car accident than a plane crash. But the ride from Johannesburg to Daroka was putting that resolve to the test.

The plane was a C-23 Sherpa, something Marsh Industries had acquired from one of their military contractor subsidiaries. It was a stout aircraft, designed for short takeoffs, but rough air had the Sherpa bouncing all over the sky like a goddamn ping pong ball. Turbulence was one thing when you were flying in some six-seater prop plane. In a military aircraft that could haul a crew of thirty fully equipped soldiers, the effect was unsettling.

One of the two co-pilots stumbled out of the cockpit, holding onto the edge of the doorway for support. Swaying like a cartoon drunk, he made his way to the Pendleton Strike Team—as London's crew was officially known—and shouted to be heard over the noise of the storm and the engines.

"We're going to have to lose altitude to get out of this turbulence," he announced. "The worst of it should clear by the time we're over Borwannah."

"Well, we're not parachuting in, so that's no problem," London answered.

"Thing is, we got word from our ground intel that Mbowi's troops are moving south. They get to the airstrip before us, things could get hairy." The co-pilot shrugged like he was breaking the news that the in-flight movie had been canceled.

"I thought the latest intel was that Mbowi was dead."

"Looks like no one clued his boys in. We got satellite photos showing a convoy headed back towards the border. That's courtesy of the UN, who is making their case for boots on the ground to protect the sovereign state of Borwannah."

"What's security like on the ground?" London asked. "We got any cover?"

"Skeleton crew, I'm afraid. The closest official military presence is in the horn of Africa, so what little there is in Daroka is mostly CIA spooks and private contractors like yourself. But hey, if they're moving to the border, that means it should be smooth sailing for your boys heading into the jungle."

"Yeah, that's looking on the bright side."

Well, that's just fucking great, London thought. *We get sent into a free-fire zone and our only backup is a bunch of CIA spooks. Typical.*

"All in a day's work, right?" The co-pilot turned and began his wobbly march back to the cockpit.

London looked at his team. Despite the announcement about possible hostile presence on the ground, they all looked cool, calm, and collected. And why not? Every mission they went on was a suicide mission. They'd fought on five continents, crossing swords with the worst of the worst. So far, their luck had held. London would have liked to think it was down to their supreme skill with weapons and tactics, but he knew better. Skill could only take you so far before Lady Luck had to do her part. And since London's team had been together, Lady Luck had been their bitch. But the thing about Lady Luck—like so many beautiful ladies—was that she was fickle. She was a free agent, always on the lookout for a new team.

And that's why, after the air calmed down, and the plane was entering Borwannah airspace, he wasn't shocked when they began taking fire from surface-to-air artillery. The Sherpa wasn't equipped to return fire, and it sure as hell wasn't designed to outmaneuver artillery. The best they could hope for was that Mbowi's troops didn't have anything bigger to lob at the plane. If they could land, London's team had an above average chance of getting past Mbowi's guys. But even the short, sharp descent towards the landing strip seemed nearly eternal as the bottom of the plane took machine gun fire.

The team took it in stride. It wasn't their first rodeo. They unbuckled from their seats and moved to the rear of the aircraft, where their equipment was stowed.

"Jesus fucking Christ!" Zantoro shouted as the plane rocked to one side. "They keep this shit up, I'm going to take it personally."

"Fucking stow the chatter and get strapped up!" London shouted, shrugging into his own backpack. He grabbed his rifle from the rack and checked it. Ready to rock 'n roll, as usual. He watched his men follow suit.

They all had their little rituals, the tics that got them locked in for combat. Vincent plugged pink balls of bubblegum into his mouth. Osbourne, the group's only religious man, kissed the silver crucifix that hung on a chain around his neck. They went through their routines so easily that London knew they were little more than reflex at this point. He realized then that he'd lost count of how many missions they'd run. Somewhere along the line, he'd quit keeping score.

He shook his head to snap himself back to the situation at hand, then reached into his hip pocket for his own talisman—a laminated photo of Bettie Page from some ancient skin magazine. His fingers groped through his right hip pocket and came up empty. He checked the left pocket and still didn't find her.

Well, Bettie, we had a good run.

London never thought of himself as superstitious, at least not the way so many soldiers of fortune were, but it was hard to have a good feeling about dropping into a firefight without Bettie in his pocket.

"When we land, we go out the back," London said, pointing to the rear of the plane. "Hopefully, our transport is still there. Rally point is the hangar. Time to rock, boys."

The plane touched down with a teeth-rattling impact, but none of London's team lost their balance. Again, not their first rodeo. The plane's brakes engaged, bringing the aircraft to bumpy halt. The rear platform hatch—a Marsh Industries modification—dropped sharply, and London's team hit the ground running.

Combat can affect perception in any number of ways. London had heard stories from guys whose senses got sharpened to such a degree that they could count the beads of sweat on the enemy's face. But for him, everything got hazy. Everything melted into a big slush of sensory input once the first shots were fired. Later, when things were calm, he could recall details with perfect clarity. But in the moment, in the thick of a pitched firefight, an eerie calm descended on him. He sometimes wondered if he'd even notice if he took a mortal wound. Would it snap him back to a more immediate sense of what was going on around him? Or would he just slide on a raft of strange calm into the afterlife? One day, he just might discover the answer. But that day was not today, he decided as he blasted away at the line of ragtag soldiers in front of the airstrip's corrugated metal tower.

Bullets hit the ground around him, throwing up small sprays of dirt. Others whizzed by his head. In his peripheral vision, he caught glimpses of the other members of the team in action. The highlight was watching Vincent pull the pins on a pair of grenades and toss them with major league pitcher precision into the backseat of one of the Jeeps. Some of Mbowi's men dove into the vehicle, hoping to get to the grenades before they blew. The others—the more sensible—turned and ran. But the outcome was the same for both groups. The grenades detonated, transforming the Jeep into a firestorm of shrapnel that reduced the men to shredded meat. More importantly, the explosion took out the mounted machine gun that had given them such a hard time during their descent.

After that, it was a foregone conclusion. Mbowi's men were loyal and vicious, but they weren't trained soldiers, and it showed. London's team dispatched them with brutal efficiency, taking shelter behind the heavy equipment scattered around the airstrip, then advancing until they were firing at the last remnants of Mbowi's attack squad. London had to give them credit: none of them retreated. They stood there and took it like men. Well, like a bunch of dumb assholes, anyway.

When the smoke had cleared, the landing strip was strewn with bodies, but London's team had come through unscathed. It looked like things might actually be okay despite the rough entry. Then London climbed back aboard the plane and had a look at the cockpit and realized that Lady Luck might have spread herself too thin.

The three-man flight crew were still in their seats in the cockpit, but they'd been shredded by shrapnel. One of Mbowi's troops lay a few feet away, his guts still dripping from the bulkhead.

London did a quick and dirty reconstruction of the events that led to the gory outcome. During the firefight, the Mbowi loyalist had somehow outflanked London's team and gotten aboard the plane. He'd made his way to the cockpit with a couple hand grenades at the ready, probably figuring that if one grenade was good, two must be excellent. Gifted with bravery that far outmatched his brains, the loyalist had managed to toss one grenade into the cockpit, but had dropped the other. Most likely, he'd been paralyzed by panic or indecision, possibly both. His brain had short-circuited for the exact amount of time that it took the grenades to detonate. Thus, the dead flight crew and the blood-splattered bulkhead.

"Goddamn it," London said.

He took out his can of Skoal and helped himself to a pinch. He let the wad of tobacco get good and juicy before he went out to break the news to his team: their exit strategy had just gotten blown to bits by a pair of hand grenades.

2

The land on this side of the border was a flat, grassy expanse, so Lia Rousseau saw the border checkpoint well in advance. It wasn't much, just a few men with guns standing around a Jeep parked in the middle of the road. If it was an officially sanctioned checkpoint, then Daroka's situation was dire indeed.

She slowed the Land Rover's speed a bit, not enough to look suspicious, but enough to reassure the vehicle's other occupants to play it cool and let her do the talking. She knew she could count on her cameraman, Max. The two of them had bribed their way past checkpoints much scarier than this over the last decade and a half. The three Americans in the backseat, well, she just hoped they could keep their mouths shut for once. The man and woman hadn't stopped arguing since Lia and Max had picked them up at the scene of a car wreck back in Borwannah. At least their kid was quiet.

The trio of men running the makeshift roadblock were exactly what Lia had expected. They were dressed in military fatigues and armed with AK-47s. But nothing about the way they carried themselves suggested that they were trained professionals. While General Mbowi's inner circle was comprised of battle-tested soldiers, these men were more than likely just ragtag amateur mercenaries who'd come from neighboring nations to make some easy money after the coup. They'd probably been strong-arming shopkeepers in Chapmantown or running truckloads of heroin to the coast before Mbowi recruited them. And now that Mbowi had gone missing, they were trying to eke out a little more cash before the UN sent in peacekeepers.

Lia lowered the driver's side window and handed over her credentials to one of the men. His lips peeled back in a smile, revealing a pair of gold incisors, as he glanced over the documents.

When he spoke, he did so in her native tongue. "You're a long way from France, Mrs. Rousseau. What brings you to Daroka?"

"We're journalists," Lia said, gesturing to the papers in his hand. "As you can see."

The mercenary folded the papers and passed them back, clearly unimpressed. Lia had him pegged as the type who thought he could mask his incompetence with an excess of swagger. By her reckoning, that sort of blowhard accounted for at least half of the planet's male population.

"If you're journalists, then you know that the situation in Daroka isn't stable," he said. "Perhaps this isn't the best time to visit the country. Maybe you should return to Paris. They have riots there too, no?"

There was an envelope stuffed with euros in the Lia's hip pocket. When they'd gone through the appropriate amount of theater, she'd pull it out and hand it over. But they weren't there, yet. After all, the mercenary hadn't commented on her femininity in a crude attempt at sexual intimidation. But that part was coming, and soon.

Right on cue, he said, "Especially it is not safe for a pretty woman like you. With that blonde hair and that body, you would be in constant danger. Many of the men in this country are not gentlemen like us. Some of them are dangerous and desperate."

His partners, their rifles propped on their hips, laughed. One of them grabbed his crotch and waggled his eyebrows.

Now, it was time to try out their intimidation tactics on Max. If they could get a strong enough reaction, maybe they might have the opportunity to put on a show of violence.

The gold-toothed mercenary poked his head into the vehicle. "Your friend doesn't look like he can handle himself in a rough situation."

Max smiled and gave a thumbs-up. When he spoke, he put on his best American accent. "Beautiful country you have here! And wow, isn't this heat something? I thought it was hot back in Chicago, but this is just out of sight!"

Lia sighed dramatically and shrugged. "He's American, so he only speaks English. Same as the people in back. They're paying me to get them into the country. Now, I'm sure we can come to a similar arrangement."

She expected to be treated to a show of feigned indignation, in which the mercenary angled for a bigger bribe. Instead, the man just nodded and extended his hand. Either he was even more amateurish than Lia had thought or he was eager to finish the transaction and get the hell out of the country. Whatever the reason, Lia slapped the envelope into his hand.

The mercenary thumbed through the bills and seemed satisfied with the amount. He motioned to his friends, who jumped into the Jeep and moved it out of the road.

"Be careful," the mercenary reminded them. "This whole country is going to hell."

Lia kept her speed reasonable as she drove down the bumpy road. She checked the rearview mirror until the mercenaries were out of sight, then put the pedal down. If the mercenaries decided to follow them, she wanted to at least make it difficult. After a few miles, she relaxed.

She looked over at Max. "You know, that accent was pretty convincing."

Max laughed. "I was trying to sound like the one from those movies about the family vacations. Chevy Chase is the best American. He should run for president."

"I don't see anything funny about what just happened," Walter, one of the actual Americans, spoke up from the backseat. "We were just robbed. And it could have been even worse. We could have been killed."

Lia rolled her eyes and switched back to English. "You call that robbery? I guess you haven't done much traveling."

"We've done mission trips to both Mexico and Brazil, thank you very much," Walter snapped. "And not in the nice parts that tourists see."

"I wish you'd give it a rest," Walter's wife said. Her name was Josie and ever since she'd climbed into the backseat of the Land Rover with her injured son clutched to her chest, the woman's face had been a mask of panic and terror.

"Oh, sure, I'll give it a rest when you admit that we should have gone back to Mexico instead of coming halfway across the world."

"Maybe we should have offered the mercenaries Walter instead of the money," Max said in French.

Lia snorted a quick laugh. "They'd pay us to take him back. We could have come out ahead on that deal."

"Don't act like you're not talking about me," Walter said. "I may not speak French, but I know what my name sounds like."

If Lia ever needed a reminder of why she never got married, a day of riding with Walter and Josie certainly provided it. She glanced at the rearview mirror and had to stifle a laugh at the sight of him. He was red-faced and pouting, his arms crossed over his chest. He looked like a bearded, balding toddler who'd just been denied the chance to eat at McDonald's. But any urge to laugh died away when

Lia checked the other two backseat passengers. Josie looked frightened to the point of hysteria. And Dominic, the couple's five year old son, was near catatonic with sickness. The boy's eyes were bloodshot and runny, with dark circles beneath. His face was pale and shiny with sweat.

"There's an old French mission a few kilometers west of here," Lia said. "It's a little out of our way, but I seem to remember that there was a hospital there. Well, what passes for a hospital in these parts, at least. The last time Max and I were here, the Red Cross was training medical staff for the mission's infirmary."

"Do you think we could find help for Dominic?" Josie asked.

"The way things are going in this country, who knows. But it's worth a try," Lia answered.

"Thank God you're familiar with the area." Josie sounded like she was on the verge of tears. "I don't know what we'd have done if you hadn't come along. You're like our guardian angel."

Walter grunted. Lia got the idea this was as close as he could bring himself to genuine gratitude. Lia had only known Walter and Josie for a few hours, but during that time, she'd gotten a pretty good idea of what their relationship was like. Most likely, when things were going his way, Walter was boisterous and full of good cheer, while his wife stood at his side, smiling meekly and nodding her head in agreement with every word he said. But once the going got rough—and no doubt about it, the going didn't get much rougher than the situation in Daroka—Walter dissolved into a bitter, accusatory asshole. Strange that the man was a Christian missionary, but if there was one thing Lia had learned during her career as a journalist, it was to never take people at face value.

The McPhersons—Walter, Josie, and little Dominic—had been doing mission work in Champs de Fleur, a village on the Borwannah-Daroka border. They were part of an interfaith humanitarian mission to get the village set up with a school, basic medical facilities, and sanitation. When their work began, it appeared that General Mbowi had zero intention of crossing the border. Champs de Fleur may have been a remote, primitive village by Western standards, but the central government of Borwannah was stable, with a well-supplied standing army. All that changed with the disaster at the Marsh Industries research center. Amid rumors of toxic chemical spills and a miasma of lab-generated germs, the Borwannah government closed ranks around the capitol city, leaving the outlying villages to fend for themselves.

According to the McPhersons' story—delivered in Josie's cracking, near hysterical voice with frequent condescending interruptions by her husband—a band of guerrillas crossed the border in the middle of the night and staged a raid on Champs de Fleur.

"They were crazed, more like animals than men," Josie had said. "Some of them weren't even armed. They just attacked us like rabid beasts."

"One of them bit our son," Walter had explained, pointing to Dominic's bandaged forearm. "We were lucky to get out of there alive."

Josie had sniffed back tears. "We managed to fight off that man who bit Dominic. Then we ran into the night. I'll never forget the look in that man's eyes. It was like he was possessed by some demon. And I'll also never forget the screams. We left everyone—all our friends—we left them all behind."

Lia wondered how much of the story was true. It wasn't that she suspected Josie and Walter of fabricating the whole incident, but Lia had made her reputation by venturing into global hot spots in search of the next big news story. And she'd learned that extreme conditions provoked extreme responses. One such response was to become hyper-focused on details. The people who responded this way made the best witnesses. They could recount every bit of their traumatic experiences with complete clarity. The other response was to recount the ordeal as if viewed through a lens of nightmare logic. In this view, people became monsters with near supernatural levels of bloodlust. Lia suspected that the McPhersons were leaning toward the latter response. And she couldn't blame them. They were, after all, a pair of activist do-gooders. They may have been up to the task of rough work in harsh conditions, but they were unprepared for a combat scenario.

They rode the remaining few kilometers without conversation. The shuddering of the vehicle's frame and they bounced over rocks and potholes seemed to be soundtrack enough. But they made it to the Mission of Our Lady of Peace without incident. No more checkpoints this far from the border.

"This place looks deserted," Max said as Lia parked outside the white stucco building that served as the infirmary.

Lia silently cursed this bit of bad luck. She'd hoped to deposit the McPhersons at the mission. The last time she and Max had visited, there had been a trio of priests, a full complement of at least a dozen nuns, a group of Peace Corps volunteers, and a staff of local workers. Nearly a hundred people if you counted the patients in the infirmary. Now, without a single soul in sight, it seemed that she was stuck with the McPhersons.

"It's been, what, four years since we were here?" Lia glanced around. Although Max's observation appeared to be correct, the place looked like it had been well-kept. If the residents had abandoned it, they'd done so recently.

"Yeah, four years sounds about right. Back when Mbowi was still a St. Pierre loyalist."

In the backseat, Walter cleared his throat. "I hate to interrupt your walk down memory lane, but if this place is abandoned, we should get moving. I mean, look around you.

This place hasn't been sitting empty for very long. The grass is mowed, the whitewash on the buildings can't be more than a few months old, and none of the windows I can see are broken. But *something* made people pick up and leave, and whatever it was, it was recent. Could be Mbowi's men took the place over. Maybe they're all out at the border, shaking people down, like your friends back there. They could be back at any minute, and I don't think it's wise to hang around and wait."

Lia and Max looked at one another. They didn't need to be telepathic to know what the other was thinking: *This guy is a world-class coward.*

Lia scooted around so she could look directly into the backseat instead of talking to the rearview mirror. "It may have been a few years since I've been in this country, but as far as I know, this is the last outpost before we get to the jungle. Yeah, I know the location of some native villages, but they're not exactly big on modern medicine. So unless you think Dominic could benefit from the prayers of a Ka'Longho shaman, I suggest we see if there are any medical supplies we can salvage. At the very least, we can refill our water supply. The Red Cross installed a filtration system last time I was here."

Walter's sour expression said that he didn't much care for a woman putting him in his place, especially not some liberal, feminist, university type. But he nodded slightly and murmured something that might have been agreement.

"Besides," Max said, reaching for the hidden compartment beneath his seat. "We got protection."

From the compartment, Max brought out a shoebox. Inside were a pair of nine millimeter pistols. He slotted a magazine into one and passed it to Lia, then he repeated the process on his own weapon.

"We only have two," Lia told Walter. "Sorry."

"I wouldn't know what to do with one anyway," Walter sniffed. "I'm a man of peace."

"And here I thought you Americans were born with a gun in each hand," Max laughed.

"I see nothing funny about the situation." Walter turned his head to stare out the window, signaling an end to his part of the conversation.

"Don't worry. We won't be long." Lia directed her words at Josie. She didn't care to speak to Walter any more than was absolutely necessary. Her distaste for the man grew every time he opened his mouth.

"No, I want to come with you." Josie didn't wait for an answer. She passed her sleeping son over to Walter.

"Oh, sure," Walter said. "First you insist that we drag the child halfway around the world so you can prove that you're a modern woman. Now you expect me to take care of him."

Lia knew she should ignore him, but she couldn't help herself. "He's your son too."

"No, he's not" Walter snapped. "Josie here got knocked up while she was still in high school. My parents nearly disowned me for marrying a disgraced woman, but I thought, through the grace of our Lord, that she could be led into the light. I prayed on it and the Lord told me that I was right. I guess maybe he sent her to me as a test of my patience. I'm like Job, asked to prove myself a faithful servant of God in the worst circumstances."

Lia gave Josie a closer look. She'd never been a good judge of ages, but she would have figured Josie for a woman in her mid-thirties, at least ten years older than a woman only five years out of high school. Then again, she could see how living with a man like Walter could prematurely age you.

"Well, let's not waste any more time." Lia opened the door and climbed out. She raised her arms above her head and stretched. It felt good to be out of the car for a moment, even if the atmosphere of the abandoned mission was ominous.

"Fucking ghost town, eh?" Max said as he stepped around the front of the vehicle. "Something weird about this place. Can't explain it."

Lia did her best to shrug it off. "It's just empty, that's all. Every small town looks spooky when it's empty."

"Yeah, but I'm glad we're not here at night."

"Okay, I'll admit you're right about that." Lia glanced over her shoulder at Josie, then said, "Come on. Let's see if we can find anything useful."

3

Ever since his team landed in Borwannah three hours ago, Mike London hadn't been able to shake the feeling that something was wrong. Every soldier who'd come through multiple combat tours intact developed something like a sixth sense that allowed them to know when the shit was getting dangerously near the fan. But he'd done his best to tamp the feeling down and focus on the job at hand. Any job that started with your exit strategy getting blown to shit by a couple of grenades was bound to leave a sick feeling in your gut, after all.

"What's that look like to you, boss?" Zantoro asked, pointing to the roadblock in the distance.

London shrugged. "I had to guess, I'd say it's some enterprising men doing their best to make some money."

Zantoro laughed. "Welcome to Daroka, the land of opportunity!"

London was driving, while Zantoro rode shotgun; Osbourne and Vincent were in the back. With their supplies packed into the rear compartment, the Jeep was a tight fit. But these operations rarely involved comfort.

"Goddamn," Osbourne said. "You think this fucking road could get any bumpier?"

"And this fucking dust, man!" Vincent scrubbed a finger over the lens of his sunglasses and leaned into the front seat to show Zantoro the layer of grit and dust he'd collected. "I told you guys we shouldn't ride with the top down."

"Shit, some of the ranch roads back in Black Mound make this look smooth as glass," London said. "And you ain't seen dust until you've been in west Texas in the middle of the summer. Then when it rains, you get mud coming down from the sky. Looks like something out of the Bible, one of those plagues sent to Egypt so that Charlton Heston and his people could be set free. But forget that bullshit for a minute and focus on this roadblock up ahead. I don't want to drop any unnecessary bodies, but I don't see that we have much of a choice. I don't want to keep looking over my shoulder the whole way to the compound."

"You hear that?" Zantoro ejected the magazine from his pistol, checked it, and then slammed it home. "The boss said we ain't paying no fucking toll."

London kept driving with both hands on the wheel. If things went bad at the roadblock, his guys would be more than enough to handle it. They'd made plenty of widows and orphans over the years. Do something long enough, it becomes routine.

He took his foot off the accelerator and let the Jeep come to a gradual stop a few yards away from the roadblock. He turned off the engine to underline the message that he wasn't getting any closer; if the three men standing in front of their own Jeep wanted to have a conversation, they were going to have to do a bit of walking. The early stop was intended to get the three men out in the open, where London could get a better look at them and spot any hidden backup. It also told London what sort of threat he was dealing with. If all three of them started walking, they were rank amateurs.

And—surprise, surprise—that's exactly what they did. After a brief conversation, all three men came down the road towards London's team. They did so with their rifles raised, but they didn't make any effort to spread out to different angles of approach. Any of the men on London's team could have picked them off in the blink of an eye.

"Look at these fucking idiots," Zantoro mused. "It's almost beneath us to waste bullets on them. I always feel bad shooting the mentally handicapped."

Vincent and Osbourne laughed.

"Put a sock in it, you fucking goofballs," London said. "Stay sharp."

He watched the trio of gunmen approach. The one in the center was the leader, London decided. He walked a half step in front of the other two, and his gait had a bit of swagger that was missing from his obvious subordinates. Also, when he came alongside the Jeep and smiled, London saw the sun glint off a pair of gold teeth. He wasn't sure, but he felt like that was a sign of dominance in some cultures. Or what the fuck, maybe he was just reading too much into the man's dental work.

Gold Teeth rattled off a string of French.

London shook his head. "Sorry, my man, but I don't *parlais Francais.*"

Behind him, Zantoro snickered.

"Where you gentlemen headed" Gold Teeth asked, this time in English.

London shrugged, keeping his hands in plain view. "Oh, nowhere in particular. Just out for a Sunday drive."

"This a bad place for that. And maybe you don't know, but it's Monday."

"You hear that, boys?" London kept his eyes fixed on Gold Teeth. It forced the man to keep his own eyes fixed on London. And that meant he couldn't see what Zantoro was up to, never mind Osbourne and Vincent. The other two gunmen were keeping their distance, but they were still standing in the middle of the road just a few feet in front of the Jeep. Once again, these guys were pure amateur hour.

"Goddamn it, I hate Mondays!" Zantoro shouted. The sudden outburst drew the attention of the two gunmen in the road. They looked like they didn't know whether to start laughing or to raise their guns and fire. Gold Teeth seemed to realize a split second too late that he was standing too close to the Jeep to raise his rifle.

The men in the Jeep didn't need a prearranged signal. London's team had been together long enough that they could feel the moment. London leaned back, giving Zantoro a clear shot at Gold Teeth, while Vincent and Osbourne stood and fired at the gunmen in the road.

It was over in a few seconds. Zantoro's bullet hit Gold Teeth right in the mouth, taking out the shiny incisors on its way through the back of his skull. The man teetered for a moment, leaking blood and brains, then went down. Vincent and Osbourne also hit their targets, firing tight clusters of nine millimeter rounds into the chests of the two remaining gunmen. By the time London straightened up in his seat and twisted the key in the Jeep's ignition, the dusty road was liberally decorated with red splatter.

"I fucking hate toll roads," Zantoro said.

4

The oldest of the four boys who reported back from advance scouting duty was fourteen. Father Xavier Arnaud had to remind himself daily that the members of his army were only boys and girls, and even in a country as violent and unstable as Daroka, they should still be going to school, playing football, or even working on the family farm. He had to remind himself, because these children carried themselves like they were much older. Especially the boys who'd been pressed into service with Mbowi's militia. They walked with confident strides, holding their weapons at the ready. And although many of them were still awaiting the first real growth spurt of puberty, they had seen more horrors than most old men. Up close, you could see it in their eyes. They had the haunted, weary eyes of soldiers who'd been away at war too long.

It made Father Xavier's heart ache to look into those eyes. But at least his children were still alive. So many kids their age had been chewed up by General Mbowi's war machine or sent to the mines in the south of the country, where companies from the West extracted from the earth raw materials for cell phone parts. Those children had haunted eyes, too. But theirs weren't the haunted eyes of hardened soldiers; they were the haunted eyes of slaves. Father Xavier knew that neither state was a decent way to spend one's childhood, but he also knew that there was no obscenity worse than slavery.

He sat at the center of camp, while the rest of his followers sat in clusters of two or three in a small clearing. The canopy of trees and vegetation above them was so dense that one could be forgiven for thinking it twilight rather than mid-afternoon.

Father Xavier rose to his feet to greet the returning scouts. The oldest, whose name was Peter, tipped him a salute and dropped a darkly stained burlap bag at on the ground at Father Xavier's feet.

"All clear to keep pushing north," Peter said. "Slow going without a path. Maybe two more days."

Father Xavier thought Peter's estimate might be a touch optimistic, but he kept that to himself. Instead, he nudged the burlap bag with his foot and asked, "How many?"

"We saw four walking dead men, but there are more out there." Peter pointed behind him, toward the smallest of the scouts, a boy who had recently celebrated his tenth birthday. "Gilbert says he could smell them. He says there are many."

"And there will be more every day. I've seen it in my dreams."

Peter glanced over his shoulder at the other three boys, then dropped his gaze to ground. He kicked at the ground. Like all the boys, he wore shoes improvised from scraps of fabric and rubber from scavenged tires.

"What is it, child?" Father Xavier asked.

"These dead men we met..." Peter looked at his companions again.

"Yes?" Father Xavier prompted.

"They weren't like the others. They were soldiers, but they were white men. They wore uniforms."

Father Xavier nodded. He'd seen this in his dreams too. It meant that the time of judgment was drawing near indeed. But there were miles left to travel before Father Xavier and his boys could rest. Many miles to walk before the black robed man took them across the river and into the Eternal City.

"It's okay, Peter. You did well. I have seen these white men in my dreams as well."

Peter made the sign of the cross over his chest, as all the boys did whenever Father Xavier mentioned his dreams, then said, "The Ka'Longho are also moving north. We saw their scouting party and tried to speak with them, but they disappeared into the trees. They really *are* like ghosts."

Father Xavier nodded. "Very good. Pass out the lunch rations. We resume our march in a half hour."

He patted each boy on the head as they trooped past him on their way to the supply wagons, which were nothing more than a pair of wheelbarrows heaped with supplies looted from the various Red Cross outposts, abandoned shops, and even off supply trucks bound for the cafeteria on the Marsh Industries compound.

When they'd moved past him, he knelt on the soft earth and opened the burlap bag. As Peter had promised, there were four heads inside. They'd been hacked away from their bodies with a machete, which had left ragged stumps where the necks had been attached. Jagged bits of shattered vertebrae and slimy strands of veins trailed from the stumps, leaking blood and spinal fluid that stained the bag's rough fabric.

The boys had managed to kill the four ghouls without firing a single shot. They were getting better and better at this sort of thing. Soon, they might even be able to sneak up on the Ka'Longho tribesmen, although that hardly mattered anymore. The Ka'Longho—the so-called "Ghost People"— had long believed in the walking dead. They were perhaps better equipped than even Father Xavier's army to deal with this strange new world.

Father Xavier made the sign of the cross over the bag and began to recite the last rites for the deceased. He wondered if it made any difference. Perhaps he should abandon the practice. But while people may die easily, old habits do not.

5

Walter shifted Dominic off his lap and laid the boy across the other half of the seat. It was one thing to endure the sweltering afternoon heat on his own, but doing it with a feverish child on his lap was intolerable. He snorted, turned his head, and spit out the open window. Dominic moaned. His belly gurgled.

"Please don't puke in this car," Walter said, glaring at the child. "At least wait until your mother and her new friends get back."

Walter wished for the hundredth time that day that he'd turned down Reverend Brother Jacob's "offer" to go on yet another mission trip. After all, this was his fifth tour of duty, and most of the people who'd worked their way from Elder to Deacon only had to put in three stints abroad before being welcomed as full members of Reverend Brother Jacob's inner circle and receiving the title of Bishop. But here was Walter, out in the middle of nowhere yet again, and still only a second-degree Deacon. He was beginning to wonder if Reverend Brother Jacob had any intention of bringing him into the fold.

Dominic's moaning was getting louder, but not loud

enough to drown out the weird growling of the boy's stomach. Walter sighed. He knew he shouldn't be so hard on the boy, but it was the only way he knew. Walter's own father had never been one to spare the rod, after all, and he'd turned out just fine. Modern parents had strayed from the Bible's teachings about child rearing, and the world had suffered for it.

"Maybe they'll find some medicine in this place, but I doubt it," Walter said, laying a hand on the boy's forehead. "Shouldn't have let your mother talk me into bringing you along. That woman has always been my downfall."

The child was burning up. No telling what sort of bug he'd picked up when that crazy native had bit him. These people were diseased, both spiritually and physically. Even the ones who'd accepted Jesus Christ into their lives still held stubbornly to some of their heathen beliefs and practices. They still indulged in hallucinogenic liquors, which they claimed help them communicate with dead ancestors. And when the moon was full, husbands and wives still copulated in the open air, in full view of one another. The first time they'd witnessed the shameful spectacle, Josie had sidled up to Walter and suggested that maybe they should join in. After all, she said, Dominic was asleep in the tent, and besides, some of the Peace Corps kids were doing it. Walter had pushed her away and told her they would do no such thing. But, to his shame, he'd lain awake all night in their tent, listening to the ecstatic grunts and cries outside and wondering what it would be like to take Josie from behind, out there in the dust and dirt like an animal.

A movement in the seat beside him ripped Walter out of his shameful reverie. Dominic was sitting bolt upright, staring at Walter. The boy's eyes were so bloodshot that they appeared bright red. His mouth hung open, and a thin line of drool ran from his bottom lip and down his chin.

"Just try to relax," Walter said, patting the boy's shoulder. "Your mom will be back soon."

Dominic snarled like a cornered dog and nipped at Walter's hand.

"Good heavens!" Walter yelped, jerking his hand away. "What devil has gotten into you, boy? If you weren't sick, I'd drag you out of this car and thrash you with my belt. I have half a mind to do it anyway. Sickness is no excuse to break the fifth commandment."

Dominic raised his injured arm and sniffed the bandage. He bit the discolored gauze and tore away a large scrap, exposing the wound beneath. A stench like rotten meat assaulted Walter's nostrils. He recoiled against the car door, transfixed by the spectacle of the boy digging a finger into the infected wound and drawing out a squirming maggot. Walter's stomach heaved as Dominic continued to probe the angry wound. His finger squelched through congealed blood and pus.

"No, son," Walter said. "You're sick. Just wait for your mother-"

The boy sprang at Walter, biting and clawing like an enraged animal. Walter was paralyzed with confusion and fear for a moment, but it was soon broken by the sudden, sharp pain of the boy biting into Walter's neck.

Walter grabbed Dominic by the ears and pulled the boy's head away. Blood flowed from the punctures on Walter's neck, but his scant knowledge of first aid told him that Dominic hadn't severed anything major. Still, the pain was blinding, and even worse, the boy's thrashing made it impossible for Walter to squirm away. Dominic didn't weigh much more than fifty pounds, but he wriggled and convulsed with bone-snapping fury. Walter held fast to the boy's ears and managed to wrap his legs around his waist. His panicked brain had formulated a plan: get a firm grip with his legs around Dominic's waist, then flip him over onto his back, where Walter would have a clear advantage. After that, he could figure out a way to restrain the child until the others returned. It was a reasonable plan, but Dominic scuttled it with one quick, violent twist of his head. Walter's eyes went wide with disgust and disbelief as Dominic's ears tore free from his head with a sound like wet Velcro separating.

Walter looked at his fists, which clutched the ragged ears, then screamed. He dropped the bloody ears and waved his hands in front of his face, as much to wave away the nightmare imagery before him as to fend off Dominic's renewed attack. He screamed until he was certain his vocal cords would snap. But his screams—shrieks, really; they were high-pitched and frantic—did nothing to slow Dominic. If anything, the noise seemed to urge him on.

The boy's teeth sank into the meaty part of Walter's left forearm, just below the elbow. A white hot spike of agony raced up Walter's arm. Adrenaline sang through his veins as he battered Dominic's head with his right fist. Again and again, his punches found their mark, smashing into the bloody, pulpy mess where his ear had been. But those clenched fist shots might as well have been playful slaps. They barely served to slow Dominic's assault.

Walter's fevered brain flashed on a memory of a video he'd seen in which a feral cat mauled a grown man. Although the man was many times the cat's size, he couldn't manage to get a grip on the animal as it lashed out, shredding the man's face with its claws. If Walter found it hard to hold onto Dominic a moment ago, it was a feat that was rapidly approaching impossible. With his wounded arm and neck pumping blood, and Dominic's open mouth leaking a steady stream of green pus, everything was too slick to grip.

Dominic squirmed through Walter's arms until they were face-to-face. Walter opened his mouth—to scream, to beg, even to just catch his breath—and was rewarded with a mouthful of the foul substance leaking from Dominic's mouth. He gagged, choking on the stinking green slime and his own vomit. His eyes filled with more of the same.

And then, finally, God looked upon Walter with a small measure of mercy, for his consciousness began to ebb away as Dominic fell upon him with snapping jaws, his tiny fingers hooked into vicious animal claws.

6

Whatever had happened at the mission to cause its inhabitants to flee, it had been sudden and caught them unaware. The tables in the cafeteria were still set for breakfast service. The pots and pans on the steam table in the kitchen were still full of food, although it was so rotten and fly-covered that Lia couldn't identify what had been on the menu. Still, with the windows open, things could get to such a state in a matter of days in this climate.

"What do you think?" Max asked, covering his nose against the stink of rotten food. "Gone five days? A week maybe?"

Lia nodded. "Sounds right."

"Was it the General's men?" Josie asked, waving away a cloud of flies that had settled on a pan of what might have once been scrambled eggs. It was a futile gesture. The flies burst into buzzing chaos, reforming into a black cloud seconds later, then returning to their feast.

"I don't think so," Lia said. "For one thing, there's no evidence of that. No bullet holes that I can see. No shell casings on the ground. No dead bodies. No evidence of looting. And for another thing, Mbowi's soldiers aren't here.

There was no one here worth kidnapping, just Red Cross volunteers, nuns, a few priests, and a bunch of locals who were either too old or too young to be of any use. The only reason Mbowi would be interested in this place is as a tactical retreat. And if that was the case, they'd still be here."

"I agree," Max said. "Whatever happened here, it was quiet. And we both know quiet isn't General Mbowi's style."

He raised his camera and rolled film on the interior of the kitchen, then moved back into the dining room. Lia didn't bother with her microphone. There was no need for narration. This was one of those cases where the images were more than enough. She took Josie by the arm and said, "Come on. The infirmary is in the next building. We'll find some medicine for your son."

"Something is wrong here," Josie said, shivering despite the summer heat. "There's an evil about this place. We shouldn't be here."

"Come on," Lia replied, tugging more insistently at the woman's elbow. "The sooner we can check the other buildings, the sooner we can get out of here."

Lia did her best to walk confidently as she led Josie back through the cafeteria and out into the blazing afternoon sunshine. But she had to admit to herself that she felt the same thing as Josie. There was something wrong about the mission. Although she wasn't given to superstition, Lia had learned long ago to trust her gut instincts, and right now, they were telling her to do a quick about-face, get back in the Land Rover, and put this place in the rearview mirror. But Dominic was sick, and probably worse off than Josie imagined. Lia had reported from plague zones. She'd peered through the clear plastic face shield of a Hazmat suit at hospital wards of Ebola victims. The feverish trembling and haunted, hollow eyes of those poor souls hadn't been too far off from what she'd seen when she looked at the American boy. While she doubted that Dominic had been exposed to Ebola or anything similar, there was no doubt that the child was very ill, perhaps even deathly so.

Max finished getting some shots of the cafeteria and followed them down the dusty path to the infirmary. Lia could hear him whistling as he trotted to catch up. It was a nervous habit of his, whistling. Most likely, it meant he was feeling the same sense of eerie, oppressive dread. That only reinforced the message Lia's gut was sending. They'd been a team for years, Lia and Max, and their communication had reached a level of near telepathy.

The look Max gave her as he held open the infirmary door told Lia all she needed to know. The photographer, whose fearlessness could border on reckless disregard for his own safety, was spooked. He gave Lia a forced smile, but his eyes told a different story.

Lia drew her pistol from the side pocket of her cargo pants, and stepped into the infirmary. Although it was quiet as a grave, you never knew what could be waiting. But the place turned out to be just as empty as the rest of the mission.

The infirmary was a high-ceilinged room with plenty of windows, most of which were open. There were two dozen beds arranged in two rows, one along each wall. About half of the beds were neatly made. The others had at some point been occupied. There were still IV stands and in some cases electronic monitoring equipment close to these beds. As they walked down the central aisle, Lia noticed that some of the sheets were dark with ominous stains. Dried pools of what might have been blood, vomit, or both crusted the floor between the beds. Chamber pots stood unemptied on the floor. Flies swarmed over them. Lia was thankful for the open windows. Otherwise, the stink of the rotten food in the cafeteria kitchen might have been a perfumed bouquet compared to this place.

"Could be some virus," Max suggested, pointing the

camera at one of the most thoroughly stained beds. "Remember Sudan? Congo? We should be in Hazmat suits."

Josie looked at Lia with panic-widened eyes. "A virus?"

Lia shook her head. "If it's Ebola or something like that, we're safe. This place has been empty too long for any of it to be hanging around, especially with the windows wide open. The supplies are in that room in the back. The sooner we check it out, the sooner we can get out of here."

The supply room was locked, but Max was able to kick the door off its hinges. It took him three attempts, and each boot-shot was like thunder in the empty infirmary. Josie plugged her ears and closed her eyes after the first one. Lia patted the woman on the back when the door fell open.

"It's okay," she said.

Josie nodded weakly. "Sorry, I'm normally not so jumpy, it's just this place…"

"I know. Come on, let's get what we need for your son."

Max stood aside and allowed the women into the cramped supply closet. "I'll wait outside. I need some fresh air."

He lowered his camera and made his way to the exit at the front of the building.

Lia ducked inside the room and began a quick inventory of the medications. She wasn't an expert, but she knew a thing or two about field medicine. In addition to reporting from disease hot spots, she'd been on the ground in combat zones. She'd seen medics mend wounds and beat back infection with improvised materials and scrounged drugs. There was a black medical bag on the counter. She unzipped it and found the usual stuff: hypodermics, first aid supplies and a stethoscope. She handed the bag to Josie.

"Here," Lia said. "Hold this open for me."

Josie nodded and stood close by while Lia tossed in anything that looked like an antibiotic or antiviral. She added some painkillers and anti-inflammatories as well. When she'd finished her selections, the bag was so full that Josie had to work to get the zipper to close.

"Do you know what you're doing with this stuff?" Josie asked.

"I'm not a doctor, if that's what you mean. But we'll do our best," Lia answered.

What she didn't say was that if they didn't get Dominic to someone with actual medical knowledge, things could get very grim. Her hope was that the Red Cross might have gone into the jungle with the Ka'Longho. Although they could be elusive, the tribe was generally hospitable towards those who didn't exude hostility. During her time with the tribe, Lia had seen none of the barbaric or cannibalistic behavior that the outside world ascribed to them. Of course, if her travels had taught her anything, it was that one man's barbarity was another's sincerely held religious belief.

They went back through the grim infirmary and joined Max in the comparatively fresh air.

"Listen," Max said, pointing down the path to the church. "Do you hear that?"

"I don't..." Lia paused. "Okay, yeah. Sounds like something's alive in there. Maybe an animal of some kind?"

The sound she heard wasn't quite howling. It was too low-pitched and steady for that. It was more like moaning. She cocked her ear toward the church and was sure she could hear something like scratching, like whatever was in there was clawing at the door, which appeared to be barred from the outside. They walked a few meters closer to the building, and Lia could see that several wide planks of wood had been nailed over the doors.

"Could be people," Max said. "Like maybe they retreated in there when Mbowi's troops came through?"

Lia shook her head. "But why? Mbowi claims to be Catholic, but I doubt his troops have any hang-ups about going into a church. They're violent psychopaths, not vampires."

"I don't know, but you know how it is sometimes. We've seen some strange shit, you and me. Might just be an animal of some kind. But it also might be people. And I don't think I could just drive off if there might be some injured people trapped in there."

"My boy is injured," Josie insisted. "We need to get back to him. And besides, who nails the door shut on something that's not dangerous? Whether it's animals or people, why would you board up the door if you weren't afraid of whatever's inside?"

Off the top of her head, Lia could think of several reasons, and they all involved the level of sadism for which General Mbowi was becoming known in the international community. She'd heard stories of entire villages of men whose hands and feet had been cut off when they dared offend the general. She'd heard rumors about women forced to copulate with farm animals until they were reduced to gibbering madness, simply for the entertainment of Mbowi's troops. But she didn't feel the need to mention any of that to Josie McPherson.

"I don't think anything that dangerous could be held back by a few boards," Max said. "The windows all look like they're intact."

"Come on, Josie," Lia said. "It won't take us long. Besides, if the people from the mission are hiding in the church, there might be a doctor among them. The Red Cross was here, after all."

Josie nodded. "Let's be quick. Dominic needs me."

The trio walked to the church. Max took the lead, holding his camera in one hand and tugging at the boards with the other. The wood was ancient and sunbaked. It was coaxed to splinters after a few good pulls. He discarded the broken scraps, tossing them into a pile on the ground. Then he turned, hand on the doorknob, and looked at the two women.

"Might want to stand back," he said. "You know, in case it is an animal."

When the doors swung open and Lia caught her first glimpse of what was within the church, she was glad for the distance between herself and the doorway. And when the stench reached her nostrils, she was doubly glad. The air was superheated and thick with the pungent stink of decay. Lia had explored the garbage dumps of slums in India. She was no stranger to the nauseating reek of rot and filth. But even those garbage dumps full of human waste and dead animals couldn't compete with the stink wafting out of the church.

Lia had no idea if the story about Mbowi's troops forcing women to have sex with farm animals was true, but it appeared the one concerning hand and foot amputation was. A number of the men shambling aimlessly through the church sanctuary had neither hands nor feet. They stalked about clumsily on the ragged stumps of their ankles, falling down after a few steps then pushing themselves up with handless forearms. The others—men, women, and children—made no effort to help their maimed companions. They stumbled around the fallen men, sometimes even walking over them. They moved as if drugged or in some sort of trance. Their mouths hung open, and green slaver dripped from their swollen tongues. Their wide, unblinking eyes were red, as if every blood vessel in their eyeballs had burst. If this was the end stage of some virus, it must be one of the worst known to man.

"Holy God, they're coming for us!" Max shouted, backpedaling. Even when confronted with the horror in the church, he reached for his camera before his gun.

"What's wrong with them?" Josie grabbed Lia's arm. "Look at them!"

Lia shoved Josie behind her. "Come on, let's get out of here. Max, I think you got enough footage."

The first group of the infected people managed to stumble through the doorway. And once that first few had managed the feat, the others followed. In a matter of moments, Lia found herself surrounded. Those with hands grabbed at the three intruders. Others poked at them with blackened stumps that dripped clots of pus. Worst of all, they snapped and bit like ravenous animals. Lia threw her elbows around, knocking a few people to the ground. She backpedaled until she was out of the ground. She looked around for Max. He was fighting his way out of the crowd, throwing punches and elbows.

"No, no, no," Josie chanted, pressing her hands to her ears and squeezing her eyes shut.

"Run!" Lia screamed, raising her gun and firing a shot into the air.

The shot had been meant as a warning, just something to scatter the horde of infected sleepwalkers. But they didn't even flinch. Lia realized she'd lost Josie. Either the woman had snapped out of it and started running as soon as Lia fired the shot or she'd gotten dragged deeper into the surging crowd. Lia looked over her shoulder. She couldn't see Josie retreating, which meant that the woman was somewhere in the swirling mass of disfigured people. When they were packed into the church, Lia couldn't have given an accurate estimate of their number. Perhaps more than a hundred, perhaps as few as fifty. And now that they were out in the open—and there were still more stumbling out of the church —it was even harder to guess their number. If Josie was in that crowd, she might as well be lost.

"Fuck," Lia said, her fight or flight instincts pulling her in two different directions.

Max struggled free of the main mass of people and

grabbed Lia, pulling her along behind him as he ran for the Land Rover.

"She's gone!" he shouted. "I saw her get dragged back into the church!"

Max and Lia weren't trained sprinters, but once they'd broken away from the crowd, they outran the infected people with ease. The infected—if indeed that's what they were—moved like they were blackout drunk, stumbling forward as much as walking. They flailed about with seemingly no coordination. Lia and Max put distance between themselves and danger with ease. Max pulled Lia into an alley between what appeared to be a dormitory and an equipment shed. He leaned against the wall of the shed and pressed a hand to his side as he panted. Lia peeked around the corner. The coast was clear, at least for the moment.

Once Max had gotten some of his wind back, he straightened up. He swung his backpack off his shoulder and unzipped it. He exchanged his camera for his gun.

When he spoke to Lia, it was in a panicked burst of French. "Okay, what the fuck is going on? What happened to those people?"

"A virus?" Lia shook her head. "I don't know."

"You think a fucking virus did that? Lia, I saw a man with his guts hanging out of his belly. I saw a woman with her face ripped off. Her tongue was hanging out of her mouth like a purple snake…"

Lia put a hand on his chest. "I don't know what's going on, my friend."

"They wanted to…" Max closed his eyes for a moment, squeezing them shut as if he could will away the memory of what he'd just witnessed. "They wanted to eat us, Lia. I swear, they were trying to bite me."

Lia thought of Dominic. Josie had said her child had been attacked by crazed natives. Now, her story not only seemed very plausible, but also very grim. If the people of the mission had been infected by some virus, it was likely that the "crazed natives" that the McPhersons had encountered had been infected by the same. It would be the height of wishful thinking to believe that virus couldn't be spread by a bite.

Lia realized she didn't have the medicine bag. She'd handed it over to Josie before they left the infirmary.

"Josie had the medicine," she told Max.

"I don't think it matters," he replied. "I know how you are with kids, Lia, but you have to know that Dominic is probably past saving. The medicine you had in that bag was the same medicine those people had access to. It didn't help them, and it won't help the boy."

Hearing the words was like punch to the gut, but Lia knew that Max was speaking the truth. Even worse was the unspoken question that was hanging between them: if the boy was indeed infected with the same virus as the people of the mission, how long would it be before he became just as dangerous? Max's eyes—sympathetic yet hard—answered that question loud and clear: not long. And now they had to contend with Walter. The man already seemed unstable. How would he react to hearing the news that his wife was lost? How would he react when faced with the hard question about his stepson?

She poked her head out of the alley again. Although she could hear the moaning of the infected, the only ones she could see were still twenty meters, maybe more, away. They were shambling aimlessly, bumping into one another as they walked with arms outstretched.

"Let's go break the news to Walter," she said, motioning to Max. "Then let's put some distance between us and this godforsaken place."

7

Josie screamed as the man hooked his arm around her waist and pulled her through the reeking crowd and into the church. He was far from gentle, digging his fingers into her sides just below her ribcage as she struggled to keep her balance. Up the central aisle they went. The man—like everyone else in the crowd, he smelled awful—pulled her to the front of the church, to the altar. Josie managed to kick free only a few feet shy of the large crucifix hanging from the back wall of the church. She flipped her sweaty hair out of her face and hugged the bag of medical supplies to her chest. She offered a quick, silent prayer to the blank-faced Jesus presiding over the reeking sanctuary, then she looked to the face of the man standing over her, and it wasn't a prayer that raced through her brain. It was stark raving terror mixed with the razor swipe of panic, a combination that could only be expressed wordlessly, with throat-shredding screams.

If the man was able to hear the screams—and they were so loud that he'd have to be stone deaf not to—he gave no indication. He simply stood there, eyeing her the way a playful cat examines a wounded mouse. His clothes were stained and torn nearly to shreds, but the Roman collar around his neck was intact.

The man had been a priest before this virus or whatever it was had robbed him of his dignity. That was the desperate cry of Josie's rational brain as it tried to wrest control back from the terror that gripped her. *Maybe he's trying to help. Yes, he looks terrible and has lost his power of speech, but maybe this man of God is still somewhere inside his rotting shell...*

"Please," she whimpered. "I have to get back to my son. In Jesus' name, please..."

Invoking the savior's name didn't even provoke a twitch from the infected priest. He stared back at her with his demonic red eyes. His jaw dropped open, and his tongue, blistered and blue-black, emerged. A green globule hung from the tip, attached by thin strand of drool. The light coming in through the stained glass windows sparkled on this disgusting tableau. Josie watched as the thin tether or drool lengthened and then broke. She scrabbled backwards to get out of the globule's trajectory, but gravity proved quicker than her crabwalk, and the wad of phlegm dropped into her lap. She stared at it, paralyzed by revulsion, and watched as a trickle of maggots squirmed out of the green slime.

That sense of revulsion was short-lived. It was replaced a second later by a sense of horror so total that it forced her out of her body. She felt as though her spirit was ripped out of her physical being and, unmoored from her earthly vessel, drifted upwards to the ceiling of the church. But rather than drift heavenward, her spiritual self was forced to turn and bear witness to what was happening below. She saw the priest fall upon her, tearing at her clothes with desperate, animalistic swipes. She saw his weight bear down on her as he straddled her pelvis. She saw his lips pull back from his teeth. And she watched as he pressed his face to her breasts, his horrible tongue sliding over her nipple as his teeth made contact with her soft flesh.

The pain brought her back to earth. Suddenly, she was no longer drifting over the ceiling and observing events with numb detachment. The grinding, tearing agony spreading across her chest reeled her back in. She let go of the medical bag and screamed as she battered the priest with her fists. He wrenched his head to one side and then the other, ripping free a mouthful of her breast. His cheeks bulged as he chewed. His constant moaning lost its pained, mournful quality and began to resemble that of a satisfied lover. Blood and phlegm-clotted saliva ran from the corners of his mouth.

Josie fought through the fog of agony. The priest, perhaps distracted by the pleasure of his dripping mouthful, loosened his grip on her shoulders. She felt his thigh muscles relax just enough for her to wrench herself sideways, dumping the priest onto the floor. He gagged, coughing up half-chewed chunks of flesh. Josie's chest was hot and slick with blood. Her vision was getting fuzzy and black at the edges. She knew she was close to losing consciousness. And she might have given in and just let it happen. After all, once she let that warm black blanket slip over her, there'd be no more pain. But the memory of her son—her sweet little Dominic—was enough to get her moving. Adrenaline did the rest.

She scooped the medical bag off the floor and pushed herself to her feet. She struggled for a moment to maintain her balance on the blood-slicked floor, then she was off, running for the front door.

She knew that the crowd was still out there, but she also knew that she was losing blood rapidly. Her French companions had left her for dead. If the medical supplies were going to make it to Dominic, there was only one way for them to get there. In her mind's eye, she saw herself lowering her shoulder and plowing her way through the crowd. Although nausea, pain, and wooziness were pulling at her, she was certain she could summon one final burst of strength. Whatever happened after that was in God's hands.

She clutched the medical bag to her side, wincing at the pain in her chest. She stumbled but didn't fall. She knew it wasn't far to the vehicle. A couple hundred yards, probably less. Through clenched teeth, she muttered feverish prayers to God for one last act of mercy.

As Josie slammed through the front doors, she realized that God had left the Mission of Our Lady of Peace far behind. The crowd of infected people hadn't dispersed enough for her to thread her way through them. In fact, they seemed to have gained strength or at least a better sense of coordination. Or maybe it was her massive loss of blood finally catching up with her. Either way, she didn't make it far before a pair of the moaning, cadaverous people dragged her to the dirt. With one last burst of strength, she heaved the medical bag in what she hoped was the direction of the Land Rover. Then she closed her eyes and waited for the end.

"I'm so sorry, Dominic," she whispered. "My sweet baby…"

She didn't scream. She was beyond that. Although she did have just enough clarity of mind to wonder if the noise she heard was thunder or automatic weapons fire. But it didn't matter. Nothing mattered anymore.

8

It had been London's idea to enter the mission from the side. If Mbowi had troops here, they'd likely be guarding the front and back of the place. A single dirt road ran through the collection of buildings, while all around the entire mission was high grass and tangled vegetation, a little preview of the jungle that sprang up only a few clicks north. Mbowi's guys would probably believe that a big assault force would have to come from the north or south, that anything big enough to be a threat would be obvious if it approached from the east or west. In most cases, they'd be right. But with just four members, London's team could move with enough stealth to be well inside the perimeter before anyone noticed their presence, but to achieve that stealth, they had to go on foot.

They left the Jeep in a stand of trees about a half kilometer from the mission and then moved along the eastern flank. Veterans of jungle and forest combat, they knew how to move quickly and quietly through dense vegetation. They also knew how to take care of a force with superior numbers, especially when that force lacked training and discipline. London figured that if Mbowi left behind some troops to hold the mission, he probably didn't leave his all-stars. There wasn't much tactical advantage this far from the action. If anything, the mission was only useful to Mbowi as a fallback point, a place to retreat if his shit really hit the fan. But when it came to crazed warlords, an abundance of caution was never a bad idea.

They entered through an alleyway between two buildings, moving silently with weapons at the ready. Near the end of the alley, London raised a fist to call a halt to their advance. He could hear something like voices and footsteps. But the voices didn't seem to be anything resembling words. In these parts, French was the official language, and although London didn't speak French, he knew what it sounded like. These voices were odd grunts and moans. And the footsteps sounded scattered, random. It was like a group of drunks stumbling around in the middle of a small town square.

He edged closer to the mouth of the alley. Then the breeze changed directions, carrying the pungent bouquet of rot to his nostrils. He stifled his gag reflex and peered around the corner. There was a crowd gathered in front of the church, but they didn't look like hostiles. No weapons in evidence and none of them were wearing uniforms. London dug his rifle scope out of his pocket and used it to get a better look at the crowd.

He turned to Zantoro and mouthed the words "What the fuck?"

Zantoro gave him a confused look then grabbed his own rifle scope. He pressed in just behind London and peered around the corner.

During his time with US government, and later with Pendleton, Mike London had seen some whacked out shit. Some of it was just weird, like heroin runners in Laos who thought they could ward off demons by eating raw bull testicles. And some of it was pure nightmare fuel, like the grieving parents in Juarez, who walked through the aftermath of a cartel shootout that had seen a group of schoolchildren caught in the crossfire. London didn't sleep soundly for a while after watching mothers and fathers try to match the body parts of their blown-apart children. But even so, he didn't know what to make of the crowd outside the Our Lady of Peace Catholic Mission.

The people were dressed in clothes that had seen better days. Most of them were shoeless and covered in dust. Typical refugee chic. But what wasn't typical—and what had provoked his disbelief—was the fact that some of the men were missing both hands and feet. He'd heard the rumors about the war crimes Mbowi's troops were supposedly committing across Daroka. That stuff was in the intelligence report he'd gotten at his briefing in DC. The fact was, London had seen similar mutilations inflicted on civilians at the behest of warlords and wannabe dictators before. But what he hadn't seen was a collection of mutilated victims walking around with what looked like untreated injuries.

He saw a man with his leg severed below the knee repeatedly try to get up and walk, seemingly confused as to why he couldn't remain upright. At the other end of the crow, a man who'd been cut open by machine gun fire was trolling along with his guts in his hands and a smile on his face. Shock and adrenaline can put on a damn strange display. But this was different. For one thing, this wasn't one or two isolated cases. A quick scan of the crowd—London figured there were between eighty and one hundred—showed a couple dozen men missing hands and feet. All of them were stumbling around on their stumps. They appeared dazed or even drugged, but their faces didn't seem to register anything like pain. In fact, their faces didn't seem to register anything at all.

London and Zantoro lowered their scopes and exchanged confused looks. Then they went back to their examination of the crowd.

The missing hands and feet were gruesome enough, but

there were other details that gave London a bad feeling about the place. The people looked like they were in the late stages of some plague. Pus and mucus ran from their slack-jawed mouths and the corners of their red eyes. Ragged wounds and sores covered the exposed portions of their bodies, crawling with flies and maggots. It was no mystery as to the source of the stink that hung over the place.

Then there were screams from within the church. High-pitched screams that carried equal notes of pain and panic. A moment later, the doors to the church burst open, and woman with a massive chest wound ran out. She was clutching some sort of knapsack, and she ran wildly into the crowd in an attempt to escape. The hollow-eyed plague victims dragged her to the ground. London watched in disbelief as two of them began tearing at the woman with their teeth.

"Fuck," he said, shoving his scope back in his pocket. "We got hostiles. Weapons free, boys, but keep your distance. Possible biohazard."

London led them out, firing a quick burst into the crowd to disperse it. But the dazed people didn't disperse. They didn't even twitch. They were so busily engaged in trying to get at the poor screaming woman that they didn't even seem to register the gunfire. Even those who were struck by bullets couldn't be bothered. They recoiled from the impact and then went back to clawing and fighting among themselves over who got the next chance to bite the woman, who had, mercifully, stopped screaming.

London didn't get it. The whole thing should have been over in a matter of seconds. Once the first shots were fired, the crowd should have dispersed in a panicked stampede. Maybe some of them could have returned fire if they were hiding weapons somewhere in the filthy rags they wore. At the very least, there should have been massive casualties among the crowd. Four semi-automatic rifles in the hands of skilled marksmen, firing at this range, should have resulted in a slaughter. But these people didn't react, even when the bullets hit them square in their chests. They didn't even attempt to lurch out of the kill box.

"What the fuck, boss?" Zantoro asked.

London called a halt to the firing and shouted, "Vincent, Osbourne, grenades!"

Vincent and Osbourne let their rifles dangle from their shoulder straps while they unhooked grenades from their belts. They pulled the pins and let the safety spoons spring free. They wound up and hurled the grenades into the center of the crowd. The twin detonations were like thunderclaps. The force of the explosions threw bodies out of the center of the crowd. London watched in disbelief as one of the targets was tossed into the air, guts unspooling from its mangled torso. It was so shredded by the shrapnel and so disfigured by disease that he couldn't even tell if it was male or female. But that sort of identification didn't matter. What mattered was that this person, who had been blown nearly in half, hit the ground and immediately began dragging itself toward him. Its waist was only attached to its body by a mangled bit of spine, and as it crawled, the two halves of its body separated. The creature—London's mind couldn't conceive that this horror was a human being—continued to claw its way forward, even as it left the lower half of its body behind.

It seemed that London and his team had the full attention of the crowd. Those who weren't too wounded to be mobile had turned in their direction and were advancing. Some, like the moaning torso crawling across the dirt road, inched along, dragging ruined body parts. Others who were lucky enough to still be mostly intact, shuffled forward on unsteady feet.

"Oh, man, fuck this." Zantoro stepped forward, took aim with his rifle, and fired at the crawling creature's head. It dissolved into a chunky spray of red and pink, and the creature finally went down.

London had never been the brightest kid in class, but he

wasn't too stupid to grasp simple cause and effect. He also thanked whatever god might be paying attention that he'd insisted that his team put in so many hours at the shooting range.

"Head shots," he called to his team.

9

Lia and Max were almost to the Land Rover near the front gate when the shooting started. They detoured into a small building that appeared to be a classroom and ducked below window level. They sat with their backs pressed against the wall as the guns thundered away.

"What do you think?" Max asked. "Mbowi's troops returning from a frolic in the park?"

"Could be," Lia said. "But that doesn't seem right. If they were holding this spot, wouldn't they have left someone behind?"

Neither of them had military backgrounds, but they'd been in enough war zones to have a basic grasp of field tactics. It's also why they didn't panic when the gunfire started. They knew the best thing to do was to get some solid walls between themselves and the stray bullets that might be flying.

The gunfire stopped for a moment. There were voices shouting, then a pair of explosions that rattled the classroom door and left Lia's ears ringing.

Lia scooted over to the door. "I'm going to have a peek."

"Be careful. It sounds like fucking Baghdad out there."

Lia reached up and turned the doorknob. She opened the door and poked her head out. Through the dust-filled air, she could see the scene unfolding up the road. A good portion of the crowd had been cut to ribbons by the grenades. But they hadn't run away in terror. In fact, the only ones who weren't advancing on the line of four gunmen were those who had been so thoroughly maimed by the grenades that they were no longer mobile. And of these, some were still clawing at the air, attempting to join their fellows in their slow attack.

Lia pulled back into the classroom, closing the door. "Max, something is very, very wrong here. We are in a world of trouble, I'm afraid."

"Mbowi's troops?" he asked.

"It's just four men. White, wearing light combat gear. Before the explosions, when they were shouting, I thought I heard American accents."

"Military? Americans?"

She shrugged. "Could be private contractors. I don't know. But right now, they're under attack by that crowd of infected people."

"Fuck them," Max said. "Let's get back to the car and get the hell out of here."

"Back to the car? Back to Dominic?" Lia let the question hang in the air for a moment before continuing, "Maybe, if these are Americans, they might have some idea of what's going on. At the very least, they might be able to help us get further north."

"North? Have you lost your mind? We need to turn around and head south until we're out of this country."

Lia scooted closer, placing a hand on Max's shoulder. "My friend, there are people out there who should be corpses, but they're up on their feet…well, those that have feet anyway… but they're walking around. In fact, their walking right through a meat grinder of bullets like it's a cloud of pesky insects. And there's American military contractors out there dispatching them. We're only a day's drive from the Marsh Industries research facility. Don't you think all this might be connected somehow?"

Max sighed. "One of these days, I'm going to wind up regretting my decision to follow you into this hellhole."

"Oh, will that be before or after we accept our Nobel Prize?"

"For that to happen, we have to get out of here with our asses intact. Try not to forget that."

Lia nudged him. "Think you can lean out that window above us and maybe get some footage of that scene? If you're scared...I mean, if you think it's too dangerous...you could give me the camera and let me try."

"And let you shoot some poorly framed, shaky bullshit with my precious camera?" Max shook his head. "I'd rather risk catching a bullet."

Lia smiled. "You're so brave."

Max got to his feet, fired up his camera, and leaned out the open window.

There was a time when she would have felt bad for flirtatiously convincing him to take risks. But after so many years working together, he knew the score. Despite the feelings Lia knew he held for her, she wasn't interested in romance; not with Max, or anyone else, for that matter. Oh, sure, there had been men in her life over the years, but they'd been there to satisfy a physical need, nothing more. She couldn't afford to have emotional attachments in her line of work.

"I've never seen anything like this," Max said. "These people, they're just walking around while the Americans shoot them in the heads. The bodies are piling up, but the people just walk right over them. It's madness."

Lia stood alongside Max and watched the scene unfold.

Although there was nothing on the Americans' uniforms indicating rank, it was clear that one of them was in charge. He was tall and broad-shouldered, the poster boy of American military might.

American-financed corporate mercenary might, Lia reminded herself. There was no official foreign military presence in Daroka. Marsh Industries had exerted all its corrupt strength to keep the UN mired in endless debate over the situation in the country. The company was corrupt to its core, using blackmail and threats when their bribes weren't enough to sway public policy. Lia had been looking for the right angle to attack Marsh Industries for years, and Daroka seemed ready made for one hell of an exposé.

Lia and Max watched for a few more moments then sat back down under the window.

"What do you think?" Max asked.

"I think we'd better hope the Americans are in the mood to play nice," she answered. "Once they're done with that slaughter, they'll probably search the other buildings. I don't think we're going to slip away unnoticed."

"Lia, what the fuck is going on here? You saw those… those people…Whatever's wrong with them, it isn't some virus. Some of them were nearly cut in half by bullets and they still kept getting up and walking right at the Americans."

"Unless they took a shot to the head. When the tall American was shouting orders, it sounded like he was calling for his men to aim for the head."

"Seriously, what the fuck?"

Lia shook her head. "I don't know, but I'm certain Marsh Industries is behind it. Whatever they were working on at that research facility got out."

"And now they've sent in this mercenary group to cover it up. Makes sense."

"Yeah, but it also means we have to play our cards

carefully with those mercenaries. Don't want to get terminated with extreme prejudice by Rambo."

"You're mixing metaphors," Max said. "Not a good look for a journalist."

<h1 style="text-align:center">10</h1>

"I think we're clear," London said, lowering the barrel of his rifle.

The air was thick with the mingled scents of cordite and rot. As soon as the gunfire stopped, a cloud of flies descended on the piles of bodies littering the road. The other three members of the team stood by silently, awaiting orders. Even Zantoro, who could usually be counted on to break the ice with a joke, was grim-faced and quiet. After all, what they'd just done was horrible, even by their standards. There hadn't been any children in the group London's team had just slaughtered, but there had been plenty of women, plenty of old folks. But London knew that the absence of children was only a mercy for him and his team. Because he knew the children of the mission had most likely faced a fate worse than a bullet to the head. They'd most likely been devoured.

"Okay, boys, check weapons and reload," London said. "We need to search the rest of this place."

To their credit, none of the team objected. Technically, there was nothing about the Our Lady of Peace Mission that fell under the umbrella of their assignment. They had one real priority, and that was getting their asses north and salvaging whatever was left of the research material at the Marsh Industries compound. Making contact with Arnaud was a distant second. But after the mess they'd just cleaned, London was starting to feel their priorities slip. Something was very wrong here. London was beginning to get a pretty clear idea of why Mikkelson and his team had fallen off the radar.

Zantoro cleared his throat. Not to tell a joke, but to ask a stupid question.

"Boss," he said, stepping close to London's side. "You think this shit has something to do with our employer? I mean, is this the mess we're cleaning up?"

"I don't know," London admitted. "But when I was briefed, no one said shit about firing into a crowd of sick civilians. Let's check the rest of this place, then get back on the road. I'd like to put some distance between ourselves and this place before nightfall."

"Copy that."

London checked his weapon. He was good to go. Their ammo supply had been meant for a quick mission with minimal engagement. They certainly hadn't planned of pacifying a crowd. Supplies weren't at a critical level yet, but if things continued on the current trajectory, they would be soon.

"Okay," London called to his team. "Building by building sweep, starting with the mission. Assume anyone we encounter is hostile unless they make it very fucking clear otherwise."

The men nodded. Again, there was no saluting, no *sir, yes, sir* bullshit. They just got down to business. Stepping over fly-swarmed corpses, they made their way across the road to the church. The heat inside the building was unbearable, and it served to amplify the stench of rot to such a degree that Zantoro gagged. He bent over, grabbing his knees as he struggled to keep his breakfast down. London didn't blame him. It was, as his granddaddy used to say, bad enough to gag a maggot.

The bare wooden floorboards were crusty with dried blood and other fluids whose origins London didn't care to think about. There were human remains scattered here and there. Nothing close to an intact corpse, just pieces.

"Looks clear," London said.

Nobody argued. They turned and headed for the exit. Compared to the interior of the church, the air outside wasn't actually so bad. At least there was a bit of a breeze to carry away some of the stench. They checked the infirmary and found nothing but some hideously stained beds and a ransacked supply closet.

When they returned to the open air, they found a pair of people waiting for them, standing in the middle of the road with their hands raised above their heads. They were dressed in light khaki cargo pants and white shirts, standard safari type outfits. The man was deeply tanned and had a riot of brown curls kept in check by a baseball cap, which he wore backwards. The woman was short but athletically built. With her sweat-slicked hair pulled into a haphazard ponytail, she looked like a female soccer star.

"Don't shoot!" she shouted. "We're not infected!"

She spoke with a French accent. London got the idea she was someone he should recognize, but he couldn't imagine why.

"Yeah, please don't liquidate us," her male companion chimed in. "Or terminate us. However you say it."

The woman shot him a look that said she would like to give him a kick in the balls for clowning around, but she kept her composure.

"My name is Lia Rousseau and he's Max Lambert," she said, lowering her hands a bit. "We're journalists."

Zantoro laughed. "Well, that's fucking great. Now we get to smash up some cameras."

"Can it, Zantoro," London snapped.

"He's got a point, boss," Vincent said. "Or have you forgotten what we just did back there? You want be the star of some CNN morning show?"

Osbourne could normally be counted on to keep his trap shut in front of civilians, but he decided to lend his support. "They're right. I don't want to be on the news firing headshots at a bunch of starving Africans."

"That's 'cause you know that if they're showing your face they didn't film your good side," Zantoro said.

"Fuck you, at least I *got* a good side."

"Keep trying, kid," Zantoro said.

London had gotten his fill of the bullshit. He did the closest thing he could do to pulling rank; he told them to kindly shut the fuck up. Then he turned his attention to the journalists.

"How long have you been in town, Ms. Rousseau?" he asked.

"Not long," she answered. "Maybe a half hour before you arrived. And please, call me Lia."

London shot Zantoro a look before he could offer any witticism.

"We hid because we thought you might with General Mbowi," she continued.

"Not a lot of pale faces in Mbowi's army."

Lia and Max exchanged a glance. "We couldn't see."

"And who knows where Mbowi might do his hiring? It wouldn't be unheard of for white mercenaries to be in Africa." Max added.

"So you couldn't see us, but you knew we were white?" London shook his head. "Vincent, give these journalists a pat-down."

"Hey, you honkies speak for yourselves and leave me out of it," Zantoro said. "My dad was from El Salvador. Didn't you notice how I fire my rifle with a Latin rhythm?"

"Just ignore him," London said to the bewildered journalists.

"You needn't bother with the pat-down," Lia continued. "We're both armed. Nine millimeter pistols in our right hip pockets."

"Nevertheless…" London gestured for Vincent to proceed.

He slung his rifle strap over his shoulder and stepped forward. After he'd gotten out of the army, Vincent had done a couple years in the secret service. He knew how to frisk a suspect. Just as Lia had said, they were carrying a pair of Glock pistols. Both were loaded and ready to rock, but they hadn't been fired. He also took a utility knife off the cameraman and a Swiss Army knife off the woman. That was the total of their arsenal. Vincent pocketed one gun and stuck the other in his belt.

"Okay, put your hands down," London said. "Now, is there anything else you'd like to share with us? For instance, was that your vehicle parked by the front gate?"

Lia and Max exchanged another look.

"Yeah," she said. "About that…"

"Well?" London prompted.

"There were people with us. Americans, like you. A husband and wife with their child. They'd been doing missionary work in Borwannah."

"They'd been working that close to the border?" Zantoro laughed. "Yeah, they must have been strong in their faith, because fucking around that close to Daroka is a good way to meet your maker."

Lia didn't acknowledge the joke. "The child had been attacked. By crazed natives, that's what the mother said. He'd been bitten on the arm and was quite sick. I knew about the mission, so we stopped here to see if there was any medical help. The boy and the father stayed in the car."

"And the mother?" London asked, although he was pretty sure he knew the answer.

"She was attacked outside the church," Lia said.

"Yeah, we saw that." London shouldered his rifle. "All right, let's go have a look."

London and Zantoro walked on either side of Lia and Max. Vincent and Osbourne followed, hanging back a couple paces. It wasn't quite the same as walking with prisoners, but even though the journalists weren't an evident threat, it was a cautious formation. After all, if Lia and Max had survived out here, they clearly weren't helpless.

The Land Rover was parked just outside the mission's front gate. From a few paces away, everything appeared normal. But then, as they drew nearer and came alongside the vehicle, London noticed the windows of the backseat. They were splattered with blood and congealing globs of gore.

London called a halt to their approach. He drew his pistol from the holster on his hip and thumbed off the safety.

"Zantoro, open the door to the backseat then fall back," he said. "Everyone else stay put."

"You got it." Zantoro stepped to the vehicle. Hand on the door, he glanced into the window. He took a step back like the door was electrified. Turning back around, he said, "Oh, man, boss...I don't think..."

"Never mind," London snapped. "I got this."

He shoved Zantoro aside and wrenched open the car door. He'd prepared himself for the worst, but the brief glimpse he caught before retreating a few paces was enough to make the bottom of his stomach drop. It reminded him that the world still had fresh horrors.

The man's body had been ripped open. The contents of his stomach cavity had been so shredded that they resembled a package of ground meat more than internal organs. The flesh had been torn away from his head, exposing a blood-slicked skull. It was gruesome shit, but London had seen worse. It wasn't the sight of the carnage that stole London's breath, however; the real horror was catching sight of what—of *who* —had caused that carnage.

Lia hadn't mentioned the boy's name. Perhaps that anonymity should have made London's job easier, but he doubted it. Whatever his name was, the boy was still just a child. When he emerged from the car, London saw that the boy wasn't much more than a toddler. He wore a pair of Adidas soccer shorts and a baby blue t-shirt emblazoned with the slogan *Mommy Loves Me and So Does Jesus!* The boy's belly was so distended that the shirt was hiked up above his navel. He was smeared with blood from head to toe. His cheeks bulged as he chewed slowly. A bit of gristle hung from his lips.

The boy looked around with red, unblinking eyes. His mouth fell open, spilling out half-chewed chunks of meat. He stepped forward, arms outstretched. His teeth snapped together as he lunged at London, who sidestepped the move with ease. The boy was like an angry drunk: aggressive but too uncoordinated to be a real threat. He moaned as his little arms flailed for balance. He spun around in a slow circle, then launched himself at London again.

"Oh, fuck me," London said, shoving the diseased child away.

London sighed, closing his eyes for a moment to gather his resolve. Then he opened them and sighted down the barrel of his pistol. He squeezed the trigger, and the top half of the child's head exploded in a shower of red and pink. London's sidearm was a .45 semiautomatic, a weapon known for its knockdown power, and the close range shot tossed the boy backwards. London knew the child was dead before he hit the ground, but that knowledge didn't keep his mind from recording the event for his memory in minute, sickening detail.

He holstered the weapon and turned away from the scene.

He squeezed his eyes shut, but the scene replayed, as if the backs of his eyelids were projection screens. A hand gripped his shoulder, and he heard Zantoro's voice.

"Hey, boss, there was nothing you could do."

"Right, right, whatever." London shrugged Zantoro's hand away. "Just give me a minute, okay?"

He walked a few paces down the road and stopped behind the Land Rover, where he was out of view. The late afternoon sun's glare was brutal, but at least they were far enough away from the church that the stink wasn't quite as thick. He leaned over and gripped his knees. His last meal was a distant memory, but he knew it wasn't too late for it to make an encore appearance. He took a deep breath and willed the nausea to subside.

Had the kid and his parents stayed back in the States, the boy would most likely be enjoying summer vacation before starting kindergarten. Maybe he'd be at day camp with his friends or at the swimming pool with other kids from the neighborhood. The family had been holy rollers of some stripe, so maybe he'd have been doing arts and crafts at vacation bible school. But instead, he was lying in the middle of a dirt road in Daroka with his head blown to bits.

Yes, it was true what Zantoro said. Given the situation, London had no choice. But it was still his finger that had squeezed the trigger, and he was certain that few days would pass when he didn't find a quiet occasion to revisit the memory. There were some things that didn't soften with age, some wounds that never healed no matter how much time passed. London knew this for a fact. He had more than his share of festering, unhealed memories. He also knew that he could carry one more. But like he told Zantoro, he just needed a minute or two to choke it down.

When his stomach had stopped fluttering, and his hands had stopped shaking, he straightened up. London fished a can of wintergreen flavored Skoal out of his back pocket. He settled a pinch into his lip, and worked it around until it was packed in.

"Back to work," he sighed.

11

Once the boys had eaten their afternoon rations and taken a half hour's rest, Father Xavier organized them into ranks, took roll call, and resumed their northward march. They could still make a few miles before nightfall.

It would have been easier to go east first, back towards the logging road that the American paper companies had cut before General Mbowi scared them out of the country. Although nature was slowly but surely reclaiming the road, it was still an easier route than hiking through the dense, treacherous jungle. There were villages here and there along the logging road. But while villages meant possible access to clean water and food, they also meant people. And these days, when dead men rose up from the dirt and walked about in search of living men to devour, it was best to avoid people altogether.

As they walked, Peter drew alongside Father Xavier. The boy clearly wanted to talk, but Father Xavier could tell he wasn't ready. So they marched for a while in silence, halting now and then so the larger boys at the front of the line could hack through walls of vegetation with their machetes. He knew the boy would speak in his own time.

When Peter did finally decide to speak, he did so in a soft, childlike voice that was at odds with the hard look in his eyes. It certainly wasn't the voice of one who'd spent his morning beheading the walking corpses of American mercenaries.

"Father Xavier, I've been having dreams," Peter said. "Many of the others have had them too. Timothy, Jean Paul, and Felix, they have all had the same dreams as me."

"Is that so?"

"Is God the one who sends us these dreams?" Peter asked. "Some of the things we see in the dreams are terrible things. Even more terrible than the things we've seen since the General took us from the villages. But sometimes, the dreams show us a place where there is still happiness."

Father Xavier smiled. "Yes, I believe the Heavenly Father gave you the gift of dreams, both good and bad. I believe these dreams were sent to show us things that have not yet come to pass, but will soon be at hand. And that is why we must continue north."

Peter considered this for a moment, his brow furrowed and his lips moving in silent internal debate as the line of child soldiers slogged onward through the jungle.

After a while, Peter asked, "Is the place in our good dreams real?"

"My faith tells me that it is," Father Xavier answered carefully.

"In my dreams, I see a river of clear water," Peter continued. "And trees full of fruit and honeybees. And there are houses, more houses than in all the villages put together. Is this place heaven, Father? Will we have to die before we go there?"

"I don't know, Peter. But I have seen this place in my dreams as well. I believe that we will reach it if we remain strong in our faith."

Peter nodded. "Yes, I believe it is heaven. And if we must

die to be there, I am not afraid. Even if it hurts to die, I am still not afraid."

In his days as a traveling priest, Father Xavier had given the Holy Mass in both French and English. He'd done so in churches so humble that they doubled as cattle barns. He'd done so in the open air, under the shade of acacia trees or on the banks of muddy rivers. In all those years of ministering to the people of Daroka, he never encountered such direct, incisive questioning as he did when speaking with the children of the countryside villages. Out in the jungle, things were no different. The boys who made up his small army were still full of questions. They'd witnessed enough horrors for ten lifetimes, but still they held onto some sense of wonder. And even more miraculously, they held onto hope.

"You are brave indeed," Father Xavier said, patting Peter's head. "I have no doubt that heaven awaits you."

12

Morton Fairbanks trembled as he climbed the ladder on the wall of the elevator shaft. Although he'd dropped a few pounds recently, it was still quite a workout to move from the safety of his rat-hole in the basement staff lounge to the third floor cafeteria. He carried a backpack that had once belonged to Whittaker. She'd used it the way some women use a purse; to carry a wild assortment of items, from makeup and feminine hygiene supplies, to packs of chewing gum and a well-thumbed book of crossword puzzles. Fairbanks used it to carry food from the cafeteria to the basement. He also used it to carry his meager supply of tools, most of which could double as weapons if it came to that. Fairbanks preferred that it didn't. He was a man of science, not some warrior.

"Almost there," he whispered, pausing to wipe the sweat from his forehead.

When the shit had hit the fan at the research facility, certain emergency procedures had been enacted. That was the only explanation for why the express elevator to the basement had lost power while the rest of the building was still up and running. It was an emergency quarantine. Perfectly logical. The basement was, after all, the zone with the highest risk level. But it hadn't worked. Somehow, the infection had leaked.

Total infection, Fairbanks thought. *All those safeguards, fail-safes, and emergency protocols amounted to so much hot air. Our creation was too perfect, and now we reap as we have sown.*

Once he ascended the sixty-plus feet from the basement, he had to squirm through the maintenance access panel on the third floor ceiling. He removed the ceiling panel and poked his head through the opening. The stepladder was still there, right where he'd left it on his last grocery shopping trip. It appeared that the coast was clear.

He reeled his head back in and climbed to the other side of the open panel so that he could descend feet first. Although he'd lost weight, the maintenance shaft was still too narrow for him to turn around. Then he lowered his feet to the ladder, wincing at the metallic creaking as he eased his weight onto the top rung.

Once on the floor, he opened his backpack and took out his best means of self-defense: a cordless power drill that someone had left in the basement staff lounge. He held it at his side like a pistol, careful to keep his finger off the trigger, lest he accidentally make some noise and attract the attention of any of the infected who might be lurking about. Next, he began the harrowing journey down the hallway to the cafeteria.

He went on tiptoe. His heart thundered, and he fought to keep his breathing as even as he could manage. His muscles tensed every time he passed a doorway or approached a corner. So far, he'd made a dozen tips from the basement to the cafeteria without incident. But Fairbanks knew that streak couldn't continue indefinitely. It wasn't a matter of luck, but rather simple probability.

The door to the cafeteria was closed, just the way he'd left it. He gripped the handle with his left hand and raised the drill with his right. He eased a deep breath into his lungs and held it as he opened the door. The dining area was still littered with overturned tables and chairs. Dismembered bodies in advancing states of decay were strewn among the broken dishes and discarded silverware. The air was full of flies that buzzed among the corpses and rotten food. Even though Fairbanks was prepared for the stench, he still recoiled when the first fumes crawled up his nose. However, he breathed those fumes out with a sigh of relief as he stepped into the cafeteria and closed the door behind him. Satisfied that he wasn't in any immediate danger, he made his way across the dining area and climbed over the serving line and into the kitchen.

Like the dining area, the kitchen looked like the aftermath of a pipe bomb explosion. Human remains—some so mangled and decayed that they were unidentifiable—were scattered among the heaps of smashed cookware and broken equipment. Roaches scattered at his approach, running for cover in the corners and under counters. Those too slow to make it to safety crunched beneath his shoes. The ever-present flies buzzed past his face like tiny zeppelins. Despite the advanced state of decay, the rotten corpses and food were still a smorgasbord for the bottom links of the food chain. Each successive generation of flies had grown fatter and bolder. It was fascinating, really.

A fat rat trundled toward Fairbanks, its mouth open and snarling like some sort of apex predator rather than lowly vermin. Despite its apparent ferocity, the rat had grown fat from a steady diet of rotten flesh, and its progress was almost comically slow. Fairbanks raised his foot and stomped on the rodent, wincing as he felt its bones snap beneath his shoe. He pressed down, grinding his foot back and forth to make sure the job was done, then continued his journey to the storage room.

He tried to make the most of the trip, filling his backpack with as much bottled water and non-perishable food as he could safely carry on the return trip. Two of the chefs employed by Marsh Industries had been from Hawaii, which accounted for the abundance of Spam in the pantry. Calorically dense and full of protein, not to mention easily portable, it had become a staple of Fairbanks' diet. Not so easy to carry, but just as tasty, were the massive cans of beans. Fairbanks selected black beans this time, having tired of the overly sweet baked beans he'd gotten on his last excursion. He selected another large can—peaches in heavy syrup— then filled the rest of the space in his backpack with liter-sized bottles of water. He zipped up the pack and shouldered it.

It was the water that weighed him down and took up the most space in his backpack. Although the sink in the staff lounge was still functional, Fairbanks had doubts about the water's purity. The water for the facility came from wells on the Marsh Industries compound. During the chaos, it might have been contaminated. Fairbanks wouldn't even wash with it.

He left the storage room reluctantly. Every time he made a trip to the third floor, he was tempted to stay. But he knew it was far less secure than the basement. Down there, he had only one door to worry about and it was securely barricaded. Plus, there was a bathroom connected to the staff lounge, which meant he could maintain his hygiene somewhat. The third floor, with its open floor plan offices and labs, was a death trap. Still, it pained Fairbanks to have to leave the stores of food and water behind. Maybe it was a necessity, maybe not. He was a clinical researcher, not a survivalist expert.

Roaches and flies had already swarmed the fresh rat carcass, and they scattered at his approach. He climbed over the serving line and was greeted by another angry rat. This one scurried forward a few steps, then stopped. It seemed to reconsider, then retreated across the room and disappeared into a heap of moldering bones that had once been one of Fairbanks' coworkers.

Fairbanks opened the door and peered into the hallway. He carefully checked both left and right like a child preparing to cross the street unaccompanied for the first time. Aside from a few rats, the hallway was empty.

So far, so good.

He always had to fight the urge to go faster on the return trip. He forced himself to make his way down the hallway at a cautious tiptoe. He was halfway there, feeling the first giddy tingles of relief, when he heard a metallic clatter followed by a guttural groan. The sounds froze him in his tracks.

He considered a retreat to the cafeteria. But he knew that the noise would only attract company, and if he ran to the cafeteria, he might be trapped in there with all that open space to worry about. Perhaps some of the infected might have already managed to open the door and be waiting for him. Steeling his resolve, he took a deep breath and ran the rest of the way. Now that the noise had started, there was no point creeping along. The backpack thumped painfully against his lower back, but Fairbanks was more concerned with what awaited him when he turned into the alcove beside the useless elevators. To survive this long had been a minor miracle, and it was almost hubris to expect it to continue for much longer, but he found himself silently praying to a god that he'd long since disavowed.

There was only one of them waiting for him in the alcove. Just a solitary ghoul dressed in a torn and stained lab coat. In life, she might have been attractive, but in her current state, it was hard to tell. Large sections of her scalp had been torn away, leaving behind scabbed bald patches. Her nose had been ripped—possibly bitten—off her face. Her right arm hung limply at her side. As she moved toward Fairbanks, it twisted and bent at odd angles. It looked to have been broken in at least five spots. Jagged bits of bone protruded through her skin. One of her feet had been similarly broken, and she shuffled forward like a B-movie mummy. Her mouth hung open, and as she moaned, a constant stream of thick mucus ran from her bottom lip.

Fairbanks tightened his grip on the drill. He waited until the former lab technician was almost close enough to grab him with her good hand, then he sidestepped her, moving to her right. Unable to pivot quickly on her ruined foot, or grab with her right hand, she was frozen in place for a moment, just long enough for Fairbanks to slip behind her.

He could hear more moans coming from the end of the hallway. Sure enough, the noise had alerted more of the infected. He grabbed a handful of what remained of the woman's hair and wrenched her head back. She made a gurgling sound, like she was gagging on her viscous drool. Fairbanks raised the drill and squeezed the trigger. He pressed the whirring bit into the woman's ear. For a moment, her gurgles turned to high-pitched wheezes. Then, as Fairbanks pressed the drill deeper and blood sprayed from her ear canal, the woman's body went limp and slid to the floor.

Fairbanks didn't wait to see how many of them were shambling down the hall. He climbed the ladder and pulled himself through the opening in the ceiling. Although he doubted the infected possessed enough coordination to follow him, he reached back through the opening and knocked the ladder over.

As he crawled back to the elevator shaft, he wondered if his food and water would hold out until a rescue party came. Then he wondered if one was coming at all.

13

The montage of images flickering over the surface of the water slowed, dimmed, and then dissolved as Charon turned from the display to gaze at its city. When it had awakened from its slumber, Charon had walked through a city that was dark, damp, and decaying. Now, the city itself was awakening. The overhead forest of stalactites was receding, the craggy fingers of rock withdrawing to reveal a deep blue sky. The surface of the streets and avenues was healing, the cracks in the cobblestones disappearing. The buildings that lined those streets and avenues were straightening their walls. The archways of the cathedrals had begun to shine with polished luster. In the parks and along the riverbank, trees had broken through the ground and were beginning to stretch their limbs toward a sky that had recently been the ceiling of a cave.

And through the city, there was a low thrumming sound, audible only to ears as patiently attuned as those of Charon. It was the sound of healing and regeneration. It was the sound of life.

Charon turned its back on the river and walked into the

city. The time was drawing near and there was still so much to do.

Part Four

The ceremony of innocence is drowned…

"He's turned so many of us into metaphorical zombies. We can't let him make us into actual zombies."

—Joseph "Spider" Barclay

1

Svetlana Kurzcyk's platinum blonde hair was stylishly short when she walked into the lobby of the hotel at the Dallas-Fort Worth airport. An hour later, when she emerged from her room, she was a redhead with curls hanging to her shoulders. She knew the importance of maintaining her anonymity when she conducted these meetings, but she wondered if maybe this wig, which itched like hell and carried the cloying fragrance of cheap perfume, might be overkill. Although she didn't mind the color. She'd always wondered how it would feel to be a redhead. She was dressed in a black t-shirt and jeans with holes in the knees. The shirt featured the logo of some obscure Norwegian black metal band. It wasn't a reflection of her musical taste—she was into analog synth stuff mostly—but the Ildjarn logo was a signal to her contact.

She used a burner cell phone that was connected to a prepaid credit account to summon an Uber. While she waited, she had a cocktail in the lobby bar, taking care to look extra bitchy to forestall any pickup attempts by the drunk idiots in business suits. It didn't work. She was only two sips into her gin and tonic when a big lunk with a receding hairline detached himself from his buddies and made his approach. He arrived in a cloud of cologne, brimming with Budweiser confidence and breath smelling of the same.

"No matter where you are, the airport bar is always the same, right?" he said, flashing a smile that probably melted hearts in Omaha or Topeka or wherever the hell he was from. Svetlana tried to ignore him, but he continued undeterred. "You down here for the logistics convention or are you with an airline? You don't mind me saying, you don't exactly look like you belong with either group. I'm with J.D. Hyde Trucking, but don't worry, I don't drive a rig or anything like that. I'm in management. Name's Dwayne."

He held out his hand to shake. Svetlana just glared at it for a moment, then said, "Dwayne, just go back to your friends and tell them I said I had a boyfriend. Or tell them you think I'm a dyke. Whatever protects your no doubt fragile ego."

Dwayne raised his hands in surrender, laughing. "Well, damn, sweetheart. I was just being friendly."

Her phone buzzed, signaling that her ride had arrived, sparing her the need to further interact with Dwayne. She killed her drink in one long swallow and stood.

"Better luck with the next one, Dwayne." She tossed a twenty on the bar and headed for the door.

According to the app, the coffee shop wasn't even twenty miles away, but the ride took over an hour. Not that she cared. The whole trip was being paid for, in a roundabout way, by Marsh Industries. Pretty funny when you thought about it, Waylon Marsh picking up the tab for his own downfall. She would have laughed, but it was hard to have a sense of humor about anything these days. Since figuring out the real purpose of the HOPE Project, she hadn't felt much like smiling, never mind laughing. But, despite the fact that she knew it was the right course of action, she just couldn't take pleasure in this betrayal. She told herself her motives were pure, but she knew better. In the end, it was just another compromise, another sell-out. She supposed that was just how life went.

The driver must have picked up on her mood—he wasn't as drunk or horny as Dwayne—because he didn't attempt conversation beyond asking if she minded the music he was playing. Even though she hated Steely Dan, she suffered through "Reelin' in the Years." Toto was up next, which was marginally less irritating. After that, it was one yacht rock hit after another. The driver didn't look the type. With his full beard and western shirt, she would have figured him for a country music fan. Nothing was what it seemed these days.

It was a good thing her contact had chosen a coffee shop for the meeting. After an hour of soft rock, she was going to need some perking up. She zoned out, closing her eyes and leaning back against the headrest. And she might have drifted off to sleep to the tune of some Michael McDonald song if the driver hadn't spoken up.

"Here we are, ma'am," he said, pulling the car over. "You have a pleasant and safe evening."

She thanked him and climbed out of the backseat.

The coffee shop was called Sufficient Grounds. Svetlana wondered if the person who came up with the name knew just how groan-inducing it was. But it was doing brisk business, even at an odd hour for a coffee shop, so maybe it wasn't such a bad thing. She found a table near the back. The place smelled of freshly ground coffee, baked goods, and buttered toast. Her stomach rumbled. Although she'd intended to just sip coffee while she waited for her contact to appear, she ended up ordering a blueberry muffin, a cream cheese Danish, and a chocolate croissant to go along with her cappuccino. Despite her slender figure, she didn't count calories. And even if she did, she would have given up on the practice after seeing the footage that she pulled off Waylon Marsh's personal computer. If the world was going to plunge into a howling abyss of horror, then Svetlana Kurzcyk was going to have a full belly when it happened. And a full bank account.

She'd demolished the both the croissant and the Danish, and was preparing to get to work on the muffin, when a man in a pair of rumpled khaki slacks and a loudly patterned Hawaiian shirt paused by her table.

"Nice shirt," he said. "But can you even name three of their songs?"

"Very funny. Have a seat." She used her foot to nudge a chair on the opposite side of the table.

He was older than she expected. For some reason, it was hard for her to envision the leader of a techno-anarchist collective as someone older than herself. This guy—she knew him by his online name Joe Slummer—looked like he could be her father's age.

"So tell me again why this meeting couldn't be an email," Joe said, taking a seat.

"Because I don't want my digital fingerprints anywhere near this thing. Marsh can be pretty paranoid about his top-level employees. Same goes for the women he sleeps with."

Joe raised an eyebrow. "And you're both those things, is that it?"

"How else would I get close enough to steal the information on this?" She slid an envelope across the table. The contents of the envelope were a clone of the hard drive of Waylon Marsh's personal laptop. "A little judgmental for an anarchist, aren't you?"

"Who said anything about judgment?" He shrugged. "So what am I looking for on this hard drive? Financial malfeasance? Crimes against the environment? Or is Waylon Marsh a closet pervert?"

"Yes to all of that, but it goes much, much deeper." Svetlana paused while a waitress approached and took Sam's order. When the waitress departed, Svetlana continued,

"You've been following all the online chatter about the HOPE Project, right?"

"Hard to miss it, but most of our people think it's a bunch of conspiracy theorist nonsense, like Q-Anon or the flat earth idiots."

"Well," Svetlana said, peeling the paper away from her muffin, "it's even worse than those conspiracy theorists have guessed. Even the nuttiest fruitcake on the internet couldn't guess at what's going on in Daroka right now."

Joe smiled at the waitress when she returned with his cup of coffee, then turned his attention back to Svetlana.

"Now you got my interest piqued," he said. "Exactly what do you want us to do with this information? And what do you expect in return?"

She shrugged. "Just get it out there. Marsh has an entire department running a disinformation campaign regarding the HOPE project. Hopefully your people can cut through the noise. As far as what I would like in return? I guess a clean conscience. Trust me when I say this: there's a time coming, and probably very soon, when that will be worth more than money."

She said it with enough conviction that she almost believed it.

Joe tilted his head to one side, like a puppy examining a new toy. "You're actually serious."

"Dead serious." She laughed at her private joke and took a bite of her muffin.

2

The front door swung open and a loud voice announced, "DJ Apocalypse Tonight is in the house!"

Waylon Marsh applauded. "Oh, shit, judgment day is at hand! DJ AT is the fucking man!"

His entourage squealed with delight, joining the applause that rippled through the crowd.

Gustav Vogel didn't know who this DJ Apocalypse Tonight was, but he did appreciate the irony of the name. Because Vogel knew that judgment day was near. After all, when the Four Horseman knocked at the door, he was the one to open it. This world, fallen and hopelessly corrupt beyond redemption, would soon pass away.

"You know the party is lit when that motherfucker shows up," Marsh said. "Just look at that dude. Pure alpha energy right there."

The man in question was dressed in a bright red jogging suit. His hair was a riot of multicolored dreadlocks. Despite the dim lighting, he wore a pair of dark sunglasses. Vogel tried to decide if the man was a cheap hoodlum masquerading as a rich person or vice versa. The crowd of young women who followed him didn't seem to care.

The fundraising party was held at a posh night club/art gallery called Club Gondola. It was hosted by a political action committee called the Foundation for American Reason and Truth, a nominally libertarian think tank that was funneling money into the midterm campaigns of senators in a dozen states. In truth, the organization was a front for several multinational corporations, Marsh Industries among them, working to ensure that government oversight in the free market was kept to a bare minimum.

Vogel felt the opulence of the setting and the richness of the food was quite overwhelming, but he got the impression he was alone in that sentiment. Most of the attendees looked bored. They sipped champagne and nibbled fancy hors d'oeuvres through their forced smiles and perfunctory conversations, sneaking glances at their watches to see how much longer they needed to circulate through the crowd before it was acceptable to make an inconspicuous exit.

"Some swanky shindig, huh?" Waylon Marsh elbowed Vogel in the ribs. "I mean, shit, it better be. The check I wrote these guys had an obscene amount of zeroes on it."

Marsh had brought along his usual entourage of social media influencers, models, and musicians, but he'd also invited Vogel to tag along. It was something of a running joke for Marsh. He'd invite the awkward and conservatively attired doctor to accompany him to some glamorous night spot or charity gala, and Vogel would, of course, decline. But tonight, he'd decided to call Marsh's bluff and accept the invitation. It *was* an occasion to celebrate, after all. The grim reaper had sharpened his scythe and would soon begin to swing it. Vogel's work would soon be at an end. He had but a few more simple tasks to complete.

"It is quite something," Vogel agreed.

They were seated in a large circular booth in the center of the room. Marsh was parked between two Brazilian supermodels, whose features suggested they'd been poured out of plastic molds rather than born. Vogel sat between an e-sports champion—a fellow who played video games, Marsh explained—and a female bodybuilder who'd been fired from her spot on the panel of a daytime talk show for joking that hunting the homeless for sport wasn't the worst idea she'd ever heard. Or perhaps she hadn't been joking. Her expression was so severe that Vogel considered that the woman might not possess even the rudiments of a sense of humor.

Vogel's discomfort was profound. Marsh seemed aware of this fact.

"Bet you didn't have this sort of stuff back in Germany. Probably just dark beer and sausage and sauerkraut." Marsh paused to snatch some sushi rolls from the platter of a passing tuxedo-clad waiter. "Check it out, Doc. Genuine Bluefin tuna rolls. Want one?"

Vogel waved away the offer. "Thank you, Mr. Marsh, but I'm not hungry."

"Suit yourself." Marsh popped one of the rolls into his mouth and continued speaking as he chewed. "You don't mind me saying so, Doc, you seem tense. That's part of the reason I brought you here tonight. I know you don't get out of the lab much. Don't get me wrong, I admire your dedication. But you might try getting laid. You know, just to take the edge off. See that woman over there?"

Vogel followed Marsh's line of sight to a woman who was hovering by the bar. Her unadorned black dress and simple pearl necklace were a stark contrast to the flashy designer dresses and gaudy jewelry worn by most of the female attendees. Her hair was grey and cut stylishly, but it was impossible for Vogel to guess her age with any sort of accuracy. He wouldn't have been surprised to learn that she was anywhere between forty and sixty years old. She had the sort of effortlessly regal bearing that he so rarely saw in this country.

"Yes," Vogel said. "I certainly do."

"Not bad for an old chick, huh?" Marsh washed his mouthful of food down with a gulp of champagne.

"She's beautiful." Vogel stated it with the same tone he'd use to read results from one of his experiments. It was a fact, simple as that.

"Well, if you're interested in her, you can forget it. I doubt even I could close that deal. Not that I'm into old chicks, but you know what I mean. Her name's Stella Kuminsky. She runs the biggest escort service in DC. Half the available women at this party are on her payroll. Let me introduce you. Once she knows you're with Marsh Industries, she'll set you up with a nice piece of ass. What do you say?"

Vogel nodded. "Perhaps some female companionship would be just the thing."

"Okay, guys," Marsh said, signaling for his crew of semi-celebrities to move. "You stay here and order another bottle. Me and the doc are going to scare up a bit of fun."

Marsh's friends laughed as they cleared out of the booth. They enjoyed spending the man's money. Even someone as socially disconnected as Vogel could see that.

Before his boss invited him to the fundraiser, Vogel had considered finding a church where he could confess his sins. He'd seen enough American movies to know that there were such places open at this late hour. But after thinking it over, he decided against it. There was no point. He was quite beyond redemption, no matter what assurances a holy man could offer. Besides, was it even proper to ask for forgiveness for something you planned to do? Vogel wasn't sure, but he believed the notion of forgiveness was entirely retroactive. So he'd given up the idea of a last-minute religious conversion, and now he was going to be introduced to a madam. There was probably a joke in there somewhere, but Vogel wasn't the man to put the pieces together. He'd never been very good with jokes.

He followed Marsh through the crowd like a small fish swimming in the wake of great white shark. The crowd parted for Marsh. Even in this crowd of politicians, judges, pundits, and celebrities, Marsh had the right of way. Vogel may have been so buried in his research that he was ignorant of most of the outside world, but he understood the situation. It wasn't that these people respected Marsh. They respected his obscene wealth.

"Ms. Kuminsky," Marsh said as he closed in on the woman. "Always a pleasure to run into you at one of these affairs. You're looking radiant as always. How about we get out of here and fuck each other's brains out?"

The woman's laughter was musical. "Oh, Waylon. You're too much."

"Stella, I want you to meet my friend." Marsh grabbed Vogel by the arm and dragged him forward. "I present Herr Doctor Gustav Vogel. He's my main man in the company research and development department. The HOPE Project wouldn't have gotten off the ground if it weren't for his tireless work. Can't beat the goddamn Krauts for quality work, right?"

Stella Kuminsky rolled her eyes as she took Vogel's hand and shook it with a surprisingly firm grip. "You're probably used to Waylon's complete lack of tact."

Vogel tried to come up with a reply, but the words tangled in his throat. He settled for a smile and a shrug.

"Fuck tact," Marsh said. "It's for pussies and poor people."

Vogel covered his embarrassment by glancing around the club. What he saw strengthened his resolve to go through with his plans. The wealth represented in the room was equal to the GDP of several small nations. The enormous power these people could wield, if they made a concerted decision to do so for the betterment of humanity, might transform the world. But rather than advance the cause of human enlightenment, they'd chosen to squander their energies on ostentatious displays of materialism. To call their behavior simple greed was to make the understatement of many centuries. If these people represented the elite, then a push of the Great Reset Button was long overdue. Walking among them erased any lingering doubts Vogel might have harbored.

Marsh elbowed him. "Hey, this is ground control calling Doctor Vogel. Can you hear us?"

Vogel realized that Ms. Kuminsky had been speaking to him. "I beg your pardon, ma'am. What were you saying?"

"Just that I'm a big admirer of your work with the HOPE Project," she said. "Those people over there can pull themselves up by their bootstraps if someone just points them in the right direction. I believe Waylon Marsh is showing them the way to join the civilized world. If you played a part in making that happen, you should be proud of yourself."

"Thank you. That's most generous, although, really, Mr. Marsh deserves all the credit."

"Hey, no shop talk," Marsh said, putting a hand on Vogel's shoulder. "Look, Stella, the doc may be too polite to say it, but I'm not. This man has put in way too much overtime and needs to get laid. Now, I'll step away and let the two of you work out the particulars. Doc, you're on my tab tonight, so sky's the limit."

Vogel's face burned red.

"Stella, see that the doc is taken care of." Marsh leaned in and planted a kiss on her cheek. "Best part of coming to DC is getting to see you, my dear."

Vogel opened his mouth to protest, but Marsh was already gone, swallowed up the tide of affluent and influential people.

"It's okay," Ms. Kuminsky said.

"I'm sorry?" Vogel asked.

"To be a bit embarrassed, I mean," she explained. "Guys like your boss, they forget that not everyone is like them."

"He is, after all, an exceptional man." Vogel nodded.

"Darling, it's safe to drop the act. Discretion is one of my better qualities." She glanced down at herself and touched her gray hair. "At my age, maybe it's my best quality. Anyway, you don't have to pretend to love your boss. He's out of earshot and I certainly won't tell him."

"Well, I suppose he can be a bit boorish," Vogel admitted.

"The man's a sexist pig, Doctor. But he's a rich sexist pig, and that makes all the difference. And since you're on his tab tonight, I suggest you figure out what it is you really want. Trust me, whatever it is, nothing is going to shock me. These politicians, you wouldn't believe some of the requests I've gotten." She averted her attention for a moment to signal the bartender. When she turned back to Vogel, a fresh glass of white wine in her hand, she asked, "Well, Doctor? What can I do to help make this a memorable night for you?"

"I would like to, ah…" He searched for the polite phrase. "I'd like to spend time with one of your most popular ladies. That is, your busiest employee, the one most likely to, shall we say, work overtime."

"I see…"

Vogel's face grew even hotter. It was suddenly impossible to look Ms. Kuminsky in the eye, so he turned to the bartender and asked for a whiskey and soda.

"Darling, all my girls are busy little beavers," she said, tipping his chin up with her forefinger. "I think what you're hinting around about is what we call a slut fetish. Am I correct in that assumption?"

Vogel forced himself to meet her gaze. He nodded. "Yes, I suppose that's correct."

"Well, that's not a problem," she said. "But are you sure that's all?"

"What do you mean?" Vogel took his cocktail from the bartender and disposed of half it in one gulp.

"The services I provide aren't cheap. They're safe, discreet, and high quality, but they are also quite expensive. Your boss, one of the richest men in the world, just told you to put your entire evening on his tab. And you just want one dirty girl to *spend time* with?"

Vogel took a deep breath and let it out. He took another sip of his drink. "Very well, then. I'd like a trio of sluts who aren't opposed to indulging in some illicit substances."

Ms. Kuminsky handed him a business card. "In fifteen minutes, call this number. A car will pick you up outside the club. Now, if you'll excuse me, I really must mingle. This is a business opportunity for me, after all."

Her departure was just as sudden as Marsh's, and it happened in the same manner. Ms. Kuminsky simply turned and let herself be swallowed by the tide of people. It seemed to Vogel that she didn't have to use her feet; she only had to relax and drift away. He finished his drink and ordered another. Fifteen minutes later, he took his cell phone from his jacket pocket and called the number on the card Ms. Kuminsky had given him.

The car that picked him up looked like any number of vehicles that ferried politicians around the city. It was a late model sports sedan, black with tinted windows. The man behind the wheel could have passed for a member of the secret service. He was tall, broad-shouldered, and wore a dark suit. His facial expression was so frozen in place that it might as well have been a plastic Halloween mask.

"Good evening, sir," he said as Vogel climbed into the backseat. "Please fasten your seatbelt and we'll get underway."

"Of course," Vogel replied.

That exchange accounted for the entirety of the conversation during the twenty minute car ride. The trip terminated at a building that looked like any other big city office space. The sign at the front of the building read "Ambassador Place." That was it. No further description. A door man ushered Vogel into a spacious lobby with a burbling fountain that emptied into a koi pond.

"Take the elevator to the fourth floor," the door man said. "Someone will meet you."

Vogel nodded his thanks, then made his way through the lobby. He wondered if he was expected to offer the doorman a cash tip. The etiquette for such things was unfamiliar. Despite having spent time in both Hamburg and Paris, he never had occasion to visit Reeperbahn or Pigalle. He'd even avoided the temptations of numerous brothels during his time in Thailand. He looked back over his shoulder, but didn't see the doorman.

Vogel rode the elevator to the fourth floor as instructed. When the doors opened, he was greeted by a pair of men who might have been clones of the driver who'd brought him to the building. Even the high and tight haircuts were the same.

"Good evening, sir," of the human gargoyles said. "I'm afraid we do have to pat you down before we can take you to the room you reserved."

"Yes, of course." Vogel got the idea it didn't matter if he consented to the search or not.

The man snapped on a pair of black nitrile gloves and began running his hands over Vogel's arms and legs. After satisfying himself that Vogel wasn't carrying any weapons, he checked the doctor's jacket pockets. He found a handful of small glass vials full of white powder. He held the vials out for his partner to examine.

"It's okay," the man said. "The name on his account is one of our elite level members."

The vials went back into Vogel's pocket, and the two men led him down the hallway. The rooms were not numbered or otherwise identified. Vogel supposed that was by design. They paused in front of one of the blank doors.

"There's a landline in the room," one of the stone-faced

men said. "Use it if you need room service or if you're ready to leave."

The other man opened the door and motioned for Vogel to enter.

The room was no different from any number of nice hotels where Vogel had stayed during his time working for Marsh Industries. The bathroom was spotless and well stocked with soaps, shampoos, and lotions, as well as clean towels. The carpet was freshly vacuumed. There was a minibar full of expensive liquor and chocolates. All very familiar. But Vogel was used to being alone in such rooms, and this time, he had company.

As Ms. Kuminsky had promised, there were three women waiting for him. They were sitting thigh-to-thigh on the edge of the king sized bed: one blonde, one brunette, and one redhead. Perhaps Ms. Kuminsky had arranged it this way since he hadn't expressed any preference. Or perhaps it was simply the result of chance. Vogel was ignorant of how these things worked, which is why, as soon as he entered the room, he froze. Thankfully, the women seemed to sense his confusion. The blonde detached herself from her companions and glided across the room. Vogel was below average in height, and the woman's high heels boosted her well above him. When she drew close, he found his face buried between her breasts.

"You like that, baby?" she asked.

In truth, Vogel did not. There was a time when the act would have brought him nearly to ecstasy, but that time was long gone. His penis didn't even twitch. He extricated himself. The blonde looked at her friends and giggled.

"My name's Candy," she said.

The redhead introduced herself as Trixie. The brunette said, "I'm Kaylee Marie."

Candy tugged the neckline of her dress lower, exposing the lacy edge of her bra. Vogel felt himself blush.

"Oh, I think he's shy," she said.

Her friends rose from the bed. As if they were obeying some silent signal, all three women began slithering out of their form-fitting dresses. Vogel found it strange that they all kept their shoes on. But again, he wasn't familiar with the way this type of thing was supposed to proceed. They were superb physical specimens, these women. They would serve their purpose.

Vogel stepped back. "Perhaps I won't be so shy if we indulge our other appetites first."

He reached into his jacket pocket and took out the glass vials. All three of the women perked up at the sight of the white powder in the vials.

"Is that what I think it is?" the redhead, Trixie, cooed.

"I believe so," Vogel answered.

It was a partial truth. Most of what was in the vials was high quality synthetic cocaine, but it was blended with a cocktail of sedatives and a crystallized form of the Daroka serum. Although it hadn't been tested, Vogel felt certain that the crystallized serum would be absorbed alongside the cocaine. Within twenty-four hours after consumption, the women would carry a fully transmissible concentration of the Daroka virus in their bodily fluids.

Vogel passed each woman a vial and stepped aside as they headed for the bathroom. From a respectful distance, he watched as they got to work tapping out lines of white powder on the counter and snorting it up. The effects were immediately apparent, and Vogel had a moment of panic as he wondered if the cocaine was perhaps too concentrated. First, the brunette, Kaylee Marie, emerged from the bathroom. She kicked off her shoes and collapsed on the bed, giggling as she ran her fingertips over her naked body.

"Yeah, that's the shit," she said.

Trixie came next. She pinched her nostrils shut and paused

on her way to the bed. She pressed her body against Vogel, running her free hand over his crotch.

"Oh, don't worry," she said, her voice comically high-pitched through her closed nostrils. "We'll wake that little guy up. You like to watch?"

She slithered onto the bed and hooked her leg over the brunette. Candy came last. Her eyes were already bloodshot. Vogel urged her to join her friends on the bed. They tried their best to put on a show for him, but their movements grew increasingly clumsy. They pawed at each other rather than caressed. Lines of drool ran from their lips. Vogel sat beside them on the bed, observing.

3

The head of Earth Force's tech department was named Joseph Barclay, but he went by Spider. A former IT consultant for the NSC and part time hacker, he'd gone off the Fed radar and joined Earth Force after an oil rig off the gulf coast of Florida had collapsed and drowned the beaches of his hometown in black sludge. Now, he lived in a solar-powered RV commune that moved through the Pacific Northwest, and managed the internet presence for Lori Lund and Earth Force. Spider was one her many secret weapons in the war against Marsh Industries.

"Shit's real, Lori," Spider said. "As far as we can tell, everything here is genuine."

"Jesus Christ, it's even worse than we thought," Lori said, staring at the laptop computer screen. "I mean, holy shit, what do we even do with this?"

Depending on one's view of time, it was either very late or very early, but Lori hadn't slept a wink since receiving the files through an anonymous email contact eight hours earlier. According to the email, the source of the files was a highly placed employee of Marsh Industries, who had managed to gain access to Waylon Marsh's personal computer. The anonymous source had attested to the files' authenticity, but Lori hadn't managed to avoid both prosecution and assassination by being careless. She'd put Spider on the case. And what he'd seen on the hard drive was enough to make him hop on his motorcycle and ride three hours straight to the Earth Force office in Arnholt, Washington.

Lori pushed her chair back from her desk and headed for the coffee maker in the corner of the room. Although she'd already poured several cups down her throat, she was still just running on fumes. She wasn't as young and energetic as she'd been when she started Earth Force nearly three decades ago. Back then, she'd run the operation out of her dorm room. Using resources borrowed from the English department, she'd produced a print newsletter that eventually became a worldwide organization. Although the focus of Earth Force had never been specific—they fought against everything from hardwood logging, to puppy mills, to offshore oil drilling— Lori had preached quite loudly that Marsh Industries was representative of all the evil in the military-industrial complex. They were, she often said, the embodiment of evil. And now, at last, she had tangible dirt on Waylon Marsh himself.

More times than she could remember, people had observed that Lori's crusade against Marsh and his company seemed less like an ideological crusade than a personal vendetta. They were correct, of course. But Lori had taken some steps to ensure that people wouldn't discover how correct they were. Amazingly, Marsh had done the same. It seemed that neither of them were eager for the world to learn of the passionate, six month long affair they'd shared during their junior year at UC-Claremont. But Lori sure as hell remembered those six months. She often wondered if Marsh recalled them in the same vivid detail. She wasn't sure which scenario roused her resentment more: Waylon Marsh remembering their time together with perfect clarity or looking back on it as some silly youthful affair he'd indulged just to anger his father.

She stirred a couple teaspoons of sugar into her coffee.

"You sure you need more coffee?" Spider asked. "You don't mind me saying so, you look like you need to catch some sleep."

"How can I sleep when I have that?" She gestured at the laptop. "I mean, I've been looking at it for hours, and I feel like I'm just scratching the surface."

Spider smiled. "Yeah, I'll admit it's pretty interesting shit. A real peek inside that billionaire brain."

Lori knocked the old coffee grounds into the trashcan and got to work brewing a new pot. As the machine gurgled and coughed steam, she glanced around her office. It really wasn't that different from the dorm room where she'd drawn the first Earth Force logo on a scrap of notebook paper. The walls were plastered with posters of slogans calling for revolution. The bookshelves were crammed to bursting. Her desk chair was draped in Native American blankets. The office was cozy, cluttered, and colorful.

"Even if that video footage is staged," Spider said, "there is enough genuine dirt on that hard drive to bury Marsh. Do you even know what you're going to leak first?"

Lori bit her bottom lip as she thought that one over. Aside from the atrocities at Daroka, the stolen hard drive contained a wealth of evidence of Marsh's criminal endeavors. Everything from bribery of elected officials, to insider trading deals and tax fraud. There were even nude photos of Marsh's various girlfriends, some of whom Lori suspected were below the age of consent. She couldn't believe that Marsh would be so cavalier with such information. And that's exactly what gave her pause. If a man as famously paranoid as Marsh would keep his laptop in a place where some staffer could grab it, was it because he'd simply gotten careless or rather that he knew he'd become untouchable by the laws that bound regular people?

"I think we leak it all," she said. "Hit Marsh with an avalanche of bad press and make him scramble to cover all his bases."

Spider nodded. "Might as well."

"Get it to the big news outlets first. Give them a few hours to break the story, and then send it to every contact we have."

"Right on."

Lori sighed. She shook her head slowly, squeezing her eyes shut.

"Hey, you okay?" Spider asked.

Lori thought that one over for a moment. She opened her eyes and looked at Spider. Despite the impressive resumé with both government work and his freelance activities, Spider was still in his twenties. He was just a kid. Lori remembered, albeit somewhat hazily, how it had felt to be touched by youth and revolutionary fire. It was a special sort of heat that narrowed your focus to a bullseye crisis point. You could see the upheaval coming, of that much you were certain. If only people would open their eyes and see. If only they would open their ears and minds to the truth of your righteous cause. You knew there were long-term consequences; after all, you'd read your share of Marx. But that kind of future felt so remote that it was hardly your concern. Yes, Lori remembered. But she knew that space between a revolutionary act and its consequences could easily collapse, just as she knew the motivations for such acts could be murky at best.

"I wonder," she said, "if the footage from Daroka is genuine, are we too late?"

"Too late?" Spider scoffed. "Come on, it's never too late to bring down a bastard like Waylon Marsh. The world needs to know the consequences of selling the planet to corporate overlords like him. They won't be able to ignore us anymore, not after this."

Lori laughed at the sound of her own words coming out of someone else's mouth. There was a time when it seemed impossible for her to talk about anything without shouting the same call-to-action slogans. But the Daroka footage made all that sloganeering and fist-in-the-air indignant rage ring hollow. She knew Spider had watched the same footage, but had they really seen the same thing?

"Zombies," she said.

"Huh?"

"You do understand that Marsh's little project resulted in reanimated human corpses, right?" She felt weird just saying it. "All this time, we thought Xavier Arnaud was speaking metaphorically, but he was trying to tell us in plain old English just what is happening over there. Now, we've lost contact with him, and there are dead people getting up and walking around. The living dead. The undead. Take your pick. Right now, in Daroka, there are actual zombies walking around."

"And that's why he has to be stopped." Spider slapped the desk for emphasis. "He's turned so many of us into metaphorical zombies. We can't let him make us into actual zombies."

Lori didn't know if she should laugh or cry. Come to think of it, that dilemma summed up most of her adult life. And she decided to proceed in her usual manner: by forging ahead. After all, she'd come this far. She might as well see Marsh's corporate machine broken down to its last cog. If there was an undead apocalypse awaiting all of humanity, at least Lori Lund would go into it with a clean conscience and the knowledge that she never quit fighting.

"Okay then, kid," she said. "Let's bring that greedy asshole to his knees."

The coffee machine beeped, signaling an end to the brewing cycle. Lori filled her own cup, then offered one to Spider. It would be morning in a few hours. And the world was going to wake up to some big news. Maybe—*just maybe* —they'd actually pay attention.

4

Stella Kuminsky thought about calling Waylon Marsh, and reading him the riot act, but after catching a few minutes of CNN's morning shows, she figured he had enough to worry about.

Serves the jittery asshole right, she thought, pouring three cups of coffee and passing them out to Candy, Trixie, and Kaylee Marie. Stella was sure her name was somewhere on that hard drive. It seemed that Marsh kept everything on his personal laptop, like an absolute idiot. But she wasn't too worried. After all, she not only had the goods on politicians from both parties, she also had plenty of dirt on reporters and on-air personalities from every major news network. If someone got overly ambitious or self-righteous, she had only to make a couple phone calls to keep her name out of it.

Meanwhile, she still had a business to run. Congress was in session, which meant her resources were stretched to the limit. Otherwise, there's no way she'd even entertain the idea of letting this trio of bedraggled bitches work. They looked to be suffering through the mother of all hangovers.

"You ladies, and I use that term very loosely, look like shit," Stella said.

"That little man might not have been able to get it up, but he had some powerful shit," Candy said, pinching the bridge of her nose. "Never had cocaine like that, not even when we were partying with the Brazilian ambassador."

There was grumbling all around as the three women tried to sip their coffee. Stella had zero sympathy. Before she'd ascended to her throne as Queen of the DC Call Girls, Stella had worked long hours on her back and knees. Her conscience didn't keep her awake nights because she could say with complete honesty that she never asked her employees to do anything she hadn't at one time or another done herself. That went for the cocaine as well as the sex. Sometimes snorting a line or two went with the territory. But there were ways of avoiding overconsumption while still making the client feel like you were down to party. Apparently those lessons hadn't resonated with these three.

"Well, I hope you're not planning on taking time off for recovery," Stella said. "Last night, I was at a party with DJ Apocalypse Tonight. He's in town for his concert with Aftershocker Crew, and they wanted to book everyone who's not already working the Foundation for American Reason and Truth convention at the Grand Gardens Hotel."

"That's okay," Candy said. "I just need a couple hours to get my shit together. Last time Aftershocker Crew was in town was my biggest tip night. Rappers are my fucking jam."

Stella shook her head. "I'm afraid not. I told Bernice, Juju, and Crystal to switch places with you. So they'll take the rappers and you three ladies will take the holy roller convention. And since those conservative types get their willies waggling earlier in the day, I'll need you over at the hotel by lunchtime."

Candy, Trixie, and Kaylee Marie looked like kids who'd just been told Christmas had been canceled. Instead of drinking top shelf liquor and champagne with a crew of rappers, they'd be working the hotel bar, hoping to score customers from the Bible-thumpers in Reverend Jimmy Kelso's political action committee. Famously stingy as tippers and seriously into the kinky stuff, Reverend Kelso's followers were the type of grunt work usually assigned to the girls lowest on Stella's totem pole. It was, in short, a shit detail.

Stella stared her three employees down, silently daring them to complain. As a boss, she like to maintain a good relationship with the staff. But sometimes she needed to remind them who was in charge of the operation. None of the three could even make eye contact. They were suddenly very interested in their cups of coffee.

"Probably won't run into much powder temptation at the convention," Stella continued. "But just in case you do get an offer too good to turn down, just remember how much you hate disappointing your boss. Dismissed."

They trooped out of office with bedraggled heads hung low.

5

"What the fuck do you mean he's disappeared?!" Waylon Marsh demanded, jabbing his finger into Ray Hollister's chest.

Hollister took a half step back. "What I mean is that the man never came back here last night."

Marsh shouldered past Hollister and stomped across the hotel room, pulling out dresser drawers and opening the closet. "All his clothes are still here."

They were standing in the middle of the suite registered to Gustav Vogel, but the man himself was nowhere to be found. Apparently, he'd managed to slip the security detail Marsh had assigned to him. According to the two members of the security team, Vogel had left the brothel shortly after midnight and had requested that the car service take him to an all-night breakfast restaurant. The security guards had parked outside the restaurant to wait for the doctor to re-emerge. But he never did. After a full hour had passed, one of the guards went inside the restaurant to get a closer look at Vogel, but he came up empty.

"Sir, it seems to me that maybe your security detail

thought it was soft duty," Hollister said. "You gotta understand it from their point of view. Following an elderly German scientist ain't exactly like tailing James Bond."

"Well, understand this, Ray: both those assholes have already been fired. They'll be lucky to get a job flipping burgers in an Arkansas truck stop after this fuck up."

"I'm sure," Hollister agreed. "They dropped the ball big time. But maybe putting Vogel together with a bunch of hookers wasn't the best idea in the world. You know as well as I do that the man isn't stable."

Anger boiled up in Marsh. He wanted to smack Hollister across his fat face. As if Marsh didn't have enough bullshit to deal with, now Hollister was shrugging off Vogel's disappearance like it was no big deal.

"Stable?" Marsh yanked open the door to the minibar and snatched a vodka from the array of tiny plastic bottles. "Do you know what we asked that man to cook up for us? You think a stable person could do that? Now, with him in the wind, who knows what might happen."

"You think he's behind this information leak?" Hollister asked.

"I don't know. Maybe?" Marsh twisted the cap off the vodka and poured the liquor into his mouth. He winced as it burned on the way down, then wound up and threw the empty bottle across the room.

"Where's that secretary of yours? Ivanka?"

Marsh paused on his way to grab another bottle from the minibar. "You leave Svetlana out of this. She'd never do anything to hurt me. Besides, I know exactly where she is. She took a few personal days to see a friend in Texas. And even though I trust her completely, I checked her GPS. She's been in Dallas, going to coffee shops, the mall, that sort of thing. Girly shit."

Hollister sighed, which only made Marsh want to strangle

him even more. That sigh, with its edge of disappointment, reminded him of his father. Leonidas Marsh could convey immense dissatisfaction with a simple sigh and had never missed an opportunity to heave one when his son didn't measure up in some way. And there had been plenty of opportunities over the years. His relationship with Lori Lund, for example. Old Leonidas had hit the fucking ceiling when he found out his son was sleeping with the leader of a student environmentalist group. The old man had threatened him with disinheritance, among other things. So Marsh had withdrawn from classes at UC-Claremont and enrolled at a school on the opposite coast. He'd left his apartment in the dead of night, without notifying any of his friends. Without notifying Lori.

It gave Marsh some comfort to remind himself that old Leonidas was dead, and that the son who'd been such a disappointment had built the family fortune into the sort of wealth amassed by the pharaohs of ancient Egypt. And just like those pharaohs, Marsh would soon come to be viewed as some sort of god on earth. Once that came to pass, he'd have no more use for Hollister or any of his yes-men. Maybe he'd execute them for entertainment. The thought made him smile.

"You okay there, sir?" Hollister asked.

"No, Ray, I'm not okay. Have you seen CNN this morning? Fox News? Hell, even the weasels at New American Media are firing shots across our bow. All this bullshit is coming right at me. Fuck!" There was no more vodka, so he settled for spiced rum. It reminded him of his father's aftershave, but he choked it down.

Hollister kicked the door to the refrigerated minibar shut and stood in front of it. "Don't worry about that information leak. There's a reason your father employed me, and it's the same reason you continue to employ me. I'm already calling in favors with our media contacts. Those that can't be bought can be blackmailed. The only news outlets who will dare publish anything substantive from that hard drive will be fringe outlets that nobody will believe. Worst case scenario, we have to do a little rebranding, maybe step back from the spotlight until the midterm elections are over. After that, we're back to sitting pretty."

Marsh dropped the empty rum bottle on the floor. Some of his anger towards Hollister melted away. It left a hollow ache in his gut.

"You know," Hollister said, clearing his throat. "We might not know who leaked the information, but we have a pretty good idea who disseminated it. Lori Lund. It might be time to reconsider our policy regarding that woman. It might be time to take some direct action. After all, it's been years. College was a long time ago."

Marsh shook his head. "Forget it. Lori is off-limits. Leave her alone. You bring her up again in my presence, I'll have you removed from the board. I don't give a fuck how much my dear dead daddy loved you."

He stared the man down until he withered.

"Don't worry, your ex-girlfriend is safe," Hollister said, looking away. "And we'll find Vogel. Besides, what kind of trouble could the old boy possibly get up to? Probably just dumped his security detail so he could go party a little more. More than likely, he got into some Viagra and needs to get some partying out of his system."

"I hope for all our sakes that you're right." Marsh took a deep breath and let it out slowly. "Because we've pinned a lot of hope on the doc. Without him, we're not quite back to square one, but our timetable is completely fucked. And that's the best case scenario. Worst case is he's the one behind this leak. Who knows? Maybe the twisted Nazi fuck developed some sense of morality and decided to go rogue. Doesn't fucking matter who leaked it. The cat's out of the bag. But I want Vogel back where he belongs."

Hollister's mouth opened like he wanted to reply, but obviously, he had nothing to offer. Marsh could at least savor the small satisfaction of putting the clown in his place.

"I don't think I need to remind you that your name is all over that hard drive too, Hollister." Marsh smiled. "Just in case you get any big ideas."

6

Charon swept through the maze of streets, running its fingers over the cool bricks and stones of the buildings. It paused before sculptures carved to commemorate the dreams which had inspired the architecture of this world. There was no sun overhead, but patches of strange iridescence shone behind the grey clouds. Lights shone from below as well; tiny rivulets of glowing yellow and orange that crawled in the cracks between the cobblestones. On the corners of the wide avenues, the trees branches sprouted lush green leaves and flowers. Other branches bent beneath the weight of fruit. Insects buzzed through the air, borne on transparent wings.

The borders of the city pushed outwards, cutting through the walls of the cave. The dark edges of Charon's kingdom thronged with unseen animal life. Birds flitted through the trees. Cats stalked through the grass. Brightly patterned lizards stretched themselves atop rocks and slipped lazily into the river. Fish leapt from the water at their approach.

Charon walked on, drinking in the scents of the new life springing forth from the dead rocks. Charon knew that, in the dark and distant void of space, the stars had at long last come into alignment.

7

Foundation For American Reason And Truth Opposes
Foreign Intervention In Daroka

Reverend James Kelso, pastor of South Carolina's Pure Faith Church and president of the Foundation for American Reason and Truth, has urged his followers to be vocal in their opposition to American intervention in Daroka.

"We can't just go around policing the world," he said during an interview on the Liberty Social podcast. "We have homeless veterans and starving children right here at home. We don't need to send our tax dollars overseas. And besides, General Mbowi may not be perfect, but the government he took down was a godless socialist regime. If the people of Daroka want to oppose their new government, let them do it themselves. Freedom isn't free, after all."

—Aaron Saint John, Media Wire Service

Posted by user Holistic Holly on the *Abduction Survivors* internet message board:

Yeah, I think that Lori Lund probably ordered that kidnapping.

Brad Carter

My mom was college roomates with her and one of the orignal members of earth force and she says Lori Lund isn't even a real human but some part alien hybrid. During my last abduction I was given a vision I saw a garden of crystals on some other planet and Lori Lund was there among the grey aliens and she told me peace be upon me and that we will all be taken from the earth soon anyway. But like I was saying lori Lund is the child of a CIA agent who fell in love with a captive alien at the facility in roswell, new Mexico and their DNA and RNA was fused into a super genome, which is why they force so many vaccines because they don't want our DNA and RNA to mingle and ascend to another plane.

Part Five

Surely some revelation is at hand…

"The biggest profits are made from death."

—Max Lambert

1

After the scene at the front gate of Our Lady of Peace, nobody felt much like talking. London had tried using the satellite phone to contact someone at Pendleton headquarters, but it seemed no one was home. That was highly unusual, and it gave London a bad feeling about the future of the entire operation. First the attack at the landing strip, then whatever the fuck that was back at the mission, and now communication had gone silent.

After those gut punches, London figured it was best to keep pushing north, and that meant going through the jungle. They'd handled Mbowi's men at the landing strip, but London had the idea that those weren't exactly the General's A-team. Going through the jungle meant they were less likely to run across more hostiles—at least not those of the highly trained variety—while detouring around the jungle meant the team would be totally exposed.

Thankfully, circumstance had dropped a guide right into their laps. According to Lia, she'd spent the better part of a year in the Darokan jungle while working on a documentary about the Ka'Longho, a famously elusive tribe known as the

Ghost People. Sure, London had maps and satellite images, but it was always better to have a guide.

"Sunset in less than two hours. I wonder how far she intends to go before we set up camp for the night." Zantoro spoke up from the passenger seat. It was the first time since they'd driven onto the bumpy, overgrown logging road.

"I guess we'll find out soon enough," London said, wincing as the Jeep bounced over a rocky patch of road. "Probably wants to make some miles before nightfall. The way this road is, we'll be lucky to do ten miles before it gets dark."

Operational security procedures stated that a Pendleton vehicle should always be in the lead position. To do otherwise was to invite ambush. But when Lia had suggested that it would be easier for her to navigate if the Land Rover was driving point, London had agreed. That weird feeling in the pit of his stomach told him that things like operational security procedures would be taking a backseat to simple survival very soon. After what he'd seen in the street in front of the mission, and in the backseat of the Land Rover, he just wanted to get this operation over with and return to the real world. Maybe it was time to step back from work. He had plenty of money to fund a lengthy sabbatical.

"Boss," Osbourne said from the backseat, nearly shouting to be heard over the rumbling vehicle and the cacophony of birds screeching overhead. "Mind if I ask you a question?"

"Fire away," London said.

"Just what the fuck did we step into over here?" Osbourne asked. "Nobody seems like they want to say anything, so I guess I'll take one for the team and just ask. So, please, if you're privy to some mission-critical info or some other such bullshit, can you just spill it? Because I've been thinking about it, trying to come up with some explanation, and I keep circling back to the fact that most of those folks who came out of that church should have been pushing up daisies. Never mind that we were firing right at them and they just kept on walking like it was no big deal. Seriously, what the fuck is going on?"

London shook his head. "Sorry, but I'm just as in the dark as you are. Far as I know, this was a simple search and destroy operation first and foremost, served up with a side helping of finding out what happened to Mikkelson's team."

"Yeah, well, maybe we should call back home and demand some answers." This time, it was Vincent who spoke up. "You sure you tried to raise them on the right frequency?"

"I know how to use a goddamn sat-phone," London snapped. "This whole operation has just gone off the rails."

"A fucking crazy train," Zantoro agreed. "Shit is insane in this country."

"Those people should have been dead," Osbourne said. "I'm telling you guys, those people should have been dead. And you want to know what I think? Marsh Industries' fingerprints are all over this. We're not part of a search and rescue or a salvage mission or anything like what we normally do. We're here to cover their asses."

"Yeah, that's exactly what I signed up for," Zantoro said. "I love covering up for some corporate asshole's fuck up. Maybe after this, we can go cover up evidence of an oil spill."

"Or maybe go force one of Waylon Marsh's mistresses to have an abortion," Vincent added.

London had heard enough. He didn't like pulling rank on his team, but certain situations demanded it. And the current situation definitely fell into that category.

"Enough of that bullshit," he barked. "It's a little late for you assholes to develop moral qualms about your chosen profession. We're here to do a job, and we're going to do it. End of story. Once we're back home drinking beers, we can speculate about what the hell is going on in this country, but right now we have to focus on what's in front of us."

Whether it was the words themselves or the no-nonsense

delivery that did the trick, London's speech had the desired effect. The team fell silent. He only wished he could quiet his own thoughts so easily. It was one thing to preach focus, but another thing to practice it, especially when his mind kept circling back to the way that kid's eyes had stared back at him when he pulled the trigger.

Dominic. Lia had said the kid's name was Dominic. She also said that the white woman who had been killed outside the church was his mother, and that the poor bastard they'd scraped out of the backseat of the Land Rover had been his stepfather. It had been one hell of a day for that family.

Nothing you could do, he thought. *The kid was beyond help.*

London focused on keeping the Jeep on the road. Even with the Land Rover in the lead, it wasn't easy. Wherever Lia planned to stop for the night, he hoped it was close. There was only so much he could take in one day. He turned his head and spit his wad of Skoal into the trees.

2

"Almost there, Max," Lia said, giving his shoulder a squeeze. "There's a clearing not too far from here. Maybe some of the shacks the logging company put up are still there. The Ka'Longho might be using them, but that wouldn't be the worst thing in the world."

She checked the rearview mirror, making sure that the Americans were still following. She felt strange leading a group of mercenaries into the jungle. The more she thought about it, the more she was sure it counted as a betrayal of her principles. But after what she'd encountered at Our Lady of Peace, she felt that she could bend her principles if it meant having some firepower on her side. The pistols that she and Max carried—which, to her amazement, the Americans had allowed them to keep—felt woefully inadequate after what she'd seen outside the church.

"I supposed it's good that you trust them," Max said. "Because I don't."

"What are you talking about?"

"Come on, Lia," he sniffed. "Don't play coy with me. The Americans. Or have you forgotten the part about how they're most likely here to bury the truth that you want to show the world? I know you're smart enough to figure this one out. They're here because Marsh Industries wants to cover its ass. You know that."

"Maybe I didn't think we had a choice," she said. "Or didn't you notice how heavily armed they are?"

"We're armed too."

Now it was her turn to sniff dismissively. "Yes, because our two pistols are an easy match for that military hardware. Besides, I think you're leaving out one very important detail."

"Oh yeah?"

"The fact that we'd most likely be dead if they hadn't just happened to show up. Max, you saw what was going on at the church." She let that one hang in the air between them for a moment, then continued, "We're a pair of tough cookies. We've seen some shit and lived to tell the tale. No compromise, no cowardice. We've always told the truth about the things we've seen. This may be the biggest story of all, and if we're not around to tell it, who will?"

Max shrugged. "I don't know, maybe the BBC News desk?"

"Of course," she laughed. "But here's something you might consider about the Americans. If they were truly interested in burying this mess that Marsh Industries has created, why didn't they shoot us on sight? Not only did they not smash your cameras, they handed us our guns back. When we went into the jungle, they asked us to take the lead. This road isn't on their map. For all they know, we could be leading them away from the research center."

They rode in silence for a few minutes. Lia considered turning on the stereo, but there was no clear radio reception this deep in the jungle, and the only other option was ABBA's *Greatest Hits*, which was stuck in the Land Rover's CD player. Lia preferred her own thoughts to "Dancing Queen." That spoke volumes about her hatred for the Swedish pop group, because her thoughts were straying into very dark corners.

Like she'd said to Max, they had seen more than their share of shit. They'd seen atrocities. Mass graves in Srebrenica. Disease-ridden Congolese refugee camps. Abandoned torture chambers of the Columbian cartels. The aftermath of countless American school shootings. Lia and Max had walked through killing fields heaped with tangible evidence of humanity's appetite for its own destruction. They'd stood bravely among the rotting bodies and bloodstained walls, and they'd reported the terrible facts. They'd shown the world its own ugliest face.

But this was something new and terrible that reached beyond simple human atrocity into something even worse. Something blasphemous. Something evil. Normally, those terms would have her rolling her eyes and muttering about hyperbole. But now, she wondered if hyperbole was even possible.

Max cleared his throat. "Lia, I want to ask you something, but I'm afraid you'll think I'm crazy."

"Go ahead," she said. "After today, I think we might have to invent a new word to describe what we saw. 'Crazy' seems a bit pathetic after that."

"They were dead, weren't they?" Max turned in his seat to stare at her as she drove. "Those people back at that mission, they should have been dead. In Uganda, when we saw people with their hands or feet cut off, those that didn't bleed out got sepsis and died within a few days. And if that was all, maybe I could put what we saw back there down to quick, skilled medical treatment. But I saw people walking around with their guts hanging out. I saw people with their throats cut and faces smashed to a pulp. And when the Americans showed up and started shooting, I saw people shot a dozen times or more. And all these people, they were just walking around."

Lia nodded. "Yes, I saw it too."

"And Josie, that poor woman…they ate her. The people who should have been dead but were walking around, they ate Josie." Max winced as if stung by the memory. "Just like her little boy ate his stepfather."

"Yes…"

"Dead people walking around, trying to devour the living. Lia, this is beyond the pale. Even for the things we've seen, this is terrible."

She looked away from the road for a moment to meet Max's gaze. There was something in his eyes that she'd never seen before. It was fear, sure, but she'd seen fear on his face plenty of times. It was something beyond that, something like absolute horror mixed with a dawning awareness. Lia felt like she was looking into a mirror.

"Of all the things we suspected about Marsh Industries," she said, turning her attention back to the bumpy road, "we were never close to the truth. How could we have even conceived of such horrors? And to what end would a company pursue this?"

"Are you serious? Lia, if there's one thing that our time together has taught me, it's that the biggest profits are made from death."

The road dipped and curved, plunging them deeper into the jungle. The canopy overhead blocked out all but the smallest slivers of light. The vehicle's automatic headlights clicked on just as Lia steered around a tight curve. The twin beams of light illuminated a pair of men standing in the middle of the road, and Lia hit the brakes.

"Shit!" she shouted as the vehicle bounced and swayed, sliding over the muddy ground until finally coming to a stop mere meters from the two men.

"Here we go again," Max sighed.

The men in the road were dressed in combat fatigues and carried AK-47 rifles. They most likely belonged to General Mbowi's Glorious Revolutionary Army. Or at least they had belonged to that bloodthirsty organization when they were still alive. Both men were riddled with bullet holes. Their camouflage shirts and pants were crusty with dried blood. Shredded bits of viscera trailed from their wounds. Their mouths hung open, and thick mucus hung like green tendrils from their bloated, black tongues. They held their rifles limply at their sides, the muzzles pointed at the ground. One of them took an unsteady step forward. His finger squeezed the trigger of his rifle, spraying a burst of rounds between his feet. He stared stupidly at the gun, then threw it into the trees and continued his shuffling advance on the Land Rover. His companion followed, dragging the barrel of his rifle through the mud.

"I can handle it," Max said, ejecting the magazine from his pistol to check the ammunition.

But before he could even open the passenger side door, one of the Americans—the wild-haired one called Zantoro— sprinted past the Land Rover. He paused in front of the vehicle, the headlights shining on him like he was a stage performer. He turned his back on the pair of mutilated soldiers and struck a pose, flexing his muscles.

"Jesus Christ, the man is crazy," Lia said.

As the two soldiers came alongside him, Zantoro grabbed each of them by their collars, holding them at arm's length. He kicked up his heels, dancing a jig between the two men.

"Come on, everyone!" Zantoro shouted. "It's time for everyone to climb aboard the Soul Train!"

"I'm going to put a stop to this bullshit," Max said, sliding out of the car.

Lia watched as Max advanced with his pistol raised. He fired two shots into the torso of the nearest soldier.

"I'm sorry, Pierre, but that ain't going to cut it," Zantoro announced.

He looked at Lia and winked. Then he brought the soldiers heads together like he was trying to crack a pair of coconuts by slamming them against one another. The collision dazed the soldiers, and Zantoro released his grip on their collars. He drew a pistol from the holster on his right hip and fired a shot into one soldier's head. Brains and fragments of skull splattered across the Land Rover's hood.

"See, these assholes can take a lickin' and keep on tickin'," Zantoro said, pressing the barrel of his gun to the other soldier's forehead. "Until you get them in their ugly fucking heads."

He pulled the trigger, sending the soldier's brains spraying from the exit wound in the back of his skull. The soldier's body dropped forward, slumping over his fallen comrade.

Zantoro bowed dramatically. On his way back to the Jeep, he paused by the Land Rover's driver's side window.

"Hey, gorgeous. Like my dance moves?" he asked.

"Quite impressive," she said.

"I thought you might like that. But listen up, my boss says if we're going to camp out here tonight, we better find a spot soon." He looked over his shoulder at Max. "Oh yeah, might want to have Pierre pull those bodies out of the road. I mean, it's only fair that he contributes to the effort, right?"

3

Zantoro never went on an operation without a deck of playing cards. It had started as a simple matter of killing time. Although the bulk of the operations the team executed were high-intensity, violent affairs, there were other tasks that were little more than glorified bodyguard duty. And since the latter variety came with plenty of downtime, it was never a bad idea to have a deck of cards hanging around. But like so many other little odds and ends the team carried, the cards had become something of a superstition. Whenever they had orders to roll out, London made sure that Zantoro had a brand new deck of Bicycle cards.

They'd used Zantoro's cards to assign night watch shifts. London had drawn the high card, so he got the last shift. It was considered a shit detail because it also included breakfast duty. Not a big deal in this case; out here in the jungle, breakfast duty meant passing out the MRE pouches.

"That's just your fucking Irish luck," Zantoro had laughed after drawing a Two of Clubs and earning himself the first shift.

"Too bad I'm not Irish," London had answered, settling into his sleeping bag.

Now, the rest of the team was snoring away while London was checking the perimeter of camp. He figured he'd let them catch another couple, maybe three hours of sleep before they continued their push north.

He made his way around the camp slowly, scanning the gaps in the vegetation. The night's soundtrack was a cacophony of animal sounds. Tree frogs croaked and burped, night birds chattered, and larger animals stalked the jungle floor. The sounds of these unseen creatures was unnerving, but nothing drew close enough to worry London. After all, it wasn't animals he had to worry about.

As he walked the east flank of camp, a quick flash of light drew his attention. It disappeared quickly and was replaced by smaller, glowing orange spot. The scent of burning tobacco cut through the heavy jungle musk, carried by a whisper of night breeze.

London smiled. *For such a seasoned jungle guide, the French woman was making an amateur mistake.*

He slipped through the vegetation, choosing his steps carefully as he came up behind her. He allowed her one last drag before he reached out and snagged the cigarette away from her lips.

"Sorry, but you can't do that at night," he said, crushing the cigarette beneath his boot. "Sniper sees the light, he knows where we are."

"Snipers?" She quieted her laughter behind her hand. "I'm sorry, but I'm not sure it's snipers we should be worried about when we keep getting attacked by dead people. But you're right. I know better. And I've been meaning to quit anyway."

London fished his can of Skoal out of his pocket. "It's how I got started on this stuff. I spent too many nights on guard duty jonesing for a smoke. The one time I decided to just say fuck it and sneak a cigarette, my sergeant caught me. He told me I might as well live up to my Texan heritage and use the smokeless stuff."

She looked at the can in his outstretched hand. "Kind of a nasty habit, isn't it?"

"Yes, ma'am, it certainly is. But less nasty than compromising a mission on account of a nicotine addiction."

"My name is Lia," she said, keeping her voice just above a whisper. "I already feel old enough without you talking to me like that."

"And you can call me Mike. Might be nice to have someone address me some way besides my last name."

She tucked a small pinch of Skoal behind her lower lip. They stood there for a moment, peering into the jungle darkness and saying nothing. Then Lia broke the spell by gagging and spitting her tiny wad of snuff onto the ground.

"I'm sorry, but that shit is foul," she said, wiping the spit from the corner of her mouth. "I don't see how you can do that."

"It takes some getting used to, I reckon." London shrugged. "Do something long enough and you don't even think about it anymore. It just becomes part of who you are."

"If I get out of this nightmare and put together a story about what happened here, I'm leading with that quote."

London raised an eyebrow. "Shit, if you're going to quote me, I bet I can come up with something better than that."

"No, it's perfect," she said. "This afternoon, when we finally made it to the front gate of the mission and we saw what was waiting for us in the car..."

"Hey," London said. "It's done. No need to revisit it."

But Lia continued as if she hadn't heard him. "Everyone was standing there, frozen by fear and uncertainty. We all knew, at least I think we knew, what had to be done, but none of us was ready to actually do it. Nobody except for you. Like you said about the chewing tobacco, doing something, even if it's terrible, has just become part of who you are."

London spat his wad of snuff into the darkness. He'd suddenly lost his taste for it.

"Let me tell you something right now," he said. "Yeah, I did what I had to do. I did it for my team, for you and your partner, and for myself. But don't think for a second that it was somehow easy. Shit like that never becomes second nature. And unless you're the worst type of person, it never becomes part of you. I'm going to see that kid's face in my dreams for the rest of my life. There's nothing noble or heroic about it. Nothing whatsoever."

"I'm sorry, but if that's the truth, why did you choose this for a job?"

Anger swelled briefly in London's chest, but he swallowed it down. After all, how could he justify anger when all she'd done was point out the truth? It was the embarrassed anger of a child caught in a lie. Sad, pathetic anger that faded away to something like shame.

"Okay, you got me there," he admitted. "Guess I should think my own bullshit through before I open my mouth."

"I'm sorry. I shouldn't have said that."

"If anyone should apologize, it should be me. Me and my team, we're not exactly the most hospitable crew. We're relying on you to guide us to our destination, but I doubt you'll hear much in the way of gratitude."

"Don't forget," she said, "it's our destination too. Only we're going there to expose the place to the world, and you're going there to cover it up. Tell me if I'm wrong."

"After today, I'm not sure what we're doing," he admitted. "We've lost contact with headquarters. The sat-phone is in good working order, so that means someone back home has decided to quit taking our calls. Our navigation satellite has gone dark, so we're relying on outdated maps. I'm starting to get the idea that something outside the scope of our little operation has gotten massively fucked up, and as a result, we've been cut loose. I haven't clued the rest of my team in about my suspicions, so I don't even know why I'm telling you all this. Maybe because ever since we landed in this country, things have just felt wrong. I can't put my finger on it, but there's something that's just *off*. And I'm starting to get the idea that maybe it's not just this country, but the entire world."

London felt like he could talk until sunrise, but the honesty of the last statement shut him up. It was like he hadn't been able to acknowledge the feeling, even to himself, until he'd actually voiced it. Lia edge closer to him until their shoulders were barely touching.

"I've felt it too," she said. "But it's hard not to feel that the world has gone crazy when you've seen dead people walking around. I haven't set foot in a church since I was a little girl, so you can't accuse me of being some religious fanatic who sees omens of the end times in every hurricane or earthquake. But this stuff, it certainly makes you think. What about you? Are you religious?"

London thought that one over for a moment before answering. "I'm superstitious, but I guess that ain't really the same thing. A couple of the guys on my team pray before we roll out on an operation, but I'm not sure that's any different than Zantoro and his deck of Bicycle cards. I can't speak for everyone else, so take this with a grain of salt, but it's hard for me to have faith in a loving, omnipotent god when I've seen the things I've seen."

"I understand. I've seen some horrible things too. Maybe even some of the same ones you're talking about."

"Before I signed on with Pendleton, I worked as a sheriff's deputy in town called Black Mound. Little place in Texas, with a population hovering around ten thousand. I grew up there, but it had been years since I'd been back. I'd just gotten out of the service, and I took the job because it seemed like a quiet gig." London shook his head. He tried for a laugh, but it came out sounding more like a cough. "Anyway, I'm about one year in, and I'm starting to think that maybe this is how it's going to be from here on. You know, a nice, peaceful, normal, regular-Joe type life. Then, one day, this guy—well, he was just a kid, really—waltzes into the elementary school with an assault rifle and starts spraying bullets."

Lia sighed. "I knew I'd heard of Black Mound."

"Yeah, my little hometown was in all the headlines before the world moved on to the next tragedy. So this fucked-up kid shoots up the joint. The damage was done before my department even got a call. Twelve kids and five adults were hit before the shooter used his gun on himself. Half the kids were DOA. Another two died on the operating table. None of the adults made it. Among those adults was a woman named Valentina Martinez. She ran the school cafeteria. I used to call her my sexy lunch lady. She got a real kick out of that."

"Oh, no," Lia whispered. "I'm so sorry."

"She was pregnant. Just a couple months along, but we were making plans." London tapped his Skoal can. He considered pinching out another dip, but decided against it and shoved the can back in his pocket. "So, that was it for me in Black Mound. After the funeral, I put in my letter of resignation and got the hell out of there. I told myself I just needed some time and distance to make my peace with what had happened, and that one day I'd go back and give the normal life another shot. But deep down, I know I never will."

"That's understandable."

"I still remember the last thing I said to her." London laughed, but there was no humor in it. "I wanted to know if she could make this chicken and rice dish that I loved for dinner. I told her I loved her cooking. But I didn't tell her I loved her. I was usually good about that, making sure she knew how I felt about her. Then, the one day I slip up and forget…"

"I'm sure she knew."

"I don't know why I'm telling you all this shit," London said. "You're a reporter, not a therapist."

"Maybe there's some similarities between the two," Lia replied. "Both professions have to deal with hard truths."

London wiped his hands on his pants. "Well, here's a hard truth for you: the sun is coming up, so we need to get our asses in gear. Come on, let's go sound the wakeup call."

As they walked the remaining distance back to camp, Lia slipped her hand into his. London nearly jumped as she laced her fingers through his, but after a few steps, he relaxed. He found himself wishing they weren't quite so close to camp.

"I'm sorry," she said, starting to pull away. "I shouldn't do that. It's not the time or place…"

He held onto her hand. "It's okay. And maybe it's exactly the time and place."

<h1 style="text-align:center">4</h1>

Father Xavier only slept because he needed the dreams to guide him. And while the dreams had grown longer and more vivid over time, the duration of his rest periods had dwindled. Since he'd gone off the grid and taken his flock into the jungle, he'd only slept for two or three hours a night. That was long enough for the dreams to show him the path his flock would follow the next day. But the dreams didn't just show the path; they also showed the destination: a rocky chasm that led to a stone staircase.

In his dreams, Father Xavier had descended this staircase a hundred or more times, but he never lost his sense of awe at the scale of its construction. The staircase was wide enough for three adults to walk abreast. They sloped gently, which, for Father Xavier, was a mercy, because there were no handrails, and the walls and vaulted ceiling were smooth stone that dripped water from tiny cracks. The staircase was lighted by the garlands of luminescent lichens which clung in patches to the walls and ceiling. The light emitted from this strange flora pulsed slowly, throwing soft shadows over the stairs.

Because the time in his dreams was unmoored from that

of his waking life, Father Xavier had no way of knowing how long it took to descend the staircase. But what he did know was that once he stepped off the staircase, he emerged into a cavern so vast that he couldn't see its borders. Overhead, what must have been a vaulted stone ceiling was so distant that it appeared to be the night sky. Patches of light—Father Xavier assumed from the same lichen that illuminated the staircase—pulsed against the distant dark surface, giving the cavern the glow of warm twilight.

A short distance from the mouth of the stairwell, a river ran through the cavern. The water passed by lazily, the current gentle and steady. As Father Xavier stood on the bank, the toes of his shoes nearly touching the water, he could see fish swimming through the shallows. They were sleek, beautiful creatures, more brightly colored than any he'd seen in his waking life. Luminescent orbs, like jellyfish without tentacles, bobbed to the surface and drifted on the current, pulsing with multicolored light before disappearing beneath the water or drifting out of sight.

Across the expanse of the river, Father Xavier saw what could be a called a city, although it was unlike any city he had ever known. The cobblestone streets were shot through with shimmering threads of light, and they snaked through a maze of buildings constructed according to architectural plans that seemed to defy gravity.

A figure emerged from the labyrinth of dizzying towers and domed cathedrals. Tall and gaunt, dressed in a black robe of fabric so thin and insubstantial that the gentle breeze pulled at it, the figure seemed to glide across the ground as much as walk. It paused on the opposite side of the river and pointed a long, bony finger at Father Xavier.

"The time is at hand," it said with a voice like the wind stirring dead leaves over a quiet street. "The stars and planets have aligned. The universe has decreed that a new age shall dawn."

Father Xavier dropped to his knees. Cool river water splashed over his legs. He wondered if he should, like some wild-haired Old Testament prophet, avert his gaze. But although he was awestruck, he wasn't afraid.

"Continue your march," the figure said. "A new world awaits."

Father Xavier awoke. The transition between sleep and waking was abrupt, like flipping the switch on a floodlight in a pitch black room. He swept the thin blanket off his legs and rose from his bed of tramped-down foliage. All about him were the slumbering members of his children's crusade, their sounds of their soft snores and gentle stirs a complement to the never-ending soundtrack of the jungle. He watched them in the pre-dawn darkness, his eyes as sharply attuned as the animals stalking through the dense vegetation.

A quartet of shadowy figures emerged from the trees. Peter and his friends, returned from their advance scouting mission. Three of the boys sat down near the center of camp, passing a canteen of water between them. They communicated through facial expressions and hand gestures, a secret, silent language they'd developed on their jungle forays.

Father Xavier folded his blanket and sat down on it, gesturing for Peter to sit at his side.

"All quiet to the north," Peter said, dropping onto the blanket. "But to the east, we saw more white people. Some dressed as soldiers."

"Like the last group of dead men you returned to God?" Father Xavier asked.

The scout nodded. "Yes. They wore the same uniform. But these were not dead men. They ate food and spoke to each other. And they had guns and cars."

"If they have cars, they'll have to follow the old logging road. That means they'll be well to the east of us, at least for another day or two."

"There's a Ka'Longho village on that road," Peter reminded him.

"Then the Ghost People will figure out what to do with these white men," Father Xavier said. "If the village hasn't been abandoned entirely."

Peter shrugged. "We didn't go that far. There were dead men in that part of the jungle. Too many for us to collect heads. But we could hear them. We could smell them."

"Some of the General's men returned from the grave."

"Yes, Father. They walk in circles like mad dogs."

"You've done well, Peter. Thank you." Father Xavier patted the boy's shoulder and told him to rest. There was still time for an hour of sleep before the camp would begin to stir to life. The scout picked his way through the maze of sleeping children and joined his friends. They passed the canteen to him as he sat down. Father Xavier watched them finish their silent conversation and settle down onto the bare ground, using their skinny forearms as pillows. The sight of these children sleeping stung Father Xavier, as it always did. Many of them hadn't slept in an actual bed in over a year. The younger ones might not even remember what that experience was like. If a new age was truly at hand, as his dreams promised, he hoped it wasn't as cruel as the current one.

Peter had given him plenty to think about. The presence of the white men was puzzling. They weren't American military or UN peacekeepers. He doubted the political dithering had reached a sudden conclusion in the weeks since Father Xavier had, in accordance with his dreams, cut ties with the world and taken his flock into the jungle. If the first world countries truly cared about Daroka, they would have stepped in as soon as General Mbowi took control of the army and killed the prime minister. The foreign governments hadn't acted in the immediate aftermath of the disaster at the Marsh Industries research center. Why would they act now? More than likely, these white men were mercenaries. Such men were like vultures. They circled the carcasses of failed states, looking to fatten themselves on the carrion of collapsed governments. In the chaotic aftermath of regime change and civil war, fortunes could be made. It was the new colonialism: all the thrill of easy exploitation with none of the tedium of treaties and trade agreements. As a nation, Daroka was as good as dead, but that didn't change the mineral rich soil on which it had been built.

Father Xavier shook his head to clear these thoughts. The time for such musings was over. He wasn't making sermons for his camcorder anymore. He'd spent much of his life pleading with the world for some measure of sanity, only to see that world edge closer and closer to madness until, finally, it plunged over the cliff. Now, it was in freefall. The dead were no longer content to lie silent in their graves. In the age old struggle between chaos and order, chaos had declared victory. All that was left was to lead his flock to safety. And all he had to guide him were his dreams, which would have, in a saner age, been a laughably flimsy basis for a pilgrimage. But what other course of action was available to him? The figure in his dream beckoned. Father Xavier felt he had no choice but to follow. The important thing was to avoid this group of mercenaries. If the heads Peter and the other scouts had collected belonged to other members of their group, the mercenaries weren't likely to be in any mood to hear explanations. Experience told Father Xavier that "shoot first, ask questions later" was practically a religious mantra for the men who fancied themselves soldiers of fortune.

"Lord, give me the strength to face another day," he sighed.

They broke camp two hours later, marching slowly northward.

5

The totem was hanging from a tree limb that extended over their camp. It was impossible to miss. The totem was no simple thing, after all. It was a complex arrangement of brightly dyed twine woven around a giant snail shell. The same twine had been used to make a garland of dried flowers and bird bones, which trailed from the bottom of the shell.

When Lia and London returned from their perimeter walk, they found Zantoro staring up at the totem, while Vincent and Osbourne peered into the trees, their rifles at the ready.

"You see this shit, boss?" Zantoro jabbed the barrel of his rifle toward the totem. "Some motherfucker is putting some sort of voodoo hex on us."

Lia climbed atop the hood of the Jeep to get a closer look. She took out her pocket knife and sawed through the knotted twine that fastened the totem to the tree limb. She examined the totem, turning it over in her hands, although she knew from first glance what it was. Unlike the hex Zantoro hypothesized, the totem was in fact meant to provide protection.

"It's not a hex at all," she said, climbing off the Jeep. "This was put here for our protection."

Zantoro laughed. "Well, shit, I guess we shouldn't have bothered taking guard duty shifts. We had that authentic native handicraft hanging over our heads. And speaking of guard duty, what the fuck were the two of you up to, huh?"

"We were just talking," Lia snapped, not caring for the defensive note in her voice. "I couldn't sleep, that's all."

"Yeah, I bet," Zantoro snickered. He looked at Vincent and Osbourne. "You boys know a good cure for insomnia?"

Max emerged from the trees, still hitching up his pants. Lia knew that he was too shy about his bathroom habits to relieve himself anywhere within earshot, and he glanced around the camp in confusion.

"What's going on?" he asked in French.

"Nothing. We just had a nighttime visit from the Ka'Longho," she answered in the same language. "They think it's some sort of voodoo curse."

The one named Vincent surprised her by joining in the conversation. He spoke French haltingly and with a strange accent, but his command of the language wasn't terrible. "And my friend Zantoro makes jokes about your woman and the boss going in the woods for a good time. Don't be angry. It's jokes only."

"See," London said, putting a hand on her shoulder. "We're not all uneducated swine. Just Zantoro."

"Awful early in the morning for flattery, but I'll take it." Zantoro bowed dramatically. "Still, the question remains. What were you doing while someone sneaked into camp, shimmied up that tree, and left behind this little decoration?"

"They're called the Ghost People for a reason," Lia said. "With all due respect to your military training, there could have been a dozen Ka'Longho tribesmen walking through this camp while you were asleep and you'd never know it."

Zantoro scoffed.

"And here's something else to consider: if they meant us any harm, we wouldn't be having this conversation," she continued.

"You believe this shit?" Zantoro glanced around for support.

"She has a point, Zantoro," London said. "After all, you were here when they shimmied up the tree and hung that ornament."

"I've always been a deep sleeper," Zantoro said.

"Yeah," Vincent laughed, "just not a deep thinker."

"Fuck you, man. You get that or need me to say it in French?"

"Knock it off, you idiots," London sighed. He turned to Lia. "So, these Ghost People, do they got a village or something like that near here?"

"They're not quite nomads, but they move around a bit," Lia explained. "But I imagine they're close by if they left us this message."

"Look, boss," Zantoro said, his face suddenly serious, "are we sure we should go looking for these Ghost People? Way I understand it, those motherfuckers are cannibals." He paused, turning to look at Lia. "And to hear you tell it, they're sneaky fuckers. Could be they got to Mikkelson and his boys."

"No," Lia insisted. "The Ka'Longho would never kill your friends. That cannibalism stuff is exaggerated nonsense. When a Ka'Longho shaman dies, part of the tribe's funeral rites involves cutting away parts of the shaman's body so that each member of the tribe can eat a part of his flesh. It's no more than a small bite. They don't practice cannibalism on a large scale, and would certainly never attempt it with someone outside the tribe."

"Yeah?" Zantoro sneered. "How do you know that?"

"Because I spent ten months living with them," she explained.

"It's true," Max said. "Maybe you saw the documentary *The World of the Ghost People*? We made that back in 1997."

Zantoro shook his head. "Hey, if it doesn't star Schwarzenegger or Van Damme, I ain't interested."

Now it was Max's turn to sneer. "Now there's a shocking revelation. The clown likes adolescent cinema."

Lia grabbed Max's arm and pulled him back. She didn't think Zantoro would attack him—London's team seemed too disciplined for that—but there was no reason to strain the relationship any further. She looked to London for support, and he gave a slight nod of agreement.

"Didn't I say knock off the bullshit?" he barked. "Break out the breakfast grub so we can eat. The sun is coming up and we got miles to cover."

The team grumbled, but they didn't argue. Osbourne selected some MRE pouches from the supply box in the Jeep and passed them out. The food was barely edible, but Lia was thankful for it nonetheless. Much of the food in the Land Rover had been splattered with blood in the aftermath of Dominic's attack on his stepfather. They'd discarded much of it, fearing possible contamination. They ate fast, and within fifteen minutes, they were back on the road.

Although Lia and Max took the lead again, this time Lia let Max drive. She told him to keep his speed low, even on the rare smooth patches of ground. She wanted to be able to scan their surroundings for signs of the Ka'Longho. She didn't have to search very hard. Although the untrained eye might have missed the signs left behind by the Ghost People, she had studied their culture with intense fascination during her time among them. And she recognized the signs left in the trees: a small cluster of ground-growing flowers left on a high tree branch, a freshly killed snake stretched across the road, and a pile of brightly dyed bird feathers on a rock. Not only had the Ka'Longho followed this road, but they'd also left behind clear signs to mark their way. Lia recognized them immediately.

"You see that?" she said, drawing Max's attention to the pile of feathers.

"They're pointing us in the direction of their village." Max nodded. "But are you sure that's really somewhere you want to bring that cowboy posse?"

"You know, for someone who's supposedly open minded about all cultures, you're making a lot of snap judgments."

"Open minded about other cultures is one thing," he said, pointedly looking away from her. "Sneaking off into the jungle to fuck someone who might have orders to kill us is something else entirely. Besides, these bastards have no culture to be open minded about."

"What the fuck, man?" Lia recoiled as if slapped. "You have no right."

He shrugged. "Maybe, maybe not."

Lia let it go. This wasn't the first time Max's jealousy had reared its ugly head. She concentrated instead on reading the signs left by the Ka'Longho. And they told her that the village was close, perhaps less than a kilometer away.

"Stop the car," she said.

Max braked gently, but maintained his icy silence.

Lia sighed. On top of everything else, Max had decided to revisit his unrequited feelings for her. When he drunkenly confessed his romantic interest—during a relatively quiet press junket covering a billionaires' conference in the Netherlands—Lia had politely rebuffed him. The following morning, through the fog of a hangover, he apologized and seemed to understand that it was a dead end street. Lia had initially feared that Max's whisky-bolstered confession would taint their working relationship, but things had gone back to normal in short order. Now it seemed that the question wasn't as settled as Lia had hoped.

"Max," she said, "this is neither the time nor the place to revisit this."

His silence continued.

"Fine," she said. "If you're not going to speak to me, then at least listen. I'm going to the village alone. Give me an hour head start, then follow me. Park the vehicles outside the village. Tell the Americans to leave their rifles behind. They can bring their pistols, but we don't want to send the wrong message."

Max glanced at her and nodded, but he didn't speak.

"Please, try behave like an adult while I'm gone. Don't pick fights."

He still had nothing to say.

"Okay, if that's how you'd like it." She jumped out of the car and walked a few paces back to the Jeep. She stopped at the driver's side door and explained the situation to London.

"Are you sure it's safe for you to go in by yourself?" he asked.

"It will be fine," she assured him. "As long as I approach the village the right way."

"And what does that mean?"

She looked at him, then at the other three Americans. She smiled. "Please keep in mind that we are all adults here. I don't have anything you haven't seen before."

In the passenger seat, Zantoro perked up. "What's that supposed to mean?"

She didn't answer. He'd get that answer soon enough.

Lia's career as an investigative journalist had taken her to some exotic locales full of fascinating people and societies far removed from what the Western world thought of as civilization. Her ability to integrate herself into herself into these far-flung and often reclusive societies was nearly unparalleled in her field. Her gender made this ability all the more astounding. Although she'd encountered some matriarchal cultures, many of those she studied tended to subscribe to the view that it was indeed a man's world. The Ka'Longho were one of the few cultures that seemed truly egalitarian when it came to gender roles. She'd spent the better part of year with the tribe, and as far as she could tell, they were as close as any culture on earth to achieving true equality. They had the same strict punishments for adultery and rape as some of the other native tribes she'd encountered, but where the Ka'Longho differed was that these laws were applied equally to men. The narration for Lia's documentary asserted that the Ka'Longho had a better concept of sexual consent than most of the so-called civilized cultures of the world. As such, she wasn't afraid to approach their village in a way the Ka'Longho understood: almost completely nude.

She rummaged through the rear of the Land Rover for her duffel bag. Sitting on the back bumper, she removed her boots and socks. Then, with a glance back at the Americans, she removed the rest of her clothes. There were whoops of approval and a smattering of applause from the Jeep, followed by London's voice ordering his men to silence. Lia replaced her shoes with a pair of sandals she'd packed for the trip.

Max climbed out of the passenger side and made his way around the Land Rover, pausing to glare at the Americans. He turned to Lia and shook his head in disapproval, then went back to the Jeep to explain exactly what was going on to the Americans. Lia could feel everyone's eyes on her, but she ignored it. They were in the jungle now, and puritanical shame had no place here.

She found a tube of benzoyl peroxide sunscreen in her duffel. It was the thick white stuff that tourists smeared on their noses at the beach. It was a far cry from the body paint that the Ka'Longho made from local plants and minerals, but she supposed it would work in a pinch. She squeezed a thick blob of it into her palm, then, working from memory, she did her best to recreate the markings of a spiritual pilgrim who comes in peace. She'd applied such markings during the making of her documentary. Max had done the same. For their first month among the Ghost People, they'd both rigorously applied the markings each morning. Eventually, once they'd gained the tribe's trust, they'd been allowed to once again wear clothing. Had the Christian missionaries who'd sought to convert the Ka'Longho stripped down and applied the proper body paint, they might not have been so roundly rejected.

She pulled her hair back into a ponytail, then marked her forehead with the symbols meaning "peace" and "visitor." Next, she drew a spiral on the left side of her chest, over her heart. The spiral was a sacred symbol for the Ka'Longho. Although their concept of god was nebulous, having more in common with pantheistic religions than anything else, the Ka'Longho used the spiral in the same way that Christians used the cross. It was a symbol that brought luck, warded off evil, and designated its wearer as a like-minded individual. She drew circles around her nipples and a series of wavy lines over her belly. These indicated that, although she was fertile and still of child bearing age, she wasn't seeking a partner. She daubed the backs of her hands with three small dots, indicating that she was willing to give aid to anyone in need. Although she wasn't sure what she could do for the tribe, it seemed like a gesture of goodwill, and given the circumstances, she figured there could never be enough goodwill.

She put the cap back on the tube of sunscreen and tossed it into her bag. London leaned out of the Jeep and called out to her.

"Good luck," he said. "Whatever happens, we'll be along shortly."

"Remember, no big guns," she reminded him. "As long as they don't feel threatened, the Ka'Longho will play nice."

He gave her a thumbs-up. She returned the gesture, then started walking.

It didn't feel strange to be headed for the village of the Ghost People; it felt strange to be doing it alone. It occurred to her as she walked that this was the first time she'd gone into such a setting without Max at her side. He'd been with her at every combat zone or crime scene or native village she'd ever visited. He'd been at her side every time she'd thrown hard questions at corrupt politicians and businessmen. He'd followed her on her undercover jobs, maintaining enough distance to remain inconspicuous, but staying close enough to act as back-up if things took a bad turn. The thought made her feel guilty. And the feeling was compounded by her relief at leaving him behind this time. Ever since that night in Utrecht, when he'd drunkenly leaned in and attempted to kiss her, things between them had been tense. For the past year, she'd been able to shrug it off, mostly because they hadn't been involved in anything that took them into the field for prolonged periods. Now that they were back to globe-trotting, the weird tension had wormed its way back to the surface of their relationship. And this time, Max couldn't blame it on liquor or jet lag.

Focus, she reminded herself. *Whether or not you have experience with the Ka'Longho, this is still a dangerous thing you're doing.*

The road ran through the middle of the village. It was impossible to tell whether the logging company had bulldozed a path through the village or if it had been constructed after Mbowi staged his coup and sent the foreign companies packing (well, except for Marsh Industries, anyway). Part of what made it hard to know was the seemingly slapdash construction of the buildings. They were little more than lean-to's, made of scrap materials left behind by the logging company. Since the Ka'Longho frequently abandoned their villages and moved to new locations according to the visions of the tribe's shaman, their structures were never built to last. An abandoned Ka'Longho village crumbled not long after the tribe moved on. As Lia understood it, the tribe never spent longer than three years in one place, and even that was considered a prolonged occupancy by their standards.

As she walked into the village, she drew a crowd of spectators. Children ran from behind the houses to walk alongside her. The adults put aside their work and turned their attention her way. Gradually, a ripple of recognition spread through the crowd. The Pale Sister—the name bestowed on her by the tribal leader—had returned. In moments, the villagers surrounded her, welcoming their friend back into their midst. The crowd ushered her to the one structure in the village that appeared to have been constructed with any care. She recognized the wizened old man who emerged from the building. His name was Hutoh, and he was the tribe's shaman.

"Pale Sister," he said, drawing her into an embrace.

Lia ransacked her memory to come up with enough of the Ka'Longho language to converse. She remembered how to greet an elder, and she did so as Hutoh released her.

"I have…" She closed her eyes, searching for the words. "I have friends coming soon. They are peaceful."

Hutoh turned and made an announcement to the rest of the village. The word was out: visitors were coming.

6

London was no expert on relationship matters, but he had a pretty good idea of why the French photographer had spent the better part of the hour glaring at him. He thought he might try explaining to Max that nothing had happened with Lia during the previous night's guard duty, but London figured it would be a waste of time.

"You getting tired of that frog eye-fucking you?" Zantoro asked. "I can go knock him around for you. He doesn't look like much, but it might be fun."

London shook his head. "Stand down. Besides, it's about time for us to roll out anyway."

"You change your mind, I'll toss my name in the hat too," Osbourne said from the backseat. "That dude is starting to piss me off. That comment about Schwarzenegger movies was way out of line."

"You guys are idiots," London laughed.

He was relieved when Max fired up the Land Rover. Another few minutes of stewing in their own boredom and London's team might decide to start a fight just to pass the time. They were used to action. Pendleton Security employed plenty of bodyguards and surveillance teams who were used to sitting around during their assignments. London's team wasn't like that. They were a strike squad, accustomed to blitzkrieg operations that were often as brutal and bloody as they were fast-paced.

The final leg of the journey to the Ka'Longho village was easy enough. They parked a minute's walk from the village, locking their rifles in the Jeep's storage compartment.

"Stay sharp, guys," London said as the team climbed out of the vehicle. "Lia says these people are friendlies, but who knows how far that courtesy extends."

Max waited for them beside the Land Rover, his arms folded over his chest. As they approached, he sniffed dismissively.

Holy shit, London thought, *this guy is living up to every stereotype.*

"Try not to embarrass us," Max said as he led the way. "Lia and I spent a long time earning their trust."

London shot Zantoro a look before he could retort. While Max had certainly earned whatever insult Zantoro was going to toss his way, it was better for all involved if someone took the high road.

Lia met them at the entrance to the village. London didn't know if he was disappointed or relieved to see that the Ka'Longho had furnished her with clothing. On one hand, he would miss seeing all she had to offer, but on the other, it was much easier to deal with his team when they didn't have a naked woman to ogle. And that didn't take into account his own embarrassment. But the truth was, Lia was awful easy on the eyes, whether she was wearing her birthday suit or the basic single-shoulder tunic the villagers had provided her. A quick glance around the village told London all he needed to know about the natives' attitude towards clothing. Simply put, they didn't seem to give two shits about modesty. The men and women both wore variations on the loincloth. A handful of the women wore something like halter tops or tunics like the one they'd given to Lia, but they were few and far between. The children ran around bare-assed, and seemed to be enjoying the sight of the visitors. A crowd of kids surrounded them as Lia led the way through the village.

"I take it we're not considered much of a threat," London said. He kept his hand on his holster, not because he felt imminent danger, but rather to keep one of the kids from having a terrible accident.

"They seemed a little wary until I met up with Hutoh, the tribe's shaman," she explained. "He told me he'd been expecting us."

"Hutoh is still alive?" Max insinuated himself between Lia and London. "I can't wait to see him."

Lia nodded. "He must be over ninety years old, but you wouldn't know it by looking at him."

"That's great!" Max's voice was full of exaggerated cheer. London figured he was feeling bad about his earlier interaction with Lia and was overcompensating.

There was a lot of hubbub in the village. London wondered how much of it was on account of the visitors. He figured nearly all of it was. A tribe known as the Ghost People, and who had a reputation for chowing down on their enemies, probably didn't get much in the way of company. But much of what London saw was familiar. A crew of local guys were carrying a trio of freshly slaughtered pigs on a massive spit through the crowd. They were heading straight for one of their buddies, who was busy stoking the coals of a fire. Like any good Texan, London knew a barbecue when he saw one. It reminded him of his childhood, when the ranch hands would spend a Saturday drinking beer and cooking *cabrito* over post oak coals. He didn't know what the Ka'Longho would serve in the way of side dishes, but some pulled pork and ribs would sure as hell be an improvement over the MREs they'd been eating.

"I swear, boss," Osbourne said, following London's line of

sight, "if these dudes have a keg of beer hidden somewhere, let's just say fuck it and go native."

Vincent and Zantoro yucked it up, letting the kids climb all over them.

"It's a big occasion," Lia explained. "Not only do they get visitors today, but there's a funeral celebration tonight."

"I take it that a funeral isn't a solemn occasion for these folks," London said.

"Hardly," Max broke in. "Just because westerners dress in black and cry doesn't mean the rest of the world works like that. I know how hard it is for Americans to remember that there's a world outside their borders."

London began to regret his decision to keep Zantoro from kicking the photographer's ass. He let the comment slide. There was a time when he might have given Max a black eye on general principle, and yeah, maybe impress Lia in the bargain. But these days, he figured it wasn't worth the effort, and besides, he'd finally figured out that most women, especially ones with brains, weren't impressed by macho bullshit. So he let Max yack for a minute about funeral customs. The short version of the lecture was that a Ka'Longho funeral was an excuse for a party. Their word for "funeral" was the same as their words for "reunion" and "homecoming."

Lia explained this quirk of vocabulary, adding, "And that's why Hutoh sees this as some sort of omen. You have me and Max reuniting with the tribe, plus a funeral service for two of the tribe's warriors."

"A double whammy, huh?" London laughed. "Well, it looks like we get a barbecue anyway."

"Yes," Lia said, "and in more than one way. The warriors are going to be cremated."

London nodded. If she wanted to shock him, she was going to have to do better than an open-air cremation. He'd seen men burned alive on more than one occasion. At least these tribal warriors were going to be dead when they went up in flames.

"And because it's such a big deal," Lia continued, "Hutoh wants to speak to you in his hut."

"Oh yeah?" London asked.

Max made something like a gagging sound and let loose with a string of rapid fire French. London didn't understand a single word, but he got the message loud and clear.

"Come on," Lia said, reaching across Max to grab London's elbow. "Hutoh's place is just over here."

London told his team to behave themselves, then he let Lia drag him through the crowd of excited kids to a small circular structure that wasn't unlike a Native American teepee. They had to squat and enter through the low doorway, one at a time. The interior was dim, illuminated only by the thin shafts of sunlight that penetrated the gaps in the thatched exterior. The ground was covered by overlapping layers of animal hide. In the center of the room sat an old man. If Max had been right about the man's age, London was impressed. Although his face was deeply lined and his eyelids were droopy, the man looked like he could still hold his own in a scrap. His shoulders were wide and his posture ramrod straight. His arms were covered in ropy muscles, his chest covered in scars.

He spoke something in his native tongue and motioned for London and Lia to have a seat.

As soon as their asses touched down, Hutoh launched into a monologue. Lia nodded and occasionally fired back a few phrases of her own. She spoke the language haltingly, but Hutoh seemed to understand just fine.

"I'm a bit rusty, but I think I got most of that," Lia said, turning slightly to speak to London. "He says that the end of the world is drawing near. There's some sort of disease that is spreading through the people of Daroka, and it has claimed several members of the tribe. He says his people are scared and that some of them have even suggested reviving the old ways in order to appease the angry gods."

"The old ways involve cannibalism, right?"

Lia nodded. "He said that the plague came to the village in the form of rats."

Hutoh spoke again. Lia interjected a few questions, and the shaman grew increasingly animated as he answered.

Lia translated, "He says that the Ka'Longho will be moving north soon, to some destination he's seen in his dreams. They've been sending advance scouting parties out ahead of their departure. The two warriors that are being cremated tonight, they'd been part of that scout party. They stumbled into the village yesterday, about a week overdue. Both men were wounded, near death, but they had enough strength to tell their story."

"This is starting to sound ominous," London said.

"Yeah, well, just wait," Lia continued, "because it gets worse. These warriors say they encountered some people in the jungle that were…"

Hutoh broke in, gesturing expansively as he spoke. Lia nodded.

"Mike," she said, "what the warriors described to Hutoh sounds a lot like what we saw at the mission. They said that they ran into a group of walking dead men who were followed by a herd of rats. These dead men, most of them were white."

"White men? Rats?" London shook his head. "Could it be some people who escaped from the research center? I mean, if they were doing medical testing up there, they probably had a bunch of lab rats, right? They still do that sort of thing, don't they?"

"I don't doubt that all of this horror can be traced back to that research facility, but Hutoh tells me that some of the dead men wore uniforms like yours."

The shaman seemed to understand. He extended a finger,

pointing at the patch on London's chest. It was the eagle perched atop a clenched fist, the Pendleton Security logo.

"Mikkelson's team..." London swallowed, his throat suddenly dry. "Fuck."

Hutoh spoke again, grabbing Lia's shoulder for emphasis. She translated, "These men attacked the warriors with such ferocity that the warriors retreated. They probably wouldn't have been able to escape, but a group of children with machetes came out of the trees and...Mike, I'm so sorry...but the children cut the white men's heads off. But you must understand, they were...infected."

"Children with machetes coming out of the trees?" London asked.

"Have you heard of Father Xavier Arnaud?"

He nodded. "When I was briefed about this operation, his name came up. My employers said he was part of some counter-insurgent group in Daroka. I figured him for some wild-eyed socialist revolutionary. We've seen guys in South America like that, priests who give out bread and wine on Sunday, then pass out the Ak-47s and the hand grenades on Monday."

"Your employers? You mean Marsh Industries?" Her laugh was short and bitter. "Yeah, they would say that."

"Lia, I'm just a guy earning a paycheck. I don't do politics."

"Well, you can keep telling yourself that, but eventually, everyone has to choose what side they're on. And let me tell you, there's really only two sides to this thing: the right side and whatever side Marsh Industries is on. You're a good man. Don't ask me how I can know that, but I do. I can feel it. But good man or not, you're on a leash. Might be time to think about who's holding the other end."

"Look, you just told me some of my coworkers got whacked by machete-toting child soldiers. Maybe take it easy on me for a minute, huh?"

"I'm sorry about your friends. Really, I am. But if you're still planning on protecting Marsh Industries, you can expect more of the same. The people of Daroka have had enough."

"You're going to get a nosebleed if you don't come down a bit from that moral high ground," London said. "And if dead people are really walking around, then all bets are off. I'm already getting the idea my company has hung us out to dry. I just want to get to that research facility and get to the bottom of this."

"Get to the bottom of it? Or help cover it up?"

"Jesus, lady, can you cut me a break here?" London shook his head in disbelief. "I swear, you're something else."

"Or maybe you're just not used to a woman not swooning instantly when you wear that uniform and speak with that accent."

"What the fuck are you even talking about?"

The sound of Hutoh's laughter was so loud and sudden that both of them jumped. The old shaman slapped his knees and barked a string of words at Lia, then laughed again.

Lia made a face then said something that made Hutoh laugh even louder.

"What did the old dude just say?" London asked.

"He asked if we were married. He said only married people argue like this. When I told him we'd only known each other for a day, he said we must have been married in a past life."

London gave Hutoh a look, then shrugged. Language barrier or not, the shaman seemed to get the message loud and clear: *women.*

"I'm sorry," Lia said, letting out a long breath. "It's just…"

"No, I get it," London said, touching her arm. "This is uncharted territory. I've seen some scary shit in my time—both of us have—but this is something way over the line. Dead people getting up and biting chunks out of people, spreading some sickness that may have been cooked up in a Marsh Industries lab for God only knows what purpose…"

Hutoh grew serious again as he spoke to Lia.

"He wants to know if we've seen an underground city in our dreams," Lia translated.

London shook his head. "Since I've been in country, I only got a handful of hours' sleep. No dreams that I can remember."

She exchanged a few words with Hutoh, then turned back to London. When she spoke, her voice was hushed, her face pale. All the indignant anger was gone, replaced by something London didn't recognize. "He wants to know if you will enter the dream world so you can see this underground city. He says that, although our paths to the city are different, it's the ultimate destination for many people. When the dead claim this world, those whose souls are worthy will begin a new world below."

London scoffed. "Let me guess, it's like an acid trip."

"It's nothing like that…" She paused. "Okay, well, maybe it's a *little* like that. There's nothing to be afraid of, though. It's just a shot of liquor made from the petals of certain flowers and dried toad skin. I've done it before. They call it the Soul Nectar."

"No way," London laughed. "Come on, *Soul Nectar*? It sounds like a bad alternative rock band."

"Please just consider it," she said. "Because I've seen the same city in my dreams."

"I've never done anything like that. Drugs aren't my thing. I'm a shot-of-whiskey-and-a-can-of-Budweiser guy. Sorry."

"Please." She scooted closer to him until their thighs touched.

London knew what she was doing, but that didn't make it any easier to refuse.

"Look, if you're scared, I understand. I was scared my first time." She put her hand on his knee. "I'll go with you. To the dream world, I mean. I'll drink the Soul Nectar too. Please, Mike. It only lasts a few hours. If nothing else, you look like you could use a nap."

Mike opened his mouth to reply, but he came up empty. He couldn't believe that he was actually considering this nonsense. But the world had clearly gone insane, and maybe, just maybe, the only sane response was to go with the flow.

Hutoh passed Lia a small bottle stoppered with a tightly rolled leather plug. Then the old man rose from his seat and left the hut, taking care to cover the entrance with a flap of animal hide.

"Well?" Lia asked, holding up the bottle.

"You first," London said.

7

During the time she spent among the Ka'Longho, Lia had taken three different "dream quests," as the tribe called them. The first one had been administered as a sort of test. Once she'd gone into the dream world and returned unscathed, she'd earned the tribe's respect and trust. According to tribal legends, an impure soul who embarked on a dream quest couldn't return to the land of the living. The unlucky owner of the soul would live out their days in a catatonic state, hovering between the dream world and waking life until death finally claimed them.

She'd assumed that what the Ka'Longho were describing was actually an overdose and proceeded with the same caution with which she'd approached LSD use during her college days. But after hearing Hutoh's description of his dreams of an underground city, she wasn't so sure the Soul Nectar was a simple hallucinogen. Since she'd witnessed the scene at the Our Lady of Peace mission, the few certainties she had were crumbling away. When the dead would no longer stay dead, what certainties could one hold onto? And besides, she *had* dreamed of the underground city. Every night since she'd come to Daroka, she'd dreamed of a city on the far bank of an underground river. A strange city full of gravity-defying architecture and streets made of smooth stone. Hutoh had described the dreams exactly, right down to the strange lights overhead and the hooded figure on the opposite side of the river beckoning, with inhumanly long arms outstretched.

She pulled the stopper from the small jug and winced as the fumes hit her nostrils. London laughed at her reaction.

"It smells worse than it tastes," she said, although she knew she was stretching the truth.

"When I was a kid, my uncle made moonshine. Whatever is in that jug can't taste any worse than Uncle Roger's strawberry rhubarb 'shine. That stuff could strip paint off the walls."

Lia raised the liquor to her lips and took a small mouthful. It burned a line of fire from her tongue to the pit of her stomach. She tried to keep her gag reflex at bay as she passed the jug to London.

"Bottoms up, huh?" His eyes widened when the liquor hit his tongue. They squeezed shut as he swallowed. He coughed and sputtered. "Holy shit goddamn. That was awful."

Lia stoppered the jug and set it aside.

"So, what now?" London asked. "Do we just wait for it to kick in?"

"It won't take long," she replied.

"I can't fucking believe I let you talk me into this."

"Just relax." Lia could already feel the Soul Nectar started to diffuse into her blood. Her vision grew fuzzy at the edges. A pleasant weightless sensation crept into her belly.

London laughed. "Yeah, I'll try to relax as I sit in a medicine man's hut in a war-torn country in Africa, where, oh yeah, there's a little problem with the living dead. Sure, I'll relax."

Lia pressed a finger to her lips. "Shhh. Just let it happen."

London's apparent discomfort began to dissolve. His

shoulders relaxed and his expression softened. He sighed and leaned back on his elbows, stretching out his legs.

"Okay, maybe this ain't so bad," he said.

Lia giggled at his understatement. As the sacred liquor worked its magic, her nerves tingled pleasantly. Her equilibrium slipped, and the hut's walls seemed to swirl around her. It had none of the sloshing seasick sensation that came with drunkenness, but rather the tranquil sense of bobbing like a cork down a gently flowing river. She swayed as she pushed herself to her feet. Her body was loose and warm. She closed her eyes and let the sensation wash over her. There was drowsiness on the horizon, but it was still too distant to drag her into the darkness of sleep. For now, her body was wide awake with pleasant sensations.

"What…" London shook his head slowly, as if still trying to fight against the effects of the liquor. "What are you doing?"

Lia realized that she'd shrugged off the simple clothing the Ka'Longho had given her. She stood in the middle of the hut, wearing nothing but a few remaining smudges of improvised body paint.

"I'm doing…" She smiled, tracing her fingers over her breasts. "I'm doing what you should be doing."

"Yeah?"

She nodded, running her hands over herself. "Feels good."

London tried to stand but stumbled and went down on his ass. He fumbled with the laces of his boots until they finally came untied. He tugged the boots off his feet and tossed them over his shoulder. His second attempt at standing was successful. Once he was upright, he swayed gently, his arms outstretched for balance.

Lia stepped forward until they were toe-to-toe. Her fingers groped blindly at his waistband until they managed to unbutton his pants. His balance grew steady enough for him to help her unbutton his shirt. Working as a team, they managed to get his shirt off. They laughed softly as he struggled to untangle his feet from his pants. Then, at long last, they pressed their naked bodies together. They kissed. It wasn't the tentative, gentle action of two people sharing their first kiss. Their tongues worked frantically against each other. When they parted, both gasped for air for a moment before going back in for an encore performance.

Lia stepped back, wiping her mouth with the back of her hand. She stood there for a moment, looking at him. His eyes were heavy-lidded and half-closed as he stared back at her. He swayed slightly on his feet, but remained upright. Lia held his gaze for a moment, then glanced down to check if his arousal was as complete as hers. His erection jutted out from his body.

"I want it," she said.

He babbled a string of nonsense syllables that sounded enthusiastic enough. She pulled him to the ground, nearly tackling him, then mounted him. The sacred liquor sang in her veins. Stars burst in the hot interior of the hut, throwing tracers of light from the ceiling to the ground, which melted into swirling pools of color. She sighed as she lowered herself. London raised his hips, pressing deeper into her. They moved in concert, moaning and grunting. The world around them melted away in drips of liquid color until there was nothing left, only the two of them.

Alone in their private universe, they burst like fireworks and dissolved into the black cocoon of slumber.

8

London's body awoke before he opened his eyes. He wiggled his fingers and toes. He took a deep breath. Everything seemed to be in working order. He opened his eyes slowly, expecting the mother of all hangovers to swing a sledgehammer at his frontal lobe. Miraculously, the sledgehammer never came. In fact, he felt pretty good. He sat up and stretched his arms over his head and yawned. Then he glanced around, bewildered by what he saw around him.

He remembered fighting unsuccessfully against the pull of sleep as he wilted inside Lia. He remembered her shuddering as she lay atop him, their heavy, animalistic panting slowly changing to the soft, regular breathing of sleep. He remembered being inside the shaman's tent. But he'd awoken alone on a riverbank. A quick glance at his surroundings told him he was inside a cave so large that it staggered the imagination. The ceiling was so high that the cave had its own clouds. Light came from overhead, although there was no sun in evidence. On the far side of the river was a city carved from stone.

London stood and walked closer to the river until the water lapped at his toes. He felt a momentary rush of shame at his nakedness until he realized that he was alone. He knew where he was, of course. He was in the dream world, visiting the mysterious locale from the Ka'Longho shaman's dream.

From Lia's dream…

He waded into the water until it rose to his waist. The current seemed gentle enough, so he started swimming toward the other bank. It was easy going. He didn't have to strain against the current. If anything, the river seemed to pull him along, carrying him forward. It only took a minute or two to reach the shallows on the other side. He stood up, naked and dripping, and walked onto the riverbank.

The stone city was even stranger when viewed from the other side of the river. The buildings had been designed by a people who followed a system of architecture completely alien to London. The structures were bizarre, yet beautiful. Some of them seemed to defy gravity, their delicate arches and complex spirals reaching out at impossible angles. Others seemed to have been carved out of single massive blocks of stone. He walked through the winding streets and avenues, the streets smooth and cool beneath his bare feet. Strange trees lined the streets, their limbs bowed with the weight of oddly-shaped, multicolored fruit, and flowers with iridescent petals.

At the center of the city was a vast open space of lush grass and wildflowers. Atop one of these hills stood a figure dressed in a hooded black robe. The breeze was gentle, but it stirred the black fabric as if it were nearly insubstantial. The figure raised an arm, and with one impossibly long, skeletal finger, beckoned London to come forward.

London took one step, then…

…awoke with a gasp. Panic took hold of him for a moment as his waking mind struggled free from the lingering traces of the dream. He glanced around the dim interior of the hut with sleep-blurry eyes, breathing deeply as his head cleared. Lia sat next to him. She was still naked, but looked bright-eyed and sober. She certainly didn't appear to have his level of hangover.

"Sort of knocks you down, doesn't it?" she said.

London nodded.

"Here." She passed him a metal flask. "It's just water. You'll feel better after you drink some."

Since his mouth felt like it was full of cotton and sand, he poured half of the flask's contents down his throat. He passed the flask back to her, wiping his mouth with the back of his free hand. He got to his feet, groaning at the soreness of his muscles. Either the liquor had some lingering effects, or the sex had been more athletic than he remembered. Probably some measure of both. It had been quite a while since his last rodeo.

"That was..." He gathered his clothes and began struggling to get them on. "Well, it was quite an experience."

"We can talk about it if you want," she offered.

London laughed. Talk? Hell, he could hardly look her in the eyes at the moment. Maybe after she got dressed.

"Not ready to open up about your feelings?" She stood, tugging her makeshift garment over her shoulders. "I guess the American cowboy hasn't gone extinct after all."

London had managed to get his socks and underpants on. His pant legs were tangled to the point that he had to shake them loose.

"You think this is the appropriate place for that?" he asked.

"I think it's entirely appropriate to talk about whatever you just saw in your dream."

He opened his mouth to respond, but was bailed out by Hutoh's return. The old shaman poked his head into the hut and rattled off a string of chatter. Then, just as suddenly, he withdrew.

"Hurry up and get dressed," Lia said. "The funeral is about to begin."

London tipped her a casual salute as he stomped into his boots. She gave him a look that he couldn't quite read, crossing her arms under breasts, and cocking her hips to one side. He thought it was equally possible that she might start laughing at his hung-over clumsiness as he dressed, or maybe launch into an angry tirade. It was his own fault, of course. Once he'd done the deed with a woman, he lost all perspective. Before their clothes came off, women were just people. Afterwards, they became inscrutable, mysterious. That probably accounted for why he'd come close to marriage without ever taking the plunge. The closer he got to a woman, the less sense she seemed to make.

Lia muttered something in French then left him alone to finish getting dressed.

9

Max Lambert found a shady spot at the edge of the village and sat. He stared at Hutoh's hut, wondering how long the old shaman would keep her in there with London. Then, when Hutoh emerged, closing the hut's door flap behind him, Max gritted his teeth and tried to keep his stomach from boiling over.

No one had ever accused him of being a genius, but Max didn't need a supercharged brain to figure out what was going on in that hut. After all, Lia wasn't the only one who'd lived among the Ka'Longho for the better part of a year. Max had been there too. He knew the shaman had probably given them a dose of Soul Nectar and left them alone so the liquor could work its magic. For all his mystical talk and spiritual mumbo jumbo, the old man was nothing but a pervert. Of course, Max would never give voice to such an observation, not when Lia thought so highly of the man. But that was just how she was. Lia Rousseau—intrepid and fearless journalist, champion of indigenous peoples, and crusader against political corruption—was, beneath all the pomp and accolades, still just a woman.

A beautiful woman who you've chased around the world,

Monsieur Lambert, he thought bitterly. *An ambitious woman who never had any use for your affection, but who has just dropped her panties for the first square-jawed American to smile at her.*

Max shook off the nagging voice in his head. It was no use crying over Lia. She'd made her position perfectly clear. It wasn't as if she'd dangled herself in front of him like bait.

"Hey, Pierre, don't look so heartbroken."

Max looked up and saw one of the Americans—the one with the big mouth, Zantoro—standing over him.

Max stood up, brushing off the seat of his pants. "I don't know what you're talking about."

"Not the first time a pretty French lady got all weak in the knees for an American in uniform," Zantoro said. "Sure, your boss lady comes off like an uptight librarian, but deep down, she's got the same dirty thoughts as the rest of us."

"Shut up. You don't know her."

Zantoro laughed. "I know she stripped down bare-ass naked in front of all of us without missing a beat. And, not that I'm some peeping Tom, but I was standing by that old dude's hut and I heard the noises going on inside. Either he's got the primate house of the nearest zoo stashed away or there was some good lovin' going on."

Max clenched his hands into fists so tightly that he was sure his nails would draw blood from his palms. But he knew better than to take a swing. For one thing, there was no telling how the Ka'Longho would react. And more importantly, he knew how the story would end. Max was no coward, but he was also no idiot. The Americans may have been knuckle-dragging barbarians, but they were mercenaries who fought for a living. Max wouldn't stand a chance in that fight. He knew it, and Zantoro sure as hell knew it.

"Pig," Max spat as he stalked past Zantoro on his way out of the village.

He stopped at the small clearing where they'd parked the vehicles. Hoisting himself onto the hood of the Land Rover, he conjured up in his mind a fantastic scenario in which he dragged Lia out of Hutoh's hut, carried her out of the village, and took her away from all this insanity. If they could cross the border into Borwannah safely, they could be in Kenya in two days, three at the most. They could catch a flight to Paris, and be sipping wine at a café by the weekend. After a couple glasses, Lia might finally accept his proposal, and they'd spend the night making love. Daroka, the American mercenaries, and the living dead would be nothing but a distant memory.

It was the sort of fantasy script he'd written for himself many times over the years, but now it seemed even more implausible. He jettisoned the happy ending for a different scenario, one in which Lia came to him, teary-eyed after being used up, and cast aside by Mike London. In this new, darker fantasy, Lia's plea for Max's love fell on deaf ears. He pushed her away, telling her that he no longer wanted a woman who would lay down with a mercenary dog. He turned his back on her and left her crying. But all this fantasy did was make *him* want to cry.

If only I could live my life again, he mused. *It would be interesting to see where I went wrong.*

The sun was dipping low. Soon it would be lost behind the jungle, and the funeral celebration for the fallen Ka'Longho warriors would begin. But there was still time for one more fantasy. This one was no less bitter than the last, but it was far more plausible. He closed his eyes and imagined himself sneaking up on the American mercenaries as they slept and shooting them one by one, saving London for last. The thought of the American begging for his life brought a smile to Max's lips.

He replayed the scenario in his mind again and again, embellishing and adding detail with each repetition. By the time he heard the first slow pounding beats of the ceremonial drums, his daydream had taken on cinematic quality. It was enough to bring the smile back to his lips as he walked toward the village.

As he made his way toward the collection of ramshackle huts, he passed Lia going the other way.

"Hey," she said, "what are you doing out here?"

He shrugged. "Nothing. What are you doing?"

"Just going to change into my regular clothes." She plucked at the rough Ka'Longho garment. "This just isn't a very flattering look, and besides, it itches."

"Easy to take off, I bet." He resumed his walk toward the village.

"What did you say?" she called after him.

"Oh, nothing." He didn't look back.

10

By the time the drums were pounding and the torches burning, London was feeling more like himself. A couple cups of fruit juice and a plate of roast pork with some sort of mashed root vegetable helped. It wasn't the best barbecue he'd ever had, but it sure as hell beat the MREs. Lia stood beside him as the first of the funeral procession began moving through the village. If dinner was the Ka'Longho equivalent of a barbecue, then the first part of the funeral was their version of a conga line.

It started somewhere on the extreme north end of the village and snaked its way to a flat spot in the middle of the dirt road. The villagers who weren't involved in the parade gathered in a semicircle around the clearing. Some held torches, while others held spears adorned with intricately painted patterns. The rest used their hands to applaud in time with the slow thumping of the drums. They chanted something low and mournful as the men at the head of the procession approached. Each of these men carried an armload of dry branches and dried weeds. They arranged this material into a rough pallet.

"They're constructing a bier for the fallen warriors," Lia

explained, whispering directly into his ear. "The chant you hear is a farewell song. It's somber right now, but later there will be dancing and joyous displays."

"But first they got to give their boys a proper send off," London said. "I get it."

London looked across the clearing to where the rest of his team stood. They appeared transfixed, watching the spectacle with wide eyes. Even Zantoro seemed subdued by the ritual. That was how it was with men in their line of work. They developed a healthy respect for death. When it's your constant companion, you learned to deal with it, to accept it, but contrary to what most people thought, you never truly got used to it. Death was the thing that lurked around every blind corner, in every roadside IED, in every forgotten minefield, and in the careful aim of every enemy combatant. Death had no allegiance. It had no rules of engagement. It was the foe who could not be vanquished. And London didn't need to be psychic to know that each member of his team was thinking over some variation on that theme.

After the first group of men had finished putting the combustible material into its proper arrangement, they stepped aside, forming another semicircle inside the one formed by the villagers.

"The men in the procession are the tribe's warriors," Lia explained. "They'll be the ones to light the fires. Among the Ka'Longho, there is no greater honor."

The chanting took on a slightly desperate note at the appearance of the next members of the funeral procession. These were the pallbearers, and they carried their fallen brothers over their heads. The dead warriors had been wrapped in shrouds woven from leaves and vines, giving them the appearance of large seed pods. The pallbearers fell to their knees and dropped these green bundles onto the pallet of dried sticks and leaves.

London recognized who came at the tail end of the

procession: his new pal Hutoh. Since their meeting in his hut, the shaman had undergone one hell of a costume change. When Lia had introduced them, Hutoh had been wearing the standard Ka'Longho outfit: a simple loincloth. Now, he was wearing a brightly colored robe, cinched at his waist with a snakeskin belt. Atop the old man's head was a headdress made of animal bones and feathers. His thin arms were extended in front of him, his hands gripping a ceramic jug.

The chanting increased in pitch and volume. Somewhere in the crowd of villagers, the unseen drummers commenced beating the hell out of their instruments. London had never heard anything like it. The rhythms were complex and interlocking, not quite chaotic but awful close to it. If the villagers were going to dance to this beat, it was going to be one hell of a display.

Hutoh paused beside the dead men. He raised his jug over his head and shouted a string of guttural syllables that left London marveling at the old man's lung capacity. When he'd finished his eulogy—London figured that's what it had to be —the shaman upended his jug over the bodies, pouring a stream of stinking liquid from head to toe. Some sort of accelerant, London guessed, although it didn't smell like any he'd ever encountered.

Lia grabbed his elbow and pulled him back a few feet. "You might want to step back if you fancy keeping your eyebrows."

The drums beat faster and faster until the rhythm reached a feverish crescendo. Then the villagers tossed their torches onto the bodies. The villagers fell abruptly silent as the liquid which Hutoh had spread over the bodies hit the flames. A fireball *whooshed* into the air. London felt the heat slap him across the face. Lia hadn't been kidding about the possibility of eyebrow loss. Even at this distance, London had to turn his face away.

Then he heard the screams.

No, that wasn't right. The sounds erupting from the funeral pyre weren't screams. They were the same sounds London had heard coming from the infected people back at the mission, only these were louder and tinged with something like bestial panic. The two green bundles, now completely engulfed in flames, thrashed wildly, flinging burning embers out into the assembled crowd.

"Holy shit, this ain't good," London said, grabbing Lia and dragging her through the outer ring of the crowd. "Those warriors weren't dead; they were infected."

"But Hutoh said…" Lia shook her head. "I don't understand…"

"Do these people have anything like a hospital?" he asked.

"They don't really see disease like…"

"I don't need a fucking anthropology lesson! I need to know where they keep the sick people!" London looked over his shoulder. He picked out what looked like a vacant hut and pulled Lia inside. "Look, you know these people. Do they keep their sick folks together?"

"Well, yes, they do."

"What about the dead people? They have something like a funeral home?"

She shrugged. "I guess you could call it that."

"Where the hell is it?" London demanded, silently cursing himself for not having his men do a thorough sweep of the village before letting their guard down.

Lia shook her head. "I don't know."

The next sounds London heard were definitely screams. They came from somewhere towards the back of the crowd, from where the procession had started. London's shoulders sagged as he put the pieces together.

"Someone left the goddamn barn door open," he said.

Lia's brow knitted in confusion. "What?"

"Wherever they were keeping those dead warriors," London said. "It wasn't just those two old boys in there. I guess regular folks don't get this sort of royal treatment for their funerals, right? But they got stashed in the same place as the dead warriors. Must have heard all the commotion and now they're all stirred up. We're getting the fuck out of here. Stay here while I gather the rest of the team."

"The hell I'm just going to stay here," she snapped. "Max is out there."

London didn't feel like arguing. Although he regretted leaving the big guns in the vehicles, he still had his sidearm. He pulled the pistol from the holster on his hip and checked it. He was fully loaded, but that didn't mean much. If the situation went south, eight rounds weren't a hell of a lot of protection.

"All right then," he said. "Let's go."

They peeked out of the hut's low doorway and glimpsed a scene that was dissolving into chaos. The panic that had started at the rear of the procession—London was pretty sure that's where the tribe's "dead" had been stored—was spreading through the crowd. That horrible moaning sound could be heard even over the screams. And then, the first gunshots.

London searched the surging crowd, and saw his team. All three had their pistols drawn and were falling back to the south end of the village, where they'd left the vehicles. But it was slow going when you couldn't open up with semi-automatic rifles.

One of the villagers staggered out of the crowd. She was screaming as she came, her face turned toward the sky as if pleading with the gods to end her suffering. London looked down to her legs and saw the source of her pain. A pair of infected children—just toddlers, really—were attached to her legs. As the woman struggled to keep walking, the two children gnawed at the meaty portions of her thighs. London raised his boot and kicked one of the children, a boy with a blood-streaked face, away. The child stumbled into the crowd, where he was knocked to the ground by the surge of panicked villagers. The woman's eyes grew wide with terror and she ripped the other child away from her leg and held him to her chest. The hollow-eyed boy, whose cheeks were already bulging, opened his jaws wide and clamped down on the woman's breast. London raised his gun, but the woman threw her free hand out protectively. She shouted something as she clutched the boy. London lowered his pistol and let her stagger away, her legs and chest streaming with blood.

"I'm going to find Max," Lia said. "We'll meet you and your men where we parked."

London knew it would be a waste of breath to argue, so he didn't. He watched her duck out of the hut and begin shoving her way through the throng of people, then turned his attention back to the situation at hand. All around him was the same feeding frenzy he'd seen at the mission. It appeared that the tribe had been keeping a fair number of infected people somewhere in the village. Or maybe the virus simply took effect more quickly in some people. Either way, it looked like the Ka'Longho were fucked.

"Well," he said, taking a deep breath, "here we go again."

Leaving the relative safety of the hut behind, he stepped into the midst of the slaughter. He did a quick assessment of the situation, and the brief glance at the small village revealed an entire battlefield's worth of horrors. Many of the villagers had fallen to the ground. Some had been dragged down by the clutching hands of the infected. Others had perhaps been knocked down in the mad stampede. Some, the very young and the very old mostly, appeared to have simply laid down to await whatever violent end was coming to them.

London felt something grab his ankle. He looked down and saw an old woman trying to bite through his boot as she writhed in the dirt. Her legs were gone, ripped right out of her hip sockets along with a portion of her buttocks, leaving behind two ragged holes. One of her arms had been so thoroughly smashed that it appeared to be held together by a few thin strands of gristle. London kicked her away, but she dragged herself back toward him, clawing at the ground with her remaining hand. London stomped on her head, wincing at the sensation of his boot crunching through her skull.

Then he waded in, punching or pistol-whipping anyone who got too close. It occurred to him that some of the faces he smashed in probably belonged to the living, but in the chaos, it was impossible to tell the difference. Besides, if what he'd witnessed at the mission was any indication, a simple punch was the least of these people's worries. He focused on moving forward. If they could make it to the vehicles before the dead folks, they might have a chance to escape. He just hoped Lia saw it the same way, and didn't hang around to try to save any of the villagers. He told himself that his concern was purely utilitarian. After all, she knew the country, and with satellite communications seemingly knocked down, she was the closest thing they had to a guide. But that wasn't quite the whole truth.

Concentrate, he told himself. *Keep thinking about Lia and you'll get yourself killed.*

London shook his head and focused on pushing through the crowd without getting bitten. It wasn't as easy as it seemed. Although the infected—*the living dead,* he reminded himself—weren't all that tough one-on-one, there were so damn many of them. And they were damn persistent. He slammed the barrel of his pistol across a dead man's jaw, and the bastard didn't even blink. The dead son of a bitch just kept drooling slime, and moaning. London made a tactical decision and fired a shot into the man's head. Maybe it was a wasted bullet, but at least it stopped the fucker's moaning.

London punched and kicked his way through the human debris, pushing onward to the edge of the village.

11

Gil Zantoro popped a pill from his secret stash of uppers. It wasn't quite the same as cocaine—his preferred method of self-medication these days—but it would do in a pinch. It was his fourth dose of the day. If this assignment stretched on too long, he might have to start rationing his supply, but for now, he didn't care.

Once he saw those dead guys start twitching and moaning on the funeral pyre, he knew shit was going to hit the fan. Goddamn, he hated being right all the time.

He was standing along the west flank, between Osbourne and Vincent, watching the horror show start to unfold. Across the crowd, he could see the boss all cozied up to the French reporter chick. The lucky bastard had gotten to know her up close and personal. Zantoro didn't need X-ray vision to know what had gone on in that medicine man's shack.

But the time for sweet loving had passed, and the time for violence had arrived. Truth be told, Zantoro preferred the latter. The rest of the team might have adopted that stoic samurai warrior philosophy bullshit, but he still got off on the sheer adrenaline kick of readily indulged violent urges. It wasn't the type of thing he would ever admit during his quarterly psych evals, but at least he could be honest with himself.

"You boys ready to rock?" he asked, shooting his elbows into his teammates' ribs.

They pulled their pistols from their holsters.

"Fuck that," Zantoro said, slipping his knife from the sheath strapped to his thigh. "This sweet lady never runs out of ammo."

Calling it a knife was a bit like calling a hand grenade a firecracker. Zantoro's weapon had a nine-inch blade, with one side honed to a razor edge, and the other cruelly serrated. It was perfectly balanced and felt good in his hand.

"Let's fucking go!" he shouted.

Without waiting for his a response from Osbourne and Vincent, he jumped into the middle of the confused crowd. At first, the people swarming around him were just regular folks, but soon enough, the living dead made their presence known. They were easy to spot with their mouths dripping slime, and their red eyes. Plus that goddamn moaning and groaning. And who could mistake that stink for anything other than rotting dead flesh? Even if Zantoro's engine wasn't cranked all the way into the red, his disgust would have been motivation enough.

"Batter up!"

He grabbed one of the shambling dead men by the neck and stabbed the knife into his ear. The blade punched through to the brain with shockingly little resistance. It made a sound like chopping raw vegetables. Zantoro yanked the blade free and let the dead man fall into a heap.

"Next!" he shouted.

He hauled one of the rotten ghouls off a screaming Ka'Longho woman. It was too late for her—the ghoul had bitten a sizeable chunk out of her neck—but Zantoro figured it was too late for all the poor bastards in the village. He sawed into the dead man's neck, severing meat and arteries neatly before the blade got caught between two vertebrae. He wrenched it back and forth until the two bones separated with a sound like a cracking walnut. When he tugged the blade free, the dead man's head flopped to one side, landing with his ear pressed flat against his shoulder. Blood and green slime ran from the gaping wound as the dead man stumbled around drunkenly. For some reason, this struck Zantoro as incredibly funny. He glanced around, trying to find Vincent and Osbourne so he could share with them the hilarious sight. But his partners seemed otherwise occupied. Too bad. Zantoro let the confused ghoul stumble away, gurgling a mouthful of its own blood and pus as its jaws snapped uselessly.

"Well, now..." Zantoro smiled. The pill was doing its thing, and his heart was like a trip hammer in his chest. "Which one of you rotten bags of guts wants some?"

A pair of the infected dead looked over, seemingly ready to answer his call. One of them was a woman, but that didn't make much difference to Zantoro. During his lifetime, he'd killed plenty of women. With one glaring exception—a prostitute who'd tried to rob him in New Orleans when he was fresh out of boot camp—they'd all been hostiles. And if a reanimated corpse with a hunger for human flesh didn't fit the definition of hostile, then Zantoro was in the wrong line of work.

Because he was a modern man who believed in gender equality and all that other bullshit, he dealt with the female ghoul first. He drove the point of his blade right between her eyes. The knife stuck, so he let her drop. Then he drew his gun and fired a point blank shot into the male ghoul's forehead.

"Hey, baby, I need that," Zantoro said, planting a boot on the female ghoul's chest and tugging his knife out of her skull.

He was just about to pick another candidate out of the

crowd when he heard London's voice calling out. Seemed the boss wanted them to fall back to the cars. Bummer. Things were just starting to get fun. Still, the boss was the boss, and orders were orders. He wiped his knife on his pants leg, cleaning off the brain juice, then slipped it back into its sheath. He elbowed his way through the heaving mass of people and ghouls and headed for the south side of the village.

12

When the funeral procession dissolved into chaos, Max slipped away from the crowd, and into the humid darkness of the jungle. Had he been carrying his camera, he might have stayed to get some footage of the slaughter, but since he was empty-handed, he saw no reason to hang around. Let the Americans be heroes. Let that square-jawed country boy Mike London impress Lia by carrying her to safety. It seemed that was what she wanted.

Max took out his pistol, just in case one of the living dead decided to wander away from the village buffet and see what delights the jungle had to offer. Sure enough, he hadn't made it more than a few meters through the tangled vegetation when one of the infected dead men stumbled down the embankment on the edge of the road. Amazingly, the dead man kept his balance and began slowly making his way toward Max, with hands outstretched as if grasping for some prize that was just out of reach.

"Come on, you bastard," Max whispered. He spread his arms wide, presenting himself for the ghoul's inspection. "I may not be a real American hero, but I'm tasty enough. Come on, take a bite."

The dead man's feet tangled in the overgrown vegetation, and he fell to the ground.

"Clumsy bastard," Max laughed, although the vegetation nearly got the better of him as he made his way to the fallen dead man.

The infected villager was like a turtle on its back. Tangled in dead weeds and thorny vines, the man struggled in vain to get to his feet. Max stood over the man and glared. The intensity of his hatred was surprising. Max had never thought of himself as capable of such anger, but he didn't find it entirely unpleasant. In fact, letting that white hot emotion rise up in him was liberating.

"If you fucking dogs would just stay dead, none of this would be happening," he said, circling the hopelessly ensnared man. "Lia and me, we'd still be on our own. We never would have picked up that family, and there'd be no American mercenary pigs standing between us. And she would…"

His train of thought had run out of track. The truth was, he didn't know what Lia would do if her new boyfriend wasn't in the picture. As much as Max would have liked to believe she would have seen the error of her ways and fallen into his arms, he knew the chances of that actually happening were slim. But it felt better to have someone other than himself to blame. And it felt good to press the barrel of his gun to the dead man's head and pull the trigger.

"Hey, Pierre, nice shot!"

Max's head snapped around at the sound of the voice. Standing at the top of the embankment was one of the Americans. The crazy one, Zantoro. Even at a few meters' distance, Max could tell the man was wild-eyed and manic.

"The boss gave the order to fall back to the vehicles," Zantoro said. "So if you're done playing grab-ass with that fucking zombie, get your ass up here. Those dead pieces of shit are busy chowing down on the natives for now, but they'll be along soon enough."

For a brief moment, Max wondered what would happen if he raised his gun and took a shot at Zantoro. There was no one close enough to witness it. He could shoot the crazy man, drag his body into the jungle, and keep going like nothing had happened. Max shook his head to dislodge the thought from his brain. He was a lot of things, but a murderer wasn't one of them. Now, maybe if it was London rather than Zantoro standing up there…

"Come on, monsieur," Zantoro called. "Move your ass."

Max took a deep breath and picked his way up the embankment. He picked his steps carefully, not wanting to risk Zantoro's laughter if he should stumble.

"Pretty smart, going downhill once shit popped off," Zantoro said when Max drew up alongside him. "Those rotten fuckers don't have much in the way of grace or balance. Of course, some of us chose to stay back there and fight, but I hear it takes all types to make the world go round and round. We can't all be badass motherfuckers."

Max glared at the man. "I was hoping to find Lia."

"Well, see, she went looking for you. Vincent and Osbourne had to practically drag her back to the car. So don't you worry about her. She's back there with the boss. He's taking good care of her. But I guess you already knew that, huh?"

Max turned his head and spat into the trees.

Zantoro laughed. "What's the matter, Pierre? Did I strike a nerve?"

"Fuck off," Max growled. "You don't know anything about it."

Zantoro kept laughing. He didn't stop until they made it all the way back to the vehicles, where London and the other two mercenaries—and yes, Lia—were waiting for them. Lia ran forward and pulled Max into an embrace.

"Oh, thank God," she said. "When I couldn't find you, I feared the worst."

"I'm fine. I can take care of myself." He pulled himself away from her.

She gave him a careful look, as if appraising him. "Yes, of course. I was just worried."

"I'm sure," Max sniffed.

London strutted in front of the group, his rifle slung over his shoulder. "Okay, folks, listen up. We still got miles to go before we reach our objective, so ammo supply is a concern. We can't afford to make a clean sweep of the village, but we need to stick to the road. So we're going to have to drive through that crowd back there. We'll ride point in the Jeep and try to clear the path. Lia will follow right on our ass. Zantoro, I want you in the Land Rover with them, just in case they need some extra firepower. Once we get through, we'll put some distance between ourselves and that village before we stop to rest. Questions?"

Nobody spoke up.

"All right then." London clapped his hands. "Let's mount up."

Max stood there for a moment, watching London and his two fellow mercenaries clamber into the Jeep. While London settled himself behind the steering wheel, the other two got busy checking their weapons. Max supposed the idea was for these two cowboys to clear a path by firing into the crowd. It sounded fine in theory, until one considered the very real possibility that there were still some of the Ka'Longho who were among the living. If they weren't hit by the Americans' bullets, they would end up devoured by the reanimated dead.

"So we're just running away?" Max said, turning to Lia. "That's it? That's the best plan your John Wayne could come up with?"

"And what would you have them do?" Lia snapped. "No one feels good about what is happening here, but our dying wouldn't improve the situation. Now get in the goddamn car."

Max turned to watch her stalk away. Zantoro was leaning against the Land Rover's passenger side door. The seemingly permanent smile on his face had taken on a particularly wicked glow.

"What's the matter, Pierre? Your lady boss getting too feisty for your taste?" The mercenary laughed as he climbed into the passenger seat.

Max cursed silently. *These goddamn cowboys. They're corporate-owned killers, and Lia looks at them like they're heroes.*

He climbed into the backseat. Although they'd done their best to clean it up after the Dominic incident, there were still bloodstains here and there. Even after all he'd seen— especially in the last two days—Max still felt his stomach lurch.

Their two-vehicle convoy went forward at a crawl. The two gunmen in the Jeep—Vincent and Osbourne—stood with their rifles held at the ready. London halted the Jeep just shy of the village. He rose from the driver's seat and hurled something into the crowd of figures blocking the road.

"Grenade," Zantoro explained. "Thought we were out, but the boss must have found one under the seat."

The detonation was like thunder. It sent bodies—and pieces of bodies—flying. Although it didn't completely clear their path, the explosion did knock the majority of the people —dead, alive, and otherwise—out of the way. Then the convoy began to move again.

"Ever driven over bodies before?" Zantoro asked.

Lia shook her head.

"It can be bumpy," Zantoro explained. "You got big tires on this thing, so it shouldn't be a problem, but it can get slippery too. Just drop it into a low gear and keep moving. And make sure the doors are locked. Last thing we need is one of those rotten fuckers trying to hitch a ride." He swiveled around in his seat. "Pierre, you just keep cool. The boss and my pals are going to clear the way, but if there needs to be any shooting from our car, you just leave it to me. I'm what you might call an expert marksman."

"My name is Max, not Pierre."

Zantoro shrugged. "Whatever you say, monsieur."

Viewed through the dirty windshield and side windows, their progress through the middle of the Ka'Longho village was a short journey through hell. Max tried to let his eyes go out of focus so that he didn't have to see the atrocities taking place all around them. But something in his brain—his conscience or maybe just sheer morbid curiosity—kept his attention. As expected, the two cowboys used their rifles to help clear the path, but they were apparently mindful of their limited supply of ammunition and only fired at targets that got within a couple meters of the Jeep. Otherwise, they let the reanimated dead go ahead with their feast.

Their feast. Max stifled the urge to vomit as his eyes took in the horror show unfolding all around him. For a moment, all his emotional turmoil regarding Lia and the Americans dissolved. There was little room in his mind for anything other than complete revulsion and disgust as he looked out the windows.

A pair of women, their bodies sill painted with the bright pigments of the funeral celebration, huddled over the body of a child. They were busy tearing handfuls of viscera from the child's chest cavity and stuffing them into their mouths.

An elderly man stumbled along the side of the road as his guts spilled from a gaping wound in his abdomen. A long coil of intestine trailed behind him like a snake slithering free from his belly.

A group of men had taken advantage of the chaos and were attempting to rape one of the reanimated women. She snapped and clawed at them like an animal as they dragged her to the ground and forced her legs apart. A burst of gunfire from Osbourne's rifle put a stop to the whole affair, blowing the dead woman's head apart like a burst melon.

An infant dragged itself across the gore-soaked ground, its tiny, toothless mouth hanging agape as it vomited a steady stream of viscous green fluid.

A young couple sat side by side, embracing as a group of red-eyed undead children bit into their backs and shoulders. The couple's eyes were closed, as if they were enjoying a private lovers' moment.

Even if Max closed his eyes to block out the visions entirely, he could still hear the horrible soundtrack. There were screams and moans, but they weren't the worst of it. There was also a constant undertone of crunching and squelching as the vehicles rolled over the bodies littering the road. Each crunch was a ribcage collapsing, a skull shattering, a femur splintering. Each wet squelch was a burst internal organ. Max couldn't block them out. He was certain that he'd hear them when he closed his eyes to sleep.

The two-vehicle convoy rolled on, finally leaving the carnage of the Ka'Longho village behind. Although the journey from one end of the village couldn't have taken more than a few minutes, Max felt as though he'd just passed an entire day in hell. Even Zantoro was silent as the massacre disappeared from sight.

13

They traveled until midnight, but poor visibility and even poorer road conditions eventually forced them to pull off the road and set up camp. London knew that the chances of the undead from the village sniffing them out were probably remote, but he still didn't feel great about spending another night in the jungle. Their mission—if such a thing still even existed—was well behind schedule. Everything was completely fucked.

They gathered around the glow of a single battery-powered lantern and ate food from what remained of the French journalists' supply. Protein bars, dried fruit, nuts, and crackers with some sort of olive spread. There were even a couple bottles of wine to share. London had no idea if the wine was any good. He was more of a beer guy, but it seemed to go along with the food just fine.

The faces illuminated by the weak glow of the lantern were somber enough already, but London knew he had to break the news about Mikkelson's squad. He kept it brief, explaining that the men had gotten caught in an ambush— either the undead or Mbowi's men—and didn't make it out alive.

"Don't tell me they got killed and then came back as those fucking things," Vincent said, shaking his head.

"Looks like that's exactly what happened," London said. "And I fucking hate it just as much as you men. But right now, we have to keep moving forward. When the mission is over and we're back stateside, we can mourn the fallen. Until then, we keep pushing to the objective."

"Oh, you gotta be fucking kidding me." Zantoro nearly spat out his mouthful of wine. "You think this mission has any objective beyond getting us out of this nightmare?"

"That's the point, Zantoro. You think if we don't get the damn deal done, Pendleton is going to offer us an exit strategy? I can't even get the motherfuckers on the phone. They might have already cut us loose for all I know. But the northern border is the only one that's friendly right now. And the route to that border takes us right through the HOPE research facility. If Pendleton gets in touch and offers us a way out, we go ahead with the mission. If they maintain radio silence, we can assume they've disavowed us."

"Yeah?" This time it was Osbourne who spoke up. "And if they have disavowed us and left us swinging in the wind, what then?"

London cut his eyes sideways, glancing at Lia. "Then we gather enough evidence to bury both Pendleton and Marsh Industries."

"Yeah, right," Zantoro said. "Waylon Marsh has more money than the Catholic church. There's no amount of bad press he can't buy his way out of."

Lia held up a finger to halt the conversation until she could finish chewing. She washed down her mouthful with some wine and said, "What I have in mind is considerably more than bad press. I have some contacts in the UN who have been looking to blow the lid off this HOPE Project thing for a long time. We were hoping to catch them doing some shady business, funding Mbowi's war crimes or skirting medical ethics, but nothing like what we've seen. What's that phrase…beyond the pale? Well, this certainly qualifies."

London thought about bringing up another point, but decided to keep it to himself. They had enough to worry about without him raising the possibility that whatever was going on in Daroka had spread beyond the small country's borders. While his team might not have considered that scenario, he was certain that Lia had. And besides, thinking of all the ways this disease—or whatever it was—could jump borders did nothing for their current situation. Still, London couldn't help but mentally compile a list of possibilities. Drug and human trafficking. Exotic animal smuggling. Refugee relocation. All of those things—and countless others—were a passport for this crisis to go worldwide.

A few hours later, when Lia crept out of her sleeping bag to join him on guard duty, London thought about discussing those grim scenarios, but Lia had other ideas. She wanted to revisit the events before things went to shit in the Ka'Longho village.

"We should talk about what happened in Hutoh's hut," she said, falling into step with him as he made a slow circuit of the camp's perimeter.

London felt his face grow hot and was grateful that the darkness hid his embarrassment.

"Hey, I know we were both geeked out on whatever was in that jug," he began.

She elbowed him playfully. "Not that, silly. Although that part was nice."

London knew she left that one hanging so he'd have time to respond, but he had no idea what to say. It had been a long time since he'd had this sort of talk.

"I mean the other part," she continued. "The dream. I know you saw the city and that figure in the black robe. I could feel you there with me, although I couldn't see you."

Again, he wasn't sure how to respond. He'd hardly had

time to think that stuff through. He cleared his throat and said, "Never had a dream that felt so real before. Guess that was the drug working. The Soul Nectar or whatever you called it."

"And in a few minutes, when your guard duty ends, do you think you'll dream of anything else? Because I'm beginning to wonder if I'll ever dream of anything but that city again."

"I don't know," London sighed, he took out his can of Skoal and tucked a pinch behind his lip. "Tired as I am, I feel sort of afraid of going to sleep. Not that it was a bad dream. Fact is, it was pleasant, walking through that cool river water and into that city. Never seen buildings like that. Or those weird lights overhead. Stuff was…well, it was beautiful. Reckon part of me is afraid that I won't go back, and another part of me is afraid I will. That doesn't make much sense does it?"

She edged closer to him. "Actually, it makes perfect sense."

"Meanwhile, back in this dimension, we got more concrete problems to deal with," he said. "Like how we're still a whole day away from our objective and we don't exactly have an infinite supply of gas or ammo."

"It's a little out of our way," Lia said, "but there's an old French chateau not far from here. You know, sort of like a plantation house in your southern states. It dates back to the colonial period, but most recently, Worldview Paper was using it as a local headquarters before General Mbowi chased them away. It might be worth a look. There might be supplies that we can use. Unless Mbowi's soldiers are still using the place, I mean."

London thought the suggestion over. He couldn't see a downside. If they scouted the place and found that it was still occupied by Mbowi's army, they'd fall back and continue pushing north. If the place was abandoned, maybe the soldiers left behind some useful supplies. And it might be nice to spend some time with a roof over their heads, if only just to regroup before the final leg of the operation.

"Sure, I think it's worth checking out," he said. "But first things first, let's get back to camp. Time for some shut-eye."

She held his hand as they walked. London didn't mind that at all.

14

Father Xavier sent his scouts back to the deeper part of the jungle. Although they'd seen plenty of horrors, there was no need for them to walk through the Ka'Longho village. Peter had protested, but Father Xavier had promised the boy everything would be fine, showing him the pistol he kept for such occasions. The priest felt that God—well, certainly *a god,* or perhaps even *gods*—had granted him protection. What other explanation was there for the dreams? The divine power was calling him onward to some yet unknown location. But until then, he kept his nine millimeter fully loaded and at the ready.

"Go now," he told Peter. "Pass out snacks to the others and see that they don't worry. I'll be back soon."

Peter nodded and made his way down the embankment at the side of the road. He disappeared into the trees with a practiced ease and silence that would have been the envy of a Special Forces soldier.

Father Xavier turned his attention back to the carnage spread out before him like a buzzard's banquet. The morning had broken still and hot. There was no breeze to push away the carrion stink, or disperse the black clouds of flies swarming over the human remains littering the ground. It reminded him of the aftermath of Mbowi's raids on border towns. The General had allowed his men to indulge in the worst bloodlust imaginable. And it wasn't long before the campaign of ethnic cleansing devolved into wholesale slaughter. Even the towns and villages that offered no resistance weren't spared the horrors of Mbowi's rise to power.

But there were obvious signs that the horrors that befell the Ka'Longho were the work of something more sinister even than the mad General's campaign of terror. Despite the work of the jungle scavengers, many of the dead still bore the signs of having been bitten by human teeth. The ground was littered with bullet casings, but the bodies weren't riddled with holes. The only apparent bullet wounds were clean shots to the head. Whoever had rolled through the village—the tire tracks were still imprinted on the ground—had been trained. And they knew enough about the living dead to have only fired head shots.

"How curious," Father Xavier said, surveying the scene.

15

Dr. Morton Fairbanks had a high tolerance for loneliness. After all, he'd spent the bulk of his life in various degrees of social isolation. There was nothing traumatic in his childhood that he could point to as a cause for his inability to forge anything beyond superficial human connections. His parents —both of them professors at the local community college— had been attentive enough. There was certainly no physical abuse in the home. Even his years in the public school system had been relatively trouble-free. It was his opinion that some people are simply born to be loners, and he was one of them. His tolerance for boredom, however, was considerably lower. And once the trousers-soiling terror of his most recent trip to the cafeteria had abated, the boredom of a life confined to the staff lounge returned with a vengeance.

He'd made his way through the lounge's stash of magazines. The two female members of the basement staff— Dr. Whittaker and Dr. Royce—had left behind a year's worth of *Cosmopolitan* and *Fashionista*, and Fairbanks had already taken all the quizzes on various sexual activities, personal hygiene routines, beauty products, and hairstyles. He'd memorized the various sports schedules in Dr. Proust's *Sports*

Illustrated issues. He'd even gotten a handle on all the soap opera storylines from Dr. Whittaker's *Soap Digest.* A few paperback books had been stashed near the sofa, and he'd already read all of them at least once. There was a functioning laptop computer in the lounge, but although the unit appeared to be in good working order, internet access had been disabled, and there were only so many hours one could waste playing Solitaire.

Fairbanks sat at the table—a round four-seater—and mulled over his situation as he scooped the contents of a can of fruit cocktail into his mouth. While his physical needs were met for the time being, his mental health would soon be in jeopardy. Without something to occupy his mind, he'd soon go insane. After all, it could be months, a year even, before someone decided to reclaim the research facility. And while Fairbanks felt good about his ability to forage for food, he wasn't so optimistic about his chances for surviving without some sort of mental stimulus.

The solution was obvious. There were over a hundred specimens milling around just outside the lounge door. And while they were dangerous when they had a numbers advantage or the element of surprise on their side, they weren't so bad one-on-one. Now that he'd dealt with the initial shock of knowing that the specimens were the reanimated dead—zombies, in common parlance—he could assess them in the calm, rational manner of a scientist. And the more he considered the situation, the more he was convinced that he could allow one of them to enter the lounge without being bitten or otherwise harmed in the process. With the few tools he had at his disposal—the power drill, an extra-large roll of duct tape, a pair of extension cords, a dust broom, and a drawer full of kitchen supplies—he could subdue and restrain the specimen with minimal risk.

And then...

Well, Fairbanks wasn't exactly sure what would happen

after that, but a soft voice from the dark recesses of his brain kept insisting that it would be best if the specimen was female.

Perhaps a female will be more docile, easier to restrain.

Yes, that's it. A female companion is just what you need.

The door to the lounge was a fire safety door made of thick metal. It was so heavy and imposing that, for most of the time when the lab was functional, the researchers chose to keep it propped open. The weight and thickness of the door meant the basement fortress was impenetrable. And now he was preparing to open it. He shook his head at the madness of his plan, but he knew true madness was what awaited him if he remained alone much longer. Even in the Garden of Eden, Adam felt lonely. And the cramped staff lounge was far from a garden paradise.

He unlocked the door as quietly as he could manage, pulling back the heavy deadbolt and then clicking the doorknob lock. Taking a deep breath to steel his nerves, he opened the door a few inches and peeked out. His entire body tensed as he prepared to leap back inside and slam the door at the first sign of danger. But the only thing to assault him was the smell. Even with the overhead filtration unit still apparently functioning—Fairbanks could hear the hum—the stink was still so putrid and thick that Fairbanks could visualize it as having weight and density. Most of the smell—at least he hoped so—was most likely coming from the shredded remains of Whittaker and Proust. Some of it was from the specimens, of course. Even before total bodily reanimation, the test subjects gave off an unpleasant odor, but it was never this strong. Fairbanks knew his future companion wouldn't smell like roses. That was why he'd readied the lounge's small cache of cleaning supplies.

The infected specimens hadn't noticed him yet. That was good. It gave him a chance to survey the scene and adjust his strategy. The lab was trashed. During the initial melee, the equipment had been overturned and smashed. Chairs, computers, and various medical devices littered the floor. When Fairbanks' presence was noticed, there would be no mad stampede. They would have to come two or three at a time through the alcove that led to the lounge. It was a chokepoint. His forays to the cafeteria had taught Fairbanks that two or three specimens at a time weren't a problem, as long as you could see them coming.

Clutching the drill in one hand, and the broom in the other, he opened the door wide.

"Okay," he said in a loud, clear voice. "Who among you would like to be my companion?"

Dozens of heads turned his way. The specimens' constant low moaning took on an insistent note, and rose in volume as they began to shamble toward him. Their movements were awkward and clumsy already, and the debris littering the floor slowed them even more. Fairbanks found himself growing impatient, but he knew he needed to stay as close to the door as possible.

The first specimen to come within striking distance was a tall, gangly male. Fairbanks poked the broomstick into his chest, pinning him to the wall. The drill whined as it punched through the specimen's skull and scrambled the brains within. Fairbanks drew back, careful to avoid the splatter as he withdrew the drill. He let the specimen's dead—well, dead *again*—body slide to the floor.

By now, a second specimen was approaching. This one was female, but her face was torn to shreds. That wouldn't do, not at all. If Fairbanks was going to all this trouble to procure a companion, the least she could do was look somewhat presentable. But he didn't have time to meditate on the topic of standards. He had the room's full attention and had to act fast. Down went the sloppy female specimen, the neatly drilled hole in the center of her forehead still spraying blood like a miniature firehose as she collapsed atop the fallen male specimen.

As luck would have it, the next specimen to step into the alcove was a perfect candidate. Well, as close to perfect as Fairbanks was likely to find. Sure, her face was covered in a thick crust of dried slime, but that could be washed away, just as the few suppurating sores on her abdomen and thighs could be patched up. And sure, some of her hair had come out in clumps, leaving her with bald patches, but he thought that perhaps he could look past that as well. Her breasts were still perfect—high and apparently firm with perky nipples. Her hips rolled seductively, even as she staggered and stumbled. Yes, this was the one.

Fairbanks waited until she was nearly close enough to grab, then he swept her feet from under her with the broom handle. He turned away just long enough to open the door to the lounge and then dragged her inside. The door slammed shut just as another pair of specimens reached the threshold.

"And the Lord God said that it was not good for the man to be alone," Fairbanks said, tossing the broom and drill onto the table. "And Adam named the woman Eve."

He turned and watched his new companion—naked and dirty and moaning—as she struggled to her feet.

"Now," Fairbanks said, looking at his supplies spread out on the kitchenette counter, "let's see if we can't make you presentable."

It took a fair amount of wrestling—during which there were some close calls—for Fairbanks to secure Eve's mouth, wrists, and ankles with duct tape. But once she could no longer snap and claw at him like an enraged animal, the fight seemed to go out of her. At least, her thrashing about became less and less frantic. It took him the better part of an hour and half a bottle of dish soap to give her a thorough sponge bath, but Fairbanks was happy with the result. Once the slime and crust had been removed from her face and wounds, she didn't look at all unattractive. Her hair was perhaps a lost cause, but Fairbanks believed he could find a way to shave it off.

There was a locker full of spare surgical scrubs in the lounge, and Fairbanks thought Whittaker had been of a similar size to Eve. Working carefully, removing the duct tape at her wrists, he managed to slip the shirt onto her. The pants weren't so easy. Eve's legs kicked like pistons, but in the end, he was able to win that fight. The pants fit at the waist, especially once the drawstring had been tied, but Eve was taller than Whittaker, and the pants stopped a few inches short of her ankle. Fairbanks rolled them into double cuffs. He felt this looked somewhat fashionable, although he'd never been an expert on such things.

When he was done, he dragged Eve onto the sofa and stepped back to admire his work. She was far from perfect, but then again, so was Fairbanks.

"Not bad," he said. "Not bad at all. But I'm afraid that you'll have to undergo a dental procedure before we can coexist happily. A full extraction of your teeth, my dear. I think we'll both feel much better when they're gone."

16

Charon sat on the marble floor of the city's grand cathedral. Constructed over millennia from the dreams of the world's greatest architects, the cathedral was such a thorough blend of contrasting designs that it appeared almost alien. But Charon loved the cathedral's dizzying array of overlapping styles, just as it loved the entirety of the eternal city. The dreams of its creators still spoke from the impossibly ancient stones and timber that made up the city's countless structures. And it was dreams that concerned Charon. Stretching its skeletal fingers toward the vaulted ceiling above, it dispatched dreams to the souls of those who were worthy of entry into the eternal city.

17

Therapist at the Fayette Hills Sleep Disorders Clinic:

From the diary of Molly Corvallo, Therapist at the Fayette Hills Sleep Disorders Clinic:

So, here we go again, diary. Today, I had three more clients talk my ear off about their recurring dreams of some underground city. It's gotten to the point where, whenever the clinic sends a patient to my office, I just know it's because of these dreams. This makes thirteen of them so far. That's nearly half of my case load. THIRTEEN! A baker's dozen, right? Now, if it was just two or three cases, I'd chalk it up to patients chatting in the waiting room or something like that. Or maybe I'd just say there's some new crazy in the air (terrible language for a therapist to use, but you, dear diary, are my most trusted confidant). But thirteen of them? I'm starting to wonder if I should even write it up in my notes anymore, because maybe people will start to think I'm losing it. You know, maybe they'd be right about that, because for the last couple nights, I've had the same dream. An underground river. A beautiful city with the strangest architecture I've ever seen. A figure in a black robe inviting me to cross the river and join him (or her?). Sounds like a nightmare, but it doesn't feel that way at all.

Probably working too many hours. Too much coffee and not enough self-care. Could be getting suggestible. I'm going to blame this summer weather. I freakin' hate this freakin' heat and humidity. I'm ready for fall weather and pumpkin spice everything. You know me, diary, underneath this bookish exterior, I'm just a basic white girl! If I can convince myself to like Taylor Swift's music, my transformation will be complete!

Speaking of basic white girl things, Scott decided we need some time apart. He says he needs to work on himself, which is guy-speak for, "I'm sick of this chick and want to see what else is out there." Fair enough. I'm not sure I can see much of a future with a guy who has a tattoo of an energy drink logo on his leg…

Partial transcript of syndicated news show *Media Rundown with Guy Howard:*

HOWARD: I think this administration's response to the situation in Daroka has been a real head-scratcher. For a president who has favored intervention across the Middle East, it seems very odd that the policy regarding Daroka has been hands-off.

"SEXY T" TODD JAMES (ACTOR/COMEDIAN): I mean, I'm just taking a shot in the dark, but you think it might have something to do with the fact that it's just a bunch of—

JORDAN PULLMAN (AUTHOR/COLUMNIST): Oh, here we go with the race card. You know, it never fails. Whatever this president accomplishes, you people find some way to—

JAMES: You people, huh?

PULLMAN: Yes, you people, as in all of you on the radical left. You—

JAMES: Damn, you think—

HOWARD: I think folks on both sides of the aisle can agree—

PULLMAN: I won't agree with anyone who defends abortion or athletes who won't stand for our national anthem.

HOWARD: Now, Jordan, come on. What does that have to do with anything?

PULLMAN: It goes to credibility.

JAMES: Credibility? You think this is a court proceeding or something?

PULLMAN: Well, you'd know all about the criminal justice system, wouldn't you?

HOWARD: Gentlemen, I think we—

JAMES: Fuck you, motherfucker! Justice for Daroka!

Part Six

*…a vast image out of Spiritus Mundi troubles my
      sight…*

"I can't sit on the sidelines for the apocalypse, no matter how old I am."

—Lori Lund

1

Candy Kane was just her professional name. She'd first started using it as a stripper back in Baltimore. When Stella Kuminsky recruited her to a new career in DC, she figured she might as well hang onto the name. It sounded better than Rhea Alice Jourgenson, which is what her parents had sobered up long enough to write on her birth certificate. But as she followed some half-drunk megachurch preacher from South Carolina into one of the suites at the Westwood Hotel, she wasn't thinking about names or her shitty parents. She wasn't thinking about much of anything besides the fierce, all-consuming hunger in the pit of her stomach.

"Hey, come on in and make yourself comfortable," Reverend Jimmy said, kicking the door shut behind them. "There's an awful fine minibar if you want to fix yourself a drink."

She shook her head. "No, I don't want a drink."

The truth was, she didn't think she could handle a drink. Although she'd had plenty of time to sober up, she still hadn't been able to keep anything down. She'd tried toast with runny eggs—her usual hangover cure—and they'd come right back up, along with the mouthful of coffee she'd used to wash them down. Now, she was so hungry that she could imagine her belly as one big yawning crater at the center of her body. Her stomach growled with such force that she wasn't just worried her john would hear it, but that he'd feel it as soon as he touched her. But so far, Reverend Jimmy didn't seem to notice. Either he was too blitzed on Bud Light and Fireball whisky to care, or the hunger noises were just a figment of her imagination. Either way, all Reverend Jimmy seemed concerned with was getting naked as quickly as possible.

"Come on, baby," he said, shrugging out of his coat and ripping off his necktie. "Let's get it on. I got to give a speech about school prayer in a couple hours. Always do my best public speaking after I blow a couple loads."

Candy did her best to shake off the gnawing hunger and focus on her job. She was a professional, after all. She cooed something seductive and kicked off her high heels. Then she shed her clothes with practiced ease.

"That's it, take it off," Reverend Jimmy slurred. He was down to nothing but an undershirt and a pair of black socks. He snapped his fingers and gestured to his half-erect penis. "How about giving Little Jimmy some attention, huh?"

Candy licked her lips. Despite the nickname, Little Jimmy was actually above average. Surprising, since so many of the loud mouth crackers she serviced while working these conventions were jumbo shrimp at best. He stood there pointing, and Candy got the idea that he was waiting for her to hit her knees. Fair enough, the carpet at this hotel was pretty soft. She knelt in front of him and got to work.

"That's it, that's it, that's it," Reverend Jimmy moaned. "Do it just like that…"

Usually, Candy hated it when they couldn't just shut the fuck up and enjoy themselves, but this time, she was thankful for Reverend Jimmy's stream of consciousness blabbermouth routine. All his jibber-jabber covered up the insistent rumbling of her stomach.

"Hey!" Reverend Jimmy shouted, pulling away. "Watch the fucking teeth, bitch!"

Candy shook her head. It felt like her skull was full of wet cotton. She wanted to chalk it up to the hangover, but there was more to it than that. Her body ached as she rose from her knees. Her ears were filled with a high-pitched whine, and her heart fluttered like a wounded hummingbird in her chest. She was wobbly on her feet and was glad she'd ditched the high heels.

"On the bed, big boy," she said, snapping her fingers. Maybe she could cover for the thing with the teeth by adopting a dominant stance. Some of these religious types really went for that kind of shit.

Reverend Jimmy flopped down on the bed. He sighed as Candy climbed on top of him and guided his dick into her. She felt dry, but he didn't seem to mind. Once she got going, things slicked up, but otherwise, Candy still felt like shit. A pounding headache had taken up residence between her eyes. Her stomach seemed to alternately tighten into a ball, and open up into a great, gurgling void.

"Yeah, that's it!" Reverend Jimmy yelped. "Come on, cowgirl, get it!"

Normally, Candy would have to bite her lip to keep from laughing, but all she could do was try to stay in rhythm while the room spun around her. The world was starting to go all swimmy. Her vision blurred and darkened at the edges until she was staring down a narrow tunnel. Reverend Jimmy bucked and writhed beneath her, but her body had grown numb apart from the knife-edge ache of her empty belly. Seasick nausea rose up in her, and before she could make a no doubt futile attempt to tamp it down, she vomited.

Distantly, as if it was coming from another room, she heard Reverend Jimmy scream. Like a camera lens opening, her vision resolved into sharp focus. She heaved again. The vomit that sprayed with firehose intensity from her mouth was thick and green, shot through with stringy clots of blood. It splattered all over Reverend Jimmy, drenching him and the bed with slime that reeked of rotten meat and ammonia. His screams turned to gurgles as the viscous slime invaded his mouth and nostrils.

When her puking finally tapered off, the hunger pains in Candy's belly were more intense than any she'd ever known.

Eat him.

It wasn't a voice in her head as much as it was a compulsion so strong that it felt instinctual.

Eat his flesh…

The urge was too strong to resist. Clenching her vagina so tight that he couldn't squirm away, she descended on Reverend Jimmy with her mouth open wide. She chomped into his gym-sculpted pectoral muscle and bit down with a strength she didn't know she possessed. Then she twisted her head from side to side until a bloody chunk tore free. Revulsion flickered somewhere in the depths of her mind, but it was dim and distant, and quickly snuffed out by the immense satisfaction of swallowing a half-chewed mouthful of human meat. She shuddered with a pleasure that made the intensity of a full-body orgasm seem trite.

Reverend Jimmy screamed again, battering her with his fists. His penis wilted inside her and slipped out.

Candy snarled as she went in for a second mouthful, this time fixing her teeth onto his throat. She bit down, and his screams dissolved into wet choking sounds. Her mouth flooded with hot blood. She couldn't swallow fast enough.

Now, the voice in her head was gone. In fact, everything was gone. Her memories, her thoughts, her identity…all of it was slipping away. There was nothing left but hunger. The warm person below her…she couldn't remember his name… could only twitch as his life ebbed away. Candy fell on him, eager to bite and chew and consume as much as he could while the body was still warm.

Her fluttering heart slowed until it stopped altogether. Candy stopped chewing long enough to attempt speech. But her brain couldn't conjure words. The best she could manage was a moan. That was okay. Everything was okay. The last threads of personality withered. Her mind dissolved until only the hunger remained.

2

Dr. Vogel awoke from a nightmare with a start. Panic seized him as he looked around the dark, crowded interior. But the intensity of his disorientation was matched by its brevity, and the world snapped back into focus. He was on a Greyhound bus, bound for…well, he couldn't quite remember. In his haste to put as much distance between himself and Waylon Marsh as possible, Vogel had bought the first available ticket out of Washington DC. He'd avoided the airport—it would be the first place Marsh checked once he realized the architect of the HOPE Project had gone rogue. By the time Marsh considered bus travel, Vogel would be long gone. That was the plan, at least.

"You okay, man?"

The question came from the young man in the aisle seat on Vogel's left.

"Quite okay." Vogel nodded. "Just a bit of a bad dream, I'm afraid."

"Yeah, dude, I know all about nightmares. Just about my whole time in DC was a nightmare. Why I'm heading back home to Atlanta. Figure I can put together a little scratch, maybe lay low for a while."

Vogel turned slightly in his seat to get a better look at his neighbor. He looked to still be in his twenties—Vogel couldn't imagine someone older having such a ridiculous haircut—but his eyes had a world-weary cast to them which suggested, at the very least, some years of hard living. The doctor didn't like to indulge in stereotypes. That was the sort of thinking used by those seeking a shortcut rather than examining evidence. This is why Vogel didn't just use the young man's appearance to come to the conclusion that he was an impoverished drug addict. But sometimes stereotypes align with the other evidence presented. Such logical shortcuts don't appear out of thin air, it seemed. And it didn't take long before the young man, whose name turned out to be Devon, offered up his tale of woe. Much of it didn't hold Vogel's interest, but he feigned interest. Sooner or later, Devon would make his pitch.

"Man, it's just hard to get clean, you know?" Devon bounced his knees in an irregular rhythm and tapped his fingers on the armrest. "I keep thinking I can do it if maybe I had just one more blast. Like, if I could score at our stop in Charlotte, I might be able to ride it out until we're in Atlanta. I got family there. But I'm broke. Spent my last dollar on this bus ride. You wouldn't happen to have any extra cash, would you? I mean, you know, so I can scare something up in Charlotte?"

Vogel shook his head. "I'm afraid I don't carry cash."

"Well, that sucks," Devon said.

"However, I might have something else that can help you."

"Oh yeah?" Devon perked up. "What's that?"

Vogel reached into his coat pocket and brought out a glass vial full of white powder. It was one of a dozen such vials that Vogel had brought on this journey. He passed it to Devon and said, "It's probably not the sort of drug you're accustomed to, but I believe it can help tide you over until you're with your family in Atlanta."

"So, what, it's methadone or something?"

"Not quite. This is an experimental drug that I've developed for cases such as yours." He paused, noting the suspicion creeping into Devon's expression. "Of course, if you're not interested, I understand completely."

"No, man, I'm definitely interested." Devon closed his hand around the vial. "It's just I didn't expect...I mean...I never scored from someone who looks like you."

Vogel shrugged. "Stereotypes often crumble when exposed to careful scrutiny."

"Yeah, man. I hear that."

3

Lori Lund had been awake for nearly two days straight when Spider and the rest of the Earth Force media crew finally persuaded her to go home. She was busy brewing up yet another pot of coffee. Spider watched her for a moment, then sighed with disapproval. There was no way that sigh could be interpreted any other way. It was loud enough to be heard over the muted percussion of keyboard-tapping and mouse clicking that filled the room.

"Lori, it's not healthy for a woman of your age to burn the candle at both ends like this," Spider said, his eyes still fixed on his laptop. "You need to trust us. We got this."

"Thanks a lot for making me feel old," she said.

The female members of the crew snickered, while the men kept their mouths judiciously shut. They clearly felt Spider needed no help. He was, after all, the senior member of the department, and as such, awkward conversations fell to him.

"Come on," he said, "you know I didn't mean it like that."

Spider might not have meant to make her feel old, but a quick glance around the office did the trick. The Earth Force social media department had six members, all of whom were under the age of thirty. Hell, a couple of them couldn't even legally buy a beer. Lori was old enough to be their mother. And in a way, that's exactly what she was. These kids—with their fashionably retro punk band t-shirts, and sleeve tattoos—were more than just team members. They were her family.

"Fine, I'll hit the couch for a couple hours," she said. "But I can't sit on the sidelines for the apocalypse, no matter how old I am."

"Lori, go home. I promise we won't start the apocalypse without you." Spider was so serious he actually quit tapping away at his keyboard and looked at her. "Take a shower and sleep in your bed. You need to recharge. Keep pouring coffee down your throat and your brain might turn to mush. Then you won't be around to see it when we bring these bastards down."

"Okay, okay, okay." She raised her hands in surrender. "But before I go, I want a status update."

There was a brief burst of chatter from all the team members before Spider cut off the overlapping voices with a baleful glance over the top of his horn-rimmed glasses. The chastened team got back to work while Spider gave the update.

"As you'd expect, a lot of the major outlets won't touch the story," he said. "Even the ones Marsh doesn't have a financial stake in are too afraid right now. But we've flooded every possible forum with the footage, and sooner or later, the big boys will have to address it. At first, it will be the Marsh fanboys claiming that the footage is fake. But it won't be long before it takes off. Twelve hours tops."

"What about your old government contacts?" she asked.

"Most of them won't return my calls. And that silence speaks volumes. But one of them—I don't know which one, because the email was from a burner account—says that a guy named Ray Hollister is meeting with the President tomorrow morning."

"Hollister…" Lori rubbed her aching forehead. "He's on the board of directors for Marsh Industries, right?"

Spider nodded. "The lone holdover from Leonidas Marsh's regime. And here's what's real interesting about that meeting: Waylon Marsh apparently isn't involved. According to my source, Waylon doesn't even know."

"He's getting back-doored."

"It certainly appears so. And right after we started our media blitz with the shit from Waylon's laptop. I guess it could be coincidence, but it seems an awful lot like we struck a nerve." Spider's eyes flicked down to his laptop for a moment, then he looked back at her and said, "Now, go home and get some sleep. Have pleasant dreams. I promise you that we're perfectly capable of running this show for a few hours."

Lori didn't argue. She espoused the view that Earth Force and other environmental organizations should be youth-oriented. After all, the young had the most skin in the game when it came to safeguarding the future of the planet. But she also had a hard time letting go, which meant trusting the biggest moment in Earth Force's history to a roomful of kids was easier said than done. Had she not been both mentally and physically exhausted, she might have put up more of a fight. Maybe age was finally mellowing her out.

It was a short walk from the office to her apartment, and ten minutes later, she was kicking the front door closed behind her and dropping her keys onto the kitchen counter. Her pet cat—an obese tabby named Spock—mewed his usual greeting/plea for food combo as he stropped himself back and forth across her legs a few times. She opened a can of Fancy Feast, and knocked the stinky mush into his bowl. The soft food was reserved for special occasions, and Lori figured the imminent downfall of Waylon Marsh certainly qualified.

"Live long and prosper, big boy," she said, giving the cat a scratch behind the ears.

Spock was too busy inhaling his food to respond, so Lori

plodded into the apartment's lone bedroom, and shucked off her clothes. She briefly considered Spider's suggestion that she take a hot shower, but rejected it. If Spock hadn't recoiled from her, she didn't stink that bad. She put on an oversized t-shirt—the ghost of boyfriends past—and collapsed into bed.

She knew before her head hit the pillow that the dream would be the same. The silent figure in the black robe would beckon her across the river, and into the beautiful underground city. It was the same dream she'd had every time she closed her eyes for the past couple weeks. And it became clearer, more vividly detailed with each repetition. It was that high-definition clarity that shook her to her core. The dream meant something. It wasn't just images conjured from her subconscious brain. There was something about the dreams that made her believe with complete certainty that they came from an external source. They were a message from someone, or something.

She wasn't like a lot of the people who belonged to her organization. Her background was in hard science. She had degrees in botany, meteorology, and environmental science. Sure, she may have gone about her day-to-day business in tie-dye t-shirts and sandals, but her wardrobe was as close as she got to the crystal-gazing, dope-smoking hippie that the media liked to portray her as being. She didn't go in for the mystical Mother Earth nonsense. It was her belief that the whole environmentalist movement had been too poorly framed for the average person to give a shit. It should never have been pitched as an effort to save the planet, but as an effort to save the humans. The planet had been here long before humans, and it would be her long after. Saving the environment was a matter of simple necessity.

But, the dream was slowly but surely tugging at the loose threads of her rational worldview. There was something in the way that…

…the thought disappeared into the black velvet sinkhole of sleep. All thoughts and worries of the waking world were replaced by the sights and sounds of a gently flowing river, and the strange city on the opposite shore.

4

Trixie followed the trio of suit-and-tie guys into the hotel room. Normally, she didn't take on group work. It required way too much multi-tasking, and no matter how quick she dodged, she always managed getting semen in her hair. The guys at these conservative conventions got all their ideas about sex from porno movies, so they did all sorts of weird shit. Of course, all felt the need to unload on her face. When it was just one dick to contend with, she could fake enthusiasm while literally taking it on the chin. But when there were multiple wangs to account for, some of that friendly fire ended up going in her hair, or worse, her eye. But the shit had hit the fan at this particular convention when their head honcho, some dude named Reverend Jimmy, hadn't shown up for his evening engagements. Now, all his buddies found themselves with a whole bunch of free time, and the supply of working girls was way out of line with the demand. As if that wasn't enough, Candy had gone missing. So, even though it was her least favorite part of the job, Trixie had agreed to a group party, just to keep up with the sudden increase in demand. And maybe it would go some way toward getting her back into Stella's good graces.

"All right, boys," she said, using her best seductive sex kitten purr, "let's get this party started."

The Grand Gardens Hotel was a top notch joint, and the minibar had just about anything you could want. Trixie grabbed a couple tiny bottles of Grey Goose vodka, and poured them down her throat in quick succession. It loosened her up a bit, although it didn't do much for the weird feeling in her stomach. Ever since she'd partied with the weird old German dude, her belly had been a rumbling, crampy mess. After her first client of the day—a quickie blowjob in the parking lot—she'd run for the bathroom, certain that she was about to shit her brains out. But despite the audible wet gurgling in her stomach, everything seemed normal. So she'd soldiered on through the afternoon. After this group thing, she had time for four, maybe five jobs and then she could call it a night when Stella sent in the reserves. Then, she could guzzle down a bottle of Pepto, and hope that quieted the rumblings down below.

She emptied the last drops from the tiny bottle into her mouth, then tossed it over her shoulder. The johns were already getting into the swing of things, laughing and backslapping with half-drunken glee as they stripped off their clothes with all the grace of brain damaged baboons. She kicked off her shoes and slipped out of her little black dress.

"Man, look at those tits," one of the johns said, elbowing his friends.

"Baby want some milk!" This one, whose gut nearly hung down to his dick, must have been the comedian of the gang.

Trixie hadn't bothered learning their names. All she knew was they were youth ministers from some church in Baton Rouge and they'd paid for this hour of fun with twenties and hundreds so crisp they must have been fresh out of the ATM. The men weren't impressive specimens, but Trixie had to give them points for being comfortable in their own skins. Outside of a porn movie set, you didn't find many guys who were cool with just standing around with other naked men. They were probably closet bisexuals.

"Here we go," one of them said, punching up some music on his phone. "Get us a soundtrack for this fuck-fest."

The music was one of those new pop country songs about rednecks sitting on their trucks' tailgates and drinking beer while they watched girls dance, and guns and freedom and all manner of bullshit. It was pure nails on a chalkboard to Trixie, but at least it covered the sound of her grumbling belly. Maybe it wasn't such a good idea to do a couple vodka shots on an empty stomach, because it felt like the room was spinning. She stumbled a half-step backwards and covered the blunder by dancing to the terrible music. Her moves, which felt clumsy and slow, drew hoots of approval from her clients.

"Yeah, shake it, girl!"

"Go on, get it!"

One of them detached himself from the group and made his move for her. She closed her eyes as she felt him press close against her.

"You're about to get some serious pleasure." His breath was a fog of liquor and hot wings. "About to feel so good..."

Trixie was a pro, but it was getting harder to ignore the strange tingling all over her body. It wasn't the pleasant buzz of good blow, but it wasn't exactly terrible. Her heartbeat had been reduced to irregular palpitations. Her vision was a watery blur. She wondered, as the other two men descended on her, if these symptoms were serious. And if they were, then what of the hunger that had taken hold of her? The growls and gurgles in her stomach were so strong they nearly doubled her over.

"You all right, girl?" one of the men asked, detaching himself from her.

She heard the voice distantly, as if the john was calling from the end of a long tunnel, rather than standing toe-to-toe with her. She shook her head, trying to clear the cobwebs, but all she succeeded in doing was bringing on a wave of nausea so severe that she didn't have time to even attempt to stifle the urge to vomit. All at once, every muscle in her abdomen contracted, and a torrent sprayed from her mouth. The man in front of her did his best to dodge the stream, but his liquor-dulled reflexes fell short, and the left side of his face was soaked in a green and red sludge that reeked of rotten bile. The other two, who'd been standing behind her, yelped and jumped away.

Trixie ignored them. The horrible spasms in her stomach had abated, but the hunger remained. It was so fierce and sharp that she couldn't resist its bestial urge. She gave in, allowing the hunger to guide her actions as she fell on the vomit-soaked john, snapping and biting like a starved animal, ripping into him with fingers hooked into claws. As her jaws strained to tear through the tough gristle in the space where his shoulder met his neck, she felt herself gradually leave her body. No longer shackled to her earthly vessel, as her Baptist preacher father had called it, she watched dispassionately as the hotel room was transformed into a slaughterhouse.

With their friend now unconscious, the other two johns threw themselves at her, desperately trying to fight her off. But their fear and revulsion made them hesitant. They wanted to help, but their minds were struggling to accept the scene unfolding in front of them, and it made them easy prey.

Trixie had one last moment of amused satisfaction before she slipped into darkness.

This is one hell of sight, isn't it?

5

The butler—or whatever you were supposed to call a male domestic servant these days—appeared seemingly out of nowhere and offered Ray Hollister another drink.

"I'm afraid the President's meeting has run long," the butler explained. "You understand how these things are, of course."

"I surely do," Hollister said. "Tell you what, I wouldn't mind another drink. It's a bit early for me, but this warm weather has me parched."

"Another mint julep, sir?"

Hollister nodded. "That sounds mighty fine."

The butler departed in the same speedy, silent manner in which he'd arrived.

When people first heard Hollister speak, many of them came away with the impression that he was just an ignorant hick from Oklahoma. That was a false impression. Although there was no mistaking the Tulsa twang in his speech, the man had the steel-trap mind of the most cunning chess master. How else could he have gotten where he was?

He liked to joke that his family came from oil money. And it was true, to a point. His father had been a rig worker—a roughneck—for three decades, until an on-site accident claimed his life just a few weeks shy of his fiftieth birthday. The insurance payout and the out of court settlement from the company had covered Ray's education—an MBA from Duke University and a Juris Doctorate from Vanderbilt—and set him up with a decent starter stock portfolio. He'd gotten a job as Leonidas Marsh's financial advisor, and within a year, found himself on the Board of Directors of Marsh Industries.

Now, he sat in a wicker chair on the patio in the lush backyard of a Martha's Vineyard estate belonging to the President's family. He was surrounded by shrubbery that had had so carefully sculpted it might have been done with kitchen shears, perfumed flower beds buzzing with fat bumblebees, and a spread of manicured grass that put the most exclusive golf courses to shame. It was a beautiful day, maybe a bit hot, but there was a breeze. All things considered, Hollister should have been enjoying himself. But he couldn't quit thinking about the reason for his visit. He'd been summoned here to plunge his dagger into Waylon Marsh's back.

Et tu, Brute?

Hollister took no pleasure in what he was doing, but he didn't shy away from it either. Taking Waylon Marsh down was simply the smartest move available. Still, the method felt less than satisfying. He would have preferred to look the man in the eyes while he stuck the knife in. Leonidas Marsh had been a great man, but his son was a spoiled brat with delusions of grandeur. Even at fifty years of age, Waylon Marsh acted like an over-indulged frat boy. Hollister had been biding his time for years, watching for his opportunity to depose the brat and claim the throne for himself. If it had to be done through back channels, so be it.

The butler reappeared and deposited the cocktail on the little table next to the chair.

"Many thanks," Hollister said.

The butler nodded and excused himself.

Hollister wondered how long they were going to keep him waiting. Maybe they were trying to get a couple drinks in him to soften him up? No, he didn't think so. This wasn't some jerkoff CEO or hedge fund asshole he was meeting with. It was the President of the goddamn United States, and his national security advisor. There was no angle for them to work.

By the time he was rattling the ice in his mostly empty glass, an ex-jock type in a black suit—he might as well have had "Secret Service Agent" stamped on his forehead— emerged from the house, and motioned for Hollister to follow him inside.

"You can leave the drink on the table," the agent said. "Someone will take care of it."

"I'll bet." Hollister placed the glass on the table at the center of the patio and followed the agent into the house.

It wasn't the White House, but the place was fancy enough. The walls were coated in immaculate white paint and adorned with paintings of various styles. Hollister was no expert, but he figured each of those paintings would fetch five—hell, six—figures at auction. The pale blue carpet beneath his feet was soft and probably saw the bottom of a vacuum cleaner twice a day. The cooled air smelled of lavender and citrus and freshly brewed coffee.

The agent led Hollister down a hallway, past a kitchen full of sparkling stainless steel appliances, and through a pair of double doors into a room that could have been called a study or a library or maybe even a plain old office. Bookshelves lined the walls. An enormous old fashioned globe sat off to one side. The middle of the room was dominated by a large hardwood desk, in front of which were four chairs arranged in a semicircle.

The agent left the room, closing the heavy doors behind him with a soft *thunk*.

The three occupants of the room were of a single demographic: old, white, and rich. They were at once just like Hollister, and vastly different. While they shared his current status as members of the wealthy elite, none of them shared his hard scrabble background. The President was the son of a former CIA director, and the heiress of a retail empire. He'd been born a millionaire and had spent his entire life being groomed for a life in politics. Scott McManus, the national security advisor, came from a family of military generals and senators. Like the President, his life had been scripted from the hour of his birth. The third man was Morris Copeland, the pastor of the nation's largest mega-church, American Faith Tabernacle, which had three locations in Florida. Copeland was widely known as the President's "spiritual advisor," but anyone with half a brain, and Hollister liked to think that group included him, understood that the relationship ran much deeper than that.

Nobody rose from their seats to greet Hollister as he entered the room.

"Sorry to keep you waiting," the President said from behind his desk. "Have a seat."

Hollister eased himself into one of the chairs and tried his best to look at ease.

"I've already wasted enough of your time, so we'll dispense with the chit chat and get right to it," the President continued. "This is quite a mess your boss has made. I mean, we can turn a blind eye to all the tax evasion and insider trading. We can even look the other way on the clear violations of UN treaties in Africa and South America. But this reanimation of the dead? Goddamn zombies, Ray? That can't stand. Not under my watch. This thing blows up, and I'll have shit thrown at me from all sides. Not just the purple haired Antifa types, but the gun-toting, church-going patriots as well. You hear what I'm saying?"

"We're doing our best to keep the story contained..." Hollister shifted in his seat.

The President whipped his glasses off his nose and tossed them onto his desk. He fixed Hollister with a look of weary disappointment. It wasn't the first time Hollister had been in the room with the President. Marsh Industries had made generous donations to both his election and re-election campaigns, and poured enough dark money into various PACs to get a seat at the table whenever the administration was shaping economic policy. Because Waylon Marsh saw himself as a "big ideas guy," he wasn't much concerned with those type of details. He'd pose with the President for photo ops and eat dinner at the White House Christmas party, but he left the boring details up to Hollister. This was his most intimate meeting with the President, and Hollister felt appropriately nervous.

"Our social media people are working around the clock," Hollister said. "We have several firms on retainer—Russians, mostly; same as we used during the last election—and they're going at it around the clock."

"Too late. The story's out there. Sure, you're running plenty of interference now, but how long can that work? Any damage control you can eke out is going to be a Band-Aid on a bullet wound at this point." The President was using his debate voice, and Hollister was starting to understand how this seemingly harmless grandfatherly type had sent the competition packing. "This shit cannot—absolutely *cannot*—continue, Ray. Not on my watch."

"Amen to that," Copeland added.

McManus' jaw tightened in a way that suggested he would like nothing more than to punch the TV preacher. Instead, he tapped the screen on a tablet computer and passed it to Hollister, saying, "Last night, there was an *incident* at the Grand Gardens Hotel in DC. Go ahead and swipe through those images and videos. They'll give you a pretty clear idea of what sort of incident we're talking about."

Hollister did as he suggested, scrolling through one gruesome image after another. It looked like scenes from some nasty horror film. And Hollister tried to think of it in those terms. It was easier to keep his breakfast down that way. But he knew exactly what he was looking at: the HOPE Project had not only gotten out of Daroka, it had jumped across the Atlantic Ocean and landed in DC.

"DC Metro Police were called in to contain what they are calling a riot," McManus explained. "But it was too much for them. I guess someone connected to Marsh Industries was at the hotel, because Pendleton Security was on the scene about fifteen minutes after the police arrived. They did a clean sweep of the building. At least that's what they're claiming. But let's be honest, there's no way they could lock down a building that size in that short amount of time. Someone got out."

"Jesus Christ," Hollister said as he swiped through the hundreds of images pulled from the hotel's security cameras.

Copeland made a sound of disapproval at the blasphemy. McManus jumped back in before the preacher could launch into a sermon. "Our intel says this thing works like a virus. Is that accurate?"

Hollister nodded. "I can't speak to all the technical details, but I'd say that's close enough. Initially, it was a serum. You know, just like a regular inoculation shot. At some point, Marsh must have decided that method was too cumbersome. He must have been holding private meetings with the researchers, because this was never disclosed to the board of directors."

That was only partially true. Hollister and a few others in the inner circle had known that the project was heading in a different direction. They just didn't know how far along—or how easily transmissible—the virus was. The last technical report that Hollister read had mentioned something about mutation, but he hadn't paid it much mind. The technical stuff was all a bunch of egghead gobbledygook. It wasn't above his paygrade; it just wasn't his department.

"And now we hear that your head scientist, Gustav Vogel, is missing," McManus continued. "Is that also accurate?"

"Yeah, it is," Hollister answered. He handed the tablet back to McManus. He'd seen more than enough of that stuff to last him a lifetime.

"Waylon Marsh is also in the wind." McManus set the tablet on the President's desk. "He's not returning our calls, if you can believe that. The man is actually ignoring calls from the White House. We have people looking, but so far, nothing. As hard as it is to believe that someone like that can actually hide, that seems to be the case."

Hollister didn't find it hard to believe at all. Waylon Marsh may have been greedy, self-centered, and stupid, but he did possess a billionaire's devious narcissism. If there was one area in which he exceled, it was self-preservation. And as far as ignoring the President's phone calls? Marsh would probably just roll his eyes and say something about how he didn't vote for the guy.

"This is a real crisis," the President said. "And for Waylon Marsh, it's a 'one strike and you're out' kind of deal. He swung for the fences and he missed. Now it's time for the next man up."

Hollister nodded, trying not to appear too eager. "Yes, sir. The board of directors has a contingency plan for this kind of situation. There are 'no confidence' clauses built into every contract. And Marsh signed off on all of them, because, well, there are plenty of reasons why. For one thing, his lawyer told him to. The other reasons all come down to pride and ego, both of which my boss has got in spades."

McManus cleared his throat and spoke up. "I'm afraid we're past that stage. There will be a hostile takeover, but it won't involve paperwork or board meetings. Do you understand what I'm saying?"

"You mean terminate with extreme prejudice or something like that?" Hollister laughed. Then he glanced at the other men and realized he was the only one who found it funny.

"That's not official terminology," McManus said.

Hollister's blood went cold. *Holy shit, I wasn't wrong. They're going to kill him. The goddamn President is putting out a hit on the brat.*

"The hour of Waylon Marsh's judgment is at hand." Copeland spoke like he was explaining a difficult Bible verse to a Sunday school full of slow children. "The man's, ah, nefarious pursuits have issued forth abominations."

"If this comes as such a shock," the President said, "perhaps you're not the right man to fill the coming power vacuum."

"No, that's not it." Hollister raised his hands defensively. "I just didn't know that…well, what I mean to say…"

"The undead must not be permitted to thrive among God's children." Copeland was speaking to no one in particular, and Hollister got the idea that the man did so a lot. "This whole sordid affair reeks of sin. Pride! Wanton hubris! For God alone can know the hour of a man's death."

McManus slapped the arm of his chair. "Well, in this case, we know it too, Morris, so how about putting a cork in it? This isn't the time for one of your sermons. Save that bullshit for the retired rubes down in Orlando."

"Why, sir, I object to your general tone-"

"Enough!" The President pounded his desk.

"Thank you, Mr. President," Copeland said, smiling expansively. "The man was well and truly out of order. Why, he was stepping dangerously close to the edge of blasphemy."

"I was talking to you, Morris. You know I appreciate all

the support you've given me over the years, but no one in this room is interested in your sales pitch. So how about dropping the goddamn carnie act for once in your life? And if that's too much to ask, I'll settle for you just shutting the hell up and letting the grownups talk."

Hollister had only known Reverend Copeland for a few minutes, but that was plenty of time for him to form an opinion about the man. And his opinion was that Copeland's head was so far up his own ass that he must exist on a steady diet of his own farts. It was a rare pleasure to see a man like that get dressed down by an authority figure.

Copeland bowed his head. "Yes, sir."

"Now," the President continued, "Scott has someone in place to do the deed. So you don't need to concern yourself with the particulars, Ray. Frankly, the less you know about the details, the better. What we need to know is if you're up to the job. Because after this, we expect to have a friend at the top of the company's food chain. Down the line, that's going to pay dividends, but right now, it means taking a big hit. You're going to grovel for the media. Fall on your own sword, so to speak. You think you can handle that?"

Hollister nodded. "I know I can."

"And this thing with the HOPE Project, it gets shut down immediately, and hard." The President leaned forward, pointing a finger right at Hollister. "And that ball is in your court. There will be no nightly news footage of zombies walking down Pennsylvania Avenue. I hope I'm very clear on that point."

"Yes, sir. It will be contained," Hollister assured him.

"You can leave Daroka to us as well," McManus said. "Our contact at Pendleton Security has already got the ball rolling there."

"So Mike London's team is being recalled?" Hollister had the sinking feeling that he already knew the answer, but he asked anyway.

"Not recalled." McManus shook his head. "Disavowed and cut loose. Maybe they end up helping us out with the containment, or maybe they're already dead. Either way, Daroka is going to be vaporized as soon as we can get the right contractors in place. Officially, it will be General Mbowi's last act in his reign of terror. Unofficially, and speaking for myself, we're finally going to do what we should have done in the first place."

6

Svetlana Kurzcyk was no longer sure how to define her role in the unfolding crisis. Was she still a whistleblower trying to topple Marsh Industries in the court of public opinion? Was she just some industrial terrorist taking down one of the richest men in the world? Or was she still a government asset in a deep cover operation? Maybe all of those things were true. When she looked in the mirror, she saw...well, not exactly a stranger, but maybe a new version of herself. It wasn't the same as having a blank slate, but it did feel liberating. One more history-altering act, and she was fee to write her own story.

"These fuckers, they want to kill me," Marsh said, his word's slurred after consuming his fourth triple vodka and energy drink cocktail. "It was all champagne and roses when I was offering up an entire continent worth of resources and stock options on the future government. But now that we've hit one little speedbump, they want to fucking kill me. It's not fair, Svetlana. You hear me? Not fucking fair."

They were in the back lounge of Marsh's luxury RV, seated on a couch upholstered in Corinthian leather. The massive vehicle was rolling through the backroads of the

Deep South, somewhere in Mississippi, staying off the radar of the enemies that Marsh had begun to see everywhere. Presumably, they were on their way to Mexico, although Marsh had begun to fear that a border crossing might be too risky. For the last hour, he'd been debating aloud with himself about whether or not he'd be able to bribe his way across the border if the President really had put out a hit on him.

"You know," Svetlana said, "you could just take his phone call. This whole thing might be some big misunderstanding and you're not in any trouble at all."

Marsh laughed. "Okay, sure. I swear, this is why women will never run the world. You're too fucking naïve. Even an ice cold bitch like yourself can't see things for what they really are."

"The twentieth century called." Svetlana brandished her cell phone. "They want their sexism back."

"I thought I told you to throw that goddamn thing away," Marsh growled.

"Relax, it's just a burner. I need to keep up with the day-to-day business stuff, even if we are in the middle of a crisis. You want things to be in order when this all blows over, don't you?" Svetlana tucked the phone into the pocket of her hoodie. Outside the RV, it was a boiling hot Dixie summer, but inside, Marsh kept the air conditioner blasting. She was thankful she'd had the foresight to pack something warmer than the yoga pants/t-shirt combo Marsh liked her to wear when it was just the two of them.

"You still think this will all blow over?" Marsh looked at her with eyes full of childlike hope. "That's what I like about you, baby. You are a beacon of optimism. Or maybe it's just a total lack of knowledge about the way the world works. But that's cute too."

"There's nothing so terrible that it can't be fixed." She'd had so much practice lying to him that her reply was instant.

"All those billions of dollars can make just about anything go away, right?"

That second part had actually been true, mostly. Marsh's billions had been able to insulate him from every conceivable scandal. But the cracks in his shell were starting to widen, and his genuine fear was written all over his face.

Svetlana touched his thigh. "You'll see. Everything will be okay."

"Yeah." Marsh's smile was the trembling, unsure expression of a nervous child on the first day of school, full of forced hope and real fear. He scooted closer and draped an arm over her shoulders. "You know, I've been thinking. Maybe when this blows over and things get back to normal, we should get married. It wouldn't be so bad to have a wife, you know? Probably go a long way towards patching things up in the PR department. Maybe we could do a reality show for a while, get you into some modeling stuff, maybe a part in a Marvel movie. Could be fun."

If Svetlana had suspected before that Marsh was losing his grip on reality, now she was certain. There wasn't a man on the planet who was less capable of matrimony than Waylon Marsh.

"Yeah, that sounds like an amazing plan," she said.

He pounced on her, pressing his mouth against hers. He tasted like alcohol and artificial sweeteners. The kiss went on and on. Svetlana's mouth began to ache. Her phone buzzed in her pocket, but Marsh didn't notice, or didn't care. His tongue continued its thorough probe of her mouth. He'd always been a clumsy, careless kisser, and that was bad enough, but now, his kisses had taken on a forceful desperation. It was almost enough to make her gag. He was practically tickling her tonsils. When he finally pulled away, his face was covered in a sheen of sweat, despite the chilly air.

He levered himself off the couch and stood unsteadily.

"I gotta go to the bathroom," he explained over his shoulder, as he stumbled out of the lounge.

Svetlana scrubbed her mouth with the back of her hand. She dug her phone out of her pocket and looked at the message on the screen.

McManus says you have the green light.

She tucked the phone into her pocket and took a deep breath. Although she'd been preparing herself for this moment since the shit hit the fan in Daroka, she couldn't believe it had actually arrived.

No going back after this, she told herself.

Her purse was on the floor beside the couch. She put it in her lap and dug into it, reaching past her wallet, keys, makeup compact, tin of breath mints, packet of facial tissues, tubes of lip balm, tampons, bottle of ibuprofen, and loose change; all the way to the concealed compartment at the bottom of the bag. The small hidden pocket contained a knife with a three inch blade. It was nothing special, just a folding knife with a single edge honed to razor sharpness. But for what she had in mind, it didn't need to be anything special.

She secreted the knife away between the couch cushions, then put her purse back on the floor. She heard the toilet flush in the closet-sized bathroom. It was almost here, the moment of truth. Strange that she wasn't nervous. Although she'd rehearsed this day in her head, dreaming of the thousands of different possible scenarios, she'd always expected to be wracked with nerves. Instead, she felt an eerie calmness as she stood up and peeled off her clothes. She shivered as her skin was exposed to the cool air.

The door to the bathroom slammed open and Marsh stood at the threshold, watching Svetlana pull down her panties and kick them across the room to where the rest of her clothes were piled.

"I thought you looked tense," she explained. "Maybe a massage would help relax you."

"Yeah, a massage and something else," he said, licking his lips.

Svetlana raised an eyebrow. "Is that right?"

"Yeah, like a fucking blowjob."

The response was just the sort that Svetlana expected. When your net worth was that of a small nation's gross domestic product, you don't need to master the art of seduction. Hell, you don't even need to make an effort.

She sat on the couch, wincing inwardly as she felt her skin adhere to the cold leather. She patted the cushion next to her. "Come sit. Take off your shirt and let me get those knots out of your back muscles."

Marsh wasn't wearing some elaborate outfit, just jogging pants and a t-shirt with the logo of a British anarcho-punk band. But even so, he had trouble getting undressed. He'd been up for nearly two days straight, ingesting nothing but energy drinks, hard liquor, and protein bars. Hence the clammy, sweaty skin, and dark circles under the eyes, and fumbling, uncoordinated fingers. He got down to his jockey shorts and socks, then sat down on the couch, draping himself over one of the arms.

"Rub me, baby," he said. "Daddy's had a hard day at the office."

"Just close your eyes and relax." She put her hands on his shoulders and started to knead. "You're so tense…"

He sighed. "It's the pressures of this job. People have no idea. They think that I have it easy. But they get to work for their paycheck at McDonald's or the car wash or the shoe store or whatever, and then they just go home and relax. Sure, they only get a measly hundred and fifty thousand, two hundred thousand a year, but they don't work under the same kind of stress as I do."

"Yeah, those fry cooks making a hundred thousand should really shut the fuck up." Normally, she kept her sarcasm in check, but Marsh's brain was so pickled with alcohol and caffeine that she knew he wouldn't even pick up on it.

"I'm telling you right now, those people would wilt if they had to put up with the bullshit I deal with on a daily basis. They'd fucking wilt, baby."

"It's good that you're so much stronger than they are." She continued kneading with her left hand while her right slipped between the sofa cushions. Her fingers closed around the knife handle.

"You know how it is in my line of work: you either get tough or die."

If Svetlana was inclined to feel sympathy or pity for Marsh, she might have hesitated. But all traces of those emotions had long since been blasted away by her years at his side. Now she just wanted to get it over with. She flipped the knife blade out of the handle with her thumb and felt it lock into place.

"Damn, baby, that feels good," Marsh sighed.

"Just relax…"

The knife was sharp, and she applied plenty of pressure as she drew it across his throat. She could tell from the amount of blood and the forcefulness of the spray that she'd severed a major artery. Marsh tried to scream, but his mouth was too choked with blood to manage more than a burbling, gagging noise. Hot blood washed over the arm of the couch and slopped onto the floor, soaking the carpet. Marsh's hands clenched into fists. He flailed his arms, but she was behind him, and the few blows that actually landed lacked any real force. She grabbed a handful of his hair, and pulled his head back as she finished slicing his neck. By now, he was starting to slow down. He'd quit making so much noise, but he was still making a hell of a mess. Svetlana glanced across the room at her pile of clothes. Despite the staggering amount of arterial spray, her clothing seemed to have been spared. That was good. She didn't relish the possibility of having to walk through the bus naked.

Once she was certain Marsh had bled out, she went into the bathroom and washed the blood off her hands and forearms. She brushed her hair and tied it back into a ponytail. A quick look in the mirror to check for any remaining traces of blood, and she was done. She slipped back into her discarded clothes. The phone, which was a burner, came with location tracking. It was still in the pocket of her sweatpants, and she dug it out, replying to the last message.

Done.

She didn't have to wait long for a reply.

Good job. Extraction team inbound.

She shoved the phone back into her pocket and headed for the front of the bus.

The driver's head turned slightly at her approach. He managed a smile, but his eyes spoke of caffeine overconsumption and highway hypnosis. According to the late Waylon Marsh, the driver had worked for rock bands, and had "seen all kinds of wild shit." To Svetlana, he just looked like a tired old dude who was ready for retirement. If that was really the case, he'd soon get his wish. When the extraction team arrived, he'd most likely be retired permanently. That almost bothered her, but she knew the score: there was always collateral damage.

"Hey, Arthur," she said.

"Good morning, pretty lady." He tipped an invisible cap. "Or shit, I guess it should be good afternoon. Easy to lose track when you're in the middle of nowhere."

She gestured over her shoulder toward the back of the bus. "The boss is taking a nap in the back lounge. He asked not to be disturbed."

Arthur nodded. "Way he's been chugging down them

energy drinks, I'm amazed he can sleep at all. Guess you build up a tolerance."

"He said you should stop at the next rest area and get some sleep yourself."

"Now, that's what I like to hear. Afraid we got a few miles to go before we get to a place where we can park this monster truck, though." He glanced up at her, then patted the passenger seat. "You feel like sitting up front for a while? I could show you how to drive this thing or maybe we could just listen to some tunes and shoot the shit."

"Why not?" She dropped into the seat and relaxed.

"You don't mind me saying, you look like you could do with a rest yourself," Arthur said.

Svetlana laughed. He had no idea.

7

WAYLON MARSH: WHEREABOUTS UNKNOWN
SEARCH FOR VENTURE CAPITALIST CONTINUES

Following a wild forty-eight hour period which saw the value of Marsh Industries stock plummet, tech billionaire Waylon Marsh has been officially declared missing. The dip in stock value has been attributed to the as yet unverified reports of widespread corruption and medical malpractice surrounding the company's presence in the war-torn African nation Daroka. A coalition of climate activists and human rights crusaders have dogged Marsh Industries' HOPE Project initiative, accusing the company of locating its research centers in Daroka in an effort to skirt medical ethics and safety standards

In related news, efforts to verify the authenticity of the so-called "Daroka Zombie" footage are ongoing. While many experts have claimed the footage shows no evidence of computer manipulation or "deep fakery," others have laughed off the possibility that the events shown in the footage are real.

"I know that there have been mistakes made by company leadership, and believe me, we have plenty of housecleaning to do,"

said Raymond Hollister, president of the Marsh Industries board of directors. "We are more than willing to have that conversation. But this zombie footage thing is just science fiction of the worst kind. It's the stuff of bad horror movies. Just silly. If Lori Lund and her Earth Force activists want to have an honest and open conversation, my door is open. We can talk about reducing the company's carbon footprint and cutting emissions. We can talk about our continued commitment to reducing fossil fuel consumption and our worldwide effort to streamline recycling. But one thing we will not discuss is zombies, because, as a rational adult, I don't indulge in that type of fantasy. And frankly, I'm surprised that I even have to say that."

When asked for his thoughts about Waylon Marsh's disappearance, Hollister said Marsh Industries was cooperating with state and national authorities as well as employing a private security firm to locate Marsh as quickly as possible.

—Alicia Frazier-Campbell, CNN

GENERAL MBOWI IS DEAD?
WARLORD REPORTEDLY SHOT IN BORWANNAH SKIRMISH

General George Mbowi, the military leader who led a bloody coup in the central African nation of Daroka two years ago, was shot and killed by a citizens' militia group patrolling the border between Daroka and neighboring Borwannah.

Mbowi, whose ruthless rise to power was decried by human rights groups, overthrew the democratically-elected socialist government. Despite widespread speculation that Mbowi received covert support from the American government, connections between the coup and any foreign government have remained unproven.

Daroka made international headlines just months prior to the coup when Marsh Industries chose the small nation as the location for its largest HOPE Project research center. Despite the criticism Marsh Industries received for choosing to continue operations in Daroka after Mbowi's coup, the company's bottom line remained healthy until the recent disappearance of Waylon Marsh, the company's president and son of founder Leonidas Marsh.

Although details regarding Mbowi's death are scant, the group claiming responsibility for the ambush, Rise Up Liberated, has promised that details are forthcoming.

—Spencer West, *The Wall Street Journal*

UNITED NATIONS TO DEBATE QUARANTINE MEASURES FOR DAROKA

After a week of intense speculation regarding the authenticity of video footage from the Marsh Industries research facility in Daroka, the United Nations has convened a special committee to explore the possibility of a quarantine for the central African nation. Following the death of General George Mbowi, there is no clear government power in Daroka. Further complicating matters is the lack of a clear consensus about who has the resources to lead any humanitarian efforts in the country. In Daroka, industry and human rights have been in constant flux, ever since the discovery in the region of large deposits of rare earth metals necessary for manufacturing of cell phones.

—Noor Abdi, Associated Press

Partial transcript from episode of *Drive Time Politics with Richie Jordan and DJ Birdsong*:

JORDAN: And have you heard this story about that housing project in Atlanta where the residents got rabies? I mean, talk about weird. And the story has just been buried by the lamestream media.

BIRDSONG: You gotta wonder if the White House's political opposition is behind it.

JORDAN: Oh, I don't wonder. I know they're behind it. Nothing they fear worse than one of their social experiments going wrong.

BIRDSONG: And the people in that community don't care. They line up to vote for these guys and this is how they get treated.

JORDAN: Our phone line is blowing up, and I promise we'll get to some of your calls in a minute.

BIRDSONG: People are ready to sound off! They're pissed!

JORDAN: And do you blame them? Hard-working Americans have been subsidizing these lazy bums in their fancy apartments for years. They go to the store and buy lobster and steak with their food stamps and they can't even bothered to vaccinate for rabies.

BIRDSONG: Hold up, do they vaccinate people for rabies?

JORDAN: Of course they do. They may not tell you that's what they're doing, but how do you know what's in that flu shot? It's not like a bag of potato chips, where they got the ingredients listed.

BIRDSONG: But you don't get a flu shot.

JORDAN: Damn right I don't! You don't know what's in it! That's my point!

BIRDSONG: Right…

JORDAN: And you don't mind me saying, buddy, you look like maybe you took one of those government-approved jabs. You feeling okay? Don't tell me you let them shoot you up with that 5G radiation tracking device.

BIRDSONG: No, man, nothing like that. Just a little dizzy. And like, I'm hungry or something, but looking at regular food makes me feel nauseous. I feel like my stomach is growling so loud that the mic is picking it up.

JORDAN: Probably something you ate. Or maybe stop going to Atlanta to find dates. Let's go to the phones…

MYSTERIOUS SHIPWRECK ON BRAZILIAN COAST

Posted anonymously to the *Truth Seeker Theory* online message board:

okay, so this is a little long I apologize in advance. I live in brazil because my dad works for an american oil company (yeah, THAT one) and he was out on one of the offshore rigs for an inspection. they got a report of a ship that was out on the water and it was like an unidentified ship because it wasn't flying any flags but they figured out it was a pirate ship. not like captain jack sparrow pirates but like real african pirates. they might have been somalia pirates i don't know my dad didn't say but here's where it gets scary. the company decides to send out boats to inspect the ship since its to close to the rig and they find nothing on board but a bunch of rats and chewed up dead bodies like the rats had been eating the people. and as if that were'nt scary enough, the rats started attacking the oil rig workers who'd come to check out the ship. like ten guys in all got bit by these killer rats and their all in the hospital now because they got real sick and the infirmory on the rig couldnt handle there symptoms so they sent them back to land. now their saying that the ship was carrying drugs smuggled out of Darkoa from genral Mbowi and the rats might have escaped from that research center that marsh industrys has in dakroa…

tl;dr there are killer rats coming out of africa and that's why the price of gas is going up and pretty soon you're going to see all this on the news

**From the diary of Molly Corvallo,
Therapist at the Fayette Hills Sleep Disorders Clinic:**

The dreams are getting longer and more detailed now. And not just for my clients, but for myself as well. I swear, when I was asleep last night, I dreamed about wandering through that underground city for hours and hours, getting lost in the maze of streets. I saw other people there, wandering just like me, with their mouths hanging open like tourists seeing New York City or Rome for the first time. I'm not sure these people could see me, and for some reason, I didn't try to speak to them.

I don't know, maybe I'm cracking up. I hear all the time about how every therapist needs a therapist. Maybe I should look into that. There's no shame in it. After all, I did intakes for two new clients today, and both of them are doctors from the clinic. Feel like taking a guess what their dreams have been about lately?

Leaked Email from Independent News Service reporter Kevin Kolzack to News Desk Editor Wallace Foreman:

Good morning, Wallace.

I just wanted to get back with you about the message you left on my voicemail about my latest piece on the Daroka situation. I'm not sure exactly why you found my article unacceptable, but I'll try and answer a few of the questions you had.

Sources in the intelligence community have assured us that General George Mbowi is currently in the custody of the Borwannah rebel group Rise Up Liberated, but out actual boots-on-the-ground sources are telling a different story. In fact, one of my sources in country tells me that Mbowi is dead, and that Rise Up Liberated is part of a CIA-backed information campaign. Since I couldn't confirm any connection, I left that part out of my story. But it certainly casts some doubt on the Marsh Industries company line.

Speaking of Marsh Industries, I couldn't help but notice

that many of the talking points you demanded I put in my article are taken straight out of the company's press release. I know that Waylon Marsh owns a controlling interest in our news service, but I also have journalistic standards to uphold. I would rather be unemployed than parrot the corporate nonsense you seem to believe is a credible source.

In closing, consider this my resignation.

Sincerely,
K. Kolzack

Part Seven

A gaze blank and pitiless as the sun…

"On a global scale, we're fucked."

—Michael K. London

1

There was no doubt about it: the Jeep was fucked. London knew it before he even popped the hood. His knowledge of automotive repair wasn't exactly encyclopedic, but he knew they were screwed as soon as the engine locked up and smoke and steam started billowing from under the hood. They were still on the logging company road, although it was rougher and even less maintained this far north.

Now, the entire group—the Pendleton team and the two French journalists—were gathered around the overheated Jeep, keeping their distance until the thick clouds of smoke pouring out of the engine had finally dissipated.

"What do you think is wrong, boss?" Zantoro asked, gesturing vaguely at the engine.

"Could be the radiator," Vincent suggested.

"Yeah? You finally putting that brain of yours to work?" Zantoro snapped.

"Hey, fuck you, Zantoro." Osbourne stepped between the two men. "Like you know anything about engines. Speaking of brains, why don't you go snort some blow and kill what's left of your brain cells. At least then we wouldn't have to hear your mouth."

"Okay, right now, tough guy." Zantoro dropped his rifle and stepped forward until he was toe-to-toe with Osbourne.

"Huh?" Suddenly, Osbourne looked less like a seasoned killer and more like the Nebraska farm boy he'd been before joining the army.

"You heard me. I said it's you and me. Now let's go."

Zantoro knocked the gun out of Osbourne's hands, then grabbed the big man around the waist with one arm. With a high, girlish laugh, he grabbed Osbourne's hand and dragged him into the world's most awkward waltz.

"Come on, spin me, big boy! Is that a nine millimeter pistol in your pocket or are you just happy to see me?" Zantoro laughed. "I'm warning you, I don't put out on the first date, even for strapping lads such as yourself."

London shook his head. "I'm stranded in the middle of the goddamn jungle with a bunch of morons."

"Hey," Vincent said. "Don't lump me in with those idiots."

"You know anything about engines?" London asked.

"Well…" Vincent looked away, watching Osbourne detach himself from Zantoro, who was hanging on with fierce determination.

"That's what I thought," London said. "You're a moron just like the other two morons. And I guess that makes me a fucking moron too, because I don't know jack shit about how to get this thing moving. And even if I did, we got no fucking tools. What about you, Lia? You know engines? Max, you a secret mechanical genius?"

The reporters shook their heads. Max said something in French, but Lia raised a hand to shut him up. He folded his arms over his chest, and turned his head to gaze into the jungle.

London chose not to acknowledge the ridiculous show that the photographer was putting on. If he wanted to pout like a spurned prom queen, that was his business. Instead, London turned to the two dance partners and told them to knock off the bullshit, then continued, "So here's a status report, gentlemen and lady. We are currently twenty four hours past our objective, and it looks like it will be at least another twenty-four until we make it to the research facility. We're down to one vehicle, which means it's going to be a tight fit for the remainder of our trip. That means we need to toss everything that isn't essential."

"Wait a second," Lia protested. "Don't we get a say in this?"

"What, you want to strand us out here?" London shook his head. "I'm sorry, babe, but that's not an option."

"Of course we won't strand you," she said.

Without stopping his intense examination of the trees, Max muttered something in French. Everyone ignored him.

"But," Lia continued, "we can't just throw out all our things. Those cameras, those boxes of files, that's our work."

"Like I said, I'm sorry, but unless it's mission critical, everything in that vehicle is getting thrown out to make room for my men and any supplies we need." He put a hand on her shoulder. "You need to understand that this isn't optional. I know how important your work is to you, but it's not more important than our lives."

"That's not what you said." She brushed his hand away. "You said 'mission critical.' You're still worried about the corporate masters on the other end of your leash."

"You're wrong about that," he said. "And you're wrong about me."

"Whatever." She stomped away, joining Max in his study of the surrounding foliage.

London sighed. He just didn't understand women. He motioned to the members of his team. "You three Mensa candidates get to work cleaning out their vehicle. Anything that's not food, water, weapons, or survival supplies goes into the Jeep. Maybe we can come back for it."

"Yeah, right," Zantoro said. "Ain't nobody ever coming back to this godforsaken spot."

"Just do it." London glanced over at Lia. "I better mend some fences before we move out again."

"That what they call it these days?" Osbourne asked. "Back in Omaha, we called it making love."

"And back in Queens, we called it fucking," Vincent added.

"The Queens version sounds like more fun," Osbourne said.

They all laughed like they'd just stumbled onto a comedy goldmine. London left them to it. He headed to the opposite side of the vehicle, where Lia and Max had stationed themselves to pout. They turned their heads and gave him a look of disapproval that London thought was particularly French. When he spoke, he felt his west Texas accent more acutely than he had in ages.

"Max, you mind giving us a minute?" he asked.

"Neither of you need my permission." Max turned his eyes back to Lia. "That has been made abundantly clear."

London thought that meant Max took the hint, but apparently, either the phrase "give us a minute" didn't translate well, or leaning against the front fender of the Land Rover was so comfortable that he was reluctant to give up his spot. Either way, the photographer didn't move.

"Okay then," London said, taking Lia by the elbow. "Let's walk down the road a ways, how about that?"

"I don't see why that's necessary, but fine."

London walked until he was relatively certain they were out of earshot, then he stopped in the middle of the road and turned to face Lia.

"Look here," he began. "I don't know what you think I'm trying to do here, but evidently you don't approve."

"Mission critical." Her tone dripped disdain that was amplified by her accent. "You should hear yourself. After everything you've seen, you still want to play soldier. And I'm not just talking about the dead people who won't stay dead, either. I'm talking about the dreams, the underground city, all of that. How can you see those things and still believe in your mission?"

London laughed. "Damn, woman."

"Is something I said funny?" She crossed her arms over her chest.

"It's just that you think that your journalistic mission is still important. Maybe you ought to think about turning some of that righteous indignation on yourself."

"And what is that supposed to mean?"

"You think I still want to complete my assignment and clean up Marsh Industries' mess?" London shook his head. "When I use the word 'mission,' that ain't at all what I'm talking about. Even if I was inclined to help them with their cover-up, it's evident that they don't even care about that anymore. You ask me, they cut us loose. I reckon we've been totally disavowed and there ain't even any record of us having ever been employed by Pendleton Security. Something is happening in the world outside this little country, and whatever it is must be big."

Her expression and posture softened. "If that's the way you feel, then what is it you think is the mission?"

"Survival. And I don't mean just our survival. I'm talking about the entire human race. Because if whatever is causing this horror movie shit in Daroka happens to get out into the rest of the world, we're fucked. On a global scale, we're fucked. So we go north. We get to that research facility and we blow it to pieces. Not to protect Waylon Marsh's reputation, but to nip this zombie bullshit in the bud."

She gave him a look, but didn't say anything. While he waited for a response, he dug his can of Skoal out of his pocket and settled a pinch behind his lower lip. Another few dips, and the can would be empty; if he rationed the remainder, he might get another full day out of it. That alone was motivation to get this mission over with.

"How do the others feel about this?" she asked.

London glanced over his shoulder at his team. They were busy moving AV equipment and boxes of documents from the Land Rover to the broken down Jeep. Max had chosen not to help. He stood at the side of the road, staring into the middle distance.

"They know the score," London said, turning back to Lia. "They know we've been sold out by our company. But they also know that freaking out and getting pissed off won't help our situation one bit. Same reason they haven't lost their shit over the rest of the team getting killed. You do this job long enough, you learn to bury your feelings until the mission is complete. Most of the time, you end up just cashing the paycheck, and thanking God you made it out alive. Guys like us can't afford to let our emotions lead us around. All that laughing and horsing around back there? It's whistling past the graveyard."

"That doesn't sound like much of a life."

"Yeah, well…" He shrugged. "It's a bit late in the game to start philosophizing."

"Whether or not you want to, sooner or later we must talk about what happened in Hutoh's hut. The dreams and…the other stuff." She didn't blush or look away when she brought up their sexual encounter.

That ran counter to London's experience with women. He thought maybe he preferred the direct approach. Or maybe he just preferred Lia. He told himself to stow that shit and focus on the mission. If, by some miracle, they made it through this ordeal, he could examine his feelings about her more closely. Until then, she was just another member of the team.

Yeah, just like Zantoro or Osbourne, only with big blue eyes, soft lips, and a body with curves in all the right places. But sure, she's just another team member. A team member you've fucked and shared dreams with, but yeah, basically just one of the guys…

The sudden noise of overlapping shouts ripped him out of his reverie. He turned toward the source of the commotion and sighed as he watched Max and Zantoro circling one another with fists raised. Osbourne and Vincent stood a short distance away, offering advice and encouragement, laughing and elbowing each other in the ribs.

"I swear," London said, "sometimes, it's like having a bunch of overgrown kids."

Lia muttered something in French. London didn't understand a word of it, but he got the meaning loud and clear. It sounded an awful lot like a lament for men's inability to grow up. London had never considered himself a feminist, but on this point, he wholeheartedly agreed. After all, it wouldn't be the worst thing in the world for Max to take a stiff shot to the chin. The guy had been acting like an asshole ever since their visit to the Ka'Longho village. Then again, Zantoro could probably do with an ass kicking himself. It was a classic no-win situation, and exactly the type of bullshit that they didn't need.

"Come on," London said, grabbing Lia's hand. "Let's go throw a bucket of cold water on these idiots."

Thankfully, the two combatants were still circling one another when London stepped between them. He knew from experience that things could be cooled down at this stage, but once blows were exchanged, there would never be a moment where Zantoro and Max weren't biding their time for the next fight. London had enough on his mind without having to keep them separated.

"What the fuck is going on here?" he demanded.

Zantoro kept his eyes on Max as he answered, "Oh, not much, boss. Just that Pierre here would rather stand there with his dick in his hand than help."

"Excuse me if I don't want to help throw my own

equipment away," Max said. He took his eyes off Zantoro and fixed them on Lia. "I can't believe you're just letting them do it."

"Max, please. You need to calm down," she said.

"Don't tell me to calm down, you slut!" he shouted.

The members of London's team had all been smiling—a fistfight was just good fun, after all—but their expressions fell at the outburst. Lia deflated, her shoulders sagging, her mouth hanging open.

"What did you say to me?" she asked.

London and his team heard her loud and clear. They looked at her for a moment then back at Max, who was now holding his pistol. It wasn't raised to take aim at anyone in particular, but it wasn't safely pointed at the ground either.

"The fuck you think you're doing with that pea-shooter?" Zantoro asked, stepping directly into the line of fire.

Max raised the gun slightly. To his credit, his hand didn't tremble too badly. He backed up a few steps, putting some distance between himself and the group.

"Max, please, this isn't the time," Lia pleaded, raising her hands in front of her. "I don't know what's come over you, but I'm sure we can work it out."

"Oh, now you want to work it out?" Max's laughter was strained. "All these years working together, you knew…"

Now it was Zantoro's turn to laugh. "I'll be damned, boss. He's mad at you for fucking his lady boss. Got to admit, I'm impressed. All this time, I had him figured for a homo. Probably because he's French, and well, you know how they are."

As he spoke, Zantoro edged forward, drawing all of Max's attention. Meanwhile, Osbourne began to fade back, moving slowly out of Max's peripheral vision. London saw what they were doing. It was a maneuver so basic that any gunman worth his bullets would see it coming from a mile away. But

Max was no gunman, and he kept his eyes—and his palpable hatred—trained on Zantoro.

"Why don't you give him a break?" London suggested. "I mean, we can't help the way we're born, can we?"

Now, Max's attention was divided, and Osbourne could move a bit faster. He took two steps back, making sure his combat boots came down toe-to-heel as quietly as possible. London saw the movement from the corner of his eye. He continued talking, trying to hold Max's attention.

"Look here, man," he said. "We're all under a lot of pressure. No doubt about it, we're in the shit. But the last thing we need is to start turning on each other. How about we just rewind a few minutes, take a deep breath, and start this thing over. No hard feelings, huh?"

"Nice speech," Max said.

He opened his mouth like he wanted to say something more, but Osbourne was close enough to make his move. He grabbed Max's wrist, and twisted until the gun dropped to the ground. Then he snaked both arms around Max's waist, and hip-tossed him. London couldn't help but wince as Max hit the dirt. London knew that Osbourne had done some wrestling in college. He also knew that Osbourne had gotten his fill of Max's emotional displays. Unlike Zantoro, Osbourne wouldn't verbalize that sort of thing, but his subtle facial tics expressed it loud and clear. Most people wouldn't have even noticed, but London had spent long hours in dangerous settings with these men. He knew that a slight narrowing of the eyes, and an even slighter furrowing of his brow, meant Osbourne was ready to dish out some punishment if the need arose.

Osbourne squatted and scooped up Max's pistol. Without looking, he tossed it to Zantoro, who snatched it from the air nonchalantly, like he was catching a fresh can of beer rather than a deadly weapon. He thumbed the hammer back, and took aim at Max.

"Scary shit, isn't it?" Zantoro asked. "Having a gun pointed at you, I mean. They say you should never aim at someone you don't intend to kill."

"No!" Lia shouted.

She lunged for Zantoro, but he sidestepped her, and she went down beside Max. Zantoro laughed and pulled the trigger.

Click.

Zantoro threw back his head and laughed at the green canopy overhead. He tossed the gun to Max.

"You think I was going to let you run around with a loaded piece? Come on, man." Zantoro glanced around at the others. "Oh, please. I grew up snatching purses and picking pockets. It was easy as hell to take his gun when he was sleeping."

2

Peter watched the scene from his hiding place in the trees. He was fifteen feet off the ground, draped over the massive limb of an ancient tree. The people that Father Xavier had told him to follow were strange. Despite the situation, they still found time to argue and fight. Peter knew that most people would think of their behavior as childish, but in his experience, it was adults who allowed negative circumstances to bring their worst instincts to the surface. Although, he had to admit, it was pretty funny. The way that Frenchman's hand shook when he raised his gun. The way the big red-faced man threw the Frenchman around like a ragdoll. The crazed laughter of the curly-haired man with the wild eyes. All of it was quite amusing. It reminded Peter of the American TV shows he'd seen at the Red Cross center, back in the days before the General drafted Peter and the other village kids into military service.

He edged further out on his limb, careful not to dislodge any leaves or twigs. He wanted to get a better view so he could make sense of what was going on below. It seemed that one of their vehicles had broken down. The people were moving things from the larger vehicle to the smaller one, which was still leaking smoke and steam from its exposed engine.

Peter waited until they'd completed the luggage transfer and piled into the Jeep before he shimmied back to the tree trunk and began his quiet descent. By the time his feet thumped softly onto the ground, the white people had left, driving off in a single vehicle. Peter gave them a few minutes' lead, and then crawled into the abandoned Jeep to take stock of what had been left behind.

Most of it was useless. Camera equipment and boxes of documents that Peter couldn't read. The only thing he found worth keeping was a protein bar that had gotten wedged under the driver's seat. He tucked it into his pocket and left the rest behind. By now, the white men and the lady were probably a full mile ahead of him, but that was okay. Even Joseph, the youngest and least skilled of the scouts in Peter's group, could have tracked them. They made next to no effort to cover their trail, and when they stopped, they were as loud as a herd of water buffalo. It was a wonder they hadn't drawn the attention of every dead person wandering the jungle. And there were so many of them out there. Peter saw them all around him. When they drew too close, he used his machete to send them back to the grave. But mostly, he evaded them. There were too many to kill.

Many of the dead people were from the General's army, both adults and children. They stumbled through the jungle in torn and bloody uniforms, some of them still clutching their weapons dumbly. Others were villagers who had wandered into the trees after returning to life. And even stranger, there were white people, many of them dressed like the doctors and relief workers from the Red Cross centers. Father Xavier said that these white people came from the research center in the north. He said that the curse that caused the dead people to walk came from this place. If that was so, Peter wondered why Father Xavier was leading the children in that direction. And he wondered why the white soldiers and the lady were also heading that way. But there were many things Peter didn't understand. It seemed there were more every day.

He set off down the road, following the tracks left by the Land Rover.

3

"You boys better hold onto something," London said as he drove the Land Rover over a particularly rough stretch of road. "It looks like things are going to be bumpy for a while."

"You mean it's been smooth so far?" Zantoro muttered.

Osbourne and Vincent groaned.

"It shouldn't be too much farther," Lia said. "If it's still standing, that is. With Mbowi, who knows? He might have burned it to the ground just for fun."

"Yeah, well, we have to try," London said. "We don't have enough water to get us through another day."

Zantoro closed his eyes, leaned against the window, and tried to tune it all out. He'd popped his last pill after embarrassing Pierre. Although the drug was doing its thing and keeping him humming along, he knew the comedown would be hard, especially because there'd be nothing to take the edge off. They were a full two days past their planned extraction date. How could he have known that he should have brought more shit into the country? It was bad enough that he hadn't had time to clean his shit up when they were stateside—too many operations in rapid succession—but he could tell that London was starting to suspect. Hell, maybe London knew. The boss may have spoken like a hayseed, but he was one sharp son of a bitch.

Now, somehow, by the grace of whatever god was in charge of this fucked up operation, Zantoro was going to have to face down withdrawal. And it looked like the first stages of that awful process were going to take place while he was crammed into the backseat of the Land Rover, alongside Vincent and Osbourne, with Pierre the Pouting Cameraman riding in the luggage space behind him. No doubt about it, he was in for one rough ride.

At the moment, he was holding onto the slim hope that they'd find this old French plantation house before they stopped for the night. And he hoped that scumbag Mbowi had left the place somewhat supplied. Maybe when this zombie shit kicked off, they'd abandoned the place in a hurry. Zantoro wished for that as hard as he'd wished for a BMX bike under the Christmas tree when he was eight years old. Not only because he didn't want to die of dehydration, but also because the intel reports on Mbowi said that he was running drugs through Daroka to help fund and arm his coup. Mostly, the shit coming through this part of Africa was heroin. It wasn't at all Zantoro's drug of choice, but he had the idea that a little toot here and there might help him limp through withdrawal until they got back home. Then, he could check himself into the clinic and clean up. It was a one in a million shot that Mbowi's boys had left anything so valuable behind, but Zantoro figured that, in a world where dead people were walking around, odds and probabilities didn't hold the same weight as they once did.

If we actually manage to get back home. Shit is looking pretty fucking grim at the moment.

Zantoro clenched his hands into fists and shoved the thought away.

Focus on the objective. Thinking long term is a distraction and it will get you killed.

And right now, Zantoro's objective was finding something to stave off the worst of the chills, nausea, and shakes until they were back in the part of the world where dead men weren't hiding behind every corner, waiting to bite a chunk out of your ass. He closed his eyes and tried to relax. It wasn't easy with his last dose of speed goosing his heart rate.

Their progress was maddeningly slow. The quality of the road fell steadily until it was little more than a narrow, rock-strewn path. On three occasions, they had to park the Land Rover and get out to clear fallen trees that blocked their way. The last such stop involved a couple hours of back-breaking labor as they cleared a massive tangle of deadfall. Zantoro figured they might actually make better time walking, but he felt sick at the grim prospect of hiking through the jungle, swatting at hummingbird-sized mosquitoes, and stepping on snakes as he faced the prospect of life without his favorite chemicals. So he worked his ass off alongside the rest of the team, hacking through branches and shoving tree trunks out of their way.

They'd barely made it another mile when they were forced to stop again. Eyes closed, Zantoro groaned. "Another goddamn tree in the road? Is Paul Bunyan hiding somewhere in this jungle?"

"Shit," London said, bringing the vehicle to a teeth-rattling halt. "We got hostiles."

"And we got a big ass SUV," Zantoro responded without opening his eyes. "Run those motherfuckers over and let's find this mansion."

Vincent elbowed him. "Might want to wake up, sunshine. Only way we're running all these motherfuckers over is with a tank."

Zantoro rolled down the window and poked his head out

to get a better view. The sight of what lay ahead made him groan.

A couple hundred feet away, the road had been carved away, leaving behind a ditch that bisected the rocky ground. It looked like a jagged scar in the earth. It was most likely made by a flood, but Zantoro supposed it could have been a small earthquake, if that sort of thing was possible. Hell, maybe the same logging company that had made the road had put it there for drainage or something. The important thing was that there was a trench bisecting the road. With dense jungle on either side, the only way for the vehicle to proceed was to drive down the steep sides of the ditch and pray that the four wheel drive could get them back out. The Land Rover had a winch kit, so the odds of pulling out of the ditch were decent.

But there was a problem with that plan: the ditch was full of the living dead. They were crammed in there, too, packed together like dirty, pus-filled sardines. Zantoro figured the ghoulish fucks had been walking down the road and had just fallen in. They didn't seem very smart, after all. And now that they were in there, they didn't have enough strength or coordination to get out. A few stragglers had managed to claw their way out, and were stumbling down the road toward the Land Rover, but the majority of them were still stuck in the shoulder-deep pit.

Zantoro drew himself back into the vehicle. "Well, ain't this a fun little situation."

"Weapons check," London said.

The team ran through their weapons supply. It didn't take long. They were down to scraps in the ammo department, and they had a single grenade.

"Slim pickings, boss," Zantoro said.

"Fuckin' a," Osbourne agreed.

London killed the ignition, and turned to look at Lia. "All right, how far off is this chateau or whatever you called it?"

"I don't really remember," she said. "It's been years."

"Rough estimate. Come on, girl, give me a ballpark figure." London drew his sidearm, preparing for the half dozen walking corpses shambling down the road.

"Maybe a couple kilometers east of here. Slightly northeast, I think. It's been years…"

London pinched the bridge of his nose like a man steeling himself for an impending migraine. "Okay, Zantoro, lock and load. We're going to clear this road so we can get a closer look at what's ahead."

"I'm coming too," Max said from the space behind the backseat. He was fiddling with the single handheld video camera he'd salvaged from his stock of equipment. "I'm still going to document this."

Zantoro opened his mouth to protest, but London cut him off.

"Fine, but just stay out of our way. And when we say it's time to go, I don't want any arguments."

Max opened the rear hatch and bailed out. He trotted around to the front of the Land Rover and started filming the dead people's approach.

London put a hand on Lia's shoulder. "Don't worry, we'll keep him safe. But after that earlier bullshit, I can't give him a gun."

She nodded. "I understand."

He glanced at the rearview mirror. "You ready, Zantoro?"

"Born ready."

They exited the vehicle with guns ready. Since their stores of rifle ammo were nearly depleted, they were sticking with handguns as much as possible; standard operating procedure when the targets weren't able to put up active resistance.

"Weapons free," London said. "Just remember we got jack shit in the pantry, so don't waste anything."

"Loud and clear, boss."

Zantoro raised his weapon and took aim. The shakes

hadn't arrived yet, but they'd be here soon enough. For now, his aim was still deadly. His first shot was a bullseye. It dropped one of the ghouls at ten meters, splattering the dirt road with gobs of shiny brains.

One down, five to go…

4

Max and Lia had once accompanied a group of storm chasers in Oklahoma on one of their tornado expeditions. Their encounter with a twister that tore across the flat, dusty expanse of an oil field was still one of the most awe-inspiring things Max had ever witnessed. The sheer power of that black vortex, tearing up the ground and tossing heavy equipment like broken toys, was something that still terrified Max. He'd always wondered how it would feel to be sucked into the center of the whirling chaos. How long could someone survive at the heart of that howling vortex?

Now, he believed he finally had an answer. Because ever since their paths had crossed with London and his cowboy mercenaries, Max felt like he was being pulled deeper and deeper into the tornado. His circumstances had spun out of his control and he was powerless to resist the churning power of the storm around him. He clung to his camera. It was the only thing that tethered him to his old life. He kept his eyes fixed on the screen, making sure to keep London and Zantoro in frame as they went to work. When they were reduced to tiny images on a digital screen, Max could almost forget how much he hated them. He could almost pretend that this was just another documentary jaunt with Lia. Almost.

He fixed eyes on the screen, the camera held out in front of his chest like a protective talisman. The images he watched were grisly and nightmarish, but he didn't flinch. He'd been looking through a camera lens at horrifying images and circumstances for years, and he'd long ago learned the secret of detachment. The trick was to just relax and keep recording.

He watched London walk straight at one of the reanimated cadavers, raising his pistol at the last second, just as the creature's outstretched hands were close enough to brush against his shirt. London's pistol was so close to the creature's face that the muzzle flash caused its hair to catch fire. It collapsed in a pool of its own blood, snuffing out the flames. Zantoro laughed at the sight, then turned his attention another ghoul. This one had once been a woman, although her breasts had been torn away, leaving two gaping holes in her chest. The wounds were so maggot-infested that they appeared animated. Zantoro's shot cleaved through her skull, filling the air with pink mist. And then it was London's turn. He snapped off one shot, then another, dropping two more of the reanimated dead. One final dead man fell to Zantoro's deadly aim. This one was tall, gaunt, and armless, hobbling on one good leg as it dragged a mangled foot through the dirt. Zantoro's shot punched through one ear and out the other, opening an exit wound so large that the man's brain slid out near fully intact. It hit the ground with a wet *plop* a fraction of a second before its former owner collapsed atop it and squished it to grey and red jelly.

London holstered his weapon and looked straight at the camera.

"Show's over, Max."

But Max didn't stop rolling. He followed the Americans to the edge of the hole in the middle of the road. He took care to walk as evenly as possible so the image would remain stable.

The stench rising from the pit made his eyes water. His gorge rose, but he continued to document the horrors that lay mere meters from where he stood.

It was difficult to accurately guess the number of reanimated dead that were crammed into the pit. They were packed shoulder-to-shoulder, squirming and wriggling against one another as they clawed at the ground to escape their predicament. Some nearly made it to the lip of the hole, only to be dragged back down by their fellows. They slid back into the crowd, some of them slipping out of sight as they were slowly trampled by the other would-be escapees.

"What do you think, boss?" Zantoro asked.

Max took a couple steps back so that the Americans were both in frame.

London glanced around. He scratched at his chin for a moment. "These sons of bitches aren't going anywhere. I say we hoof it to the plantation house and see if we can't find something to bridge this hole. Maybe we get lucky and there's some scrap lumber hanging around. It was a lumber company that was in the house, right? Or maybe we get even luckier and there's a vehicle we can steal."

"On foot through the jungle?" Zantoro groaned. "Man, that sounds like a real party."

"It's just a couple clicks."

"Yeah, if your girlfriend remembers right, and she didn't sound so sure."

London looked directly at the camera, then turned his attention back to Zantoro. "You got any better ideas, I'm all ears. But there's no way we're driving through the jungle. We wouldn't make it more than a few feet. And there's no way we can drive across this fucking hole. So I don't see another way, and we best get our asses is gear. Daylight's burning."

That last line seemed like a good enough place for ending the scene, so Max turned the camera off and headed back to the Land Rover.

5

Two clicks turned out to be closer to five, and it took hours of slogging through the jungle, but they eventually found the chateau. One minute, they were hacking their way through tangled vines, and tripping over gnarled tree roots, and the next, they were standing at the edge of a valley, at the center of which was a colonial mansion. The jungle vegetation grew thickly on the walls of the valley, but the ground at the bottom had been cleared, leaving behind acres of flat grassland. It was as if the jungle had been drawn aside like a curtain to reveal a portion of the French countryside. There was even a beautiful sunset, tracing lines of red and orange over the top of the jungle that surrounded the clearing. London had to rub his eyes to make sure he wasn't seeing some deep jungle version of a mirage.

They descended the treacherous, boulder-strewn slope and stood just inside the tree line, looking at the enormous house. London dug his binoculars out of his backpack and raised them to his eyes. From the outside, the place looked deserted. There was a Jeep parked in the courtyard between the main house and a much smaller building that could have been servants' quarters or just an oversized storage shed. But

London didn't think that was an indication that the place was occupied. For one thing, the grass around the vehicle had grown so high that it covered the tires. And for another, the figure sitting behind the steering wheel was little more than a skeleton dressed in rags that might have once been a military uniform.

"Well, it seems we've arrived," he said. "Gentlemen, keep your heads on a swivel. We don't know what's waiting for us in there. Lia, you and Max might want to hang back until we clear the house."

Max shook his head. "No way. If this was one of Mbowi's headquarters, I want to get some footage of the interior before you go stomping around and disturbing the atmosphere."

"Atmosphere?" Zantoro laughed, but it sounded too forced to contain even a drop of humor. "You gotta be fucking kidding me. Some of those goddamn zombie things in there probably. You'll get your ass bitten off."

Max growled something in French.

"Oh, fuck off, Pierre," Zantoro said.

London stepped between them before the conflict could escalate. The last thing he needed was these two whipping out their dicks and pissing on each others' legs. Zantoro was starting to show signs of cracking up. Even by Zantoro's standards, his behavior was getting erratic. And he looked like shit. Of course, London reminded himself, they all looked like shit. Sweaty and dressed in filthy clothes, none of them looked like they'd be strutting across the stage at a beauty pageant anytime soon. But there was something about the dark circles under Zantoro's eyes that spoke of a problem beyond a simple lack of hygiene. London cursed himself for not sending Zantoro for a mandatory vacation at Pendleton's medical clinic.

"Cool it, you two," London said, shrugging against the weight of his backpack. The Thunderball explosives wouldn't have felt heavy during a regular stroll, but lugging them through the jungle was a different story. "Okay, we all go in. Looks like there are two levels. If the downstairs is clear, Max and Lia can start filming down there while we sweep the upstairs. If the coast is clear up top, Osbourne and I will check out that second building while Zantoro and Vincent search the place for supplies. If that Jeep isn't dead, we'll roll out in the morning. If it can't be saved, we'll explore other options. The main thing is water. We're down to our canteens. It's still another day's march at least before we locate that facility, so if we don't find something to drink out here, we're fucked. One last thing: we make our approach to the house single file, and with extreme caution."

"What, you thinking there might be landmines?" Zantoro asked.

London shrugged. "You never know. Any questions?"

No one spoke up, so London gave the signal to move out.

Birds burst from the high grass as the group made their way to the house. London wondered how many varieties of snakes were slithering around their ankles. In places, the grass and weeds had grown waist-high, and progress through the clearing became nearly as difficult as the trek through the jungle. The ground was spongy and wet. It sucked at London's boots as he trudged toward their objective.

It felt strange entering a house after spending their nights camping rough in the jungle, but the front door was unlocked, and they made their way into the place without incident. The air inside was hot and stale. All the windows were closed, and the ceiling fans were motionless. During their approach, London had noticed a generator on the east side of the house, but it was either turned off or out of fuel.

The house was a nice example of colonial arrogance. Out here in the middle of the jungle, the French could have easily made something simple, functional, and suited to the environment. Instead, they'd constructed the type of oversized manor house that looked like it belonged on a wealthy nineteenth century French vineyard. The double front doors opened into an enormous open foyer with a high ceiling. To the left was a wide staircase leading to a balcony that encircled the second floor.

A quick look around the foyer told him that the intel about this being a headquarters for General Mbowi's army was correct. The more utilitarian furniture—dining tables and chairs—had been repurposed as desks for computers and radio equipment. The other furniture—couches and armchairs—had been shoved into the corners of the room. If London had to guess, he'd say that this big room served as the General's communications center. The remainder of the first level would most likely be their mess hall, while the upstairs would have served as the barracks. It was a big house, and soldiers were used to packing in to make the best use of available space. At one time, this house might have quartered over a hundred soldiers. But now, it looked to be completely deserted.

Max fired up his camera and started filming. Lia walked alongside him, narrating in French into a small microphone. London sighed. If the rest of the house wasn't as deserted as the main rooms of the first floor, then whoever might be lurking elsewhere knew they had company.

"Goddamn Frenchies are like bulls in a china shop," Zantoro said.

London nudged him. "You and Vincent head upstairs. See if you can find anything useful. But watch your ass. We still don't know for sure we're alone in here."

"Come on, man," Zantoro said, heading for the staircase. "Let's see if there's anything worth stealing in this dump."

London made his way through a series of large rooms that were filled with needlessly expensive antique furniture. He imagined a man like George Mbowi might have enjoyed surrounding himself with such opulence, eating his dinner off fine china and drinking from crystal goblets just a few feet from where his soldiers coordinated his reign of terror. It certainly fit with everything London had heard about the General.

In a speech that had become a viral sensation, Mbowi had claimed to be the reincarnation of Vlad Tepes, the Impaler. People had laughed at the idea of this rotund bald guy with the Elton John sunglasses who thought he was a descendant of the historical Dracula. But that shit had ceased to be funny when Mbowi quickly transformed from the leader of a fringe, quasi-religious/political group, to the commander of a vicious guerilla army that ripped through the country and toppled what had been a stable government. Of course, such a transformation might easily be explained by the involvement of Waylon Marsh. Such stories, however, were completely unproven. But London knew that proof didn't matter when it came to men like Waylon Marsh. When you had that much money, you could buy public opinion. You could buy anything. Including a group of highly trained, battle tested mercenaries who would gladly charge into a war-torn region of the world and clean up your mess.

Little late in the game to start second guessing those career choices, ain't it? The thought made London laugh. *You go for one roll in the hay with some rabble-rousing French activist, and suddenly you're awash in radical thoughts about class struggle. Meanwhile, there are zombies—actual fucking* zombies *—possibly lurking around every corner, ready to have you for supper.*

"What's so funny, boss?" Osbourne asked.

"Oh, just some private joke," London answered.

They moved from a lavishly furnished sitting room into the kitchen. A quick survey of the pantry was enough to convince them that their food supply was no longer a problem. Although all the food was canned, it was abundant. If the amount of equipment and paperwork left behind hadn't been enough indication, the amount of food was enough to convince London that Mbowi's troops had abandoned this place in a hurry.

The faucet over the deep porcelain sink coughed and groaned when London twisted the handle. The water ran brown and rusty, but it cleared up after a moment. As long as everyone remembered to pack their water purification tablets, they wouldn't die of thirst.

Osbourne set his rifle on the counter and stuck his hands into the flow of water. He cupped some in his palms and splashed it on his face.

"Shit, that feels good," he said, shaking droplets off like a dog. "Spending the night here will be like the Holiday Inn compared to that damn jungle."

"Don't get too comfortable. We still got a lot of ground to cover before we can rest."

Osbourne nodded. "Yeah, you're right."

London leaned against the counter. He could hear Zantoro and Vincent moving about overhead. They were trained to be quiet, but in such an old house (and one that had been sitting for so long in unforgiving conditions), total stealth was an impossibility. The floors creaked under the faintest pressure. He could also hear Lia and Max moving through the rooms near the front of the house. Lia was spitting a stream of French narration, pausing now and then to riffle through some of the papers that had been left behind. It amazed him that, despite everything that had transpired in the last few days, those two were still playing journalist.

And you're still playing soldier, ain't you?

There was a window over the sink, and London surveyed the area on the north side of the house. Like the land on the south side, it was a tangle of overgrown grass and weeds. Maybe a couple hundred meters from the back porch to the edge of the jungle. It was easy to see why Mbowi liked this place. Aside from the relative comfort of the house, it was nearly impossible to approach without being seen.

"We're losing the light," London said. "Why don't you go out there to the east side of the house and see about that generator. If we're staying here tonight, might as well have some power if we can manage it. After that, have a look at that Jeep, see if the engine will turn over. I'll stroll over to that other building and see what's up with it."

Osbourne nodded. "You sure you don't need back up?"

"I'll take a quick peek inside. If anything looks like it might be too much for me to handle, I'll get my ass back here."

"Okay, boss. Be careful."

"Yeah," London said. "And you watch your ass too."

6

As soon as they were upstairs, Zantoro told Vincent he thought it would go a lot faster if they split up.

"I don't know, man..." Vincent looked down the hallway of closed doors.

"Look, it's about to be dark out there and we got no power," Zantoro said. "You really want to be clearing all these rooms with nothing but flashlights?"

Vincent looked doubtful, but he also knew better than to argue. The team may not have been organized like the military, but there was still a clear pecking order, and in it, Zantoro outranked Vincent.

"You got a gun, right?" Zantoro added, just in case Vincent needed a little extra persuasion. "And this house is big, but it's not *that* big. You run into anything you can't handle, just holler and I'll be there. But I don't think there's anything to worry about. This place is empty. It's fucking dead in here, man."

"Yeah, that's what I'm afraid of," Vincent said.

Zantoro conjured up a laugh, although he was starting to get antsy, and just wanted Vincent to give him some space. Finally, Vincent obliged, heading around the balcony to the other side of the house. Once he was out of sight, Zantoro got to work.

He made his way from room to room, giving each one a cursory look. They were bedrooms that had been converted into barracks. Some had metal cots with footlockers, much like a boot camp setup. Others had sleeping bags placed on the floor. All of them were unoccupied, and it looked like whoever had left the house had expected to return. Nobody had bothered to pack their personal items or stow them away. And there had been plenty of residents. Judging from the amount of beds and sleeping bags, these guys had been packed together eight or more to a room. Given what Zantoro had seen of the rest of the country, he doubted the soldiers had minded all that much. This place was a relative luxury resort, with a roof overhead and running water. Hell, there were even bathrooms with toilets and showers.

Zantoro paused at the head of the staircase after his initial inspection. It was one those good news/bad news situations. The good news was that there had been plenty of Mbowi's soldiers here and they'd all left their possessions behind. And that meant the chances of contraband being present were high. While the sort of thing he was after might be rare among professional soldiers, Mbowi's guys were famously ragtag. If that perception held true, it was likely that some of them had gotten their hands on some of the drugs the General was moving through the country. All of that was good news. The bad news was that it would take a while to look through everything. There were so many backpacks, rucksacks, and footlockers that it would take him hours to do a thorough search. Good thing they were staying overnight.

He shouldered his rifle and called out to Vincent, "Clear on the North side!"

A few seconds later, Vincent answered, "South is clear!"

7

It was a breach of protocol for London to leave the house by himself, but he figured protocol went out the window when dead people started getting up and walking around. Besides, despite the operation having become a complete clusterfuck, he was still the team captain, and if he wanted to breach protocol, that was his decision. He stepped onto the wide front porch and settled his last pinch of Skoal into his mouth. He shook his head and sighed, then tossed the empty container over his shoulder. It was a hell of a way to have to quit, but he'd been telling himself for the past couple years that he'd give the habit up. Could be the best thing to come out of this fucking operation.

Now, that ain't true. That take-no-prisoners French lady is the best thing to come out of it. Hell, she's probably the only good thing to happen to your life in ages.

The thought took him by surprise. Maybe his feelings for Lia ran a little deeper than he'd like to admit. This was the first time he'd actually given the possibility any consideration before banishing it to the back of his mind. He'd been telling himself that the mission came first, and that anything to do with Lia would just have to wait until they were out of

Daroka. But it was looking more and more like they might not actually make it out. If that was the case, he wasn't sure it mattered if he left things hanging between the two of them.

Yeah, but you don't want it to go that way. And then there are those damn dreams…

By the time his mind tossed the idea of the dreams his way, he'd almost made it to the smaller building. It saved him any further internal debate. London wasn't accustomed to that sort of thing, and he found it exhausting.

The doors to the building were on its west side, perpendicular to the house's front porch. They were like barn doors: tall and opening in the middle. With both of them open, you could easily drive a large vehicle into the building. London supposed that it had originally been intended to house heavy equipment. There was a thick latch but no lock. It was rusty but had seen enough recent use that it opened easily. He eased the doors apart just enough to put his foot in the gap, then drew his pistol in one hand and his flashlight in the other. Taking a slow, deep breath, he stepped back quickly, using his foot to throw the doors open wide.

The rapidly dying daylight didn't penetrate much beyond the threshold, but London's flashlight cut a bright swath through the darkness of the interior. As he swept the beam from left to right, the hot air inside the building drifted over him, bringing with it the unmistakable reek of death and decay. But London was prepared for it. He was beginning to think that a few more days in Daroka might make his nose immune to it entirely.

The scene revealed by the white glow of his flashlight's beam was that of a human abattoir. The concrete floor was littered with bodies in various stages of decomposition. The hot air was swarmed with obese, droning black flies. Disturbed by his intrusion into their dining hall, they buzzed through the air before returning to their feast. But these horrors, as repulsive and repellant as they were, had become commonplace during his time in Daroka, and he would have simply closed the doors and walked away, if not for the figure at the center of the scene.

Set among the bloated, mutilated bodies was an oversized, high-backed chair that was so ornately decorated that you could call it a throne. London figured that it had probably been part of the house's collection. It certainly had the same Old World antique appearance of what he'd seen inside. The figure occupying this throne was none other than the conqueror of Daroka, General George Mbowi. London shone his flashlight beam on the man like a spotlight, unsure at first if he was really looking at the man who'd kicked off a staggeringly brutal reign of terror.

No doubt about it. The man who sat there as, still as a statue, was the General himself.

London was no news junkie, but even so, he was familiar with Mbowi's outlandish physical appearance. The man was pretty hard to mistake. His size alone was memorable enough. *Time* magazine's profile of Mbowi listed the General's measurements as just under seven feet tall and five hundred-plus pounds. As if that wasn't enough to make him stand out, Mbowi's wardrobe was outlandish. While he favored military camo pants and combat boots, he chose to pair them with bright, floral-patterned shirts. He wore a diamond-encrusted Rolex on each wrist. His head was bald and appeared enormous, even atop his massive frame. He was rarely photographed without his trademark sunglasses, which had thick gold frames and diamond accents. The man seated in the chair fit that description precisely.

He also appeared to have been infected by the same virus that was ravaging the country whose government he'd uprooted and smashed in a series of bombings and assassinations. London played his flashlight's beam over the General, taking stock of each horrible detail. Mbowi's sunglasses were missing one lens, and the exposed eye was red, crusty, and unblinking. The front of his Hawaiian shirt was stained with dried blood and vomit. As he stared at London, the General's mouth hung open. Clotted gobs of green slime rolled over his bottom lip, spilling onto his lap.

"Jesus Christ, what the fuck happened in here?" London whispered.

He was no expert in forensics, but if he had to guess, he'd say that once the virus took hold of the General, he'd set himself up a buffet of his own soldiers and started chowing down. London wondered if he'd overpowered them first, maybe knocking them out before the feasting began. Or had they willingly laid down their lives for their leader? The word on Mbowi was that he had a strange hold over his followers. Maybe he was like a cult leader who could talk his congregation into swallowing the strychnine Kool-Aid. It seemed insane, but then again, Daroka wasn't exactly a bastion of sanity these days.

An overfed rat emerged from a shadowy corner of the room and waddled through the maze of corpses. The rodent's backside was so fat that London wondered if the thing could manage anything approaching a run anymore. It was the size of a small cat and wheezed audibly as it trundled over to the General's feet. In a show of strength and agility that surprised London, the creature climbed up the General's leg and onto his lap. If the General felt any pain as the rat's claws sunk into his flesh, he gave no indication. If it wasn't for the groans and gurgles coming from the General's mouth in a cheek-and-lip-flapping chorus, London would have figured the man was as dead as those littering the floor.

The rat sat there for a moment, regarding the General with its beady black eyes. Then it moved aside the flaps of the shirt, exposing a gaping hole in the man's belly. The rat poked its head into the wound, nudging the ragged skin apart as it burrowed its way inside. The General's belly swelled even further as the rat settled itself inside and nested in the putrid scraps of his internal organs. Mbowi's face remained expressionless throughout.

London stepped over the threshold and picked his way over the tangle of corpses. He swept his flashlight around in a slow arc as he went, just to be sure that there were no surprises lurking in the corners of the room. He stopped a few feet from Mbowi's throne. The late General shifted around in his seat and reached one hand toward London. For a moment, the dead man's groans took on a slight sense of urgency as he struggled in vain to rise from his throne.

Sic semper tyrannis, London thought as he raised his gun and took careful aim at the center of the General's forehead.

The report of the gun was deafening in the enclosed space, but the high-pitched sound that London heard in its aftermath wasn't his own ears ringing. It was enraged squealing of the rat. Maybe it sensed an abrupt change in its environment, or maybe it just didn't like the noise, but either way, the rat poked its head out of the hole in Mbowi's massive gut and bared its teeth at London. Its forelegs flailed as it tried to work itself free. London gave the rodent the same treatment he'd given its host. The gun thundered again, splattering the obese rat's head against Mbowi's already filthy shirt. The acrid smell of cordite hung in the air, fighting for space with the pungent stench of decay.

London turned his back on the grisly scene. He closed the doors behind him on his way out. While he was inside the building, the last embers of sunset had burned away, leaving behind the pitch blackness of a night far removed from the glow of civilization.

He entered the house and found the rest of the group in one of the dining rooms. They were seated around a large oval table, upon which sat a pair of glowing battery-powered lanterns. The white light of these lanterns was sharp, and the shadows it created spilled out of the open doorways and into the other rooms. Also on the table were stacks of ammunition boxes alongside what looked like an arsenal of firearms: mostly AK-47 rifles, but also an odd assortment of handguns.

"Well, there's running water and plenty of weapons," Zantoro announced. He had his feet propped up on the table, and was fiddling with a bullet, rolling it across his knuckles like a magician doing a coin trick. "So there's a couple problems solved. Plenty of food in the pantry also, but it looks like the stove is electric, and the generator wouldn't do much more than cough. So if you're in the mood for Spam and lukewarm pork and beans, you've come to the right place."

London shrugged. "Not much different from those damn MREs if you want my opinion."

"The good news is that the Jeep has plenty of gas," Osbourne said. "Full tank, plus two spare five gallon cans strapped to the back. Syphoned it out of the generator once I figured out that the damn thing was busted. But the bad news is that the Jeep won't start. I cracked open the steering column and tried to get her started with a screwdriver, but she won't turn over."

"Think you can get it going?" London asked.

"Don't know." Osbourne sighed. "Sorry, boss, but I ain't much of a mechanic."

"We'll see what can be done in the morning," London said. "If you get it started, great. If not, worst case scenario is we walk out. Can't be more than a few clicks to the research center. And the way the road is getting, it might not make much difference even if we get the damn thing started."

"So what did you find in that other building?" Zantoro asked.

London gave a brief recap of the horrors he'd just seen.

"We'll need to film it," Lia said. "Something like that must be documented."

"It's as dark as a well-digger's asshole out there right now," London said. "You can get some shots in the morning, but I want to be on the road as soon as possible, so you'll have to make it quick. Now, let's crack open the pork and beans. There are honest-to-God beds in this place, and I intend to get as much rack time as possible."

After they ate, they filled their water bottles from the kitchen sink. They also filled their backpacks with food from the pantry. It struck London as funny that his pack was heavy with Spam and high powered explosives. It seemed like an odd combination, even in a world that had been turned upside down. Add to that the fact that they were eating beans for dinner, and you probably had the makings of a good joke. But jokes were Zantoro's territory, and London didn't feel much like laughing anyway.

8

Since becoming a scout in Father Xavier's army, Peter had developed the ability to see in the dark. He wasn't like one of the jungle's nocturnal animals or like the Ka'Longho warriors, who were rumored to have eyes like those of a leopard. But Peter's eyes had become accustomed to searching the darkness and the shadows for movement. He could see dark shapes move against an even darker background, and his other senses—sharpened by long hours spent hiding in dangerous spaces—could fill in the details his eyes missed. And that's how he knew, from his hiding place high in the tree, that the shapes emerging from the tree line and slogging through the high grass were those of walking dead men. Although their shapes were indistinct in the darkness, their constant low groaning and their reek of pungent decay were unmistakable.

He scanned the tree line and the field surrounding the house. He stopped counting the dead men after he got to thirty. There were too many for him to even attempt to kill. His only weapon was his machete, and as good as he'd become at using it to separate the dead men from their heads, he knew he would be overwhelmed by their numbers.

He was safe in his tree perch. The walking dead may have been tireless and always hungry, but they weren't capable of climbing a tree. The people in the house—the ones Father Xavier had tasked him with following—might be in danger. There were lights coming from the first floor windows, but they were faint. He suspected that the Americans had posted one of their men on guard duty, and the lights were kept low enough that the guard could see out the windows. If so, the guard might not see the dead men until they were nearly right outside the house.

Peter had no way to signal them. All he could do was watch and wait.

9

Zantoro volunteered for the second guard shift. He wanted to make sure everyone was down for the count before he started his search for contraband. With first shift, people were still settling down. The boss and Lia had taken a room together, so he assumed they'd spend at least part of that first shift fucking themselves silly. But by the second shift, they should have gotten their jollies and fallen into a post-sex stupor. So when it was time for his shift, he gave Osbourne a few minutes to set sail for dreamland, then got down to business.

He didn't bother with the usual guard duty bullshit. It was unlikely that there was anyone with miles of this place, and if there was someone out there, they were probably camped for the night. Besides, the house was locked up tight. They were the safest they'd been since landing in Daroka.

He narrowed the beam of his flashlight and crept up the stairs. Lia and the boss had taken one of the master bedrooms with an attached bathroom. Max, Osbourne, and Vincent had each taken separate rooms. After nights of camping shoulder-to-shoulder, people had been eager to spread out. Well, the ones who weren't fucking, anyway. It had seemed to Zantoro that Lia and the boss had been pretty damn eager to sleep shoulder-to-shoulder, maybe even closer. He paused outside their bedroom, just to make sure they'd finished doing the deed. Once he heard them snoring in stereo, he moved on. There were four unoccupied bedrooms and two bathrooms to search.

The first three bedrooms were a complete bust. For soldiers of a rebel army, Mbowi's guys sure seemed boring. A search of their backpacks, footlockers, and closets yielded next to nothing of interest. A few packs of cigarettes, some bottles of liquor, and a handful of well-loved nudie magazines, but nothing in the way of hard drugs.

Bunch of bitch-ass choir boys, Zantoro thought. *No wonder a bunch of dead people kicked the shit out of you.*

Zantoro was starting to get a bad feeling in the pit of his stomach. It could have been the first symptoms of his dreaded withdrawal or it could have been the evening's Spam and beans dinner working its way through his system. But more likely, it was the thought that he might be stranded in this hellhole without a crutch to get him through. He cursed himself for not smuggling more speed pills into the country, but how was he to know that the operation would last so long? They should have been gone days ago.

Finally, he hit pay dirt while searching the bathroom. In one of the cabinets, hidden behind a stack of dusty, mildewed towels, were three gallon-size plastic bags packed full of white tablets. The bags were labeled with a piece of white tape on which the words "LES SOLDATS NE DORMENT PAS" had been printed in large block lettering. Zantoro didn't know French, but he'd been raised by his Spanish-speaking grandmother, and he'd heard that the two languages were similar enough. And *Les soldats ne dorment pas* looked an awful lot like *Los soldados no duermen.*

"Soldiers don't sleep?" Zantoro whispered, turning one of the bags over in his hand.

It didn't take a genius to connect the dots. There were

times in any boots-on-the-ground operation when sleep was an impossibility, and during those times, soldiers often received some chemical assistance. It looked like Mbowi's guerillas were no different than actual soldiers in that respect.

"Better living through chemistry."

Zantoro opened the bag. He dumped some of the tablets onto the counter, considered the amount, then added a few more for good measure. Then he put the bag back into the cabinet and took his pill bottle from his hip pocket. The tablets filled it nearly to the top. He figured that was plenty. If they were still in Daroka after he burned through that supply, there would be problems even bigger than withdrawal. He popped one pill in his mouth and swallowed it dry. He wasn't taking chances with the water from the bathroom sink. Although he knew it would be some time before the drugs could disperse through his system, the relief he felt was instantaneous. Maybe their luck with this doomed operation was finally starting to turn around. He popped a second pill for good measure. He figured his tolerance was higher than that of the average Mbowi guerilla. And considering the journey ahead of him, a good jolt was damn near a necessity.

He tip-toed down the hallway and down the stairs to the first floor. The single lantern in the center of the foyer had been dialed back to its lowest setting, but it cut the darkness just enough that he could kill his flashlight. Now that he'd checked off the biggest thing on his to-do list, he felt like he deserved a treat, and there was a can of fruit cocktail in heavy syrup in the kitchen with his name on it. He strolled around the edge of the room, intending to fulfill his duties as night guard with a few cursory glances out the windows on his way to the kitchen.

But what he saw through the windows erased his thoughts of fruit cocktail in heavy syrup. The small traces of cautious optimism leaked out of him like air from a leaky balloon. He ran across the room and checked the view from the other windows. The situation was the same on the west and south sides of the house. He ran into the kitchen and peered out those windows. The west side view was no different.

"Oh, shit," he said.

There were hostiles aplenty. Dead hostiles from the look of things, but they had an overwhelming numbers advantage and they were on the move. They were stumbling out of the jungle, slogging through the tall grass on a steady march toward the house.

"Rise and shine, people!" He thundered up the stairs, shouting as he went. "Hostiles incoming! Hostiles incoming!"

The drug may not have had time to take effect, but that didn't matter. Good old fashioned adrenaline was doing the trick just fine.

10

London and Lia had taken a room together without any prior discussion. After dinner, when it was time to turn in, they'd simply stepped into the same room, as if it was a foregone conclusion. There had been a bit of talk about the possibility that they'd once again share the dream of the underground city. It was mostly on her part, while they were settling into the room by lantern light. She'd spoken of it while they brushed their teeth, talking about the strange architecture and the mysterious robed figure through a mouthful of toothpaste foam. London had limited his part of the conversation to nods, noncommittal grunts, and shrugs. It wasn't that he didn't want to contribute or that he was afraid to discuss what the dreams might mean. It was just that he couldn't force his brain to engage such nebulous concepts, not when there were more immediate concerns. Specifically, how they planned on getting out of the country alive.

In the end, it didn't matter much. They'd stepped into the shower, and the time for talking was over.

The water temperature didn't rise above lukewarm and the soap left behind by the room's former occupant would never be mistaken for a luxury brand, but that didn't much matter to a pair of people who'd been sleeping rough in the jungle for the better part of a week. The water streaming off their bodies looked like mud. It took a while before it eventually ran clear. They sighed as they soaped one another's backs, closing their eyes as the layers of grime and old sweat sloughed off.

But one thing soon led to another, and what they began in the shower, they finished atop the creaky bed. Afterwards, they lay tangled in the damp sheets, breathing deeply as their racing hearts gradually slowed.

"What are we doing?" Lia asked as she turned onto her side, settling into the crook of his arm. "What is going to happen with us, I mean?"

London winced, partially because he knew this was the sort of thing that she was going to say. His knowledge of women wasn't encyclopedic, but he knew these were the sorts of open-ended questions they loved. He also winced because the same questions were hovering in the back of his mind. In less than twenty-four hours, they'd likely be at the Marsh Industries research center, the international hub of the controversial HOPE Project. Although the mission objective was still the same—blow the place to smithereens—the purpose behind it had changed. Whatever was taking place stateside—and hell, maybe it went beyond those borders— had thrown a wrench into the works. Now, they were swinging in the wind. There was no exit strategy. There was a very real possibility that the people at Pendleton would be looking to liquidate their bad assets. Plenty of scenarios, and none of them were particularly pleasant.

He tried in vain to come up with some satisfying answer, but when he couldn't, he decided to go with the truth. "I don't know. I suppose we just have to take it day by day."

"And when we fall asleep and have the same dream of the underground city?"

"I don't know what that means either. I suppose it's a

bridge we'll have to cross if we, by some miracle, find ourselves alive after we detonate the explosives I've been lugging around since we stepped into this nightmare."

The answers felt paper thin, but they seemed to be enough for Lia. She pressed closer to him and sighed, her body relaxing as she drifted to sleep. London closed his eyes, intending to follow her, but before the darkness could claim him, Zantoro started shouting, and everything went to hell. A couple minutes later, they were dressed and downstairs. Their lovers' afterglow had been blasted away by a red alert adrenaline rush.

Zantoro and Osbourne were in the dining room, loading the AK-47s. Vincent was in the foyer, peering out the window and shaking his head in disbelief. Max stood at his side, muttering in French as he fucked around with his camera.

"Zantoro, status report," London said as he and Lia stepped off the staircase.

"We got hostiles incoming. I'd say they got us outnumbered fifteen, maybe even twenty to one," he answered, stepping out of the dining room with a rifle in each hand. "But you know, they're dead and fucked up, while we still got functioning brains."

"Might want to walk that back a bit," Vincent called over his shoulder. "Some of these hostiles appear to be armed."

"What the fuck?" Zantoro handed a rifle to London. He hesitated a beat or two, then handed the other one to Lia. "You can handle this thing?"

She nodded. "I think so."

He disappeared into the dining room and came back with another AK. His pockets bulged with spare magazines. In the dim lantern light, it was hard to see clearly, but London didn't care for the way his second-in-command looked. Zantoro's face was covered in a sheen of sweat, and the dark circles under his eyes spoke of more than just sleep deprivation. As he handed over a pair of extra magazines, London noticed his hands were shaking.

"Yeah," Vincent called from the next room. "We definitely got some armed opposition out there."

"So it's not all dead folks?" London watched Zantoro for another few seconds, then joined Vincent at the window next to the front door.

"See for yourself." Vincent stepped aside.

London peered out the window. His stomach dropped at the scene he beheld. A crowd of men wearing military fatigues was lurching across the field that separated the house from the road. They had the same stumbling, drunken gait of the reanimated dead from the mission and the Ka'Longho village, but some of them did indeed carry weapons. Others were dragging what appeared to be dead bodies. Whether they were the bodies of other reanimated dead men or the bodies of the recently deceased was impossible to tell. But from what London could see, the soldiers dragging the bodies were heading for Mbowi's throne room in the storage building, while the armed contingent was heading for the house. They'd emerged from the tree line in a bunch, but now that they were in the open, they were spreading out. Their movements were clumsy and slow, but it looked an awful lot like they were moving to flank the house. London shook his head in disbelief at the notion. It certainly added a new wrinkle to the situation, and a terrible one at that. Maybe if these reanimated corpses hung around long enough, they got smart. Maybe it was some sort of reverse decay in which their bodies rotted to scraps of maggot meat while their brains started to regenerate.

If that's the case, he thought, *then we're fucked. If they can master basic weapons and tactics, these dead assholes will be running the show in no time flat.*

Osbourne checked the view from the window on the other side of the room. "Looks like Mbowi's guys. Maybe they're just holding onto those guns out of some sort of instinct. Like maybe some kind of rigor mortis has fucked up their hands and now they can't let go of whatever they were holding onto when they died."

"Better not make any assumptions," London said. "We don't know what they're capable of. Guns like that, you don't have to be an expert marksman to do some major damage."

As if they were eager to settle the question, a pair of Mbowi's dead soldiers raised their weapons and fired a quick burst in the general direction of the house. The bullets shattered one of the upstairs windows. Across the field, another snapped off a shot from a pistol. The bullet hit the packed dirt of the driveway, sending a tiny cloud of dust into the air.

"You see what I mean?" London shook his head. "If they can fire those weapons, we're going to have to rethink this. Maybe we use this as a defensive position…"

"Fuck that. They're fucking dead. Those shots are just reflexes or something. No way those pus brains can aim," Osbourne replied. "You want to see some shooting, watch this. I'll show you what *I'm* capable of."

The sudden outburst caught London off guard. It was the sort of insubordinate bullshit he'd come to expect from Zantoro, but Osbourne's voice rarely rose above a polite conversational tone. London wouldn't have been more shocked if Osbourne had punched him in the face. If he'd had time to reflect on the situation, London might have seen it coming. The operation had gone to shit days ago. The men had been laboring under the cloud of Pendleton Security's probable disavowal, with no exit strategy, and with no clear plan of action beyond their original objective. Everyone was running on fumes. It was amazing that the cracks in the dam had taken so long to appear, but now that they had, and the floodwaters were bursting forth.

London didn't have time to recover before Osbourne

wrenched open the front door and stepped onto the porch. Vincent wasn't far beyond, charging across the room at full sprint to join Osbourne.

"You with me?" Osbourne asked.

Vincent slammed a magazine into his AK, raised it to his shoulder, and sighted down the barrel. "I'm with you, brother."

Osbourne turned his head to look over his shoulder at the rest of the group, who stood just inside the doorway, too shocked to do anything else.

"It's time to rock and roll," he said. "Y'all get to that Jeep. We'll hold these assholes off long enough for you to see if you can get it moving."

London briefly considered the fact that he could, at least in theory, overrule this course of action. He was still the one in command, after all. But the truth was, all that chain of command/rules of engagement stuff was starting to seem like a relic from a world that ceased to exist the moment dead men refused to stay down. And now that those same dead men had somehow learned to fire automatic weapons, maybe all bets were truly off.

"Come and get it, motherfuckers!" Osbourne shouted.

The loose formation of armed dead men was closer now, well within range of the AKs. The others were nearing the shed. They ignored the house, intent on carrying their burdens to the smaller building. The leader of the pack, a man whose head rested on his shoulder as if his neck had been broken, reached the building ahead of the group and began fumbling at the latch. London felt his stomach knot with disgust as he connected the dots on what he was witnessing. The soldiers who were dragging the bodies were doing so in order to feed their leader. Even after death, General Mbowi's infamous gluttony continued, and his soldiers made sure his appetites were indulged.

Standing shoulder-to-shoulder, Osbourne and Vincent

opened up with their guns. Their first burst of fire ripped through the front line of dead soldiers, but head shots were next to impossible at this range. The best they could hope for was slowing Mbowi's forces down enough to escape.

"Okay, everyone, grab your luggage and we'll hit the road," London said.

Zantoro and Lia hurried to the kitchen, where they'd left their food and water supplies. Max stayed put, his camera held out in front of him as he documented the scene.

"Come on, Max," London said. "We gotta move, man."

"Fuck you." Max didn't budge. "You're not my commanding officer."

London knew exactly where the hostility was coming from, and there was even a time when he would have been sympathetic. But that time was past. He slapped the camera out of Max's hand, then grabbed a handful of his shirt and threw him against the wall.

"Look here," he growled, pressing his forearm against Max's neck. "If it was up to me, I'd let you stay here and film this horror show until your heart's content. You understand me? I would gladly leave your ass behind. But Lia still has a soft spot for you, so I have to drag you along with us."

Max tried in vain to shove London away.

"Now, I'm going to let you go," London continued. "And when I do, you're going to pick up your camera and put it in your pocket. Then you're going to follow us out the door to the Jeep. Like it or not, you're with us until the end. Got it?"

Max sneered like he wanted to argue the point, but in the end, he nodded.

"What's going on here?"

London turned at the sound of Lia's voice. He eased his forearm off Max's chest and took a step back.

"Nothing, babe," he said. "I was just helping Max get ready to leave."

11

Zantoro remained in the kitchen while Lia took off to see what all the raised voices in the other room were about. He needed a moment to collect himself. And that involved leaning over the sink to vomit up and mouthful of slimy green stuff. He gagged at the smell of the slime as it splattered against the bottom of the sink. He wiped his nose with the back of his hand and winced at the sight of blood. Although his heart rate was up and his head had the slightest edge of dizziness, he was starting to get the idea that the pills he'd found in the upstairs bathroom weren't actually amphetamines.

"Fuck me," he said, and another wave of nausea socked him in the gut. He puked more of the green stuff into the sink.

The insistent chatter of gunfire was louder now, coming from three sides of the house. Zantoro splashed some water on his face and looked out the window over the sink. He shook his head in disbelief. Those rotten motherfuckers were actually shooting at them. True, they couldn't aim for shit, and their weapons' recoil jerked them around like puppets, but they *were* dead, after all. He'd seen plenty of living people who weren't much better with firearms.

His stomach clenched again. He grabbed the edge of the sink and puked a third time. The slime came pouring out of him with such force that he was sure his eyeballs were going to pop out of his skull. When it finally stopped, he was left gasping for air. His stomach rolled over again, but this time the sensation was different. As strange as it was after just having puked his guts out, he felt almost hungry.

So this is how it ends, huh? Your mother and your two ex-wives told you the drugs would eventually catch up to you, but somehow I don't think even they saw this one coming. Fuck it. We were never getting out of here alive anyway.

He slumped to the floor and leaned back against the cabinets. Maybe it was time to call it a day and just relax for a while. He couldn't complain. He'd had a good run, after all. He'd packed a lot of living into his thirty-two years on this planet. He'd traveled the world and seen shit that most people couldn't conjure up in their wildest dreams. Of course, he'd seen (and done) shit that was pure nightmare fuel, but if it took choking down all the bad times to earn the good times, then he was okay with *that*.

"Zantoro!" London shouted from the foyer. "Get your ass in gear!"

He opened his mouth to tell the boss that he'd hit the wall and they were going to have to push ahead to the finish line without him. But the words stuck in his throat. Surrender had never been part of his vocabulary.

Fuck it. Let's see this thing through.

He took a deep breath and levered himself off the floor. The room seemed to spin around him. He felt like his body was being pulled in a hundred different directions, as if he'd been plopped into a whirling centrifuge that was tearing him to pieces. He dug the bottle of pills out of his pocket and shook a couple into his hand.

Might as well go all in.

He tossed the pills into his mouth and washed them down

with a mouthful of water from the sink. The pills traced a line of fire from his throat to his belly so hot that he thought his innards might melt. But the room stopped spinning, and the nausea finally stopped squeezing his stomach like a stress relief ball. That was fine with him. Whatever was around the corner wasn't so fine, but he'd burn that bridge when he got to it. The thought of stumbling around like one of those dumb fucks outside wasn't the most appealing thing in the world, but you never knew, did you? Maybe it would be bliss. Besides, there was no other choice, was there? Suicide just wasn't his style.

12

"What the fuck, man?" London said, watching Zantoro shuffle into the room. "We got a small army out there taking shots at us. Move your ass!"

Zantoro shouted a reply, but it was drowned out by the noise of gunfire as Osbourne and Vincent let loose with another salvo. The bullets knocked down the front line of dead soldiers, but London knew they'd be back on their feet in short order. To complicate things further, it looked like the dead men on food delivery detail were finally getting wise to the fact that General was gone for good this time. They were milling about in front of the open shed, seemingly confused as to what their next course of action should be. London didn't feel like hanging around until they sorted it out. There was already a small crowd around the Jeep. A half dozen dead soldiers were climbing all over it. One was sitting behind the wheel, like he might start driving. Things had already gone to shit, but that didn't mean they couldn't get worse. If dead soldiers could still fire their weapons, how long before they remembered how to drive?

London waited until Osbourne and Vincent paused in their assault then stepped out onto the porch.

"Think the Jeep might be fucked," he said. "Aim for those spare gas cans in the back and light it up. We'll use the fire to cover our escape."

"We're walking out of here?" Osbourne paused his portion of the firefight to look at London. "Aren't you worried about those landmines you mentioned earlier?"

"Yeah, but I'm more concerned about the goddamn zombies firing automatic weapons at us," London said. "I don't think we can hold them off long enough for us to figure out auto repair. Now light that fucking Jeep up so we can get the hell out of here."

Osbourne and Vincent changed their rifles to full auto and dumped two magazines' worth of bullets into the Jeep in a matter of seconds. The gas spilled and splattered, soaking the vehicle and the ground near it. Sparks flew as bullets pinged off metal. The gasoline fumes ignited, and a fireball woofed skyward. Flames roared, engulfing the dead soldiers climbing over the vehicle. They stumbled in drunken circles, human torches lighting up everyone and everything in their path. If the other soldiers had any sense of self-preservation, they didn't display it. They simply pressed forward, closing in on the house. Those who were armed continued their clumsy assault, firing their weapons without bothering to aim. London wondered if they had spare ammo to reload. He wondered if they even knew how. But his curiosity wasn't enough to make him want to hang around to find out.

"Zantoro, you and me are on point. Osbourne, Vincent, you're the rear guard. Lia and Max, keep close. We head north until we get to high ground. Once we're out of this valley, we'll figure out our next move, but right now we're getting the fuck out of here. Let's move!" he shouted.

London didn't allow time for discussion. As soon as Zantoro drew up alongside him, he led the charge off the porch.

The dead were emerging from the dark edges of the jungle

on all sides. With only the moon and stars to light their way, London and his team weren't much faster than the enemy. Slogging through the high grass wasn't easy, especially when they were weighed down with their backpacks full of freshly plundered supplies of food and ammunition. It wasn't quite the same as being dropped into a war zone. No heavy artillery fire. No snipers with pinpoint accuracy. No air support. But there were still bullets flying overhead and tearing up the ground. The best the dead soldiers could manage seemed to be firing off random bursts in the team's general direction, but London knew that even wild shots sometimes found their target. He'd heard that a million monkeys banging on a million typewriters would eventually write a Shakespeare sonnet. He figured a hundred zombies firing off thousands of rounds might eventually hit something.

Now that ammo was no longer a concern, he didn't hold back. While only a shot to the head would put one of the dead soldiers down for the count, a tight cluster of bullets aimed at center mass would sure as hell knock them down. The other members of the team followed his example, clearing a path through the reeking crowd of reanimated corpses with indiscriminate aim. The dead soldiers were even less precise with their targets, and didn't mind shooting one another.

Behind them, the Jeep exploded. They were well away from the house, but the hot force of the explosion shoved London forward. He belly-flopped into the knee-high grass, coming face-to-face with one of the soldiers who'd been torn apart by friendly fire. Although it was little more than a torso with a head and a single arm, its jaws snapped as it moaned with bestial hunger. London rolled away and sprang to his feet. He brought the butt of his rifle down on the soldier's skull, smashing it open like a ripe melon.

Before he could resume leading their escape, he noticed that something was wrong with Vincent. The kid had dropped his rifle, and was standing there with the air of someone who'd just learned a terrible secret.

"One in a million chance, boss," Vincent said, pressing a hand to his stomach. "I mean, those fuckers can't aim, can they?"

Blood squelched from between Vincent's fingers as he took one hesitant step forward then fell to his knees.

"No!" Osbourne screamed. He grabbed a fistful of Vincent's shirt and began trying to haul the wounded man to his feet. "Come on, man. Come on, we got to keep moving. It's just a scratch. You can do it…"

Vincent yelped in pain and slipped from Osbourne's grasp. He went face-down in the grass, exposing a back that had been shredded by machine gun fire.

"Fuck you!" Zantoro roared. He planted his feet in a shooter's stance and fired at the nearest soldier, dropping him with a clean forehead shot. "Fucking rotten bags of shit! I'll kill all of you!"

London shared the sentiment, but he knew better. They were too outnumbered. Undead soldiers were still emerging from the jungle to their southeast. If they didn't haul ass, sooner or later, those rotten bags of shit would be all over them. There wasn't enough time or ammo to deal with their sheer number. He glanced at Lia, who was holding her gun at the ready, but not firing. Max stood beside her, camera held in front of him to capture every possible angle of the scene unfolding around them.

"Come and get it, motherfuckers!" Zantoro tossed off his empty magazine and loaded another. He laid down a fresh burst of rounds, taking some of the dead soldiers off their feet for the moment.

"Goddamn it," London muttered, touching Lia's arm. He stepped away from her and crouched beside Vincent.

London rolled the kid onto his back as gently as he could manage, but he what he saw confirmed what he already knew: Vincent was dead. And since Pendleton Security wasn't a branch of the military, there were no dog tags to send home to his family. There would be no flag-draped coffin for Vincent's parents to bury. There wouldn't even be an official record of how or where he died. He simply wouldn't come home. That was part of the contract they all signed when they took the job. Hell, it wasn't even hidden in the fine print. Like the rest of them, Vincent cashed the paycheck. And now he'd paid the price.

London stood up. "Zantoro! Osbourne! Move out!"

To their credit, the two men ceased fire and got their asses in gear. It seemed that, even when all hell was breaking loose, London still had command of his unit. It wasn't much to hold onto, but a drowning man shouldn't bitch about the color of the life raft.

13

Peter had seen enough.

Once the fire spread from the Jeep to the house, he shimmied down the tree trunk, and began his retreat through the jungle. Although it was pitch black under the thick canopy, he moved with the stealthy speed of a jungle cat. Father Xavier and the others were camped a few hours' hike from the old farmhouse, so Peter felt reasonably certain that they were safe from the dead army. But he needed to tell Father Xavier about what he'd seen. He could hardly believe it himself.

The dead men had been using guns to attack the Americans! If the dead men from General Mbowi's learned how to use weapons, they'd be just as bad as when they were alive. Worse, maybe.

14

The light on his camera wasn't strong enough for Max to choose which shots would work best, so he gave up on filming any wide cinematic angles and settled for capturing whatever he could. Although he would have liked to pull back in order to convey the true scale of the battle, there wasn't much hope of that with his little handheld camera.

Maybe if those fucking cowboys hadn't forced you to abandon the rest of your equipment…

Even amidst the chaos, Max found himself seething with anger. The fucking Americans; it was so typical the way they threw their weight around and took charge of the situation. Especially that fucking Texas cowboy, Mike London.

Max had gotten a good shot of London getting his feet tangled in the grass and falling down face-first. Sure, he'd popped right back up and smashed a zombie's head in for good measure, but it hadn't exactly been done with the graceful power of the action hero that the man so clearly thought he was. But the best scene Max captured was the death of Vincent, the youngest of the American mercenaries. It was pure luck that Max had been doing a slow sweep of the scene when he paused to get a shot of Vincent firing his rifle into the slowly advancing army of the dead. By happenstance, Max captured the moment when a burst of automatic weapons fire caught Vincent in the back. Vincent jerked like a puppet experiencing a seizure. He dropped his rifle and clutched his stomach as blood poured from the exit wounds. It was a true hero's death scene, the sort of thing that would play well to any audience once some appropriate music had been edited in. Maybe Lia could offer some narration. Or maybe she would think it was best to let the images speak for themselves.

Or maybe she's too busy fucking her new boyfriend to care…

Max turned the camera on Lia. She winced as the light hit her eyes, throwing a hand in front of her face to shield herself.

"What the hell are you doing?" she demanded in French, closing the distance between them in three angry steps. "You'll give us night blindness with your stupid light."

"I can't film with no light," he said. "Leave me alone."

She drew back the hand that had been shielding her eyes and slapped him.

"Idiot! Do you really think we're still making a documentary?"

The force of the blow staggered him, but he kept the camera trained on her. "What else am I supposed to do? Your boyfriend doesn't trust me with a gun."

"Because you've been acting erratically. I wouldn't give you one either. Now turn off that stupid light before you get us all killed."

"I told you to leave me alone!" he shouted over the thunder of gunfire. "Why don't you go fuck your cowboy hero some more and leave the journalism to those of us who still have some integrity."

"You're a selfish son of a bitch," she spat.

"And you're a disloyal cunt. After all these years, we finally know where we stand."

Max stepped out of slapping range, then he turned his

back on her and resumed filming. He steeled himself for a moment, preparing himself for her to retaliate. But after a few seconds without any response, he relaxed and turned his full attention back to his work. There was a panorama of horrors all around him, and he intended to document as much of it as possible. Now that the house was engulfed in flames, he actually had enough light to get some wider shots. It wasn't ideal, but he could focus on some of the subjects who were more than a few meters away.

He zoomed in on one of the dead soldiers. In life, the man had been quite a specimen, covered in thick muscles, towering head and shoulders over most of the others around him. Death had reduced him somewhat. Max supposed that was only natural. The giant soldier was missing most of his left arm. A jagged scrap of bone dangled from his shoulder, the shredded muscles and ligaments having withered and dried until they resembled the scraps of beef jerky that London and his mercenaries ate. The soldier's face looked like it had been worked over with heavy duty sandpaper. His lips were gone, exposing a mouthful of crooked teeth. One of his ears dangled off the side of his head.

Max zoomed in as close as his camera would allow.

"You are impressive," he whispered. "You could be on the movie poster."

The soldier seemed to stare back at him with red, unblinking eyes. Max was so preoccupied with capturing the image in as much detail as possible that he didn't immediately notice that the soldier was using his remaining arm to raise a gun. But when Max zoomed out slightly, he saw that the gun was aimed right at him. Max knew he should move. He knew he should drop to the ground, out of the line of fire. But the image was so powerful that he couldn't look away. And besides, the reanimated dead couldn't really aim, could they? The shots that had taken down Vincent were one in a million.

The first shot caught Max in the shoulder and spun him around. His camera flew from his hand. He watched it tumble through the air and fall into the grass.

I guess that makes two in a million, he thought.

The second shot kicked him square in the ass, propelling him forward. He fell to the ground, coming to rest right beside his camera.

Three in a million? No end to your bad luck in this country.

As the pain washed over him, he stared into the lens. He wondered if the camera was still on, if it was still capturing images. It occurred to him that, after all his years filming documentaries, this would be the first time he'd ever been on the other side of the camera.

"Probably will get left on the editing room floor," he whispered, closing his eyes.

15

Morton Fairbanks' lower back was sore. His heart was beating jackrabbit-fast in his chest. Sweat streamed down his face despite the air conditioned room. He felt like he might collapse at any moment, but he continued to thrust himself as deeply as he could manage into Eve. Her vagina was pleasantly tight, if a bit dry. He'd lubricated it with some rose-scented hand lotion Dr. Whittaker had left in the staff lounge, but he'd done so sparingly. There were only a few ounces of lotion in the bottle, after all, and Eve's body would never again have the ability to self-lubricate.

"Come on, come on, come on," he grunted with each thrust.

For her part, Eve wasn't much of a lover anymore. During their first few couplings, she'd struggled against him, clawing and biting against her duct tape restraints like an enraged animal. Her deep, monotone moans were impossible to mistake for sounds of pleasure, but they'd added a certain something to the thrill. But the following day, when Fairbanks had dropped his pants and mounted her, all that fight was gone. She lay beneath him, staring blankly at the ceiling while he pumped and grunted. While that passivity did hold a certain thrill for

Fairbanks, the novelty soon wore off and it became almost tiresome. But there wasn't much else in the way of entertainment in his basement home, so he carried on as best he could.

Eve stared up at him blankly. Her red eyes held no passion or pleasure, but they were also blessedly free of judgment. Her flesh was cool yet pliant beneath him. If not for the soft moans, she might have been a cadaver. And while that particular kink had always excited Fairbanks as a fantasy, the reality was less than satisfying.

"You won't thrash around and try to bite me, will you?" he asked, pausing his rhythmic thrusts just long enough to rip the duct tape off her mouth. It came away trailing a scrap of flesh from her bottom lip, but she didn't seem to register any pain. Although he'd removed her teeth before their initial coupling, he found that she still tried to bite him if she wasn't gagged. While she couldn't do any damage, the extra wrestling made the carnal act too much of a workout. So he carefully applied duct tape each time he got the urge to fulfill his duty as a husband.

Fairbanks tossed the wadded-up ball of tape over his shoulder and drew back, prepared to jump away from her if she showed a high level of aggression. But she continued to lie there, seemingly uninterested in anything. This new development was perplexing enough to wilt the doctor's erection. He climbed off her, shoving her legs to the floor and hauling her to a seated position. Then he sat beside her on the sofa, breathing heavily. His mind worked through the various hypotheses. And although he had no way to test them, the likely conclusions weren't elusive.

The serum worked like a virus, pirating the body's cells and reproducing feverishly until they'd taken complete control. But viruses are, if nothing else, endlessly adaptive, finding ways to jump from one host organism to another. The Daroka serum was supposed to have fail safe measures to prevent unchecked mutation, but those measures had already proved to be ineffective, if they were ever meant to work at all (and Fairbanks had strong suspicions they were not). The viral component of the serum had already mutated to be orally transmittable. Sexual transmission wasn't much of a leap from there.

Fairbanks laughed. He looked down at his penis. "You really are the cause of all my troubles, aren't you?"

It was true: If it wasn't for his deviant sexual appetites, Marsh Industries wouldn't have been in a position to blackmail him into participating in the HOPE Project. But it hardly mattered anymore. Fairbanks was a realist. Now that the virus had broken containment, there was little chance that it wouldn't continue to spread. If he had access to his computer, he could have run the data through a modeling program and gotten a more accurate picture of what the future held, but again, it didn't matter.

He looked at Eve and smiled. "You know something, darling? I knew you'd give it to me. I'm a lot of things, but an idiot isn't one of them. I knew the risks. Maybe, deep down in some dark part of my subconscious, I wanted it to happen. Maybe I wanted to be part of the group."

Eve stared at the ceiling and moaned.

"Right, darling," Fairbanks continued. "You're not a therapist, are you?"

He stood up and went into the bathroom. His discarded clothing was piled on the floor and he began sorting through it and getting dressed. When he'd finished putting on his clothes, he paused in front of the mirror that hung over the sink. As he ran a comb through his thinning hair, he peered at his reflection, searching for telltale signs of infection. There were circles under his eyes, but that wasn't surprising. He'd been living like a rat in a bolt hole, with the faintly buzzing fluorescent fixtures overhead as his only source of light. That could account for the dark circles and even the bloodshot quality of his eyes.

There was, of course, one way to be absolutely certain.

He walked out of the bathroom and paused in front of the sofa, where Eve sat like an exhibit in the horror section of a wax museum. He waved a hand in front of her face. When there was no response, he leaned in close and pressed his mouth against hers, kissing her with as much passion as he could muster, licking her cracked lips and probing her dry mouth with his tongue.

He pulled away, straightened up, and wiped his mouth with his hand. "Darling, I think it's time to go out for a stroll. Don't wait up."

Without hesitation, he crossed the room and opened the door. He stepped over the threshold and into the lab.

Eve's friends were scattered throughout the trashed room. Some were stumbling around aimlessly, walking in circles or wandering in and out of the open cells. Others lay on the floor, as if they'd fallen and didn't possess the necessary motivation to stand back up. As Fairbanks walked into the room, they turned to look at him. For a terrible moment, their constant moaning stopped and they regarded him with their blood-red eyes. They seemed to sniff him as he approached, like they were wary dogs. But they didn't attack him. In fact, once they'd gotten a good look and sniff, they didn't even seem all that interested. They went back to their aimless routines and resumed their low moaning. He walked among them untouched.

"Well, then," he said, shaking one of the reanimated specimens out of his old chair at the computer desk. The specimen, a male whose face looked like it had been worked over with steel wool, fell to the floor, and crawled away.

"I reckon that it's only a matter of time until I'm a full-fledged member of this new society," Fairbanks announced, leaning back in his chair. "Until then, carry on."

It occurred to him as he put his feet up on the desk that his reaction should be different. Panic, perhaps, would have been more appropriate, or all-consuming sadness and regret. Maybe he should have put on a big show of grief. Some of that wailing and gnashing of teeth spoken of in the Bible. But really, if he felt anything at all, it was relief. For the first time in years—maybe even the first time ever—he could truly relax. He closed his eyes and breathed deeply, imagining that he could feel his life ebbing away with each exhalation.

Things were going to be okay. He'd said that to himself many times, but this was the first time he actually believed it. He leaned back in the chair and closed his eyes. He laughed and laughed until his sides ached.

16

A CALL TO ARMS FOR ALL PATRIOTS!!!

Wake up, sheeple. This whole thing is just some government psy-op to force you into giving up more of your natural rights. The deep state is behind Waylon Marsh's death, and I'm willing to bet that bitch Lori Lund is somehow connected to it. You know that rumor about how she's really one of Leonidas Marsh's illegitimate children? That's not a rumor!!! The bitch has had it out for Waylon Marsh since day one because she wasn't strong or smart enough to be a real Marsh. The new world order is coming. Get ready for mask mandates and travel restrictions and gas prices through the roof. And get ready for another vaccine, because that's coming too. Well, I won't comply. I won't be taking their 5G microchip or nanotech spyware into my veins. Give me liberty or give me death!!!

—Fred Stanopolos, Op-Ed columnist for *Elder Statesman* magazine

New York Times **headlines:**

CONGRESS EMERGENCY SESSION DEBATES RESPONSE TO EPIDEMIC CONCERNS

MARSH INDUSTRIES STOCK REBOUNDS UNDER NEW LEADERSHIP: *HOPE PROJECT FACILITIES SHUT DOWN IN UKRAINE, INDIA, BRAZIL*

CONTINUED UNREST IN BRAZIL: *DEATH TOLL RISES*

CHINESE GOVERNMENT DENIES EPIDEMIC

Just wanted to know if anyone has any tips for fighting off this virus that's going around. A little about me: I'm a proud home-schooling mama bear with six little angels, all completely unvaxxed pureblood! We're an organic household and we stick to a gluten-free, raw milk, vegan lifestyle. Currently, three of my little ones are experiencing flu-like symptoms with high fever, heavy mucus, and vomiting. So far I've tried a raw honey-garlic-ginger syrup and high doses of bee pollen, but nothing seems to be working. Any advice?

—posted by username ATL_Organic to the *Holistic Fam* internet message board.

Partial transcript of DEA wiretap of suspected Baltimore, MD drug dealer Teddy "Poonman" Sotos:

POONMAN: Yeah, I got no fucking idea where the shit came from, homes. But shit was real, you heard. I had some bitches over to party last night and shared out a few grams. Almost made me wish I ain't sold the rest off.

UNIDENTIFIED CALLER: Word? Where you get it?

POONMAN: It's fucking wild, bro. (coughing) You remember that shit went down in DC at that fucking hotel?

UNIDENTIFIED CALLER: You talking about the white church people who had that fucking riot?

POONMAN: (coughing) Yeah, one of my girls was there and got out before the police showed up. (unintelligible) Bitch name Kaylee Marie.

UNIDENTIFIED CALLER: Yeah, white girl, high class ho. She work for Madame Stella, right?

POONMAN: Yeah. Couple her friends got killed in that hotel. She went to check on them and there was just blood all over the room. (coughing) Looked like a fucking horror movie.

UNIDENTIFIED CALLER: Shit…

POONMAN: Anyway, girl was shook, so I told her come over. You know, I was going to comfort the girl, because we go back. Bitch was fucking scared, right? Anyway, she the one who brought me the shit. Said she had a job fucking some old dude and he's the one had the shit. She lifted it off him. Good shit like that, I wish she'd have just shot his ass and taken everything he had!

UNIDENTIFIED CALLER: Well, thanks for sharing, bro. I did a few lines with my boys (unintelligible) and goddamn…

POONMAN: Yeah, I…(coughing) Sorry, bro. Think I'm coming down with a fucking cold or some shit. Got all sorts of green fucking snot…(unintelligible)…fucking gross.

UNIDENTIFIED CALLER: Yeah, I ain't feeling right myself. Some cold going around. Saw some shit on the news about a virus…(unintelligible)…I don't (unintelligible)…fucking puke my brains out. Goddamn (unintelligible) shit was everywhere. Ruined the fucking carpet. You see that shit I was talking about on the news? Rabies or some shit…

POONMAN: Aw, fuck the news. Always talking some shit about a virus…

Part Eight

The darkness drops again…

"This world of money and status and privilege and superficial beauty is about to be devoured by an army of the living dead."

—Svetlana Kurzcyk

1

Vogel was at the Amplitude Music Festival when they finally caught up to him. The festival, which featured a lineup of reunited punk and new wave bands, was being held at the Leonidas Marsh Memorial Amphitheater just outside Austin, Texas. The irony of Marsh Industries' goons finally tracking him down at an amphitheater named for the Marsh family patriarch wasn't lost on Vogel. In fact, he'd been hoping they might find him when he chose this place as his destination. His supply of the powdered serum was gone. He'd traded two of his last three for his ticket to the festival, then snorted the contents of the final vial in the venue's restroom. The sedatives and cocaine in the powdered serum were competing for control of his system. The effect wasn't entirely unpleasant.

"What took you so long?" he asked the two bounty hunters who grabbed his elbows and hauled him out of his seat.

They were dressed in blue jeans and freshly purchased t-shirts featuring logos of the festival's headlining act. If it was their best attempt at blending in with the crowd, it was pathetic. Even to Vogel's untrained eyes, they looked like undercover narcotics cops.

"Don't make a scene," one of them ordered.

Vogel stood up. "You sure we don't have time to stay and listen to the music?"

His two new friends just stared at him.

"No, I don't suppose you look like the type to have much interest in the arts," he said. "It's not my preferred genre, of course, but it's never a bad idea to step outside one's comfort zone. I doubt it would make a difference in the grand scheme of things if we stay for just a song or two."

"Don't make this any harder than it has to be," one of them answered.

Vogel shrugged. "Oh, well."

They hustled him out of the amphitheater, walking on either side of him. Vogel found it amusing, the way they pressed so close. It was like they thought he was some fleet-footed fugitive rather than a seventy-three year old man carrying thirty pounds of extra weight atop two bad knees. He supposed they were trained to stay close to their quarry and to treat every prisoner as if he were armed and dangerous. It was the only way they knew, and like most people, they acted according to their nature.

They guided him to the edge of the parking lot, where a pair of massive black SUVs sat idling. As they approached, the leading vehicle's rear passenger side door flew open. The goons shoved Vogel into the backseat, then slammed the door. Vogel glanced around at the vehicle's other occupants. Another pair of muscle-heads sat in the front seat, although these had been spared the indignity of having to wear casual clothes and were dressed in black military-style tactical outfits. He imagined they were the type who would feel comfortable wearing similar outfits as pajamas. The person sharing the backseat was Ray Hollister, who was wearing his customary grey suit, sipping from a glass of what Vogel guessed was very expensive whiskey.

"Well, Doc, it seems you've been a bad boy," Hollister said.

The SUV lurched out of the parking lot and gathered speed as it headed for the interstate.

"Now that your boss is dead, I suppose you'll be the one calling me Doc," Vogel sighed.

Although not for long, he added silently. *I can already feel the serum working its way through my system.*

"So you heard the news about Marsh, eh?" Hollister loosened his tie and took a sip of his drink. "You know what they say: that's life."

"Well," Vogel said, "it's death, at any rate."

Hollister must not have found the joke funny. He didn't laugh. "You're in deep shit, Doc. After the bullshit in Daroka….and that mess at the hotel in DC and whatever the fuck is going on in Atlanta and now I'm hearing about the trouble in Brazil..." Hollister paused to finish off his whiskey. "Someone is going to have to fall on his own sword, Doc. And that person is going to be you. There are people—very important, powerful people—who believe that this whole mess is a result of sabotage on your part."

"Oh?" Vogel put a hand to his heart, doing his best to feign shock. "Falling on one's sword sounds quite painful."

"*Oh?*" Hollister might have been aiming to mock Vogel's German accent, but it sounded prissy. "Yeah, you're going to do that very thing, because otherwise, your future prospects are very grim."

"I should imagine they'll want to put me in prison for the rest of my life. How could it be any grimmer than that?"

Hollister leaned forward to hand his glass to the front seat passenger, who got busy pouring a refill. "Really? Do I need to remind you about our facility in Kyrvyiv? Or what about that little house of horrors you were running in India? Those places may be shut down for the moment, but once this bullshit blows over, they'll be up and running again. I'm sure the new research staff would welcome a new specimen."

Vogel shuddered dramatically and forced himself to keep a straight face. "No, not those places…"

"Yes, Doc. *Those places.*" Hollister accepted his glass from the man in the front seat. He took a sip, and smiled at Vogel. "I bet you'd much rather do your time in a minimum security federal prison than go anywhere near your old stomping grounds."

"Yes, I see your point. Thank you for putting things in perspective."

Hollister's posture relaxed. "Good, that's settled. Soon as we get to the airport, we're taking you back to DC, where you'll surrender to the secret service. It seems the President would like a word before you're handed over to the FBI. You'll have an attorney assigned, and I suggest you adopt a policy of listening to his advice and speaking when spoken to."

"Yes, that does seem to be the best course of action."

Hollister tapped the back of the front passenger seat and told the square jawed fellow in the tactical gear to pour the doctor a couple fingers of bourbon. Vogel accepted the glass and took a sip. The spirit burned his throat. His stomach rumbled, and Vogel wondered how much longer he had before he started to vomit uncontrollably. He hoped he could make to DC. The dose he'd taken was small enough that he should still have a few hours.

"One thing I've been wondering," Hollister said. "Why the hell did you do it? I just can't figure it out. I know Marsh paid you well. By just about any standard, you're a rich man. But I don't think it was about money. Far as I can tell, you don't even care about that. You got a house on the west coast, but it's not much more than a bungalow. You keep apartments in Mumbai and Ukraine, but they're just for the few hours of sleep you get when you're not busy in your labs. So why? What was the point of this little apocalypse?"

Vogel turned to look out the window at the blurred scenery. He thought of the many answers he could give Hollister. He could tell him that humanity was so deeply flawed that it was past redemption. That every scientific advancement would either be weaponized or priced out of the reach of those whom it would benefit most. That even if a project to end world hunger was successful, it would never be implemented, because those occupying the seats of power believed it was necessary for many to starve in order to ensure that a select few could wallow in obscene wealth. That even in the midst of abundance, with the makings of a literal utopia within reach, most people would choose to draw and redraw borders, divide themselves into tribes, and send their young people to maim and kill one another in the name of whatever Bronze Age mythology their nation favored. That hatred and fear had become the daily bread of billions, while love and compassion were held up as signs of weakness to be mocked. That greed and ignorance had soured humanity's collective soul to the point that it was no longer worthy of salvation, and the only hope was to wipe the slate clean and start from zero.

Yes, Vogel believed all of that with unwavering conviction, and could very well have told Hollister so. But it would have been a waste of breath. Instead, he put the question to Hollister.

"Why did *you* do what you did?" he asked. "I assume Mr. Marsh didn't die of natural causes."

"Because a great man sometimes needs to be replaced by a greater man. But you still haven't answered my question."

Vogel smiled. *Because you answered it for yourself. A world that lifts up men like Waylon Marsh and Ray Hollister doesn't deserve to continue.*

"Come on, Doc," Hollister said. "How about an answer?"

Vogel shrugged. "Maybe I just wanted to see what would happen when control of this world was taken out of the hands of a few rich men. And you must admit, the results have been quite exciting."

"Crazy goddamn Kraut." Hollister sneered. "Tell you what, Doc, I'm done with you. We got another half hour in this car, then it's a three hour flight to DC. I don't want to hear another word out of your mouth during that time. First word you say, I'll have someone break your goddamn kneecaps and you can go to your meeting with the President in a fucking wheelchair."

Vogel leaned back in his seat. He closed his eyes and listened to the gurgling sounds in his stomach.

2

Lori Lund awoke slowly. She sat up in bed and glanced around at her room, trying to find her bearings. Spock jumped onto the bed and paced back and forth, meowing a demand for his morning meal.

"All right, fat boy," she said, throwing back the blanket and sliding out of bed.

On the way into the kitchen, she scooped the remote control off the counter and turned on the TV. She filled Spock's bowl and fired up the coffee maker. While the machine gurgled to life, she dropped a couple slices of bread in the toaster. The usual morning soundtrack filled the apartment: the gurgle-hiss of the coffee maker, the crunch-purr of Spock tucking into his kibble, and the drone of overly-enunciated newscaster speech from the TV. It was mostly just aural wallpaper, a bit of background noise to drive away the temptation to crawl back into bed for another couple hours' sleep. She reached for the ceiling and stretched her back muscles. One last big yawn, and it was time for that first cup of coffee.

Then the bottom fell out of her world. One of the

newscasters' voices swam out of the background noise and tossed off a sentence that turned Lori's knees to jelly.

"Once again, we have confirmation of the death of international business tycoon Waylon Marsh," the morning news anchor said in clipped, yet almost breezy tones. "Marsh, aged 52, has courted controversy for much of his adult life, turning risky tech ventures into Wall Street darlings as he swelled the fortune left to him by his father, Leonidas Marsh. During his time as president and CEO of Marsh Industries, Waylon Marsh clashed with everyone from labor union leaders and environmentalists, to the Catholic Church and pro-life groups. His flashy lifestyle, high-energy personality, and unconventional approach to business made him a favorite subject of the media, which he often derided as exploitative and dishonest. Marsh's body was discovered in an abandoned RV at a rest area near Meridian, Mississippi. Local authorities are cooperating with the FBI in an ongoing investigation."

Lori staggered into the living room and stared at the TV screen as the sheriff of Podunk County explained to a gaggle of reporters that there few details about the investigation that he could disclose, although there was evidence of foul play and Marsh's death had been ruled a homicide.

"You colossal asshole," she said to the image of Waylon Marsh on the TV screen. "You'll never even know it was me that finally brought you down."

Once she'd regained some sense of equilibrium, she threw on some clothes, poured her coffee into a to-go mug, and headed for the Earth Force office.

When she'd left the office eight hours earlier, it had been a hive of activity, filled with her social media team and tech specialists. The place had been a noisy symphony of overlapping, excited conversation backed by a percussion section of keystrokes and mouse clicks. Now, the place was nearly silent except for the faint hum of the overhead lights and the ancient refrigerator in the lounge. It was also deserted, save for her faithful assistant Spider, who sat at the paperwork-strewn conference table, sipping a cup of coffee and staring at the screen of his laptop.

He turned at the sound of her entering the room and raised his cup in a toast. "Ding dong, the witch is dead, huh? Can't fucking believe it. Of course, there will be someone just as bad ready to step into his spot. A power vacuum, right? Or maybe an evil asshole vacuum. We'll be ready."

Lori looked around the empty office. "Where is everybody?"

"Once the news broke, I sent them home," Spider said. "I mean, we were working around the clock to destroy Waylon Marsh, and now he's dead. I figure people deserve a break. Seems like we've been after that guy forever, so people are kind of at a loss for the moment."

"Yeah…" Lori took a seat at the table.

"Besides, lots of people want to go to the protest in Portland," Spider continued, turning his eyes back to his laptop screen. "Fucking cops shot someone trying to get help at the emergency room. The official statement is that some homeless dude was showing signs of a rabies infection and acting aggressively towards the hospital staff. Ridiculous, right? I mean, rabies? It's like they're not even trying anymore. It's just typical victim blaming. Okay, the poor guy might have bitten a nurse or two, but should that be a death sentence? I mean…" He glanced up from his computer. "Lori, you okay?"

She forced a smile. "Yeah, sure. Still a little tired, I guess. Plus, this news…"

"It's like Captain Ahab finally getting the whale, right? Pretty cool."

She didn't bother telling him that the whale dragged Ahab to his death. She wasn't much in the mood for discussing literature, and besides, she didn't want to rain on Spider's parade. He'd put in long hours in Earth Force's campaign against Waylon Marsh. He deserved to enjoy the moment.

"Look," she said. "You've been working your ass off lately. Why don't you take a few days off and relax. Head over to Portland if you want or maybe just chill out and binge watch one of those Japanese cartoons you like so much."

"You mean anime," he said, his patient expression and tone of voice like those of a parent gently correcting a slow child. "We don't call them cartoons."

"I'll clean up around here. Next week, we'll have a general meeting and figure out where to go from here. Sound good?"

"Yeah, sure." Spider closed his laptop and stood. He gave her an uncertain look, then squeezed her shoulder. "We did it, Lori. We brought him down. The word on the street is that the new CEO is pulling the plug on the HOPE Project. You should be proud."

She nodded. The smile she conjured up felt like a plastic Halloween mask on her face. Thankfully, she didn't have to wear it long. Spider shoved his laptop into his messenger bag and headed for the exit, leaving her alone in the office. She sat there staring at the littered surface of the table. Mountains of paperwork, discarded coffee cups, takeout boxes from the Chinese restaurant across the street, empty soda cans…all the refuse you'd expect from a group of mostly twenty-somethings pulling an all-nighter. She thought about cleaning it up, but couldn't muster the energy.

Instead, she just sat there, wondering what Captain Ahab's post-Moby Dick life would have looked like if Melville hadn't sent the captain to his grave in the briny deep? Would he have carried on with the same determination, finding a new terror at which to aim his rage? Would he give up the nautical life and haunt the harbor town taverns, nursing mug after mug of beer while he told his tale to anyone unlucky enough to be within earshot? Or would he simply fade away, growing thinner and more insubstantial with each passing day in the absence of the Great White Whale? Would he pine for the days of endless pursuit?

She was so wrapped up in her musings, so absorbed by herself, that she didn't hear the woman enter the office. She didn't even notice the presence of another human being until the woman—a tall Nordic blonde—took a seat in Spider's recently vacated swivel chair. The woman's sudden appearance was so strange that it caught Lori off-guard, and she said the first absurdity that popped into her head.

"That's Spider's special chair. He says he does all his best thinking in it, and that's why no one else is allowed to sit there."

"Is that so?" The blonde woman cocked her head to one side, like she was listening to a strange new type of music and couldn't decide whether or not she enjoyed it. "It's pretty comfortable, but I don't think it does anything for my thought process. If it bothers you, I'm happy to move."

Lori shook her head. "No, that's okay."

"Fair enough. My name is Svetlana." She offered her hand. Still too shaken by the weirdness of the encounter, Lori shook it and introduced herself. Svetlana smiled as she replied, "Oh, of course I know who you are. Otherwise I wouldn't be here."

"Yes," Lori said, "of course."

"When I was in college, I had a poster of you on my dorm room wall. It was that photo from *Time* magazine. You know, the one where you were chained to a tree while the cops and men from the logging company were shouting at you?"

Lori nodded. "That tree is still standing."

"Well, I suppose you've heard the news by now. You don't wear makeup, but I can still tell you've been crying."

Lori wiped her cheeks. She stared at her moist fingertips. "I hadn't even realized…"

"He always spoke highly of you," Svetlana said. "No, that's an understatement. He spoke of you with something like reverence. Even when he was railing about how much he hated you, it was obvious that his feelings were very far from hate. He admired you, and he said so quite often. Only when he was with those he truly trusted, you understand. With everyone else, there was a lot of bluster about how you were just another frigid repressed lesbo with an axe to grind. He'd say you were terrified of his alpha masculinity and hated success. All the usual nonsense. But when we were alone, and usually after he'd had a few drinks, his tune would change. He admired your persistence. And the way he smiled when he talked about you, well, let's just say I'm certain he never smiled that way when he spoke about me. Or about any of the other women in his orbit."

"Don't tell me you loved him." Lori laughed bitterly.

"Maybe I did, in a way. But whatever feelings I might have once had for Waylon withered and died long ago, about the time that I realized I could never compete with your ghost."

"That's ridiculous. We were only together for one semester and part of a summer vacation, and it was ages ago. We were just kids."

"And yet here we sit." Svetlana settled her purse in her lap. She unzipped it and dug out a tube of lip balm, which she carefully applied. Once she'd rubbed her lips together, she reached back into her purse and traded the lip balm for a pistol. It was a compact thing, not some hand cannon, but the way she held it told Lori that the weapon was just as deadly.

"I thought you would never get to the point," Lori said.

"I'm sorry, it's just that I've wondered for so long what it would be like to actually talk to you. When I stole that hard drive from Waylon, I deleted some files before I handed it over to my contact. There was one that was a type of diary, and each entry was addressed to you. He wanted to justify himself, and he spent hundreds of thousands of words on a one sided argument with a woman whose bed he'd shared for a few months, back when he was just twenty years old. It's actually amazing. It's the sort of thing you think only exists in bad paperback novels or tear-jerker movies."

Lori shook her head. "There's no justification for what he became."

"I suppose that's true. He could be quite a monster," Svetlana admitted. "Still, history is mostly shaped by monstrous men. Once I accepted that fact, I achieved some sort of clarity."

"And that clarity gave you such insight that you're running errands for whatever monster stepped up to take Waylon's place." Lori said. "Sister, you aren't enlightened by some special wisdom. You're a contract killer. That's one step below whore."

"That's not very nice. And I'm not sure it's the sort of thing a feminist icon should say."

Lori had her own sudden flash of insight. "It was you that killed Waylon, wasn't it?"

Svetlana nodded. "He'd gone too far. Once I figured out the true nature of the HOPE Project, I knew it was only a matter of time before his world came crashing down and buried me in the rubble right alongside him. So I decided to get ahead of the curve. I put that hard drive out there, knowing it would find its way to you. Then, I stepped back and waited for my next opportunity to reveal itself."

"And now you're here to tie up all the loose ends. Let me guess, it's that fucking redneck Hollister, isn't it? He's the one pulling your leash now that Waylon is out of the way. I hope he's paying you well," Lori said.

"Oh, it's not so much the money as it is the security," Svetlana replied. "We managed to stop the HOPE Project, but I think we were too late. The genie is out of the fucking bottle, and it's not going back in. Ray Hollister and his pals on Wall Street and his cronies in Washington DC may think they can still turn this thing around, but I doubt it. This world of money and status and privilege and superficial beauty is about to be devoured by an army of the living dead. Some people will manage to survive and rebuild society from the ground up. I intend to be one of them. Men had their chance at running the show, and they bungled it."

"No argument there, but something tells me that if the women who step in to take their place are anything like you, the difference will be negligible."

"Now you're just being mean." Svetlana sighed. "You keep talking like that and you might hurt my feelings."

"Then I guess you'd better get on with it," Lori said.

Svetlana stood. She raised the gun and pointed it at Lori's head.

"Well?" Lori prompted.

"Don't worry," Svetlana said. "It won't hurt."

Lori closed her eyes and took a deep breath. Svetlana was right.

3

Partial transcript of satellite radio show *Market Watch with Money Madman Mike:*

MONEY MADMAN MIKE: You heard it here first, folks: now is the time to buy Marsh Industries stock. Normally, when you see a media controversy about a company and then there's a leadership change, you're thinking it's time to sell, sell, sell. But if yesterday's numbers are any indication, the price for Marsh Industries is going to remain strong.

CALLER: They're still in my portfolio, but the news about what's going on in DC and Atlanta is giving me second thoughts. And now we're hearing something about Portland and Austin…

MONEY MADMAN MIKE: Once again, this is just one of those tempest in a teapot situations. The government always likes to make a big deal about every little flu bug like it's some apocalypse level event. This isn't a pandemic folks! It's just a bug that's going around, same as it ever was.

USA Today headlines:

RUSSIAN PUNK BAND VAGINA DENTATA DETAINED DURING PROTEST OVER GOVERNMENT'S RESPONSE TO DAROKA

MEXICAN GOVERNMENT CONSIDERS BORDER CLOSURE AS OUTBREAKS CONTINUE IN SOUTH TEXAS

Part Nine

And what rough beast, its hour come round at last,
Slouches towards Bethlehem to be born?

"People who create something like this plague, they're not normal."

—Gilbert Zantoro

1

Father Xavier listened to Peter's account of the events he'd witnessed at the farmhouse with growing concern. Had anyone but his most trusted scout told such a wild tale, Father Xavier would have chalked a great deal of it up to simple embellishment. Children were prone to such things, after all, and although his army had seen much and traveled far, they were still children. But Peter was a special case, even among the battle-hardened, world-weary children that made up Father Xavier's flock.

"But they survived?" Father Xavier asked. "The Americans and the French journalists, they survived and continued north?"

"One of the Americans was killed," Peter said. "And the French man, he was hurt. The others had to carry him out of the valley. But the others, they survived."

"And they took to open jungle rather than the old logging road?"

Peter nodded. "The road was full of the dead. If they had gone that way, even the Americans' guns would not have been enough."

"Then we shall continue to avoid the road as well." Father

Xavier patted the boy on the shoulder and told him to eat and rest. Sunrise was still another hour away, and it would be another hour after that until the entire army was ready to move. They were camped in the thick jungle, perhaps two kilometers from the logging road. Father Xavier was relieved to know that his instinct to keep away from the road had been correct. There had been times over the last few days, when their progress had been so slow he'd begun to wonder if he wasn't being overly cautious in his choice of route. But now he knew the Americans were still pressing north, towards the research facility, and there could be no doubt.

The mercenaries were pilgrims leading the way to the new Holy Land.

2

They walked for a couple hours before London finally called a halt. Even under better circumstances, the hike would have been brutal. It felt like a death march.

They found a rocky outcropping and took shelter. The space was too open and shallow to be called a cave, but it would be a decent defensive position when things went south. And after the way their brief stay at the farmhouse had ended, London was keeping "worst case scenario" firmly in mind.

As the group huddled beneath the damp rocky ceiling, London took stock of their situation. The good news: supplies of food, water, and ammo were all good. The bad news: just about everything else.

Since Vincent's death, Osbourne had become grim and silent. His shoulders sagged and his eyes were fixed in a constant thousand yard stare.

Zantoro was clearly sick. London hoped it was just withdrawal symptoms, but he'd begun to fear that it could be much worse. Once they'd retreated to a safe position, Zantoro had excused himself to step behind a tree and puke his guts out. London knew it was serious when Zantoro didn't have a ready-made quip upon his return.

Max was hanging in there, but just barely. Osbourne had done his best to patch the Frenchman up, but those bullet wounds were beyond the reach of even a skilled combat medic. Osbourne had managed to dig the bullet out of Max's, ass and stitch up the hole, but even after bathing the wound in a generous amount of antibiotic, infection was a near certainty. The other bullet had punched straight through, clipping a good chunk of Max's shoulder blade on its way out. The wound, which Osbourne had stitched, was still full of tiny pieces of bone. Again, infection was practically assured. The flesh around the wound was angry and swollen. Beads of congealed pus studded the spaces between stitches.

Lia looked like someone on the verge of combat shock. Although she'd witnessed many atrocities during her years in the field, the horrors she'd seen over the last few days were a new level of violence and brutality. She gripped her rifle the way a child holds a security blanket, clutching it to her chest with both hands.

All things considered, the outlook was grim.

They drank from their freshly filled canteens and ate unheated pork and beans straight from the can. They were too tired to even consider making a fire. They were too tired to do much of anything. Max groaned and whimpered through a few mouthfuls of food, then laid down, using Osbourne's backpack as a pillow. Osbourne, the closest thing they had to a medic, looked down at him and shook his head. Zantoro wandered away from the camp, claiming that he needed to relieve himself, but London suspected that there was more to it than that. He considered confronting Zantoro about his drug use, but this wasn't the time for an intervention.

London set his can of beans aside and leaned against the rock wall. "Probably not much more than a few clicks north.

We can camp here for a few hours, but we move out at full light. With any luck, we'll be there in the afternoon."

"And then what?" Lia asked.

"And then we do what we came here to do," London answered. "We blow that place to hell and hope that it's enough to stop the spread of this thing. But before we do it, we gather enough evidence to bury the sons of bitches that cooked it up in the first place. And if that isn't an option, we use it as a bargaining chip to save our asses."

"You saw how many of those things there were at the farmhouse." She closed her eyes and shook her head slowly, like she was trying to dislodge the memory. "There's no stopping it now."

"Then after we blow it to hell, we make for the border. There's an American embassy somewhere. If I can get on the horn with someone from Pendleton, they have enough juice with the US government to call in an airstrike. Then, we explore our options for using the information we gathered at the facility."

"So you trust them enough to help us?" Lia opened her eyes and stared right at him. "Your company, I mean. After they abandoned you and your team, you think they even care?"

"Oh, I know they don't give a rat's ass about us. But they'll do whatever's necessary to protect themselves and their clients. Which is why, once we make that phone call, we'd better disappear. I doubt they'll be in the mood to leave any loose ends dangling. The kind of bargaining we'll do with that incriminating evidence will be remote, through back channels." London paused to return her stare. "You got any better ideas, I'm all ears."

She sighed. "I don't know."

Zantoro made his way back to camp, crashing through the underbrush without even a token effort at stealth. He groaned as he sat down, pressing a hand to his abdomen. Without a word, he leaned back against the wall of their shelter and fell asleep.

"Might as well just kill them now," Osbourne muttered.

"The fuck did you just say?" London asked.

"These two." Osbourne pointed at Zantoro, then at Max. "These two won't make it very much longer out here. Max will hardly be able to walk tomorrow. I have some morphine in my medical kit, but that will just knock him out. It will take a miracle for him to avoid sepsis. And Zantoro…I don't think he's telling us everything. I know he was popping amphetamines like candy, but this isn't just withdrawal. Something back at that farmhouse made him sick. If I didn't know better, I'd say he got bitten by one of those zombie things. His symptoms look an awful lot like we saw from those missionaries' kid."

London gave him a hard look, but he knew Osbourne was making sense.

"They just have to hang on until we make it to the research center," London said. "If there's a cure for this thing —a vaccine or something—it's bound to be there. At the very least, there should be an infirmary where they can get some medication…"

He paused and looked from Osbourne to Lia, then back. Their faces were full of pity. He was grasping at straws, desperate to find some silver lining to keep them going, but they saw him for exactly what he was: full of shit.

"Anyway," London said, "you guys better get some sleep. I'll take first watch."

Lia grabbed his arm. "This is a problem you can't shoot your way out of."

"I know."

He ducked as he left the shelter of the outcropping, then shouldered his recently acquired AK-4. Reflexively, he reached for his can of Skoal, although it was long gone. Too bad Mbowi's army hadn't left any tobacco in the kitchen. He supposed he could have rifled through all the rucksacks and footlockers in search of something to scratch the itch. Hell, that was probably what Zantoro was doing while he was supposedly on guard detail.

London winced at the thought of Zantoro. Lia was right: it was a problem that he would have to face - sooner rather than later.

3

Morton Fairbanks was ripped from the velvet womb of dreamless sleep by the insistent blatting of the facility's alarm system.

"What fresh hell is this?" he muttered as he sat up on the sofa.

From her spot in the corner, Eve moaned. Since she didn't sleep, Fairbanks kept her there when he couldn't supervise her. He tethered her to the coatrack with his belt to keep her from endlessly pacing back and forth. She was harmless, really, but the sound of her shuffling footsteps kept him awake.

"Let's go see what all the fuss is about, shall we?" he asked.

Eve answered with a groan.

Fairbanks grabbed his backpack and shoved his arms through the straps. Although he now had nothing to fear from the building's residents, one could never tell when an improvised weapon might come in handy. It was a new world, after all, and one in which the rules shifted constantly. Besides, he liked the weight of the power drill. It was reassuring.

He unbuckled the belt from around Eve's hands, and moved it to her neck. If it was too tight or uncomfortable, she gave no indication. He led her to the door of the staff lounge, and opened it. The air of the basement lab's decaying population was rancid, but Fairbanks no longer found it quite so offensive.

He strolled through the basement of the research center like the proud monarch of a rotten kingdom. His subjects were loyal and obedient, stepping aside to allow him to pass as he made his way to the elevator. Eve followed close behind. She had a tendency to stray, likely still overwhelmed by her rise from a member of the common rabble to royal consort, hence the necessity of the leash. But it took no more than a gentle tug to correct her course, and she followed him into the elevator easily enough. Now that he no longer had anything to fear from the research center's infected populace, he'd had time to get the elevator working again. Trips to the upper levels were easy enough.

A couple of the other basement dwellers tried to hitch a ride with them, but Fairbanks shooed them away. Although his nose had grown somewhat accustomed to Eve's scent, he didn't care much for the idea of sharing a tight space with the others. Some of them had grown quite ripe as decay set in.

The doors slid shut, and Fairbanks pushed the button for the first floor. Behind him, Eve shuffled into a corner and stood there, clawing half-heartedly at the wall.

"Don't worry, darling," Fairbanks said. "We'll get this little disturbance sorted out."

The elevator came to a stop and the doors opened. Fairbanks gave the leash a gentle tug and led Eve out into the lobby. A large crowd of the infected had gathered there. Many of them pressed against the front doors, which had been locked during the initial outbreak. Others paced aimlessly around the open floor. The green slime leaking from their gaping mouths splattered the concrete floor. As he made his way across the room, Fairbanks was careful not to slip in any of the green puddles. He didn't want to fall and hurt himself. He had a bad disc in his lower back, after all, and a slip could aggravate it, although he suspected that, very soon, his lower back would be the least of his concerns.

His senses seemed to still be in good working order, but his fine motor skills were beginning to diminish. His hands shook, and his feet felt heavy when he walked. The constant headache that had started as a pinprick of pain in the center of his forehead had spread across the top half of his face. Each thud of his pulse seemed to press against the back of his eyeballs. In the pit of his stomach, there was a constant, sharp emptiness that no amount of food could quiet. And during his morning constitutional, he'd noticed blood and mucus in his stool. Most distressingly, his penis was showing signs of bruised discoloration. And though the utter lack of sensation in that area had at first been discouraging, perhaps it was merciful, given the grating pains that wracked the rest of his body.

He stepped behind the semi-circular security desk, and sat down in one of the three empty chairs. Eve chose to remain standing. Amazingly, all three monitors on the desk were still functioning, their screens displaying images taken by the facility's numerous surveillance cameras. Each screen was divided into four sections that switched between separate feeds every five seconds.

"Let's see who's knocking at our door, shall we?" Fairbanks mused.

He hummed a jaunty tune as he swept the litter of paperwork, coffee cups, and food wrappers off the desk.

It took him a moment to get the hang of checking each monitor. The one on his left displayed images from the interior of the research facility, while the one in the middle showed the camera feeds from the outside area surrounding the building. The monitor on the right side showed aerial views of the entire compound. As with everything on the Marsh Industries property, no expense had been spared when it came to the surveillance equipment. The images were crystal clear, as sharp as any high-definition TV screen. The system was also relatively simple. It only took Fairbanks a few keystrokes and mouse clicks to find and enhance the camera feed he sought. Another couple mouse clicks and he had a full-screen image of the newly arrived visitors.

"Could it be, my dear?" Fairbanks tugged Eve closer to him. "Could it be that there is a group of heroes here to rescue us?"

He threw back his head and laughed. Part of him was disturbed by the crazed edge that his laughter had taken on, but the other part wasn't bothered at all. It was this latter part that was growing stronger with each passing minute. It was just another symptom of the virus spreading through his system. He'd observed signs of cognitive decline, confusion, and instability in plenty of specimens. Now he was experiencing it firsthand.

"Let's have a look at this band of heroes…" He tapped a few keys and the image onscreen zoomed in.

They were a disheveled quintet: three fellows in some sort of military uniform alongside a man and woman in standard issue safari dress. One of the men in uniform appeared to be suffering from the same symptoms as Fairbanks. The man in civilian attire was wounded, his shoulder heavily bandaged. The remaining three seemed to be relatively unscathed, although they looked like they'd had a rough go of it. They all carried firearms, however, and they'd managed to get through the south gate without incident. But they had a long way to go, if they were headed for the research center, and that way was swarmed with the infected.

When the facility had been operational, it employed nearly two hundred scientists and researchers. There was an equal number of support staff and security personnel, plus the men General Mbowi had stationed there to act as liaisons with the local population. Fairbanks estimated that the infection rate for those who hadn't died during the initial chaos to be one hundred percent. Many of them were still trapped inside the building with Fairbanks, but there were plenty scattered across the compound.

"This should be interesting," Fairbanks said, settling back to watch the new arrivals fight their way across the open ground. He tugged Eve's leash until she sat in the chair next to him, then he slung his arm around her shoulders. "If only we had some popcorn."

4

The alarm started up as soon as they breached the perimeter fence. It was an insistent, monotonous honking that startled the birds from their trees. London didn't care for their presence being so loudly announced, but at least the fence wasn't electrified. He finished cutting away a section of the chain link, then slipped the bolt cutters into his backpack.

They were standing at the south entrance to the Marsh Industries compound. The place had been carved out of the Darokan jungle, and covered nearly two square miles. The perimeter of the compound was surrounded by high chain link fencing topped with razor wire. Just inside the gate was a guard shack. It wasn't just some little pre-fab building, either. This guard shack looked as spacious and well-appointed as London's first apartment. Waylon Marsh had certainly spared no expense setting this place up.

"If anyone's alive in there, at least they know we're here," Lia shouted over the alarm.

"Yeah, but so do the hostiles," London said, turning to face the group. "Okay, we're on the south side of the compound, and our objective is northeast of our position."

Max did his best to stand up straight and tip a mock salute. "Sir, yes, sir."

The compound was set up like a military base, with barracks and a mess hall and a command center. A road had been carved through the dense foliage, and London could see that it led to a building looming over the tree line. London figured they probably had nice civilian names for the various buildings on the compound, and no doubt the accommodations were nicer, but their function was the same. According to the maps he'd seen during the intelligence briefing, there was staff housing to their immediate north. London figured that was the building just up the road.

"I always thought the element of surprise was overrated anyway," Zantoro said, his voice little more than a hoarse croak.

Osbourne pressed in next to him and pointed to an area a few meters inside the fence, where a white metal pole stood. "See that lamp post? How much you want to bet that's surveillance?"

"Smile, you're on candid camera." Zantoro's laughter dissolved into a coughing fit. He stepped back from the group and spat a wad of phlegm into the bushes.

"Yeah, well, I doubt anyone's home to watch the show," London said. "This place looks dead."

As if on cue, the door to the guard house swung open, and a trio of men in military style uniforms stumbled out. Two of them looked like they'd been worked over with a chainsaw. They had ragged holes in their abdomens from which desiccated ropes of intestines hung like grey garlands. The third appeared unscathed from the neck down, but his face had been ravaged to the point that it was little more than exposed skull with a few leathery scraps of muscle attached. One of his eyes was gone, and as he shuffled alongside his two companions, a small army of insects spilled from the empty socket.

"Jesus Christ," Lia said, gagging at the sight of a shiny black beetle burrowing its way into the man's nostril.

"Jesus left this place long ago," Max replied.

London turned to look at him. Max was dripping sweat and had dark circles under his eyes. The walk from their camp to the Marsh Industries compound had reduced him to a trembling, feeble wreck. Just as Osbourne had predicted, infection had set in, and Max's wounds were leaking yellowish pus. London wondered if shooting him might be an act of mercy, but he knew he could never suggest such a thing to Lia. And for some reason, that consideration took priority. London forced himself back to the situation at hand.

"With that alarm going full blast, we might as well go in hot," he said.

That was all the invitation Osbourne and Zantoro needed. They raised their weapons and opened fire. Three heads exploded in a brief burst of automatic weapon fire, showering the ground with gore.

"Osbourne, see if you can't find something in that guard shack to silence the alarm," London said, pulling aside the cut section of fence to allow Lia and Max to scramble through.

"Right," Osbourne said, ducking through the hole. Zantoro was close behind.

London took a deep breath and stepped through. "Here we go…"

It took Osbourne less than a minute to disable the alarm, but that was enough time for a gang of half-rotten ghouls to slink out of the trees and onto the road. There were a dozen, maybe fifteen of them, moving in a tight group. From the looks of them, they'd been civilian researchers, since they were dressed in casual American-style clothing.

Tough day at the office, I guess, London thought.

He and Zantoro moved forward, closing the gap between themselves and the ghouls while firing at them. Now that there was no longer a need to conserve ammo, some of their shots missed the mark. The AKs they'd taken from Mbowi's stash weren't quite as accurate as the top of the line M4s that Pendleton provided, but they packed plenty of punch. They reduced the small crowd to shredded meat in seconds.

London ejected the spent magazine from his rifle, tossed it over his shoulder, and started walking. It was a bullshit action film star move, wasting a perfectly good magazine, but with the finish line in sight, his patience was dwindling. Besides, his backpack was heavy enough already.

"Come on, let's move it before we attract more." He slapped a fresh magazine into the AK. "I don't know about you, but I'm ready to get this damn thing done."

Their progress was slowed by Max's injuries. At best, he could manage to hobble along, but the pain was clearly cutting through the painkillers Osbourne had been feeding him all day. Max's breathing was raspy and labored. He was so sweaty that he looked like he'd been caught in the rain without an umbrella.

London stopped walking, and grabbed Osbourne. "You got any more of those pills?"

"Gave him the last one about an hour ago," Osbourne said. "But that ain't the worst of it. He's already burning up with fever. Out here, in this heat, he might collapse at any second. If there's a housing unit ahead, maybe we can find a place to stash him until we're ready to make for the northern border."

London glanced over his shoulder and watched Lia trot back down the road a few paces to help Max. At first, Max shrugged her off, but she tugged his arm over her shoulder and pulled him along.

"Yeah," London sighed. "I bet that's going to go over just peachy with him."

"Fucking Pierre," Zantoro said, shaking his head.

Yeah, you're not looking so great yourself, London thought, as he looked Zantoro over. *Maybe we should stash you right alongside Max.*

Lia and Max drew up alongside them. Max was panting like a dog, his mouth open wide to gulp air. Sweat dripped from his curly hair. His shirt was soaked through. He looked like he'd just finished a hard sprint rather than a short walk.

"Maybe we can find you a spot to rest at the housing unit," London said.

"No way." Max shook his head. He pulled away from Lia, and crossed his arms over his chest like a petulant child. "You're not leaving me behind. I know you want to get rid of me, but I'm not going to let you."

The thought crossed London's mind that he could just have Zantoro shoot Max and be done with it. But he'd never run his operations that way, and it wasn't a little late in the game to turn over a new leaf, so he just shrugged and said, "Okay, Max, suit yourself. But we're not going to carry you."

"Fine," Max said. "But I want a weapon."

"After the shit you pulled last time you had one?" London shook his head. "Hard enough to keep from getting eaten by a bunch of dead folks without having to worry about you trying to shoot us. Stay close and you'll be fine, but you lost your right to bear arms."

Max stared daggers back at him, but said nothing.

London gave the signal to move out.

5

Fairbanks' knowledge of anything related to combat was scant at best, but it seemed to him that the three men in uniform were masters of their chosen profession. At first, he was disheartened to see that there were only three of them, but once they squirmed through the hole in the fence and began their advance up the road leading from the south gate to the barracks, he felt his spirits lift. Within minutes, they'd managed to disable the alarm and dispatch a group of the infected with brutal precision.

"Do you see that, darling?" Fairbanks tugged Eve's leash so that her head faced the monitor. "They are coming for us. Oh, how exciting."

The wounded man in civilian clothes was having trouble keeping up. His limp was so pronounced that he appeared to stumble with every step. Twice, the leader of the group had to call a halt to their progress to allow the wounded man to catch up. There appeared to be an argument of some kind, but the group continued their march, albeit at a slightly slower pace.

Fairbanks lost them for a moment as they walked out of the camera's range. He grabbed the mouse and clicked through a few screens until he found them again. They were just entering the barracks, so he had to click through again until he found the feed from the barracks' interior cameras.

"If I get the hang of this, perhaps I can get a job working this desk," he said. "It's much nicer up here than it is in that stuffy basement."

Eve moaned a response. A glob of green mucus dropped from her bottom lip and splattered on the desk.

6

Buzz Osbourne had grown up on a pig farm in Iowa, so he was familiar with the many pungent stenches that nature could produce. But even his experience shoveling animal excrement and cleaning slaughterhouses wasn't enough to prepare him for the rancid stink inside the Marsh Industries housing unit. Even compared to some of the hellish smells he'd sniffed during his time in Daroka, this one was bad. For some unfathomable reason, the air conditioning had been turned off, and the building had become a giant sauna filled with corpses. The still, heavy air was thick with flies, and an army of oversized rats occupied the first floor lobby. The combined efforts of the flies and rats had reduced the bodies littering the floor to little more than heaps of bones scattered over a crusty, stained floor.

The assault on his senses was enough to make Osbourne gag. One of the rats, a big son of a bitch with patchy brown fur and a ragged stump of a tail, walked right up to him and sniffed his boots. Osbourne drew back his foot, and delivered a kick that sent the rodent sailing across the room. It thumped heavily against one of the lobby's many overturned potted plants. The rat untangled itself from the plant's leaves and regarded Osbourne warily. Then it scampered back across the room, making a beeline for Osbourne.

"To hell with this," he said, raising his rifle and taking aim at the rat. He pulled the trigger, and the rat exploded.

Osbourne felt a hand on his shoulder and heard London's voice. "Keep it together, Buzz. We're almost to the finish line."

Osbourne nodded. "I'm good, boss. It's just…"

"Yeah, it's fucked," London agreed. "But we need to sweep the building. Unlikely that there's any survivors lurking in here, but I need to be sure. We got three floors here. You take the first floor, Zantoro will take the second, and I'll head for the penthouse suites. Max isn't in any shape to help out, so I'm stashing him down here and leaving Lia to keep an eye on him. Sound good?"

Osbourne wanted to tell him that nothing had sounded good in days, not since their boots hit Darokan soil, but he kept that to himself. No need to state the obvious. Doing solo sweeps of the building wasn't the best idea from a tactical point of view, but Osbourne figured London wanted to get it over with as quickly as possible. On that point, Osbourne agreed. Both Max and Zantoro looked like they could fall apart at any moment. Every second they spent in this building was that much longer they delayed any sort of medical care. Not that Osbourne had much hope for that either. This place was dead, and it was over twenty miles to the border.

"You happen upon any hostiles in numbers you can't handle, you get your ass back downstairs," London continued. "That goes for you too, Zantoro. The lobby is the fall back point if you run into anything you can't handle on your own."

"Fuck it. Let's get this shit over with," Osbourne said.

While London relayed the plan to the rest of the group, Osbourne glanced around the lobby, taking stock of his surroundings. If not for the sights and smells of carnage, the place might have been an apartment building in a semi-affluent part of a small city. The furniture, now covered in scraps of rotten meat and crusted with dried blood, had once been top quality. There were potted ficus trees in southwest-style pots in each corner. Most of them had been overturned, leaving dark piles of potting soil on the floor. The reception desk in the center of the room was made of hardwood and faux marble. It was occupied by the eviscerated corpse that had once been a young man. A group of chittering rats were picking their way over what remained of his body.

As Osbourne passed the desk on his way across the room, he noticed that there was still a nametag pinned to the scrap of shirt that clung to the body. Beneath the Marsh Industries logo was the name Matt Harding. Osbourne wondered, as he passed the desk and headed down a hallway lined with apartments, if poor Matt had signed up for a job in Daroka thinking it would be an adventure. Maybe he'd just wanted a few stories to tell his buddies back home. Or maybe he thought it would be an easy way to see the world.

Tough break, man, Osbourne thought.

He paused at the first door on his left, wondering if he should bang on it like a cop serving a warrant, or if he should just kick it in. The latter seemed more appropriate, so he stepped back and raised his boot. Then he paused, lowered his foot, and tried the doorknob. It turned easily enough. He pushed the door open and stepped inside. He glanced around, gun at the ready. It took a moment for the information his eyes relayed to his brain to truly register. And once it did, Osbourne felt like a rapidly deflating balloon.

The room wasn't an apartment at all. It was a nursery. Osbourne supposed it made sense. After all, according to the briefing London had given them, the Marsh Industries compound had been going full steam for well over two years, operating with a staff of more than two hundred employees, plus security and service personnel. It stood to reason that pregnancies and childbirth would be an eventuality for a group, especially one so isolated and living in close proximity. The nursery's presence made sense. But its current state was the stuff of nightmares.

When Osbourne was a teenager, he enjoyed reading H.P. Lovecraft stories, and he'd always wondered what sort of unnamable, indescribable horrors could reduce the characters to gibbering madness or catatonia. He's always wondered if maybe Lovecraft wasn't just using that stuff as a cop-out. Standing in the doorway of that nursery, Osbourne understood all too well that there were some horrors that are simply too much to take.

The corpse of a woman lay in the center of the room, her face frozen in a rictus of terror and agony. She was dressed in hospital scrubs that were so thoroughly bloodstained that it was almost impossible to discern their original color. Her abdomen had been ripped open, and her organs were strewn about the floor. She wasn't alone. The corpses of other victims were scattered through the room, their twisted bodies lying among piles of toys, crayons, and stuffed animals. But these corpses were much smaller. Some of them still wore diapers.

Suddenly, on one side of the room, a closet door swung open, and the perpetrators of the carnage stepped out. There were six of them. The oldest couldn't have been more than two or three years old. He was wearing Batman pajamas, and clutching a teddy bear in the crook of his left arm. His right arm had been torn off, and a ragged scrap of empty pajama sleeve hung at his side. His face was covered in a crust of dried blood and mucus. His mouth hung open as he moaned. His companions were just as grim. Three of them were little girls dressed in Disney princess pajamas. One of them dragged her leg as she walked, her little foot so thoroughly mangled that it hung limply from her ankle. The others held fistfuls of what might have been pieces of the disemboweled woman. Green mucus ran in a steady stream from their gaping mouths. The final two members of the group were too young to walk. They dragged themselves across the carpet with their hands, as if their legs were no longer capable of crawling. They looked at Osbourne with eyes so bloodshot they were completely red. Their chubby cheeks were mottled with purple bruises.

"Oh, no…" Osbourne took an involuntary step back. "Not this. Please, God, not this…"

The six dead children advanced towards him, moaning and grunting as they kicked through the mess of discarded toys. Viscous streams of green slime ran from their mouths, dripping from the tips of their swollen black tongues. Their cracked lips pulled back, exposing baby teeth stained pink with blood.

Osbourne knew what he had to do. He knew it was for the best, that no child deserved to carry on in such a state and that dispatching them would be an act of mercy. But knowing that didn't make it any easier. It didn't stop his hand from shaking as he pulled his pistol from its holster. And it didn't stop the hollow feeling in the pit of his stomach from expanding outward until it seemed to fill him from head to toe.

I don't want to be here anymore.

It wasn't the thought of a petulant child or a mopey adolescent. It was a realization. Osbourne no longer cared to be part of a world where such horrors could exist.

7

Max was sick, in every sense of the word. He was sick of being taken for granted by Lia. He was sick of being treated like a misbehaving child by the Americans. He was sick of pretending that the current situation was something that could be escaped. And he was also *sick.* He was burning up with fever and his head throbbed with such intensity that he was starting to believe his brain might liquefy and leak out of his ears. There was a gnawing pain in the pit of his stomach that was too sharp to be called nausea. While the bullet wound in his shoulder was still pulsing with white hot agony, the one in his ass had gone completely numb to such a degree that he could barely walk without falling down. He let Lia lead him to one of the sofas in the lobby, then sat down gingerly, keeping his weight off his wounded side as much as possible.

"When was the last time you had any painkillers?" Lia asked.

"It seems like a long time ago. Zantoro gave me something that was supposed to keep me going. It was a white pill, like aspirin. I don't think it was a painkiller..." Max tried to remember, but the details of the last few hours were foggy.

Zantoro had slipped him a plastic baggie of pills and told him they would keep him moving. Max had lost count of how many he'd taken.

"Let me check behind the desk for a first aid kit," Lia said, brushing his sweaty hair away from his forehead.

"Fine," he muttered.

As she searched, he closed his eyes and tried to ignore the clenching sensation in the pit of his stomach. His pulse thudded in his ears. His thoughts swam with fevered confusion, but they coalesced around one idea: the situation was hopeless. He wanted to put an end to this miserable charade once and for all. More than that, he wanted to show the others that they never should have underestimated him and treated him like some misbehaving child.

Lia returned with a bottle of disinfectant, a tube of antibiotic ointment, and a roll of gauze bandage. She leaned her rifle against the bench, then sat beside him and began removing the sweat-and-blood stained dressing from his wounded shoulder. As soon as the bandage was off, Max could smell the rancid infection.

"I don't know why you waste your time," he said, his voice thick with phlegm and nausea. "I'm a lost cause and you know it."

"Just try to relax," she said. "I know this might sting a little bit, but we need to clean it."

He winced as she poured disinfectant on the bullet hole in his shoulder, dousing both the entrance and exit wound. "Come on, Lia. Why bother? I'm probably going to die, so you might as well drop the act. You never cared about me, never loved me. You can stop pretending now."

"For God's sake, Max, would you give the self-pity a rest?" She waved a hand over his shoulder, trying to dry the bubbling disinfectant.

"I love you, Lia." His shoulder throbbed. He glanced down at the wound. The disinfectant solution was a bubbling white froth dripping over a hardened black crust. At the center of the wound, like the pupil of some alien eye, was a congealed glob of green and red pus.

"Stop it, please." She wrinkled her nose at the stink coming off his shoulder.

"Stop what? Telling you that I still love you? That I still want you more than anything in the world?" He shook his head. "No. I will never stop."

"This isn't you. It's the fever talking."

"But this *is* me, Lia. I've felt like this for years, but you've been too wrapped up in your work to notice. All these years, you could never see what was right in front of you."

"This isn't the time or place for this discussion." She squeezed a thick glob of antibiotic ointment from the tube and spread it over his shoulder.

"It's the end of the world. Hardly the time for you to start a love affair with G.I. Joe, but that didn't stop you from fucking him, did it?"

"You…"

Max smiled. "Don't worry. I'll take you with me once I'm finished. Maybe, if we survive this, you can learn to appreciate my love for you."

"Finished? What are you talking about?"

Max leaned in, as if preparing to impart some deep secret, then smashed his forehead against the bridge of her nose. She cried out, clapping her hands to her face as she slid off the bench, and went sprawling onto the floor. Max pounced, throwing himself on top of her. She fought back, nearly wrestling away from him, but he snaked his good arm around her neck and wrapped his legs around her waist.

"Just go to sleep," he said, pressing against the artery in her neck. "When you wake up, all this will be over. Just the two of us again. Just the two of us…"

He repeated the words like a mantra until she stopped fighting.

"You'll see, Lia. This is for the best. In time, you'll see…"

When he was sure she was really out, he released the pressure on her neck and wriggled away from her. It took quite an effort to get her back onto the bench with only one good arm, but Max managed. He did love her, after all, and it would have been wrong to leave her lying on the hard floor. Once he had her positioned comfortably, he picked up her rifle, and eased the shoulder strap over his head. It would be hard to fire the gun one-handed, but he thought he could manage. He was sufficiently motivated.

All the exertion had stirred his sour stomach to a nauseated whirlpool. He swallowed a few times, trying in vain to fight back the urge to vomit, then turned his head away from where Lia lay and spewed what felt like liters of green slime from his mouth. His stomach heaved so hard that the vertebrae in his lower back crackled and popped. Another stream of stinking green fluid poured out of his mouth. It splashed and splattered on the hard floor. Finally, the spasms wracking his midsection abated, although the seasick sensation remained.

He scrubbed his mouth with the back of his hand and began his slow march across the lobby. Black dots swam across his vision, and each step felt like he was teetering on the edge of some yawning abyss, but he managed to put one foot in front of the other. He was so close to the end of his struggle. Hatred prodded him onward. Hatred for the Americans who'd come between him and Lia. Hatred for this hellish country where the dead refused to just lie down and rot. Hatred for this world where greed and brute strength could flourish while love—true selfless love—was cast aside and trampled into the dirt.

His jaws ached as he ground his teeth. His stomach growled like a caged beast. The nausea ebbed away with each passing second, replaced by a hunger so fierce it was like being stabbed in the belly by an ice cold blade.

Clamping the butt of the rifle in his armpit and wrapping his fingers around the grip, he turned into the hallway where Osbourne had gone. He checked the rifle's safety, making sure it was off.

Lia, I'm doing this for you, he thought. *I'm saving you from your own worst impulses. One day, you'll understand…*

He almost laughed at the thought. Deep down, he knew there was no future for him. But something like survival instinct swirled into his bitter hatred, and drove him on. The first door on his left was standing open. He paused to take a deep breath, then raised the rifle, and stepped over the threshold.

Inside, Osbourne was sitting on the floor with his head in his hands. His rifle lay across his knees. Arrayed in a semi-circle around him were the bodies of children, two of them no more than infants. Each of them had been shot through the center of the forehead, and their brains were splattered across the brightly patterned carpet. Osbourne's shoulders hitched. He sniffed, then blew his nose on the sleeve of his uniform.

"They were just babies, man," he said without looking up at Max. "Just fucking babies… and I had to…"

For a brief moment, Max felt a twinge of doubt. Maybe he didn't have to go through with his plan. After all, Osbourne wasn't so bad. Sure, he was part of Mike London's mercenary crew, but of all the Americans, he seemed the least threatening. He'd practically carried Max out of the valley, even as Zantoro muttered threats to leave him behind. And now, here he was, crying for the mercy killings he'd been compelled to commit. But Max shoved these thoughts away. Osbourne may have seemed sympathetic, but he was guilty by his association with the mercenaries. While the deaths of the children had reduced the big man to tears, no doubt he'd committed many acts of brutal violence at the behest of his corporate masters. A man truly deserving of Max's sympathy would never have set foot in Daroka on the orders of Marsh

Industries. A man truly deserving of mercy wouldn't have stood by while London pressured Lia into spreading her legs. He would have recognized that Max was far more deserving of her love.

"I'm sorry," Max said. "But you just stood by and watched him steal her away from me. You shouldn't have done that."

Osbourne finally looked up at him. His face barely had time to register confusion before Max opened fire.

8

If Fairbanks' appetite hadn't completely disappeared, he might have wished for a bucket of popcorn and an ice-cold soda or beer to wash it down. The video feed from inside the barracks was more thrilling than any television show. He shook his head in amazement at each new development.

"I wonder, my dear," he said, putting an affectionate hand on Eve's backside, "if our brave rescue party will even reach our doorstep. It seems they might be turning on one another."

There was certainly one member of the party who would not turn on anyone, and he was currently lying in a pool of his own blood on the floor of the nursery. The limping man in civilian clothes lowered the smoking barrel of his rifle and stood over the dead man, as if admiring his handiwork. Then, the limping man fell upon his victim, clawed through the shredded remains of his shirt, and plunged his face into one of the gaping wounds in the dead man's bullet-riddled abdomen.

At the sound of his voice, several of the aimlessly shuffling infected turned their heads to regard him with their red eyes. They seemed to sniff the air, as if suddenly wondering if this man was a food source. But they were reassured by whatever sense they possessed that allowed them to differentiate between those who were infected and those who were not, and went back to milling about the lobby.

"It seems that man with the limp has joined the ranks of your fellows, my dear," Fairbanks said, giving Eve's rear a playful squeeze. "Just as I shall do in short order, I suppose. Yes, very soon I'll be a full-fledged member of the undead."

Saying it aloud gave Fairbanks pause. It was the first time he'd given voice to what he'd known since he got his first glimpse of his discolored manhood. He was a dead man. Sure, his lungs still breathed air, and his heart still pumped blood into this arteries, but for how long? He was simply passing the time until the virus replicated to such an extent that his life functions ceased. There was no doubt death would soon claim him. A matter of hours, perhaps. Certainly not more than a day.

And how is that different than any other human being? He wondered. *Aren't we all just passing time until the reaper knocks at our door?*

He shook his head to clear away the philosophical musings. They didn't matter much, especially when there was such good entertainment on the security monitors. He laughed, squeezing Eve's ass even harder with one hand, and slapping the desk with the other. There was a quiet voice in the back of his head urging him to get a grip, struggling to remind him that he was Morton Fairbanks, MD, not some voyeuristic pervert. But that voice was washed away by the giddy rush of lunacy. The laughter that erupted from his throat had a crazed, ragged edge to it, and though some part of him knew it was alarming, he could not quiet it. The infected crowd in the lobby groaned in response.

He turned his attention back to the screen, staring intently at the scene in the nursery. The man in civilian clothes was now tearing into the dead man with real gusto, pulling handfuls of guts from the man's abdomen and shoving them into his mouth. The civilian's throat bulged as he swallowed each mouthful. Gobs of half-chewed viscera flew from his mouth as he chomped. Fairbanks, who hadn't had much of an appetite until this moment, clutched his stomach as it growled. His mouth watered so heavily that drool ran down his chin. And although the idea of consuming human flesh still repulsed him on some level, he found that he could not help wishing that he might soon partake in the feast.

Only a matter of time…

9

Zantoro knew something was wrong when he heard the sudden tornado chug of fully-automatic gunfire. That was a panic response, shooting like that, and the impulse to panic under extreme conditions had been trained out of the strike team long ago. Either Osbourne was trying to alert them, or another person was firing one of the AKs. Zantoro didn't think the boss' new girlfriend was down there popping off rounds, so that left…

"Fucking Pierre," Zantoro growled.

He paused in the middle of the hallway, then turned around and headed for the stairs. His search of the second floor apartments had so far turned up nothing but empty rooms and a few dead bodies. Whatever was happening downstairs seemed more important. He took the stairs two at a time. Although his headache was making him dizzy, he was still able to focus on reaching his objective. As London liked to say, when the going gets rough, the training takes over.

But no amount of training could have prepared Zantoro for what he found downstairs.

First, he saw Lia sprawled on one of the lobby's cushioned benches. From the way she was positioned—arms flung out, one leg bent back beneath her—he feared the worst. But a quick check showed that she was still breathing. Pierre, however, was unaccounted for.

"Max!" Zantoro shouted, using the photographer's real name to let him know that playtime was over. "Front and center, asshole!"

Zantoro turned in a slow circle, checking the corners of the room for movement. The place seemed quiet. Then, Max finally made an appearance. He emerged from the hallway on the north side of the building, moving with a slow, shambling gait that left little doubt about his current condition. And if his clumsy walk and jerky movements left any doubt, his bloody clothes and face eradicated it altogether.

"Goddamn, Pierre," Zantoro said, raising his rifle and drawing a bead on Max's forehead. "I wish I could say this was going to hurt me more than it was going to hurt you, but what the hell…"

Zantoro knew this moment would come. Ever since Max swallowed the first white pill from Zantoro's stash, this outcome was assured. But Zantoro had no idea it would come so soon. It made Zantoro wonder how much time he himself had left.

"See you on the other side, Pierre…"

If Max saw it coming, he gave no indication. He just stood there, groaning as bits of gore fell from his mouth, while Zantoro took careful aim. Zantoro squeezed the trigger, and Max's head exploded in a shower of bone fragments, and chunks of grey matter. A faint pink mist hung in the air as Max's body collapsed to the floor.

The sound of the single shot was enough to bring Lia back to consciousness. She sat up, pressing a hand to her forehead. She muttered something that sounded vaguely interrogative as she stood. Zantoro steeled himself for an oncoming storm of grief, but when Lia's eyes alighted on Max's nearly headless corpse, her shoulders merely sagged, and she shook her head slowly.

"I thought he was trying to strangle me," she explained, her voice soft and almost uncertain. "He wasn't thinking straight..."

"He came from over there." Zantoro gestured toward the hallway. "I need to go check on Osbourne. Why don't you have a seat and wait?"

"No," she said. "I won't be left alone again in this place. Whatever is down that hallway, I can handle it."

Zantoro shrugged and started walking. "Suit yourself."

It didn't take them long to find Osbourne, or rather what was left of him. His body was laid out in the middle of slaughterhouse that appeared to have once been a nursery. The floor was littered with bodies, most of them children. Lia gasped, covering her mouth with her hand.

"My God," she whispered.

"God has left the building," Zantoro said. He stepped out of the room and shut the door. "Come on, it's time to blow this joint."

"But we can't just leave him there..."

"Why the hell not? He signed up for this, same as the rest of us. When I'm gone—and yeah, I know that check is in the fucking mail—you have my permission to leave me where I fall. Now let's get out of here." He paused to spit a wad of green phlegm onto the floor then started walking.

"Hey," Lia said, grabbing his elbow. "I'm sorry about Osbourne. And Vincent."

He stopped, but didn't turn to face her. "And believe it or not, I'm sorry about Max. I know I gave him shit, but he didn't deserve to end up like that. Nobody does."

"Look, I know you're scared, but maybe we'll get some answers at the research center."

"Scared? Bullshit, lady. I ain't scared of nothing." He coughed then spit more green slime. His chest felt like it had taken a stiff shot from someone who knew how to fight. He winced. "But you know what? There are no answers. Seriously. I'm dead and you know it. That's okay. We all have to go sometime. My number was just up, that's all. But let's get our asses moving while I can still be of some use."

They moved out of the hallway and into the lobby just as London was emerging from the staircase. London paused when he saw Max's body.

"Shit," he said, looking at Lia. "You okay?"

She nodded.

"What's our status?" he said, turning to Zantoro.

"Boss, we lost Osbourne. Max must have..." Zantoro shrugged.

"But he wasn't bitten or infected," London said.

"He'd lost his mind," Lia explained. "He tried to kill me, and then he killed Osbourne. He must have thought..."

Zantoro considered owning up to his part in Max's disintegration, but decided there was no point. It was just one more item on the list of things he'd have to answer for in hell.

London sighed. His shoulders sagged as he pinched the bridge of his nose. For Zantoro, seeing the boss so defeated was somehow worse than the pain in his chest and his head. As long as they'd known each other, London had never been anything other than rock solid. The team had experienced casualties before. In Rwanda, they'd lost Harris. In Columbia, they'd lost both Otis and Pittman. Through all of it, London had maintained a stoic warrior's philosophy. They'd all signed up for work in some of the world's most dangerous places, carrying out missions where they were vastly outgunned and outnumbered. But they'd done it with the knowledge that they had a home to which they could return; that civilization still awaited them when the shooting was over. Now, Zantoro had a strong suspicion that civilization might not be at the end of this rainbow. They'd been disavowed, cut loose. And the people who'd made that call weren't the type that were willing to shake hands and let everyone go their separate ways. If London and his girlfriend survived Daroka, Pendleton Securities wouldn't just let them walk away. As for himself, Zantoro wasn't leaving this jungle.

London took a deep breath and seemed to snap out of it. He unslung his backpack from his shoulders and unzipped it. "This place is dead, but I'd prefer not to take chances. Let's blow it to hell and be on our way."

Zantoro smiled as he watched London pull out one of the Thunderballs. "Now you're talking. I've been itching to see what these things can do."

London stripped away layers of foam padding and bubble wrap, tossing the material to the floor. The explosive looked like a black golf ball the size of a grapefruit. It wasn't a perfect sphere; it had a flattened base to keep it from rolling. There were no distinguishing features on its surface. Nobody would even suspect it was an incendiary device with enough explosive power to level a building. But London knew, and he handled it with obvious care.

"You ever felt nervous carrying those things around all this time?" Zantoro asked.

"Every fucking minute of every day," London said. He placed the Thunderball on the reception desk and backed away. "Okay, let's take this place down."

They didn't run for the exit, but it was apparent that they were all eager to get out of the barracks. Even the stabbing pain in Zantoro's chest did little to slow his pace. He pushed through the front doors and gulped a lungful of fresh air. The deep breath brought on another coughing fit. This time, he didn't just bring up a small wad of the green stuff, he gagged out two mouthfuls that were shot through with streaks of red and solid giblets. His eyes watered as he doubled over. His stomach contracted in tight spasms that felt like they might snap his spine. Just when he was sure the spell wouldn't pass, and that he was in the final throes of whatever transformation was coming, the pain subsided enough for him to straighten up.

"You okay to move?" London asked, placing a hand on his shoulder.

Zantoro nodded. "Yeah, I think I got a few miles left on these tires. Fuck it, let's go."

London's only answer was a forehead-creasing look of concern. Lia chimed in silently with a look of mingled pity and worry.

"I said I'm good to go," Zantoro said, shrugging off London's hand. "Now let's get down the road. I've been itching to see something blow up."

They moved out with no further discussion. Without having to slow their pace to allow Max to limp along, they put distance between themselves and the barracks with ease. London called a halt to the march after a half click. He rummaged through his backpack and came out with something that looked like an old TV remote. The Thunderball had a dedicated detonator that made it less likely to be accidentally triggered by a random signal from a radio or cell phone. Zantoro wasn't sure what the technology was, and he really didn't give a shit. The giant black golf ball was about to go boom, and that was good enough for him.

"All right, buckle up," London said.

Lia clapped her hands over her ears and closed her eyes.

"Enough fucking foreplay. Blow that motherfucker to hell." Zantoro flashed a thumbs-up.

London punched a six digit code onto the keypad, then covered his ears.

Nothing happened.

He punched the code in again, this time not bothering to protect his hearing.

Still nothing.

"Fuck," he growled as he punched the code in a third time.

"You sure you got the code right?" Zantoro asked.

"Hell yes, I'm sure. I set the fucking thing myself. I made sure it was something I wouldn't forget, so I used my own birthday."

"What does that mean?" Lia asked, looking from Zantoro to London and back again.

"It means we can't detonate these things remotely," London said. "And that's a problem, because we have to take down that research center. If we don't blow that place to bits, who knows how far this thing might spread. And then this whole nightmare was for nothing. Vincent, Osbourne, Max..." He shook his head. "Goddamn it."

"Hey, cheer up," Zantoro said. "There's always another way. Every explosive has a manual trigger, right?"

"Yeah, but I have no idea how to set a timer if the remote is fucked," London replied.

"That's what you get for throwing out the instruction booklet. I swear, you tough guys just think you know it all." Zantoro smiled, but he didn't laugh, just in case it brought on another coughing fit. "Luckily, you got me. I can be your trigger man."

"But that would mean..." Lia grabbed London's elbow. "Mike, you can't let him do that."

"Hey, mademoiselle, I appreciate the sentiment," Zantoro said. "But we all know I'm dead either way. I popped some pills that I found back at Mbowi's farmhouse. Thought it was speed, but now I think it was a dose of whatever turned Mbowi's boys into gun-toting zombies. Hell of a way to break an addiction, huh?"

"But there might be a way to reverse it," Lia argued.

Zantoro shook his head. "I doubt it. I mean, you'd think that the people who created this thing would have cooked up an antidote, right? That's what any normal person would do. But that's the thing. People who create something like this plague, they're not normal. Because normal people don't spend billions finding a germ to reanimate the dead, and then just let that germ get out because they have a little oopsy-daisy in their lab."

"He's right," London said.

"Fucking-A," Zantoro continued. "We came here to take that research center down, and that's what we're going to do. We're going to find enough evidence to bury Marsh Industries, and then you guys are going to get that evidence out there. I'm going to stay behind and blow Frankenstein's laboratory to hell."

10

"Well, my dear," Fairbanks said, standing up, "I believe the time has arrived for us to give our visitors a proper welcome."

He gave Eve's leash a gentle tug, and she followed him across the lobby. They had to shove their way through the growing crowd of the reanimated dead, but that didn't bother Fairbanks. He'd gotten used to the smell, and when their hunger wasn't aroused, they were quite docile. It didn't take much to move them aside, although once the front doors were opened, they seemed to wake up somewhat. At first, they watched Fairbanks and Eve pass through the doorway with their usual glazed detachment. But once they figured out that they too could step into the open air, they followed the doctor and his bride into the late summer sunshine.

After so many days spent in the cool air and soft fluorescent lighting of the building, the hot, humid air, and the fierce sunlight were disorienting. Fairbanks' equilibrium was already skewed by his steadily climbing fever and dehydration, and the sudden change of environment caused him to fling his arms out just to maintain his balance. Eve turned to look at him with her typically blank expression. She groaned as she watched him stagger a few steps.

"Oh, my heavens," he gasped. "It certainly is muggy out here today. And bright! Not a cloud in the sky. A beautiful day to receive visitors. But first, perhaps we should make our castle a bit more welcoming."

Behind him, dozens of the infected tottered out of the building, and into the afternoon sunshine. It seemed that the word was out about the open doors, and the building's entire population was eager to get some fresh air.

Fairbanks slipped his backpack off his shoulders and let it drop to the ground. He knelt and unzipped it, pulling out his power drill. He gave the trigger an experimental squeeze. The drill responded with a sharp whine as the threaded bit spun. Fairbanks nodded, satisfied with the tool's response.

"Ah, American craftsmanship," he said, standing up. "You simply cannot beat it."

Eve groaned.

"Yes, I'm afraid you may find this operation distasteful," Fairbanks said. "But it is necessary for the safety of our guests."

Taking a deep breath, he turned to the nearest member of his rotten kingdom. This specimen was a male, and he must have been among the first wave of the infected, because the virus had progress to such an extent that the specimen had sloughed away nearly all of its skin. The exposed muscles looked dry and cracked, like old leather left too long in the sun. Its mouth hung open, exposing teeth that were almost entirely black.

Interesting, Fairbanks thought. He wondered what the end stage of this decay might look like. Would the specimen simply continue to walk around until it collapsed into a pile of bones? Or would the viral load inside its body reach some critical mass and cause the specimen to explode, like some poisonous mushroom releasing its spores? He sighed wistfully at the thought that he would never know the answers to these questions, then he raised the drill, pressed it to the specimen's leathery skull, and bored a hole into its frontal lobe. The specimen twitched. Its red eyes rolled back into its head. A gout of thick blood erupted around the whirring bit, showering Fairbanks with droplets of gore.

Good thing I decided to wear scrubs today!

He pulled back on the drill as the specimen collapsed to the ground. "Well, that's one down, and roughly a hundred to go."

Pulling Eve along with him, he got to work. The infected specimen's survival instinct was limited to feeding their unnatural hunger, and even that was probably just a function of the virus. From what he could tell, the specimens required no nourishment. Taking in nutrients didn't seem to arrest the process of decay. In fact, they…

Fairbanks laughed, shaking his head. Even now, he was still thinking like a scientist. The laughter brought on a coughing fit. Each cough was a hammer blow to his chest that brought up what felt like liters of thick green phlegm. Fairbanks spat it onto the dusty ground. His vision swam for a moment as he struggled to catch his breath.

Prognosis grim, my friend. Better keep your mind on the job at hand.

He didn't have to go far to find his next candidate. This specimen was a Caucasian female. Her clothing—tattered, torn, and stained though it was—indicated that she had at one time been a Marsh Industries employee. Her ID badge was still clipped to the collar of her blouse. According to it, her name was Eileen Daniels, and she worked in the biotech division. As he drilled into her brain, Fairbanks wondered if he and Eileen's paths had ever crossed. Perhaps they'd passed one another in the cafeteria, or maybe participated in one of the team-building exercises at the semi-annual staff picnics. He wondered if her presence in Daroka was a calculated career move or if, like Fairbanks and so many of the others, she'd been blackmailed into working on the HOPE Project. In the end, it mattered little who Eileen Daniels had once been. Now, she was nothing more than a collection of bones buried in layers of rotten tissue.

The next specimen to fall victim to Fairbanks' drill was also female. This one appeared to be in the later stages of infection, though she wasn't as far gone as the skinless male specimen. It was impossible to determine what her age had been at the time of her death. Like Eileen, she appeared to have been an employee at the facility, but her ID badge was nowhere to be found. That was fine with Fairbanks. It was easier when they didn't have names. Like the others, she offered no resistance and showed no fear, even as the drill bit began to chew its way into her skull. Her body twitched with involuntary spasms as Fairbanks scrambled her brains. And once the drill had done sufficient damage, she went limp, and fell to the ground.

Fairbanks wiped his forehead with the sleeve of his lab coat. It was a hot day, even by Daroka standards, and he still had quite a bit of work ahead of him.

Once he got into a rhythm, it didn't take long to finish the job. Although some of the specimens had begun to wander around the open space between the building and jungle, most of them still seemed content to mill about in a loose grouping. Perhaps the heat was making them sluggish, or maybe it was the absence of uninfected people. Whatever the cause of this undead ennui, it certainly made Fairbanks' work easier. He could put down several specimens in the space of a minute without exerting himself. And before he knew it, he was done. Sure, some of them had eluded euthanasia via power tool by wandering into the trees, but they were of no consequence, really. If they happened to find their way back to the facility by the time the guests arrived, the specimens would no doubt fall to the guests' guns.

For now, all that remained of the reanimated dead was Eve.

"I'd best get moving, dear," he said, giving Eve's leash a gentle tug. "Our guests are well-armed and have itchy trigger fingers. I should go greet them, lest I be shot by mistake. And that brings me to another point, and one that I'm sad to make. I'm afraid that the time for us to part ways has arrived."

He dropped her leash and gestured toward the tree line.

She groaned.

"I must insist," he said.

She reeled in her leash and stared dumbly at it. She held it up, the end dangling from her hand, as if offering it to Fairbanks. The gesture made him smile.

"No, my dear, there's no talking our way around this one. We're just too different, you and me. I'm a man of science, and you are, after all, just reanimated dead tissue. There's no future where both of us can be happy. Now, it's off to the jungle with you."

For a moment, it was almost as if some sort of recognition crossed her features. A twinge of regret made Fairbanks soften his tone. He reached out to caress Eve's cheek and said, "Well, perhaps we can table the discussion until later. But I must insist that you stay here while I go out to meet our guests."

Eve regarded him with red, unblinking eyes. She stood there, unmoving.

He turned his back on her, and set off down the road.

11

London raised his rifle and took aim at the figure walking toward them. But when the figure—a man dressed in stained hospital scrubs and a white lab coat—raised his hands in a gesture of surrender, London lowered his weapon.

"Hello there!" the man in the lab coat shouted. "Please don't shoot me! I promise I'm one of the good guys!"

"Well, I'll be damned." Zantoro whistled appreciatively. "It's a survivor. I bet this guy has quite a story to tell."

"Yeah, but be careful," London said.

"Why?" Lia asked. "He's still alive."

"Because he could be infected…" London cut his eyes sideways, looking at Zantoro. "Or maybe he's lost his marbles. Staying alive through something like this is bound to take a toll."

"Like Max," she said.

London said nothing by way of reply. He started walking toward the man in the lab coat. They met in the center of the road, pausing to look one another over before they spoke.

"If you're a rescue party, you certainly took your time getting here," the man said, offering his hand to shake. "My name is Dr. Morton Fairbanks. I'm all that remains of the Marsh Industries workforce here in scenic, sunny Daroka."

"I'm not sure that you could call us a rescue party. We're more like a cleanup crew." London declined the handshake, leaving the man standing there with his hand awkwardly outstretched. "I'm Mike London. The smiling son of a bitch on my right is Gil Zantoro, and the pretty lady to my left is Lia Rousseau."

Fairbanks finally got the idea that the handshake wasn't going to happen, and dropped his arm back to his side. His brow furrowed. "*The* Lia Rousseau? The one who made that documentary about the drug cartel in Cartagena?"

Lia nodded. "Yes, that's me."

"A celebrity!" Fairbanks smiled. "Whatever brings you to Daroka? Are you back to do another documentary about the Ka'Longho tribe? The first one was fascinating."

"I'm here to do an exposé on Marsh Industries' HOPE Project," she answered.

"Marvelous." Fairbanks' smile spread even wider, exposing a mouthful of pink teeth. "I'll be happy to tell you whatever you need to know. As long as I receive proper credit, of course."

"Um…" Lia looked at London for a moment, then turned back to Fairbanks. "Of course. It's just that most of my sources prefer to remain anonymous…"

The way the doctor giggled with excitement confirmed London's suspicions: this guy had fucking lost it. And the crusty stains on his scrubs plus his extremely bloodshot eyes suggested that Fairbanks was infected. Not surprising. It was an occupational hazard for someone working inside ground zero.

"If you'd like to follow me, I can take you to the research center," Fairbanks said. "But I must warn you, the population of the facility will greet you with open arms and open mouths, if you take my meaning."

Before London could answer, another figure lurched into view, walking unsteadily around a bend in the road. This one was a woman. She was dressed in scrubs like the ones Fairbanks wore, but her feet were bare and there was some sort of collar around her neck. A leash was clipped to the collar, its length hanging against her chest like a necktie as she shuffled forward.

Fairbanks' head swiveled around, following London's line of sight.

"Oh, dear," the doctor said. "It seems that my wife has decided to follow me. I asked her to stay back at the research center and wait for my return, but she must have been too excited to wait. You're our first visitors, after all, and, well, you know women." He turned back and smiled at Lia. He reached out and touched her shoulder. "No offense, Madame Rousseau."

She jumped back, recoiling at his touch.

"Excuse me for a moment," Fairbanks said. He turned and trotted down the road to meet the approaching woman.

"Boss, this dude is bat shit fucking insane," Zantoro said. "And he's got the bug, same as me. I can…I don't know…*smell* it on him."

"Yeah, but he's also willing to help us get the goods on Marsh Industries, so maybe we indulge his eccentricities for the time being," London said. "Lia, make sure you keep your distance from this guy. No telling what he might do. Zantoro, first sign this guy is about to jump squirrely, you put a bullet in his brain."

"Goddam right." Zantoro slapped his AK for emphasis.

London looked down the road, and shook his head in disbelief at the scene unfolding a short distance away. Fairbanks stood in front of the infected woman, holding her by the shoulders as he spoke to her. London couldn't hear what Fairbanks was saying, but it wasn't hard to get the gist of it, especially when the doctor drew the woman into an embrace. The woman didn't respond. She didn't return the show of affection, but she didn't try to bite a chunk out of him either.

"Oh, man," Zantoro snickered. "This just gets better and better. This fucking guy has been slipping a zombie his sausage."

"Come on," London said. "Let's get this thing over with."

By the time they reached Fairbanks and his companion, the reunion was over. The doctor stood at the woman's side, gripping the leash in his fist. As the trio approached, Fairbanks raised a hand and cautioned them to keep their distance. The woman stared at them for a moment, then sprang forward, straining at the leash. Her fingers hooked into claws as she swiped at the air between herself and London. When she opened her mouth, London saw that her teeth had been removed. A swollen black tongue lolled between her lips.

"Yes, you may have noticed that Eve has no teeth," Fairbanks said. "A precautionary measure I took during the early stages of our courtship. Sadly unnecessary, as I soon discovered."

"What do you mean?" Lia asked.

Zantoro snorted. "He means that he didn't want her biting him while he gave her the goods. But then he figured out that this virus he and his fellow mad scientists cooked up could also be sexually transmitted. And by 'figured out,' I mean he learned it the hard way. No pun intended. Now that the virus has crawled up his dick and into the rest of him, it doesn't matter if she has teeth or not, because these goddamn walking cadavers don't chow down on each other. Since he's on his way to becoming one of them, she doesn't find him so appetizing anymore."

"My God…" Lia put a hand to her mouth.

"I'm afraid that your friend's hypothesis is accurate," Fairbanks said. "Vulgar, but accurate nonetheless. You know,

Mr. Zantoro, you really could soften your tone. I happen to love Eve, and our relationship, while unconventional, is perfectly harmonious."

"Oh, relax, Dr. Love. I'm in the same boat as you." Zantoro stepped forward and waved a hand in front of Eve's face. While she still strained at her leash and grabbed for London and Lia, she ignored the hand just inches from her mouth. "It's just that I didn't pick up the bug by doing the horizontal tango with a dead woman."

London gave up trying to conceal his disgust. In a world that had gone insane, he figured it was just fine to dispense with social grace. Besides, now they were so close to the end that the finish line was in sight. One last push, and they'd blow the research center to smithereens and walk away with enough dirt to bury Marsh Industries for good. And then…

And then what? he wondered. *Ride off into the sunset with your woman at your side? That's bullshit and you know it. There is no happy ending. You're just pushing forward because you don't know what else to do.*

"Are you ready to continue your journey?" Fairbanks asked. "The missus and I will be happy to escort you to the facility. But, as I said, you should be prepared for some danger. I've dealt with all the specimens that presented themselves, but I'm sure that there are still plenty lurking about. It is a large building with plenty of nooks and crannies in which to hide. I sense that you, Mr. London, are the leader of the group. Far be it from me to speak out of turn, but I'd suggest that Mr. Zantoro take the lead once we reach the facility. I'm afraid there will be a large number of the infected waiting to greet us. Mr. Zantoro and I will be able to make our way unmolested, because we'll be viewed as members of their tribe, whereas they'll see you and Madame Rousseau as…well, a late lunch."

London nodded. "Sounds like a solid plan."

"This is so very exciting," Fairbanks said. "A group of real-life action heroes…"

They started walking. Fairbanks and his undead companion took the lead, while Zantoro followed close behind. London and Lia hung a few meters back, their rifles held at the ready. Although Fairbanks claimed he'd cleared out the specimens, as he called them, London wasn't about to let his guard down.

"If you've come this far, I can only assume that you've encountered the infected before." Fairbanks called over his shoulder.

London didn't like the idea of shouting back and forth; it went against his years of training. If there were hostiles lurking about, their voices would draw them.

"We've run into our fair share of these zombies or whatever you call them," London answered. "Saw them up close and personal at an abandoned Catholic mission, in a Ka'Longho village, and at a French farmhouse that General Mbowi was using as a headquarters."

"Ah, yes," Fairbanks said. "George Mbowi has cast a long shadow over this land."

"Well, he's fucking dead now." London checked his rifle's magazine. They were getting close enough now that the stink of the undead hung heavy in the air.

"That's good news. A bit late, but good nonetheless."

London closed the distance between them a bit. If they were going to converse while they walked, they might as well not have to shout.

Lia leaned in and whispered into his ear, "This man is a mad scientist straight out of a bad horror movie."

"Zantoro was right," London whispered back. "The guy's fucking insane. But we're not exactly in a position to be picky about the company we keep."

"Can I assume, Madame Rousseau, that you'll be wanting to interview me about the nefarious dealings at the research facility?" Fairbanks asked. "Because I was party to some perversions of science that would make Mengele blush. And I'm willing to tell you all about them. Call it absolution, if you will. The virus to which I was exposed-"

"You mean the virus you stuck your dick into," Zantoro said.

Fairbanks turned to the toothless ghoul on the leash. "I'm sorry, my dear, but this man is a soldier, and their manner of speech can be coarse indeed. I promise you that he means no offense."

Lia shot London a wide-eyed look. She shook her head and whispered, "Totally insane."

"As I was saying," Fairbanks continued, "the virus is replicating within me at the standard rate, which means I'll most likely lose my powers of reason within the next twenty-four hours. If your mission had been delayed by another day's time, you might well have found me in a state not unlike my bride. I expect that the viral load in my body will reach a critical state within twenty-four hours."

"Your bride?" Zantoro started to laugh but ended up coughing instead. "Man, I've been horny and desperate in my day, but goddamn."

"Give it a rest, Zantoro," London said. It wasn't that he was worried about offending Fairbanks. As far as London was concerned, the man deserved every bit of the abuse and more. But for the moment, they needed the man's help, and if that meant masking some of their disgust, so be it.

"Sorry, boss," Zantoro replied.

The road ended in a flat, dusty expanse. It looked like a few acres of desolation dropped in the center of the jungle. The ground was littered with bodies. No doubt these were the "specimens" that Fairbanks had dealt with. Some appeared to have been in advanced states of decay at the time of their second deaths. They looked like they'd been put through a meat grinder. Some of them looked to have lost their flesh entirely. Others looked relatively fresh. Apart from their red eyes and faces crusted with dried mucus, some of them still looked like normal people. The one commonality between all the bodies London examined was a dime-sized hole in the center of their foreheads. The holes were of such uniform size and so neatly placed that they might have been done by machine.

"There's a cordless power drill in my backpack," Fairbanks explained as they picked their way through the litter of bodies. "It's quite easy to dispatch the infected specimens with such a tool."

"And they just stood there and waited their turn to have their brains drilled out?" London asked. So much blood and bodily fluids had been sprayed over the ground that there were puddles of mud near some of the bodies. The mud sucked at the soles of his combat boots as he walked through it.

"As I said, I became infected with the same virus..." Fairbanks paused, turning to regard Zantoro, as if he was waiting for a knowing snicker or perhaps a dirty joke. But when Zantoro offered nothing, Fairbanks pulled his tethered companion closer to his side and continued, "My hypothesis, which will sadly not undergo rigorous testing during my lifetime, is that those whose viral load has reached a certain level are able to perceive the presence of the virus in others, even if those others do not yet carry a sufficient viral load to have undergone death and reanimation. It's quite fascinating. It's almost as if the reanimation process results in a type of sixth sense. There's so much left to study about the process, but alas..."

London nodded. It made sense. Hadn't Zantoro said something about being able to smell the virus on Fairbanks?

The Marsh Industries Research Center Daroka Division (as the sign at the front of the building proclaimed) looked like your average glass and metal corporate office building.

London had seen photos of the building in the mission dossier, but he still found the bland edifice surprising. Knowing the nature of the atrocities that took place within, it was jarring to see that the building could have been air lifted out of the urban sprawl of Dallas or Chicago and dropped into the middle of a war-torn African nation. The place could have been the corporate headquarters of a bank or an advertising agency. But London supposed that's just how it was. Evil didn't come from gothic castles where mad scientists labored through the stormy night in laboratories crowded with arcane devices and buzzing electrodes. It came from corporate boardrooms and political think tanks and church pulpits, and it was dreamed up by suit and tie businessmen with MBAs and political ambitions. A man like Fairbanks may have been the brains behind the nuts and bolts of the HOPE Project, but it took a money man like Waylon Marsh to set the thing in motion.

Fairbanks paused at the double doors that led into the building. "Perhaps this is the time to remind you once again that the building is still somewhat occupied. Is 'lock and load' a phrase that applies or is that just something said in action films?"

"It's the latter, but I understand the sentiment," London said, hefting his AK.

"Lock and load?" Zantoro shook his head. "I'm going to remember that one. Drop it into casual conversation. Fucking Vincent will crack up when I do it in my Schwarzenegger voice."

Lia gave London a look. She mouthed the name Vincent.

London nodded. He supposed it was a symptom of the virus. Some sort of cognitive decline. Zantoro was coughing up horrible green shit. He was shaking and sweating excessively, despite the heat and humidity of the jungle. How long before other, more alarming and even dangerous, symptoms manifested?

Fairbanks opened the doors and pushed his companion inside. A blast of cool air hit London in the face.

"The emergency power runs on solar," Fairbanks explained as he stepped over the threshold. "I keep the air cool, mostly because it seems to make the infected specimens more docile, although, as I say, that's no longer an area of concern for me."

The lobby might as well have been the killing floor of a cannibal slaughterhouse. The floor was stained with black patches of dried blood. Bodies, and pieces of bodies were strewn throughout the room. Flies buzzed from one maggot-infested carcass to the next. London thanked God for the functioning air conditioner. His nostrils still burned from the stink of the housing unit.

A trio of oversized rats emerged from a corner of the room. They trundled along with unhurried clumsiness, like they were drugged.

"Excuse me," Fairbanks said, tugging his companion along behind him as he crossed the room to meet the rats. He called back over his shoulder, "Strange thing about this virus, it can move from rats to human, and vice versa. That probably accounts for how quickly the virus spread. This place is crawling with rodents. Some of them from the jungle, others from our own laboratories. They're quite the nuisance, but they're also dealt with easily enough."

Fairbanks pulled his drill from his backpack. He squatted beside the rats, who regarded him with red-rimmed beady eyes. One after another, the rats succumbed to Fairbanks' drill. The whirring bit obliterated their small skulls.

"Now, where were we?" Fairbanks said as he returned to the group. "Ah, yes. You want some background on the project, a little mud to sling at Marsh Industries. If you'll accompany me to the third floor, I can allow you into the administrative offices. Waylon Marsh was quite paranoid about industrial thievery, so very little was stored online. But there are hard drives and hard copies aplenty. I'd imagine there's more than enough for your purposes. And as I said, I'm more than willing to answer any questions you might have."

Fairbanks led them to the elevator. He stabbed the "Up" arrow button and began to whistle a jaunty tune. When the doors whooshed open, he shoved his undead lover into the elevator with a stern warning to behave herself during the ride.

London didn't care much for sharing the small space with the ghoul, but Fairbanks held her by the collar and kept her face pointed into the corner.

"It's okay, I assure you," he said, noticing their reluctance to ride with one of the infected. "She's becoming more and more docile as time goes on. And if she acts out of line, there's always the drill. Just between us, I'm not sure our relationship is built for the long haul anyway."

Lia looked at London and shrugged.

"Fuck it," Zantoro said, stepping inside. "It beats walking up a bunch of stairs."

They rode to the third floor in silence. Despite the absurdity of the situation, once the elevator doors shut, everyone behaved like it was a normal elevator ride. They stood facing forwards, watching the illuminated numbers above the door. Even the doctor's zombie wife stood in her corner quietly. The ride was brief.

12

Father Xavier could have sent Peter to follow the trio of pilgrims, but he knew that this was something he needed to witness with his own eyes. So he left his scout in charge of the army and set off through the jungle to follow the pilgrims onto the Marsh Industries compound. He moved as quietly as he could manage through the jungle, making his way parallel to the road. He kept some distance between himself and the group in order to remain undetected, but he was careful not to lose track of them. His dreams told him that miraculous events were drawing near, events in which the pilgrims' roles were critical, and he didn't want to miss a single moment.

He watched with growing excitement as the group entered the housing facility, but his heart sank when they emerged a short time later with their number reduced by two. Still, his faith was strong. Since the tyrant George Mbowi had forged an alliance with the rapacious tycoon Waylon Marsh, the dreams hadn't led Father Xavier astray. His nightly visions had kept him and his child army alive when the rest of the nation had succumbed to the undead plague. If his dreams told him that these unlikely pilgrims would open the gateway to another world, then it was surely so.

And then, the pilgrims were confronted by a man in scrubs and a lab coat. This madman was walking an undead woman like a dog on a leash. When she came abreast of the pilgrims, she began to snarl and claw at the air, and the madman pulled at her leash, keeping her well away from the other people. Eventually, she calmed down, as if coming to grips with the fact that she would not be allowed to devour these people.

Father Xavier crept through the trees until he was close enough to the surviving trio to hear them speak to the madman who wore the clothing of a doctor. What Father Xavier gleaned from their words was that the madman and one of the pilgrims carried within them the plague, although they had yet to die and be reborn as members of the undead horde. He wondered why the pilgrims' leader—the man who introduced himself as Mike London—didn't take the obvious course of action and kill those who'd been infected. It would be an act of mercy, after all.

For a moment, their conversation was drowned out by the increasing volume of the dead woman's groans. Although she seemed to have accepted the fact that the pilgrims were off the menu, she seemed impatient. Then, the party of five set off down the road, walking toward the research facility. Father Xavier waited a short interval, long enough for them to get a lead, then picked his way out of the trees. He followed them at a distance, intrigued by this strange assortment of individuals. If the divine power had chosen this motley assortment to blaze the trail to the new world, then perhaps it was true that the ways of God were mysterious.

When he arrived at the Marsh Industries compound, Father Xavier marveled at the carnage littering the field between the end of the road and the front doors of the research center. A hundred or more bodies lay in rapidly drying pools of blood. The air was swarmed with flies. Vultures circled overhead. Soon enough, scavengers would emerge from the trees and reduce the bodies to piles of bones. It was the way of things, after all, and he had seen more than his share of bodies left to rot during the days since General Mbowi seized power. But even so, it was a shock to see so much human carnage in one space. He supposed that it would be worse to become numb to such things. When one's sense of outrage at such violence left, it took with it a piece of one's humanity. That was the crux of a sermon Father Xavier Arnaud had preached many times, and although he'd been forced to reevaluate many of his beliefs, that was one he still held firmly.

He watched from the edge of the field as the madman led the pilgrims into the building. His heart quickened at the sight. A sense of familiarity washed over him. He'd been here before, in his dreams. It was as if some prophecy had been fulfilled. The end was near, and he had only to wait a short time until the divine power revealed itself.

13

Lia had always suspected that Marsh Industries' presence in Africa was far less altruistic than Waylon Marsh claimed. But even she couldn't have guessed at the true extent of the cruel inhumanity behind the HOPE Project. She certainly couldn't have imagined the depths of the depravity underlying it.

She was seated behind a desk that had once belonged to Alexander Remington, the head of research operations for Marsh Industries in Daroka. As she picked through a stack of paperwork she'd pulled from one of the office's file cabinets, she wondered if Mr. Remington was among those who'd gotten up close and personal with Dr. Fairbanks' power drill. After all, nearly half of the bodies she'd seen were still wearing tattered and stained lab coats or scrubs.

London and Fairbanks sat on the other side of the desk, seated in padded swivel chairs, while Zantoro, and the undead woman were in a staff lounge a couple doors down the hall. There was a small couch in there, and Zantoro had collapsed onto it, telling them he preferred to rest while they searched through the files. His sickness was getting worse by the minute, and Lia could hear his coughing fits growing in frequency and duration. Fairbanks had wanted to bring the dead woman into the office, but London had refused to be in an enclosed space with her stench.

"A short elevator ride is one thing," he'd said, "but I'm not sitting in that office while she stinks up the joint. It smells bad enough in here already."

Fairbanks had looked hurt, but he acquiesced. He handed the makeshift leash to Zantoro and asked him to keep an eye on her.

Now, Lia busied herself by scanning through a stack of files containing everything from inter-office memos to expense reports to lab results. There were even photos of human test subjects who'd undergone horrific mutations. It was a jumbled mess. She knew she couldn't take everything, but there was no time to scan the documents. Normally, these types of investigations involved finding the damning needles in a haystack of bloated corporate nonsense. But here, even the daily financial reports contained evidence of atrocities. It was enough to bury Waylon Marsh, sure, but London had told her she only had a matter of minutes to collect what she needed.

Meanwhile, Fairbanks droned on about his time in Daroka.

"Many of us came to this godforsaken place because Marsh Industries dangled the promise of a clean slate in front of us," Fairbanks explained. "For me, the idea of being to finally emerge from the dark shadow of my past sexual indiscretions was more than enough motivation to cross the Atlantic. I imagine that most of my colleagues were eager to purge their own closets of some equally embarrassing skeletons. But most of us were also devotees of the work of a man named Gustav Vogel. You won't have to dig through much of that paperwork before you come across his name."

"I've heard of him," London said. "He was mentioned in

our mission dossier. Some sort of disgraced German scientist."

"That's correct," Fairbanks said. "He *was* disgraced. However, he was also brilliant, and his research did have world-altering implications, even if he had to skirt plenty of ethical concerns to carry it out."

Lia resisted the urge to tell the men to quit talking as if they were the only ones in the room who knew anything about the HOPE Project. She'd done her research before coming to Daroka. Although the initial focus of her documentary was to be General George Mbowi's coup, it was impossible to tell that story without delving into some of the dirt on Marsh Industries. It had quickly become apparent that Mbowi's regime and the HOPE Project were so thoroughly entangled that they were, in fact, one and the same.

"We were offered the chance to work in an environment completely unfettered by government oversight, unbound by the hypocritical standards of scientific institutions," Fairbanks continued. "Any true scientist would jump at the chance."

"I think you're letting yourself off the hook pretty damn easy," London said. "Plenty of people still have ethical standards."

"So says the man who kills people for money," Fairbanks said.

Lia looked up from the paperwork, interested to see how London would react to the barb Fairbanks had just tossed his way.

"Yeah, I'm going to hell just the same as you, I suppose." London looked back at her. "But it's a little late for regrets."

"Just so," Fairbanks said. "You must understand that, until very recently, we believed the true purpose of the project justified the means. Waylon Marsh spoke of ending world hunger, easing overpopulation, and fostering a new age of global prosperity. If a few ethical standards had to fall by the wayside to achieve those things, wouldn't you say it's worth it? I sincerely believed so when I boarded the plane bound for Daroka."

London shrugged. "You want absolution, better go look for a priest."

Lia turned her attention back to the stack of papers in front of her. A cursory look was enough to paint a nightmarish portrait of what had transpired in the facility. It was like Waylon Marsh had discarded every single standard of medical and business ethics in a bid to leverage control of an entire continent's resources.

Fairbanks reached across the desk and tapped the computer in front of Lia. "You'll want the hard drive from this machine, although I suspect the contents are encrypted. Here, let me help you."

Using the same drill that had recently dispatched a couple hundred reanimated dead people, Fairbanks removed the back of the computer tower, unplugged the hard drive, and handed it over.

"The initial work was done in the United States," Fairbanks said. "At that point, we were just moving onto testing with primates. We had a facility in Mississippi, where oversight was minimal. Marsh had a couple congressional representatives in his pocket. But no amount of political palm-greasing is going to allow for experimentation on humans, and since that was always where Marsh wanted to take things, he saw an opportunity with General Mbowi. One little nudge, and the country was in chaos."

"So what was it all about, the HOPE Project?" Lia asked. "Because it couldn't be ending world hunger and fighting disease and all the other platitudes Waylon Marsh was pushing."

Fairbanks shrugged. "In the beginning, it was about cell phones."

"What the fuck?" London shook his head. "I don't get it."

"He means that the natural resources necessary for the manufacturing of cell phones are found in great abundance in this country. Rare earth metals, things like that," Lia said. "Waylon Marsh has interests in all sorts of industries. Automotive, aviation, pharmaceutical, even publishing. But tech has always been the biggest money maker. And if he could control the resources necessary for the phones, he'd have a virtual monopoly on the market."

Fairbanks leaned forward in his chair. "Not only could he control the market for Daroka's natural resources, but he could also tap into a ready-made work force to extract those resources."

"Zombies working the mines." Lia shook her head. "Why bother with a slave labor force that might revolt at any moment when you can train dead people to do the work?"

"This whole thing…civil war, political corruption, multi-billion dollar stock market deals, a steadily increasing body count…" London closed his eyes and pinched the bridge of his nose. "This whole goddamn things was about some rich asshole wanting to corner the market on fucking cell phones?"

"Quit acting surprised," Lia said. "I know you keep saying you're just a hired gun, but you can't possibly be that naïve about the type of people you work for."

She felt bad about saying it so directly, but it was the truth. It was also true that she'd developed feelings for the man, but that didn't mean she could turn a blind eye to who he was. To *what* he was.

"Fucking cell phones." London repeated it, as if trying to make sense of the situation.

And this is the way the world ends, Lia thought, slipping another file folder into her backpack. *Not with a bang, but a bunch of hollow-eyed consumers watching an endless parade of fifteen second videos of cute kittens, teenage pranks, dance routines in public spaces, celebrity gossip, and a thousand other inanities.*

Pretty soon, these reanimated dead people will be indistinguishable from the drooling idiots who are still alive.

Fairbanks slapped London on the shoulder. "She's one smart cookie, huh? Put all the pieces together like it was nothing. We were brought here to pursue several paths of gaining control of the population. At first, I thought we were simply creating a sterilization program to depopulate the country. But that wasn't it at all. In the end, we were working to create a disease that could wipe out the local population, and then bring them back as mindless drone workers. Miners who are already dead don't need a paycheck, and they certainly never go on strike. And if the disease turned out to be communicable, then that was just an added benefit, because Marsh Industries would hold the patent on the vaccine."

"Only this disease got out into the world before you had the vaccine ready," London said.

"You may not be quite as sharp as this lady," Fairbanks said, "but you're no idiot. The virus *has* mutated. In fact, it's still mutating. It's a shame that I won't be around to see some of the changes, but I'm certain that the loss of cognitive function in those infected with newer strains might not decline so sharply."

"You mean like these zombies shooting automatic rifles at people?" London sighed. "Because we've seen that."

"Fascinating," Fairbanks said. "Simply fascinating. Although I don't see how-"

The doctor was interrupted by shouts coming from the hallway outside the office.

"Shit, that's Zantoro," London said, standing up.

There was a burst of gunfire, followed by more shouting.

Lia stood as well. She shouldered her backpack and checked her rifle.

"No, you should stay here with the doctor," London said, gesturing for her to sit down. "I'm going to check this out. If

I'm not back in a few minutes, get the hell out of here, because I'm triggering the explosives."

Lia shook her head. "No way. You know better than that. I'm not some shrinking violet. And I'm sure as hell not letting you out of my sight. We're in this together, until the end."

"Wait," Fairbanks said. "What explosives?"

14

Zantoro wondered how much time he had left. It was a hell of a thing, knowing that you could measure the rest of your life in minutes, but he was starting to look forward to crossing the finish line. Every time he coughed, his guts contracted into a tight ball of agony, and stars burst across the backs of his eyelids, so bright that they drove spikes into his brain. The coughing fits brought up mouthfuls of green slime that were so acidic they steamed when he spat them into the trash can beside the sofa. And while he lay there, wondering how much longer London and his girlfriend would dilly-dally in that office, Fairbanks' dead lover stood over him, staring down at him with red eyes.

"Fuck you looking at, bitch?" Zantoro said, wiping green globules from the corners of his mouth. "

She responded by tugging the leash out of his hand.

"Fine with me," he said. "Not much place you can wander off to."

He clenched his jaw shut, gritting his teeth against another coughing fit. His efforts to stifle the fit were in vain, and he was soon curled up in the fetal position, spitting out mouthful after mouthful of steaming, stinking slime. He no longer even aimed for the trash can. He spat the stuff onto the floor, half-expecting it to melt through the thin carpet. Through his tear-streaked vision, he saw the dead woman—Eve was what the crazy doctor had called her—walk over to the door of the lounge. She fumbled with the doorknob for a few seconds, then managed to open the door and walk out.

"Hey, the fuck you think you're going?" Zantoro said, still wincing at the pain that the last coughing fit had brought. "Goddamn it…"

His rib cage felt like it was straining to keep his organs in the proper alignment. He scooped his AK off the floor and used it for support as he levered himself off the couch. One by one, the vertebrae in his spine popped. The sound reminded him of snapping the bubbles on sheets of plastic packing material.

Limping along, he used his rifle like a cane as he followed Eve out of the lounge and into the hallway. He caught sight of her, and shouted for her to stop. If she understood him or even heard him, she didn't give any indication. She just kept plodding unsteadily to the T-junction at the end of the hallway. She seemed to be going back the way they'd came, heading for the elevator.

"What the hell, man?" His voice was hoarse. His throat burned from the noxious vomit. What he wouldn't have given for a piece of chewing gum or even some of that stinking tobacco that London shoved into his lower lip.

He paused outside the door, wondering if he should follow Eve or go alert the others. Drawing in a slow breath, cautious not to provoke another coughing fit, he decided to go after Eve. She was still wearing that belt around her neck like a leash, and weak as Zantoro felt, he figured he could drag her back without much problem. This time, he'd tie that belt to something so she couldn't wander off. Then maybe he could relax until it was time to set off the Thunderballs and blow the building.

And yourself along with it, don't forget.

But he found that the thought of his impending death didn't really move him anymore. If he felt anything about it at all, it was simple gratitude that it would be over quickly.

He went down the hallway as quickly as he could manage. His equilibrium was out of whack, probably a result of his steadily increasing fever. He felt so hot that he was afraid he might spontaneously combust, but he could no longer sweat. His skin was dry. Patches of it had begun to flake away, like he was recovering from the world's worst case of sunburn. Clear fluid wept from the cracks left behind by the skin he'd sloughed off.

Not much longer, pal. Once you start leaking like that, the end can't be far off.

He found Eve standing in front of the elevator. The numbers above the door indicated that the compartment was rising from the basement level. Eve turned to look at him. Although her eyes remained as blank and vacant as ever, her expression changed. Her mouth, which normally hung agape, just like all the other reanimated dead, closed. Her cracked lips pressed together. The corners of her mouth rose ever so slightly as she regarded him.

What the fuck? Is she…smiling?

The elevator dinged, and the doors slid open. The sight of what was waiting behind those doors made Zantoro stagger back a couple steps. The elevator compartment was packed with ghouls. They were crammed into every inch of available space, from floor to ceiling. Their limbs were folded at unnatural angles to fit into the tight corners. Zantoro's fevered brain conjured memories of old photos of college students packed into phone booths. And as the ghouls untangled themselves from one another and tumbled onto the floor, he remembered the time he'd gone to the circus as a child and watched a seemingly endless parade of clowns emerge from a tiny car. At a time in the not too distant past, the absurdity of the two mental images would have compelled him to make some joke, to throw back his head and laugh. But his capacity for humor had withered and fallen away, just like the pieces of dead skin dropping from his arms, neck, and face.

"Holy shit!" He shouted as he raised his rifle, fumbling with the safety. His manual dexterity seemed to have gone the way of his balance. "Hey, boss! Might want to get your ass in gear, because we got some fucking company!"

Despite the coughing that his shouts provoked, he managed to fire two bursts from the AK into the pile of writhing, groaning ghouls. His hands were shaking too badly for him to aim. If he managed any head shots, it was only through dumb luck. He backpedaled, but the movement felt like dragging his feet through wet cement. Eve turned slowly. Her strange half-smile was still fixed on her face. She raised her hand and extended one finger to point at him. She blinked her eyes with exaggerated slowness.

"Fuck you, bitch!" Zantoro shouted.

He fired a burst of rounds at her. The bullets raked a trench through her abdomen, and she staggered back as withered organs spilled from the wound. But her hand remained outstretched, and her smile didn't falter. He squeezed the trigger again, but the chamber clicked empty. He'd left his supply of spare magazines in the staff lounge, so he went back to using the rifle as a walking stick.

He turned away from the still-unfolding spectacle of the ghouls emerging from the elevator and stumbled back the way he'd come. What he saw coming from the other side of the T-junction was enough to goose his failing endocrine system to dump its final reserves of adrenaline into his infected bloodstream.

Hundreds, maybe thousands, of mutated lab animals were scrabbling across the tiled floor. Mice, rats, rabbits, guinea pigs, and even a few rhesus monkeys, all of them covered in patchy fur matted with dried blood and vomit. Their beady eyes were so red they seemed to glow. They crawled over one another, their claws ripping into flesh and drawing forth a sludge of coagulated blood and pus. The roadkill stench of the rotten menagerie was so thick Zantoro could practically see it as a yellow haze. The pathetic creatures chittered and growled as they advanced. The first wave of ghouls to emerge from the elevator had found their feet. They began to stagger toward him. Any second now, the two undead armies—the dead humans and the dead animals—would converge. Zantoro was certain of one thing: he didn't want to hang around to watch the two groups meet.

He turned and fled down the hallway. He no longer possessed enough strength or coordination to run, but he staggered as fast as he could.

15

London stepped out of the office and was immediately assaulted by a rotten stench so thick that it had overpowered the building's air conditioning system. His sense of hearing was likewise assaulted by a cacophony of overlapping grunts and growls, both human and animal. The walls of the administrative office must have been somewhat soundproofed, because sounds that were distant and muted while London was seated in the office were suddenly like the din of a full-scale riot.

"Jesus Christ, it sounds like all hell's broken loose down there," he said.

Lia pressed close to his side. "Are those animals?"

They took a few steps forward, but the sight of Zantoro emerging from around the corner at the end of the hallway stopped them. He wasn't exactly running, more like stumbling very quickly. His mouth was working, but whatever he was shouting was rendered indecipherable by the rest of the noise. His frantic gesticulations were clear enough: he was motioning for them to return to the office. At first, London felt frozen by his confusion. But that didn't last long. After a few moments, the reason for Zantoro's panicked hand gestures became very clear. From one side of the T-junction behind Zantoro came a parade of strange creatures, lab animals that had been ravaged by injections of the virus. From the other side came a shambling army of reanimated corpses, human test subjects who'd undergone similar treatment. The two groups converged into a single migrating mass of mutants. Some of them moved on four legs, others on two, but their intent seemed to be the same. They knew that London and Lia were alive and not infected. Somehow these reanimated creatures, both human and animal, could sense it, and their ravenous hunger for living flesh was urging them forward.

The office door swung open behind them, and Fairbanks emerged.

"Where's Eve?" he asked, shouldering past London. "Where's my darling bride?"

"Doc, you're going to want to get back in that office," London said, grabbing the man by the elbow. "That's no Sunday school picnic coming down the hallway."

Fairbanks ripped his arm from London's grasp. "How dare you? I welcomed you into my home and now you've-"

The doctor's outraged monologue was cut short by an outburst of violent coughing that nearly doubled him over. When he'd finished hacking up several golf ball-sized wads of bloody phlegm, he straightened up and gave London a wounded look before shuffling off to meet the oncoming tide of the dead.

Lia started after him, but London pulled her back.

"Let him go," he said. "The man is as good as dead anyway. He might as well spend whatever time he has left with his zombie wife. Jesus, I can't believe I just said that."

Max kept accusing of you of behaving like you were in an action movie, London Thought to himself, *but he was wrong. You're in a fucking* horror *movie!*

It was almost enough to make him laugh.

"Why are you smiling at a time like this?" Lia asked.

He shook his head. "Nothing. I'll tell you later."

He watched as Zantoro and Fairbanks passed each other in the hallway. They exchanged words, but London still couldn't make out anything over the noise of the rotten crowd that was drawing nearer with each moment.

Finally, when Zantoro was within a few meters of them, his hoarse voice became intelligible.

"I think our timetable for finishing this thing has moved up..." He glanced over his shoulder, then looked back to London. "Significantly. The sons of bitches took the elevator if you can believe that."

London stepped back into the office, holding the door open for Lia and Zantoro. They stepped through, and London slammed the door, locking it for good measure. He wasn't sure if he understood everything Fairbanks had said about cognitive abilities in the undead, but he hoped that they hadn't learned to pick locks. Zantoro had just said that they could use the elevator, so London supposed it was entirely possible.

Zantoro turned his head and coughed. Then he took a slow breath and said, "Hate to say it, but I think you guys are going to have to go out the window. There's enough of them out there that you'll never be able to shoot your way out."

You, not we, London thought. *He's so fucking calm about the fact that he's not leaving this building.*

"Out the window?" Lia's voice had a note of panic.

"Should be some rope in the boss' backpack." Zantoro shrugged. "Standard field supply kit for Pendleton operatives includes fifty feet of nylon fiber rope."

"Yes, but..." She swallowed. "I'm frightened of heights, that's all."

London and Zantoro looked at one another. London tried to keep the smile off his face. He knew, once he smiled that

Zantoro would start laughing, which would provoke another bout of coughing.

"For real?" Zantoro's shoulders hitched as he tried to stifle laughter. "Lady, there is a goddamn army of reanimated dead people and zombie animals heading our way as we speak. I get that we've been living with the idea of undead humans for a while now, so the shock has sort of worn off. But there are a bunch of zombie rats and monkeys out there among those undead humans. Motherfucking zombie monkeys, lady. I saw them with my own eyes, and trust me, you don't want to get up close and personal."

London was taken aback by the outburst. Not because it was outrageous. In fact, it was exactly the sort of thing he'd come to expect after years of working alongside Zantoro. But it was shocking that the man was still capable of such a rant. For London, it brought home the fact that Zantoro was his friend; one who would soon be dead. The realization landed with all the subtlety of a kick to the balls.

"I suppose I can confront my fear," Lia said.

This time, London couldn't contain his laughter. When Zantoro joined in, he was able to limit his coughing to a brief burst.

"Boss," Zantoro said once they'd gotten control of themselves. "I hate to say it, but we better get this show on the road. I'm not feeling so good, and I want to make sure I have enough gas left in the tank to do what needs to be done. You get what I'm saying?"

London nodded. "Loud and clear. Let's get this damn thing done."

The office window overlooked the open expanse between the building's front entrance, and the edge of the jungle. London gave it an experimental jab with the butt of his rifle. The result was as he expected. The window was made of shatterproof safety glass. He doubted it was bulletproof, however, and he asked Lia and Zantoro to stand clear while he fired a burst of rounds at the window. The bullets punched holes in the glass, around which dense spider webs of cracks appeared. A little gentle persuasion with the rifle butt was enough to knock what remained of the window out of the frame.

Lia poked her head out of the window and looked down. She said something in her native language. London didn't speak much French, but he got her meaning loud and clear.

"Ever done any mountain climbing?" he asked as he fished a tightly coiled rope from his pack of supplies. "Rappelling, maybe?"

She pulled her head back in. "Didn't you hear me say I'm afraid of heights?"

London tied the rope to one of the legs of the desk. Then he pitched the rest of the length out the window. It unspooled, the dangling end flapping against the side of the building like a lazy snake.

Outside the office, the dead parade was slowing. London watched them through the office's lone interior window. The vanguard of the dead had come to a halt, and they stared through the glass at him. At first, there was only a pair of them, then another three stopped their slow march. The leader of the group pressed his hands against the window. A rat scurried up his chest, its claws punching neat little holes in the ghoul's skin.

"You guys better think about getting your asses in gear," Zantoro said, emptying the contents of London's backpack onto the desk. There wasn't much left in the way of supplies, just a half-dozen magazines for the AK, a few cans of beans lifted from Mbowi's pantry, a stainless steel canteen, and a roll of duct tape. And the Thunderballs, of course. There were three of the black, spherical explosives. Zantoro picked one of them up and held it at eye level.

"The trigger is just under that flat part. The cover unscrews. Once you've hit the manual trigger, there's a fifteen second delay, but there's no way to take it back. Once you flip that switch, you're committed," London said. He felt pretty stupid saying it. The delay could have been fifteen minutes or five seconds; either way, it made no difference for Zantoro.

"Know what I'm going to do?" Zantoro smiled, picking up another of the Thunderballs with his free hand. "I'm going to fire them all up and then go bowling. Maybe drop one down the elevator shaft. These things work as well as you say they're supposed to, there won't even be rubble to sift through."

"Yeah." London nodded.

Zantoro gave him a look, seeming to read London's mind. He set the explosives on the desk and put his hands on London's shoulders.

"Look, boss," he said, "let's not drag this thing out. It sucks, but what can you do? I mean, I had a good run. I can't complain. And you know something, I think I'm ready. Been ready for a while. Not even afraid."

London opened his mouth to respond, but Zantoro shook his head and told him to be quiet. Good thing, because London had no idea what he was going to say.

"It's been a hell of a ride, boss." Zantoro turned away, gazing out the interior window at the growing crowd of undead humans and animals. "You and your lady be sure to give 'em hell for me, huh? You guys ever have a kid together, don't name him after me. Gilbert is a lame fucking name. Call him something like Snake or Axel."

London let Zantoro have the last word. He knew how much Zantoro liked ending every conversation with his best one-liner. He turned to Lia and began giving her a crash course in rope climbing. Mostly, it involved not strangling him during their descent as she rode piggyback.

"You can close your eyes if that will help," he said. "But

try to be mindful of the fact that I'm climbing with an extra, what, hundred and fifty pounds on my back."

"I beg your pardon?" Lia sniffed. "One hundred seventeen. Probably less after being in this jungle for so long."

"Hey, I was making allowances for those files you're bringing along," he said.

16

Zantoro waited until he heard the boss and his girlfriend go out the window, before he turned away from the crowd outside the office and sat down behind the desk. The stinky fuckers in the hallway seemed pretty disappointed that the uninfected people were gone. Now that it was just him in the office, they quit pounding on the window and simply stood there, milling around aimlessly.

"Well, fuck you too," he said, waving his middle finger at the pair of ghouls who were staring at him. "You're not such hot shit yourself, you know? But you're about to be. Hot shit, I mean. We all are."

He reached out and touched one of the Thunderballs. The metal casing was smooth, almost slick. The explosive contained within—something so top secret that even the United States military wasn't privy to its secrets—was the most powerful incendiary device in human history. Pound for pound, it made thermite look like a glass of ice water. And the explosive trigger—a stabilized azidoazide derivative, according to the accompanying instruction booklet—had more than enough power to level a building ten times the size of the research center. It was truly amazing how much of mankind's genius had been channeled into something so destructive. Zantoro didn't know whether to be awed or disgusted. He supposed it didn't matter much either way. His opinion hadn't counted for much up to this point, so he didn't see why it should start now.

He checked his watch. He'd told the boss that he'd give him a thirty minute head start. Hopefully, it would be enough time for them to get out of the blast radius.

"*Ka-boom*, motherfucker," he said, patting the Thunderball.

He closed his eyes and waited. His lungs burned with each shallow breath he drew. His slow, measured exhalations rattled in his chest, each one threatening to bring on another coughing fit, another mouthful of thick, reeking phlegm. The headache throbbing in the center of his forehead was edging into migraine territory as it spread over the rest of his face. Everything hurt. His joints felt tight, as if his ligaments and tendons were drawing up. His heart fluttered in his chest like a wounded bird.

In short, he was dying. And it wasn't the sort of blissful, light-at-the-end-of-the-dark-tunnel, new age journey to total enlightenment. It hurt. It hurt like hell. Worse than anything he'd ever before felt.

His body began to shake. It was like shivering, although he also felt like his skin was on fire. His teeth chattered. He held one of the Thunderballs close to his chest, counting the minutes down until he could open the control panel on the device, activate the trigger manually, and slip into merciful oblivion.

He opened one gummy eyelid and checked his watch. Not long now. As he shifted in his seat, searching in vain for a comfortable position, he caught a glimpse of a face pressed against the office's interior window, staring at him. It was one of the reanimated lab animals, a monkey who'd been brought back from the dead. Its fur was crusty with dried blood, vomit, and mucus. Its eyes were red and cloudy. But otherwise, it might have been a monkey in a zoo. Zantoro raised one trembling hand and waved. The monkey responded by extending a single finger and probing the depths of its nostril. It dug out a dripping nugget of congealed mucus and smeared it across the window.

Although it hurt like hell, Zantoro had to laugh.

Fairbanks felt like a salmon swimming upstream as he fought his way through the parade of infected specimens that was making its way down the hallway. As he pushed and shoved through the crowd, he scanned their faces, searching for Eve.

He found her standing outside the elevator, perhaps waiting for it to bring up another load of the infected. As he approached, calling out her name, she turned slowly and fixed him with her red-eyed, unblinking stare.

"My dear," he said, his breathing fast and raspy. "I thought you were lost."

She cocked her head to one side like dog trying to puzzle out a new command.

"We must be quick," he said. "Our castle is no longer safe, and we must flee ahead of its destruction. I thought perhaps we should stay here and let events take their course. But I've changed my mind. I want to take you away from this place."

Fairbanks didn't know if it was some primitive survival instinct taking over or if his fevered brain had lost the capacity for rational thought, but he no longer had any desire to go down with the Marsh Industries ship. He understood that the virus was running rampant through his body, but that was a bridge he could cross once he and his beloved were safe. If what London and Madame Rousseau had said about cognitive increases were true, then perhaps all they had to do was wait it out. And since Eve was already so far ahead of him, she could care for him as he progressed through the virus' stages, just as he had cared for her.

"Perhaps there is a future, after all," he said, taking her hands in his. "Perhaps all we need to do is embrace our new world…"

She pulled her hands away and took a step back, continuing to regard him with her head tilted. Then, without taking her eyes off him, she unbuckled the belt around her neck and slipped it off.

"Yes, yes, my dear." Fairbanks nodded eagerly. "There's no need for such things any longer."

She looped the belt back through the buckle, then stepped forward and dropped the loop over Fairbanks' head.

"What…" He reached out to touch her face. "What are you doing?"

She straightened up. Her eyes narrowed as she looked at him.

"I have no need of-"

She silenced him with an abrupt yank on the belt's dangling end, cinching it around Fairbanks' neck so tightly that it choked off his air supply. He clawed at the leather strap, desperate to get his fingers under it. But Eve pulled harder, and the noose tightened.

Fairbanks gagged. His knees trembled, then buckled, and he sank to the floor. Eve stood over him, the belt clutched in her hand. Fairbanks' eyes bulged. His vision swam, the edges of the world growing dark and blurry. His sight narrowed until it was a single spotlight on Eve's face. The corners of her mouth pulled upward ever so slightly, as if she was smiling at the punchline to some private joke.

He reached up to touch her face one final time.

18

London and Lia ran down the road, through a jungle that was giving up its dead. Some appeared to have once been Marsh Industries employees, others victims of the HOPE Project's medical deviance. Animals came with them, but London was unable to determine if they were infected, or simply joining the mass exodus. When the first few ghouls slouched out of the tree line, London raised his rifle and shot two of them cleanly through the head. But it soon became apparent that there were too many of them to simply shoot down. But, strangely, it didn't seem to matter. Most of them appeared uninterested in trying to devour him and Lia. The red-eyed ghouls just plodded down the road, heading for the research center. When one of them strayed too close, London shot it in the head, but he let those who kept their distance carry on. It didn't matter anymore. If they were headed for the research center, they'd all be permanently dead soon.

"Why are they just ignoring us?" Lia asked, clutching her own rifle to her chest.

"Who knows?" London shrugged. "And who cares? As long as they're not trying to eat us, I say we let them go get blown to bits. Not our problem."

"Yes, but..." She turned around and walked backward for a few paces, watching the dead parade make its way toward the research facility, toward the birthplace of the plague.

"Let it go, Lia. This is one mystery you're not going to solve."

"It could be important. Something I need for my..." She turned back around. "Well, something important anyway."

London took his eyes off the passing line of ghouls just long enough to look at Lia's face. What he saw told him that she was starting to come to the same conclusion he'd reached when he'd stepped out of the housing unit. Or maybe he'd gotten there even earlier and just refused to acknowledge it. That conclusion was that none of this mattered anymore. They'd been cut off from the outside world since they set foot on Darokan soil. Who could tell how far this thing had spread in the meantime? Completing the mission at this point was most likely a futile gesture. It was a Pyrrhic victory at best. They'd lost Vincent, Osbourne, and Max. Soon enough, they could add Zantoro to that list. And for what? The flimsy hope that they could somehow make it back to civilization and put their evidence in front of someone who actually gave a shit?

"I've been thinking about those dreams," London said. "About that underground city."

"Yeah?"

"Be nice if that was a real place."

"Who knows? Maybe it is." Lia smiled, but her eyes were sad. "I'm beginning to think it was just a delusion. The world has gone insane and we're just following along."

"Well," London said, "wherever we're going, we better pick up the pace. It's not too much longer until Zantoro pulls the pin and turns that place into a crater. We got a few minutes before the big bang."

He reached out and took her hand. It wasn't the sort of thing one normally did in this type of situation. Hand holding wasn't anywhere in the combat tactics manual. But London didn't care. As they got farther away from the research facility, the number of ghouls on the road began to dwindle, until there were only a few stragglers making their north, drawn back to ground zero by some silent siren call.

London tried running, but neither he nor Lia could keep up the pace for long. They jogged for a short distance, until that too became more than they could manage. They slowed their pace until they were strolling along as if they were a couple of lovers enjoying a quiet evening.

London was wiped out. And Lia appeared to be just as spent. Here, at the end of the line, he'd expected some sense of relief, some feeling of closure. But all he felt was tired. More than that, actually. He felt completely drained. Since setting foot in Daroka, he'd been moving from one horror to the next, in a waking nightmare. It had finally caught up with him.

"Think we put enough distance between ourselves and the bomb?" Lia asked.

"They're highly experimental explosives, so who knows?" London sighed.

"Maybe we could go into the jungle," Lia suggested. "We could find a nice quiet spot to rest before we continue."

To London's ears, it sounded a lot like she was suggesting they give up. But he found that he didn't mind that so much. They stepped off the road and into the jungle. The thick canopy choked off the sunlight. In the pleasant dimness, London felt even wearier. Each step took a mountain climber's determination. His shoulders felt heavy. There was something strange about the atmosphere. It took London's tired brain a few minutes to puzzle it out, but it eventually dawned on him that the jungle was quiet. Normally, the place was full of sound. The shrieks and squawks of birds and primates. The buzzing and chirping of insects. The snapping and cracking of dead tree limbs. The growling of unseen predators. But all that was gone, leaving in its wake a silence so hollow that it seemed to pull London into its depths.

They paused by silent agreement in a small clearing full of brightly colored flowers. The rainbow flora hung from the crisscrossed limbs overhead and blanketed the ground underfoot. Lia dropped her rifle and shrugged off her backpack. London dropped his rifle as well. They embraced, holding each other close as they kissed.

"Do you think it's safe to rest here?" Lia asked as she pulled away slightly.

"Whether it's safe or not, I'm about to fucking collapse," London answered. "Call me crazy, but it feels like we're the only ones left in this little patch of jungle."

"Yeah, I feel it too."

"These flowers, they sure are pretty," he said. "I wonder how many times I've walked past flowers like these, and never noticed."

"They certainly are beautiful," she said.

They sat down, each of them wincing at the various aches and pains they'd acquired through their ordeal. The flowers beneath them were cool and soft. London lay back, sighing as his cheek brushed against the fragrant petals. Lia snuggled into the crook of his arm, laying her head on his chest. Their breathing fell into sync. She murmured something in French, her voice little more than a whisper. London opened his mouth to ask for a translation, but decided against it. Even if he didn't know her words' exact definitions, he knew the sentiment behind them, and he agreed. He pulled her even closer. His eyelids felt heavy. Whether he wanted it or not, sleep was overtaking him. He offered up a silent prayer that whatever dreams awaited him, they were half as pleasant as lying in a patch of flowers with Lia.

Just as his eyes closed, and consciousness began to ebb away, the ground shook with a thunderclap louder than any

London had ever heard. His eyes snapped open. Even through the dense canopy overhead, London could see the flash of fire that filled the sky. The ground continued to rumble and shake beneath them. Lia's body stiffened, then relaxed again. London squeezed his eyes shut. The world around them burned and shook, but he just wanted to sleep.

19

Father Xavier sat on the riverbank and sighed contentedly. He scooped a handful of pebbles off the ground and rolled them around in his palm. Some were shiny black onyx, others nearly transparent and streaked with ribbons of bright color. All had been worn smooth by centuries of tumbling through the gentle flow of the river. He tossed them one by one into the water, enjoying the faint *plop* and the slow spread of ripples across the river's smooth surface.

On the far shore, his child army was slowly dispersing. Some were running and playing games. Others were wading through the shallows, pointing out the strange and beautiful creatures that swam through the gentle current. Others were lying on the sand-and-pebble bank, gazing up at the iridescent sky overhead. They'd discarded their weapons before crossing the river. They'd done so without his prompting. Their guns, machetes, knives, and clubs lay in a tangled heap behind Father Xavier, where they would gather dust and, he prayed, eventually decay. He glanced over at the small arsenal, and decided they should bury it. The weapons were relics of a chapter that had just ended. It was a chapter best forgotten.

He turned his attention to the two figures slumbering on his right. They still clung to one another, just as they had when Father Xavier had found them in the jungle. He knew that he would have to wake them soon. He was, after all, eager to cross the river and join his children on the other side. But for now, he was content to sit at the water's edge and listen to the sound of children's laughter.

In the distance, the city awaited their arrival. And somewhere in that tangled maze of streets was a figure in black robes, who waited for Father Xavier. But there was time enough for that, just as there was time enough for everything that was to come. There were other pilgrims out there, people from the old world who would find their way to Daroka and descend into the mouth of the crater that had once been the Marsh Industries compound. There were hundreds of them, perhaps event thousands, people who had shared the dreams of the underground city and who had felt the robed figure beckoning to them. Soon enough, the city would be filled with life, and the new world could begin to write its own history.

Until then, it was nice enough to just sit by the river.

20

Charon stepped out of its cathedral and was greeted by the musical chimes of childrens' laughter, mingling with gentle song of the river's current. Gathering its black robes around itself, it set off through the maze of streets, quickening its pace as it neared the source of the sounds.

Epilogue

There was a time when Ray Hollister would have been overawed, almost giddy, at the prospect of a private meeting in the Oval Office. But that time had passed. Now that he'd had a good long peek at the man behind the curtain, Hollister viewed the President as no more than another stuffed suit in a world full of them. The man was just an annoyance, really, but unfortunately a necessary one.

A hulking secret service agent led him through the silent hallways of the building. The place had been closed to tourist traffic for the past week, ever since Washington DC initiated lockdowm measures. All the nonessential staff—which, if Hollister was any judge, appeared to be most of them—had been sent home.

"Place is a fucking ghost town, huh?" Hollister said.

"Yes, sir," the agent said. His tone was respectful, but his expression told a different story. Even though his eyes were hidden behind the dark lenses of his sunglasses, the agent's stare radiated pure distaste. And that was okay with Hollister. He didn't give a fuck whether or not this particular steroid junkie respected him. People like that weren't worthy of his anger. They were so far beneath him that their opinion was no more important than the field mouse's opinion of the snake that devours it.

"You're a pretty cool character," Hollister said. "Wearing those shades indoors, you could be in some goddamn action movie."

"Yes, sir." This time, the agent didn't even look his way.

Hollister shrugged and kept walking. Despite being the seat of power, the White House struck him as nothing more than a dump that got repainted and had new carpeting put down every few years. Some of the artwork was nice enough, but Hollister didn't really give a shit about that. Like so many things in his life, the reality of the White House just didn't stand up to his dreams of the place. He supposed that was how it went.

The agent paused to open the doorway to the Oval Office and allow Hollister to step inside. Hollister expected the agent to accompany him into the room, but was mildly surprised when the door clicked shut, leaving him alone with the President.

"They must trust me," Hollister said. "Leaving me alone with you like this. Yeah, they put me through the metal detector and gave me a pat-down, but who's to say I couldn't just grab a pen off your desk and stab you in the neck with it?"

The President didn't laugh. He was seated behind his desk, but his back was turned to Hollister. He appeared to be staring out the window.

"Nice weather we're having, huh?" Hollister laughed. The day was anything but nice. It had been pissing down rain for the last few days. The sun was hidden behind a thick grey curtain of clouds. Every few minutes, the wind would kick up, and fat drops of rain would slap against the windows. It was the sort of rain that Hollister's father would have called, "A real gulley washer."

"Have a seat," the President said.

His voice was rough, like he had an oncoming bout with bronchitis. Maybe he'd just been yelling at his staff too much. Hollister supposed the latter might very well be the case. Plenty of shit had hit the fan over the past month, and a lot of that shit was being blown directly back at the administration. The news networks were having a field day, pumping nonstop footage of the widespread unrest in the cities while they tossed all sorts of accusations at the President.

Hollister took a seat in one of the chairs by the fireplace. The chair was more comfortable than it looked, which wasn't saying much.

"Give me a status report on the vaccine," the President said.

Hollister didn't care for the fact that the man still had his back turned. He supposed it was some sort of petty power play. He made a mental note to try it out next time he needed to read one of his staff the riot act.

"We're ready to go to human trials within the week," Hollister said.

"Trials? I think we're past the need to exercise any kind of caution," the President croaked. "Maybe you haven't turned on CNN in the last couple days, but martial law has been declared in this country. Thirty-seven states are under full quarantine as we speak."

Hollister tried to conjure up the proper response. He knew he should be say something that would convey a sense of grave concern, but the truth of the matter was that he didn't really give a shit. Africa was engulfed in war, and South America was heading that way, but there were still plenty of options, and most of them just looked like opportunities for him to turn a profit. He didn't care about the politics behind the dollar signs. If he had to move operations overseas, so be it. He figured Switzerland was nice this time of year.

"This shit is everywhere," the President continued. "And before you start thinking you can just take your ball and run off to some European country, you might want to look at the intelligence reports in that folder on my desk."

"I seem to have forgotten my reading glasses, sir." Hollister said. This was some pathetic display. He knew the President was technically a lame duck, but until now, he'd never known how true that really was. In fact, lame was too kind a word for this old man.

"Imagine that." The President paused to cough for what seemed like a full minute. When he finally got ahold of himself enough to speak again, his voice was even raspier. "Let me give you the highlights, Ray. I know you set fire to your facility in Ukraine, but it seems you were a little late. Something crawled out of there and slimed its way across most of Eastern Europe. Russia is not amused. Saint Petersburg is burning to the ground as we speak. So far, they've kept a media lid on the stories, but that won't last much longer. We got people seriously discussing their nuclear options. And not the usual fringe loonies, Ray. We're talking NATO countries here. Do we even want to speculate about that fat fuck in North Korea? The son of a bitch has been itching to fuck with China, and this might be his excuse."

"Well, that's certainly grim." Hollister didn't care much for the news about Eastern Europe. Russia had been his safety valve, and now it sounded like even he might not be able to buy his way in. But still, he had options.

"This vaccine," the President said, "how much longer?"

"We're going as fast as we can, but it takes time to synthesize. Maybe a six weeks. A month if we get lucky. And I guess I don't need to tell you how expensive it is."

"I'm sorry, Ray, but that's not good enough."

Now Hollister was starting to get annoyed. "Yeah, well, that's the best I can do. You act like I'm the one in the lab putting chemicals in test tubes. I can only tell you what my technicians tell me."

Finally, the President turned around to face Hollister.

"For obvious reasons, your best is just not going to cut it, Ray. I'm afraid it's time you had some extra motivation."

The President's face was covered in ruptured boils that leaked a green substance. His shirt and tie were crusty and stained. His eyes were so bloodshot they looked completely red. He opened his mouth and licked his lips with a tongue that had turned black.

Hollister shot out of his chair, and bolted for the door. But it was locked, and the knob wouldn't turn. He beat on the door, and called for someone to let him out. His cries went unanswered.

"Please!" he screamed. "Someone let me out of here!"

He backed up a few steps, and threw himself at the door in a desperate bid to break it down. But the impact of his shoulder barely even rattled the door in its frame. He tried again, but all he succeeded in doing was dislocating his shoulder. The pain doubled him over, and he fell to the floor.

"It's no use, Ray," the President said as he crossed the room in a slow, unsteady walk. "This administration is a united front. No one is coming to help you."

Ray whimpered, scooting back on his ass until his back was pressed against the wall.

"Don't worry, I'm just giving you a little extra motivation," the President said, looming over him. "It won't hurt, not really. And it'll be over quick, I promise."

But Ray, like so many of the promises Ray had made during his lifetime, that was a lie.

Pale Death beats equally at the poor man's gate and at the palaces of kings.

— Horace

Afterword

If you survived to the end of this book, you're most likely a fan of the film *Hell of the Living Dead* (or *Virus*, as it was originally known). And if you're a fan of the film, you might well be scratching your head and wondering what the hell this book has to do with the movie you love. Sure, there are some familiar scenes and characters, but for the most part, this novelization departs from the source material in just about every way. There's a reason for that.

When David Gregory of Severin Films first pitched me the idea of turning *Hell of the Living Dead* into a film novelization, I eagerly accepted. I'd already written a few such books for Severin (*Night of the Demon, Mardi Gras Massacre,* and the ill-fated *Cruel Jaws*), and each was more fun than the last, to say nothing of the fact that I'm a massive fan of Italian horror, including all the strange and wonderful gems in the Bruno Mattei/Claudio Fragasso/Rossella Drudi filmography. Each time I've written a novelization for Severin, David has given me a long leash as far as altering the source material to better fit the novel format. After all, films and novels are completely different art forms. What works on the screen might not work on the page, and vice versa. And, more importantly for the low budget features that I've novelized, there are no budget constraints for the plot of a book. That means no limits on cast, running time, special effects, or locations. I've always approached the process of turning a movie into a novel with the mindset of rendering the source material in a way that the producers, directors, and screenwriters might have done if given the budget of a Spielberg blockbuster. As long as I remained true to the spirit of the film, I felt comfortable stretching the narrative to include new characters, subplots, and even endings. But this time, David asked me to take that approach a step further, and that meant going back to the original source material.

As originally conceived by screenwriter Rossella Drudi, *Virus* was a true zombie epic, stuffed with wild characters, social commentary, and some idiosyncratic mystical imagery that catapulted the narrative into realms far beyond what had been attempted in other zombie movies. Alas, this original story suffered a death of a thousand budget cuts, and most of her story was stripped away, leaving a bare bones, albeit highly entertaining, version of her vision. David was aware of this bit of background, and saw my novelization as a means for bringing that vision to an audience that could appreciate the scope and audacity of an alternate version of the film they loved.

I got excited just talking about it. Hell, I'm getting excited just typing these words, and I've already written the goddamn thing!

The first step was getting in touch with Rossella and Claudio. After all, if this book was going to take her original vision, which was already pretty damn big, and expand it from a film treatment into a full blown novel, I needed to get some notes from the creators. After some correspondence with Rossella (and some help from a translator to bridge the language gap), I had a better idea of what she originally intended, and I was able to start the process of combining her initial treatment, and some of my own material (as well as a few bits from the film) to bring you the book you've just read.

The Charon storyline, with its references to the underground city and an afterlife, as well as that of Father Xavier Arnaud were carried over from Rossella's original treatment. She also fleshed out the character of Lia Rousseau and widened the scope of the setting. I added most of the portions that take place in the United States, giving a face to the corporation that kickstarts the zombie apocalypse. Lori Lund, Waylon Marsh, Doctor Vogel, and Ray Hollister are characters I brought to the table. Rossella had plenty of ideas about fleshing out the research center storyline with more three-dimensional characters, so I added the doctors and researchers. I also moved the story into the present day. Since Rossella felt the social commentary of the original treatment was mostly lost in the film, I wanted to emphasize those aspects in the novel, and I find it's easier done in a present day setting. If I couldn't remain 100% faithful to her original ideas, I did my best to hew as closely as I could to their spirit. The book had to be scary, gory, and exciting, but it also had to carry some serious weight. Of course, it would be impossible to pull off without a bit of humor to act as a leavening agent.

The process was a tricky balancing act. My aim was to write a book that would make Claudio and Rossella proud, but I also wanted to deliver something memorable for the fans of the film and newcomers alike. And, as has been the case with all the film novelizations I've written, I wanted it to be a fun read. Writing the Great American Novel is a fine goal for some writers, but it's not for me. I want to write the books that people actually *want* to read. Yes, there is some social commentary, but it's buried in plenty of gratuitous violence, gore, and sex.

I want to take the opportunity to thank David for making this happen. Getting to work with Rossella and Claudio was a dream come true, and having the chance to adapt one of my favorite zombie movies into an epic was an experience I'll always cherish.

Hopefully, you, the reader, have enjoyed this fresh take on a beloved film. If not, I'm sure I'll hear all about it!

Brad Carter
Rogers, AR
May-October 2023

The following pages feature images from the film *Hell of the Living Dead*. Used by permission.

THEY CRAVE THE LIVING
ALL NEW
NIGHT OF THE ZOMBIES
MOTION PICTURE MARKETING
Presents
"NIGHT OF THE ZOMBIES"
starring FRANK GARFEELD · MARGIT NEWTON · SELAN KARAY
directed by VINCENT DAWN · music by GOLBIN
director of photography JOHN CABRERA
An MPM Release 1983
THIS FILM CONTAINS SCENES WHICH MAY BE CONSIDERED SHOCKING. NO ONE UNDER 17 WILL BE ADMITTED.
STARTS FRIDAY
AT A THEATRE OR DRIVE-IN NEAR YOU

LAMBERTO FORNI PRESENTA
VIRUS

L'F
"L'INFERNO DEI MORTI VIVENTI"

MARGI EVELYN NEWTON · FRANK GARFEELD · SELAN KARAY · ROBERT O' NEIL
GABY RENOM · LUIS FONOLL · Musiche dei "GOBLIN"
Regia di VINCENT DAWN
PRIMA VISIONE L.F. FILM · WIDESCREEN · VERSIONE INTEGRALE

When the Creeping Dead
devour the living flesh!

ZOMBIE
CREEPING
FLESH

Starring
Magrit Evelyn Newton, Frank Garfeeld,
Robert O'Neil and Selan Karay

Directed by Vincent Dawn   Produced by Sergio Cortona

WARNING: 'X' Certificate — Not to be rented or sold to persons under 18

VIDEO

NIGHT OF THE ZOMBIES

MOTION PICTURE MARKETING
Presents
"NIGHT OF THE ZOMBIES"
starring FRANK GARFIELD · MARGIT NEWTON · SELAN KARAY
directed by VINCENT DAWN   music by GOLBIN
director of photography JOHN CABRERA
An MPM Release

FRIDAY THE 13th WEEKEND
GORE O'RAMA
MOVIE MARATHON
IN COLOR!
"WHEN THE MOON TURNS RED THE DEAD SHALL RISE"
THE GATES OF HELL
THIS FILM CONTAINS SCENES WHICH MAY BE CONSIDERED SHOCKING. NO ONE UNDER 17 WILL BE ADMITTED
HERE'S THE (RAW) BEEF!
Some things never rest in peace.
CENTURIES OF EVIL HAVE JUST AWAKENED
THEY EAT THE LIVING
NIGHT OF THE ZOMBIES
FUNERAL HOME
MAUSOLEUM
WE'LL MAKE YOUR FLESH-DANCE
FRI.-SAT. ONLY
Show at Dusk
GRAND ISLAND
DRIVE IN THEATRE
TELEPHONE 382-8398
Box Office Opens Around 7 P.M.
R RESTRICTED

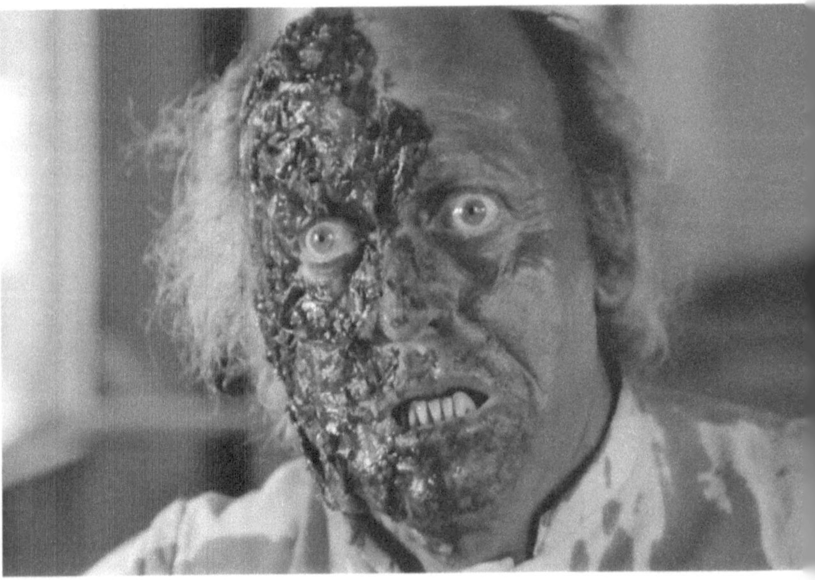

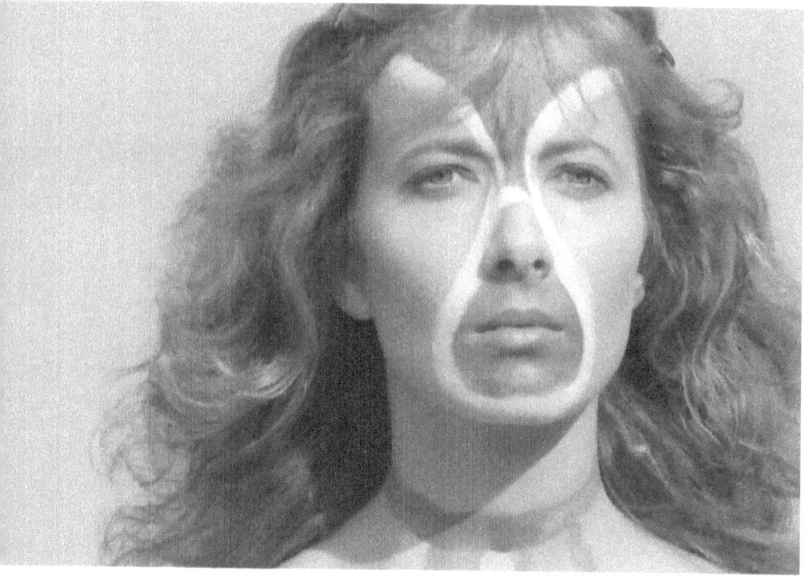

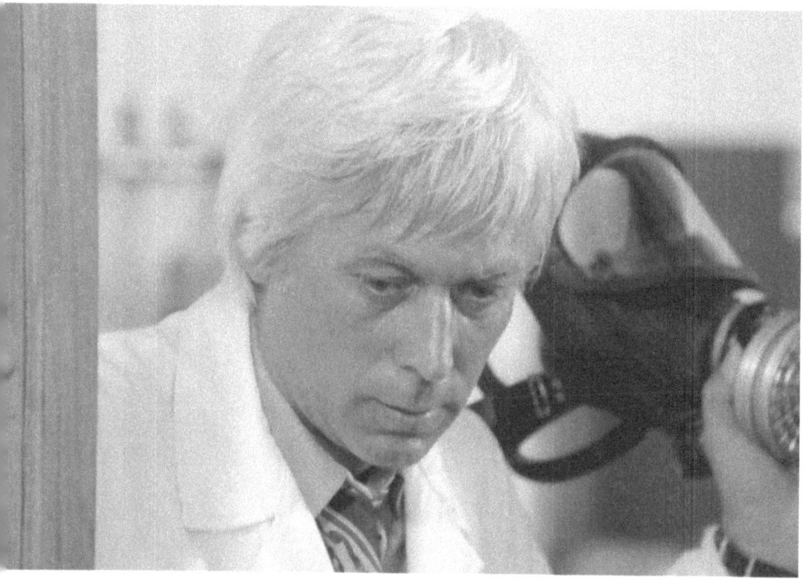

About the Author

Brad Carter lives in Arkansas with his wife and daughters. They encourage him to write, because it keeps him out of trouble.

Also from Brad Carter
(dis)Comfort Food
Saturday Night of the Living Dead
Only Things
Uncle Leroy's Coffin
Human Resources
Cruel Jaws
Rats: Night of Terror

THE RETRO MASS MARKET COLLECTION

COLLECT THEM ALL!

- ☐ HELLRAISER: THE TOLL
- ☐ FRIGHT NIGHT
- ☐ RE-ANIMATOR
- ☐ HARDCORE
- ☐ WISHMASTER
- ☐ HELLRAISER: BLOODLINE
- ☐ TITAN FIND
- ☐ CREATURE
- ☐ VAMP
- ☐ SCARED TO DEATH
- ☐ OF UNKNOWN ORIGIN
- ☐ MANBORG
- ☐ ATTACK OF THE KILLER TOMATOES
- ☐ THE SPECIAL
- ☐ TAMARA
- ☐ FORBIDDEN ZONE
- ☐ COMMANDO NINJA
- ☐ LONG WEEKEND
- ☐ THE ODD JOB
- ☐ BLUE SUNSHINE
- ☐ THE BARN
- ☐ MOTORBOAT
- ☐ HOUSE SHARK
- ☐ HOUSE SQUATCH
- ☐ SHE KILLS
- ☐ AMITYVILLE DEATH TOILET
- ☐ SQUIRM
- ☐ PUPPET SHARK
- ☐ COCAINE SHARK
- ☐ CRUEL JAWS
- ☐ SPLICE
- ☐ ROBOT NINJA

- ☐ PLAN 9 FROM OUTER SPACE
- ☐ CIRCUS OF THE DEAD
- ☐ NIGHT OF THE DEMON
- ☐ MARDI GRAS MASSACRE
- ☐ LIFE CYCLE
- ☐ CHOPPING MALL
- ☐ ALL THROUGH THE HOUSE
- ☐ CHRISTMAS WITH THE DEAD
- ☐ FLESH EATERS
- ☑ VIRUS
- ☐ RATS: NIGHT OF TERROR
- ☐ CUBE*
- ☐ DEADGIRL*
- ☐ SLEEPAWAY CAMP*
- ☐ SHREDDER ORPHEUS*
- ☐ THE AMAZING BULK*
- ☐ THE RETURN OF THE AMAZING BULK*
- ☐ SWITCHBLADE SISTERS*
- ☐ THE DEAD NEXT DOOR
- ☐ REDNECK ZOMBIES*
- ☐ SPIDER BABY*

*Coming Soon

ENCYCLOPOCALYPSE

PUBLICATIONS